A TALE OF BLOOD AND BLOSSOMS

VOL. 1

MEGAN FATHEREE

ISBN: 978-1-7359411-2-7 (paperback)

To all the girls who are soft, kind, forgiving, and sometimes naive.
You are special. Those are your superpowers.

The War's End

War. Painful and prolonged war. It wreaked havoc throughout the realms and brought to their knees the weaker tribes. Where once all had lived in peace, no longer would peace bless their homes. The strong ruled over the oppressed. The winners gloated to the losers.

And, yet, in the midst of all the chaos, one tribe remained pure and impartial.

Hidden by fogs and guarded by plants and people, alike, the inhabitants of Amaryl existed within a paradise of their own.

An understanding tribe by nature, the Amaryl elders could not fathom deciding which side of the war had the right to win. Perhaps one had provoked the other. Perhaps both had wounds that ran too deep to avoid their conflict. Whatever the case, Amaryl never sent soldiers and never expected to help either side. They merely existed, while the clash of nations ravaged the world around them.

When the war ended, so too did it change how the outside world treated those from Amaryl.

Before the war, Tribe Amaryl had been known for their medicines and herbs. For their ability to heal any sickness. After, the rumors began. The talk and jabs at the healers who did not help the dying.

From there, it became a serious problem. Traders appeared, ready and willing to capture any Amarylite and sell their knowledge... for a hefty price. The people of Amaryl became a sideshow. Something to be gaped at and bartered over. Something valueless.

The elders tried to negotiate with those rumormongers. When that didn't work, they sought one of the two nations that had been established at war's end. That nation refused to help, believing instead the rumors of Amaryl's cold hearts.

Because of that, the rumors escalated. Amarylites began to be harmed. Beaten. Sold as slaves.

To avoid the conflicts, the Amaryl Elders closed off their borders and used their knowledge of local flora and fauna to protect themselves. To exit, any Amarylite must have a letter of passage from the elders. To enter, any outsider must endure the effects of hallucinogenic gasses released by their fog barrier. Few dared to venture into Amaryl lands.

And yet, a wise Amaryl Elder foresaw the futility of their actions. Though it might protect them for a moment, what would happen if one day a captured Amarylite betrayed his tribesmen? Would the forest and fields burn to ashes? Would the war prevailing outside their closed borders come to take their lives, as well? They could not survive for long, isolated from the world outside.

So, the elder journeyed beyond their borders to see the state of the world. What he found concerned him more than what he had imagined.

The Amaryl Elders had known about the division of two nations. What they had not realized was the severity of the war's outcome.

For the kingdom from whom they had sought help paid tribute to another.

The Amaryl lands existed in the foothills and forests of the Draiochta Mountains. Since the beginning of time, Amaryl had thrived alongside the flora and fauna. They had no need to suspect their neighbors who thrived in the mountain range's heights. In hindsight, they should have been aware of the ferocity residing there.

Qranbu had, in the end, become victors. Now, they lorded over all around them, taking tribute in place of lives and devouring the freedom of those who rebelled against them. Even the other victors in the war quivered in fear at the mention of Qranbu's Dragon Tribe. They were not human, the rumors said, but heartless demons. Monsters without emotions, raised only to kill and destroy. They held no affinity for anyone, no familial connections or romantic feelings. They were bred for war.

That Dragon Tribe had not invaded the Amaryl ancestral lands surprised the journeying elder. Delighted him, in many ways. But under no circumstances could he trust things would continue on in such a way. One day, Dragon Tribe would require Amaryl's expertise. When they did, they would undoubtedly find a way to rule the bit of the world that hadn't fallen under their thumb.

The Amaryl Elder couldn't concoct a decent countermeasure. So he returned home, discussed with his fellow elders, and together they prayed for their nation's safety.

The prayer worked for years to come. But they had all known their peace couldn't last forever. When one never left their borders for fear of being captured alive and sold, it was only a matter of time until one's greatest fear became reality.

CHAPTER ONE
Lada

A whisper of wind snaked through the leaves above and caressed the grass below. Flowers bowed their respect. Birds stretched their wings skyward. Sunlight graced the tips of every living thing, drawing it all in for a burst of life.

In the midst of this border oasis, a spritely woman bent to smooth a palm over the moss on an ancient elm. Her plaited hair tumbled over one shoulder as she stooped, a single petal falling from one of the blossoms holding her hair in place. The roughly-woven basket on her arm, alight with leaves and vines, swung against her knee with a *thud*.

Lada gingerly plucked the moss away from the elm's bark. "Don't fret. I'll take this and you can grow more. It's for a good cause, I assure you."

The elm, of course, did not answer. The trees never did.

Lada spoke to them because she had been told all living things could hear. If that were the case, the trees must appreciate her explanation when she took things they so cautiously helped to grow. If she explained, wouldn't the trees happily give her what she sought?

As carefully as she had peeled the moss away, Lada settled it in the corner of her basket. She had other things to gather. Herbs, spices, and blossoms. If she didn't make haste, the sun would set before she accomplished her goal. If she didn't accomplish her goal, she would have to stay out after dark to procure the rest of the items on her list.

Lada shuddered at the thought. She hated the dark.

Thus, with one last smile and a soft thank you, Lada rose to her feet and skipped off to find the next item. Red-Crown Mushrooms shouldn't be hard to locate in this part of Amaryl's lands.

Her toes sank into the rain-softened ground as Lada skipped her way to the next grove of trees. They grew in pockets here, making any path more like a maze than a way out. As a native Amarylite, Lada didn't pay much mind to it. She could navigate the forest as easily as she could concoct Euphoria Tea. Navigating the labyrinthine path came second nature to her.

She had found the Red-Crown mushrooms and harvested half when a noise caught her attention.

Lada froze, hand halfway to her basket. As far as she knew, no one ventured into these woods, close to the foggy border of Amaryl lands. Even her mother had been wary of entering the area.

A bush rustled, stirred by an intruder large enough to move every branch.

Lada held her breath, waiting for them to show themselves.

The bush rustled a second time. Its leaves parted, split in half by the newcomer's emergence.

A relieved breath settled on Lada's lips.

The White Deer stalked its way into the cove of trees, each step calculated and regal. Strange, that such a noble creature would find its way to this part of the forest, but a White Deer always bespoke good omens.

Lada rose to her feet and dipped a curtsy to the royal creature. It had clearly decided to trust her, if it deemed the copse safe enough to show itself. She should return the favor by treating it as Forest Royalty. For all intents and purposes, Lada had invaded his home, not the other way around. She should be polite to the homeowner.

The White Deer tilted its head, studying Lada for a long moment before it took a step closer.

Lada remained still. If she moved, she might scare the creature away. White Deer were known for their chivalry and generosity. It wouldn't hurt her, especially if Lada remained quiet.

The White Deer stopped directly in front of Lada. Its head lowered toward her basket, its nose taking a sniff.

Lada slowly raised her basket and peered down into it.

The White Deer's head followed. He must want something she had harvested.

Lada perused all the plants in her care. What could he want from such a diverse collection? Having never met a White Deer before, Lada had no idea what it would eat. Regular deer ate grass and leaves, but White Deer were far from regular. Taking a wild guess, Lada lifted a Wild Rose plant from the corner of her basket. She held it out toward the White Deer, blossom, leaves, and roots alike.

"Is this what you want?"

The White Deer gave one more sniff, took hold of the plant, and began to chew.

Lada stood still, smiling as the majestic creature ate out of her hand. In a small voice, meant to soothe the animal, Lada asked the most prominent question in her mind.

"If you don't mind my asking, sir, why are you so close to the border? It doesn't seem safe at all. You'll get caught if you cross out of the forest."

The White Deer kept munching, down the plant's stem and to the ground leaves. Not that Lada had expected him to answer, but majestic beasts could surprise anyone.

The White Deer swallowed the end of the plant, craned its neck, and gave a shake of its head. Then it gave Lada's skirts a nudge.

Could it be a form of communication? Intuition told Lada the White Deer wanted her to leave. To move on.

A second nudge only served to confirm her suspicions.

Lada didn't live by superstitions, but when a rare and sacred animal communicated with a human, she should listen. Majestic beasts such as this one were rarely seen by human eyes. Even less often did they offer help or warnings.

"I'll go home, then," Lada agreed.

The White Deer shook its head, saying goodbye in a way only an animal could.

Lada shuffled off toward Inner Amaryl, taking a different path than those she had walked upon to reach the borderlands.

The White Deer watched her leave, standing guard over her until Lada disappeared into the forest.

Though Lada didn't recognize it at the time, the White Deer did indeed guard her. For lost in the vestiges of fog and the border foliage's darkness, a pair of beady eyes followed the whole exchange.

Only when the White Deer turned to stalk off did the intruder move, following the animal's footprints into the forest's denser areas.

CHAPTER TWO
Davorin

Shuttered by tapestries and warmed by twin fireplaces as wide as their opposing walls, The War Chamber swirled with whispers and sighs. Windows had been secured. Doors had been reinforced. Now, the room's inhabitants waited for only one purpose. One person.

At the far end of the table, a pair of royal ministers kept to themselves. They had been there longest and knew the most about these council sessions. They had seen generations of leaders call these sessions to order. Had heard every command passed down for execution. Had survived their peers by keeping silent when the time came.

Judging by the state of things, today would be one of those days where silence would save lives. Unfortunately, they saw the pride their younger peers walked in. Blood would spill by day's end.

The door burst inward.

The whispers ceased.

Shrouded in layers of shimmering black silk, their ruler billowed into the chamber. A circlet as black as his garb and as sharp as his commands perched heavy on his head. The firelight lent it an ominous, foreboding gleam. The rasp of his robes echoed like the murmurs of a thousand ghosts returned from the battlefield. No one in the chamber dared greet him by name, but they all knew his identity.

Davorin Astrophel, Dragon Supreme.

One by one, rippling as he passed, the royal ministers bowed their silent greeting.

Dragon Supreme settled into the porous Coal Coral chair at the head of the table, his sleeves draping over the arms and trailing along the ground.

His constant companion, as close to Davorin as a shadow, took a stance behind and to the right of the seat. Cadfael by name, no one had ever successfully passed him or turned him in order to overthrow Davorin Astrophel. His reputation preceded him, inferior only to the invincible man he protected.

One of Dragon Supreme's hands lifted, his fingers splaying to signal the others to begin.

The eldest ministers kept their lips firmly in place.

The younger ministers had not yet learned their lesson.

One of the young ministers, a cousin to Davorin and a noble in his own right, rose to his feet. "My Lord, Dragon Supreme." He pressed his hands in a bird-like shape over his heart, a salute to show his respect for the title and the man holding it. Within Qranbu's borders, they referred it as the phoenix symbol. "Dare we ask why this war council has been summoned today?"

The posed question hung like a veil over the atmosphere, swirling like mystic smoke above their heads. Davorin surveyed the room, keen dark eyes piercing every man's gaze.

No one dared to maintain eye contact with Dragon Supreme. In turn, each looked away, hoping beyond hope their leader didn't see the thoughts dancing through their minds.

Minutes passed like hours. Every man at the table held his breath, waiting for their demise.

Davorin lifted his haughty chin, eyes staring straight instead of at any one man. "I've set my sights on Amaryl."

A murmur of discontent swelled in the silence. No one dared say what first came to their mind. Especially not the elder ministers.

But everyone knew.

One did not casually trifle with the nation of Amaryl. They had survived the Great War and had managed to hide their lands from the world for thirty years after. Amaryl did not consist of normal people. Those who had been taken and sold had proved that much. The world around Amaryl had changed, but the people within their mysterious borders somehow remained the same. To cross them could bring bad luck, or worse.

Davorin's cousin cleared his throat. "My Lord, Dragon Supreme. Amaryl? That's a bit..."

"A bit... *what*?"

"It's an unwise decision."

Davorin rose to his feet, his presence growing and imposing on every man in the room. Then he turned to Cadfael.

Dragon Supreme wrapped his hand around the hilt of Cadfael's weapon, preparing to pull it from its sheath. Cadfael's sword swung in Davorin's hand, backward toward his cousin. A single, clean line through the cousin's throat sent him into a heap on the floor. Dead.

Davorin re-sheathed Cadfael's sword and turned back to the stunned and frozen ministers. "Does anyone else dare question my wisdom?"

Chairs scraped the floor. Ministers scrambled to their feet. Hands flew to chests, resting in the phoenix symbol over their hearts, their heads bowed in fear and respect.

"We dare not question Dragon Supreme's judgment," one of the eldest ministers answered.

He had learned what the younger ones had not. To question meant death, no matter one's status. When Dragon Supreme laid out a plan, everyone went along with it. The choice belonged to them: obey and live or rebel and die.

Davorin's cousin had chosen poorly.

Satisfied with the obedience he saw, Davorin sank back into his seat.

One of the elder ministers gathered his courage to speak. If not him, one of the younger ministers would say something rash. He felt it in his old, weary bones.

"Your Lordship," the elder began reverently, "you say you've set your sights on Amaryl?"

"Did I stutter?" Dragon Supreme's gaze landed on the minister.

The minister bent his head to avoid the glare. "No, My Lord. But as you've brought it up, would you wish for us to inform you of their tactical advantages?"

Davorin's fingers flitted through the air, a precursory movement that released everyone's held breath.

With the offered permission, the minister continued. "They are accomplished healers, but isolated themselves during the Great War. Amaryl is difficult to enter, even if one does locate their border. None have entered and returned alive."

Davorin's eyebrows raised. Without a word, everyone knew what he would say. *None yet.*

One of the younger ministers rose to assist his elder. "Aside from lands in the foothills, wherein rare creatures are found, they don't seem to have much to offer."

Davorin ignored the insult behind the young minister's words. "Tell me of their people."

"We know little else but what the Amaryl slaves in Orafel have told. They are surprisingly loyal to their tribe." The younger minister cast an unsteady glance to the other ministers.

The elder minister took up the gauntlet once more. "As little is known, perhaps My Lord would allow a scouting exhibition. Only then would we be able to map a battle plan worthy of your ideals."

The excuse sounded weak to the elder's ears, but perhaps the intent would please Dragon Supreme. If he had set his sights on Amaryl, nothing and no one would stop him before he accomplished his goal. Their nation, Qranbu, had won the war. They would not be thwarted by a mere tribal land.

Dragon Supreme thought for many minutes, during which all the ministers remained still as statues. Any interruption to his train of thought could bring on another flash of temper. None could chance such a thing.

Davorin Astrophel's shoulders rose, then settled. "A month is not too short a time. You must be thorough."

Granted, their wish for time. A rare generosity from their great and strict leader. Every minister bent their deference to him, a chorus of "your magnanimity abounds" echoing in the hall.

Davorin beckoned Cadfael forward, pointing to the body on the floor nearby. A flick of his fingers denoted his command.

Cadfael alerted the guards at the door, who rushed forward to dispose of Dragon Supreme's deceased cousin.

Out of sight, out of mind. That's what happened in Isonpool fortress. The cousin's family would take care of the funeral rites.

Davorin's attention turned to the others. He calmly lifted a hand to inspect the iron claw rings thereupon. "You had other business to discuss."

"My Lord, Dragon Supreme." Another of the elders rose to present the most pressing order of business. "It has come to the time of year for Orafel to present tribute."

A sigh of relief floated through the air like the warmth of a fire. Tribute. A topic safe to discuss.

Orafel had been offering tribute to Dragon Tribe every year since the Great War's end. It had become customary, to the point that Dragon Tribe's children looked forward to the glimpses they caught of the Tribute Parade. They may never see such fine things for the rest of their life.

"Receive it as always," Davorin commanded.

"But, Your Lordship..." the elder shut his mouth, realizing that saying anything further may earn him the same end as Davorin's cousin.

Instead of death, Davorin offered rare lenience. "But... *what*?"

"As per the Treaty, this year the tribute will include a bride."

It had been written long ago, the agreement between Orafel and Dragon Tribe. Each term had been meant to ensure the safety of Orafel's interests, the supremacy of Dragon Tribe's reign. With the treaty in place, the time had now come.

To ensure Orafel lived on peacefully, Dragon Supreme would allow a woman of Orafel nobility to marry into his household. If Dragon Tribe rejected her, Orafel could take Draiochta Mountain. If Orafel did not send her or the bride never reached her destination, Dragon Tribe could demand a bride of their own choosing from Orafel.

Davorin's head lifted and lowered, a nod that bespoke the racing of his mind as it considered all his options. He had so few when it came to receiving this bride.

"I will receive Tribute personally this year." Davorin rose from the table.

No one had expected less. It may not be a joyous occasion, this marriage, but it was necessary.

Without another word, Davorin sailed from the room, his trusted guard five steps behind.

For the good of all, they would continue the farce of the treaty. Everyone knew, if he wanted, Davorin Astrophel could conquer Orafel at any time he wished. He simply hadn't wished it yet.

CHAPTER THREE

A Complicated Character

"His Lordship, Dragon Supreme will receive Tribute in person."

The whispers and rumors spread throughout Isonpool Fortress as quickly as water through cracks. How could they not, when it had been so long since a Dragon Supreme had taken part in the Tribute Celebration? By nightfall, all of Isonpool Palace had heard. By next morning, Isonpool Fortress buzzed with the news.

For common subjects, it meant only that their celebration would be livelier and grander than ever before. Those who grew up in noble families—those who knew the War Treaty's contents—viewed the news rather differently.

An outsider as a bride. They all knew the consequences. Undoubtedly, Orafel would send a woman whose loyalty to her country ran deep. They wouldn't miss their chance to plant a spy in Isonpool Palace. Nor should they, tactically speaking. Dragon Tribe wouldn't fault them for wanting the upper hand, but all knew they could not willingly give such an advantage to Orafel.

In the heart of Isonpool Fortress, surrounded by mansion walls built nearly a century prior, the news reached the ears of one such noblewoman.

Nerys Galashiel descended from a long line of loyal Dragon Tribe nobility. Her grandfather had served as a Royal Aide in Isonpool Palace. Her father, a trusted Military General, had given his life during a rebel skirmish in order to protect Isonpool Fortress. Nerys had been but a heartbeat within her mother's womb at the time. In all her twenty-seven years, she had only known her father through stories and paintings.

Without any male descendants in her immediate family, Nerys had naturally inherited everything her ancestors worked hard to build. Fame, wealth, prestige. A certain amount of sway at court, with every minister except the one that mattered. No one, not even his own mother, could sway Davorin Astrophel.

Nerys had just begun her breakfast when her chambermaid came scurrying into the room. A quiet but devoted young woman, Nerys's chambermaid rarely came out of the woodwork. For her to arrive looking frazzled should have tipped Nerys off to the severity of the news.

"Something must have happened," Nerys deduced aloud.

The chambermaid nodded, swallowed, and finally opened her mouth. "His Majesty, Dragon Supreme will personally receive Tribute this year."

Nerys paused, a piece of medium-rare meat halfway to her lips. A quick count of the years gone by confirmed her suspicions. This would be the year.

Tamping down her innermost reaction, Nerys settled the meat in her mouth, chewed it slowly, and swallowed without fuss.

"Perhaps His Lordship wanted to join the fun. He isolates himself so often, it must tempt him."

The chambermaid worried her lower lip between her teeth. Glanced around the room. And finally took a step closer to lower her voice. "They say there's a bride coming, my lady."

"What of it?" Nerys worked on cutting another bite of her breakfast.

"Forgive my saying so, but we all know who suits Dragon Supreme best. What's to become of you if he marries some Orafel minx?"

Nerys hid her smile behind a bite of food. "Watch your words. Who are we to interfere in His Lordship's personal affairs?"

"It's not a personal affair, my lady." the chambermaid shook her head, big eyes clearly forlorn. "It's a matter of state. The whole nation is involved in this decision, and if someone from Orafel enters Isonpool Palace..."

"If His Lordship, Dragon Supreme heard you speaking of his affairs so casually, he would surely slice out your tongue." Nerys set her fork down on her plate, turned a dark gaze to the chambermaid, and gave a practiced huff. "If you're concerned, what do you propose we do about it?"

The chambermaid lowered her head. She hadn't thought far enough ahead to be saying those things as confidently as she had said them. Her brazenness would be scolded if not for the accuracy of her statements. An Orafel bride would upset the entire balance of Qranbu's hierarchy.

Nerys lifted her napkin to her lips, calculating the risk of the plan simmering in her head. It would have to remain a secret, but the nobles were excellent at keeping those. How else would they have kept it from the commoners about the Orafel bride? The fewer who knew, the more room they had to manipulate the situation.

"Call the Eight High Nobles together," Nerys instructed.

"The Eight High Nobles?"

"Your words, however inappropriate, do hold weight." That's what sparked such a splendid idea in Nerys's head. The Eight High Nobles wouldn't allow an Orafel spy to waltz into their walls so easily. Nerys would ensure it. "I will speak with them myself at their earliest convenience."

"Where should I tell them to gather?" the chambermaid asked.

Nerys stretched her arms high above her head, reaching for the ceiling above her though she knew she could never touch it. "The usual place. I will arrive in two hours. Make sure they are summoned promptly."

The chambermaid gave a curtsy and scrambled to do what her mistress had commanded.

Nerys lifted her crystal goblet to inspect the red liquid inside. She had been clearing the path before her Dragon Supreme for as many years as she had been at court. This would not deviate her from her final goal.

An Orafel bride? The treaty had been clearly written, but everything had its loopholes. Nerys had never met a situation she couldn't turn around in her favor. Nor had she ever failed to attain what she set her sights upon.

Not even a deity would stand in Nerys's way. Let alone a royal from a country they had already outwitted. One way or another, the Orafel bride would never enter Isonpool Fortress.

CHAPTER FOUR
Catalystic

The melody of a songbird rang through the morning dew. Somewhere, a chipmunk chattered, scolding the songbird for waking him. A beam of sunlight peeked out to kiss Lada's cheek. The warmth and song woke her from a peaceful slumber.

Lada stretched her arms up over her head, basking in the serenity her morning offered.

For as long as she remembered, Lada had enjoyed the benefits of waking up in Flora Master's Hall. Her mother, and her mother's mother, and her mother's mother's mother had passed down their knowledge of plants, spices, and herbs from one generation to the next. Each had risen in ranks to become the Flora Master of their time.

The Amaryl Elders had yet to name the next Flora Master, after the passing of Lada's mother. Everyone expected Lada to be promoted as

Flora Master, though no news had come almost a year after her mother's death.

The Elders knew best. Lada trusted their decisions with her whole heart. If they had not declared a successor to Flora Master's Hall, there must be a legitimate reason for their hesitation. Perhaps the time for grief had not yet passed. Perhaps establishing a new Flora Master now would only remind the people of the emptiness left in the wake of Lada's mother.

So, for now, Lada resided in Flora Master's Hall as the apprentice she had been since her childhood. Lada didn't need titles. Flora Master's Hall was her home. Her family, anyone who came to seek treatment.

The drip of dew from the four corners of the Hall's roof slowed with the sun's rising. Lada swung her feet out of her bed and rose to greet the morning. Beneath her, moss and leaves crunched softly, the only form of carpet in the entire Flora Master's Hall.

Along Lada's bedroom walls, outlined by the windows on all sides, plants with varying degrees of illness perked up in their pots. Touched by morning sun and forest dew, how could they not feel better than they had the day before?

Lada greeted each plant with a touch of her fingertips and a whisper of encouragement.

"You're looking better."

"Your roots have less rot today."

"Look at all your new petals!"

In turn, each ailing flower and herb received their morning greetings. As if they had waited for that very thing all night, each piece of vegetation recovered more every morning. When they were healthy again, Lada would return them to their rightful places in the yard.

By the time Lada finished her greetings, the sun had risen nearly to the treetops.

"I still have to find the last flower on my list today," Lada pouted at the late morning sun. "Couldn't you have moved a little slower?"

The sun merely twinkled through the leaves atop the nearest grove of trees, as suns are wont to do.

She couldn't bargain with the sun, so Lada raced around gathering the things she would need. Only on her way out the door did she remember to turn back around and change into suitable outdoor clothing. A night-gown would simply not be appropriate for flitting about in the forest.

With her clothes in place and her hair held back by freshly-plucked blossoms, Lada snatched up her basket from beside the door and set off into the woods she knew so well.

The scent of blossoms and nighttime rainfall—her old bosom friends—greeted her. Lada picked her steps carefully. Her destination had but one path leading to it. If not for the sake that it was the year's only blooming season for this plant, Lada wouldn't take the treacherous journey.

In the heart of the forest, Lada came to the entrance of a tunnel formed by overhanging trees and vines. Without prior knowledge of its existence, one would be fortunate to encounter such a sight.

A rare specimen lied on the other side of that tunnel, known only to the Flora Masters and the Amaryl Elders. It had been her family's secret for generations. A key that could be used to unlock good or evil, depending on the owner's intent.

The Elders had asked to use the plant only once, years ago. Those who resided in Flora Master's Hall kept it on their person if they ventured beyond the safety of the borders. Lada meant to follow in the tradition, after she offered the year's harvest to The Elders first.

"I'll be visiting for a while," Lada informed the ominous foliage tunnel before her, in case it had any nefarious plans of closing in on her.

She used a whole minute to summon her courage. After all, the impenetrable vines and leaves made the tunnel quite dark. If not for the necessity of harvesting the plant at the other end, Lada would never venture into such a gloomy place.

The lack of light lowered the temperature inside the tunnel. Another thing Lada despised. Cold.

A shiver worked over Lada's spine as she traversed the mysterious path. Old, dead leaves crunched underfoot. Earth-dwelling insects scurried to and fro, displaced by the feminine intruder.

Step by cautious step, Lada worked her way up the incline. Over fallen limbs and leaf-buried roots. Through layers of vines, hung in a living curtain before her.

Finally, Lada stepped out of the far end of the tunnel.

The space at this end could be measured by a man's height. Made by a single stone jutting out from the mountain's side, the platform dropped off into a ravine so deep none would survive the fall.

Lada didn't worry about falling. She had climbed more precarious ledges. Rather, her focus landed on a pair of red flowers rising from a single stem.

The Mirror Flower.

Lada set her basket on the stone beneath her. She had come at last, and it had bloomed as it should. The graciousness of such a rare specimen to provide this magical harvest year after year was not lost on Lada. The Mirror Flower had earned its reputation, indeed.

"Hello, old friend," Lada greeted the plant as she knelt beside it. "It's come to that time of year. Would you like to come with me to Flora Master's Hall?"

A gentle breeze stirred the plant, making it seem as though the blossoms nodded their agreement.

Lada set to work.

First, the needles. Mirror Flower's pollen wrapped itself around a single needle perfectly placed in the bloom's center. Lada retrieved them carefully, sure to place them inside the embroidered satchel at her waist without pricking herself.

Next, her hands lowered to the dirt beneath the stem, moving and digging until she had exposed Mirror Flower's roots. After that, moving the flower into her basket required only a little finagling.

The whole process took less time than the movement of a sundial from one notch to the next.

Satisfied that she had done her duty, Lada turned to the twin plant on the other side of the rock. "Grow well and I will see you next year."

Having given all her greetings, Lada clutched her basket to her chest and headed back down the path. Though ominous and foreboding, the vines and trees didn't swallow her up. Lada accepted it as a small victory. No matter their temperament, her plants recognized their friend.

Lada returned to her normal forest route without trouble from the trees.

She had only gone past a few copses when he came up alongside her. The Great White Deer who had accompanied her the evening prior.

Lada stopped in her tracks, a smile lighting on her lips. She had never expected to become friends with such a creature, but it seemed he had taken a liking to her.

"Is your home in this part of the forest?"

It would make sense for a noble creature to reside nearby a rare plant. In their own paradise, away from prying eyes and greedy hands, they must dwell peacefully alongside one another.

The Great White Deer tossed his head.

Lada giggled. Her friend the Great White Deer liked to respond in that way.

Something snapped in the underbrush nearby.

Lada and the deer, alike, stopped to listen.

To an outsider, the forest sounded quiet. Only the usual chirping of insects and singing of birds filled the air.

Lada and the Great White Deer were at home in such a place. They had heard the forest sounds every waking moment of their lives. They knew how the forest air felt on their skin. How the soil gave way underfoot. They knew when someone had entered their sacred grounds. No matter how still one remained, they couldn't be absolutely silent.

Lada heard it first. The sound of creaking leather and wood. Her head lifted, her eyes turning toward the source.

She spotted him immediately. A human trying to hide among trees, with one arm lifted before him and the other pulled back.

His arrow pointed at the friend by her side.

"Run," Lada breathed, hoping the Great White Deer would hear her and take flight.

He pranced on his hooves, but the deer did not leave her side.

Lada gave her new friend a shove. "Run!"

This time, the Great White Deer heeded her advice.

The arrow sailed through where the creature had been standing, barely missing Lada before it embedded into a tree trunk.

With the deer gone, the man set his sights on the girl instead.

She had encountered so few strangers in her life. None of them had harbored good intentions. Never could she allow anyone to harm her friend, The Great White Deer. She must do whatever it took to draw away his attention.

Lada ran.

As far and as swiftly as her feet would carry her, she ran.

All the while, Lada heard the man pursuing her. His clothes didn't sound like they had come from Amaryl. They rustled too heavily and creaked like his weapon.

A second arrow pierced a bush by Lada's side.

With a screech, Lada stumbled and fell, her basket rolling away from her across the mossy forest floor.

Lada didn't care about the basket. She could make another. She scrambled, instead, to snatch the Mirror Flower from its perch inside. Only when she had a firm hold on it did Lada set off again.

Her feet pounded over the familiar forest floor, her skirts flying around her and her arms pumping at her sides.

It was no match for the booted footfalls fast approaching behind her.

Lada jumped over a log, turned a corner, and raced in the direction of Flora Master's Hall.

A brutal arm wrapped around her waist and gave a tug.

Lada's back hit a hard tunic, unlike any tunic she had seen before. Her feet rose up off the ground, leaving her completely at her captor's mercy.

Still, Lada fought. She shoved at the arm holding her aloft. Kicked at the legs behind her. Screamed at the top of her lungs.

No matter what effort she gave, all remained futile. With a single arm, he had subdued her.

The hunter's free hand came up with a flourish, dousing Lada's face in a dust she recognized by its smell. Bit by bit, her limbs went weak. Her fight lost its luster. Her fingers loosened, dropping the Mirror Flower to the ground below her feet. Then, with a final cry to alert the forest about her mistreatment, Lada went limp in her captor's hold.

Fully alert but unable to move, Lada could only whimper in response to the big man's malicious chuckle.

CHAPTER FIVE

Amaryl Elders

"Elders! Elders!" A gasping and panting Amarylite woodsman came clambering into the hall, his eyes wide and his face white as ash.

The oldest, most influential elder lifted a hand to calm the poor boy. So few times had any seen a woodsman panic. For him to come barging in, something must be terribly wrong within Amaryl's isolated borders.

"Be calm, child, and tell us. What has happened?"

The man gulped a series of deep breaths, but his limbs shook and his eyes shone with fearful tears. "Lada of Flora Master's Hall has been taken."

If not for the way he phrased it, The Elders may not have listened to the man's announcement. Had he said Lada went missing, they may not have questioned it. Lada sometimes went off into the woods for days on end, only to return as soon as they worried.

But the man said that Lada had been taken. Those three words implied more than a mere disappearance. Those words had the power to tear down everything Amaryl so carefully protected.

"Taken?" One of the elders questioned.

The woodsman nodded, his hands flying around his person as if he didn't know what to do with them. "I saw it myself! A strange man in a hardened tunic carried her out through the Border Fog. He certainly didn't belong to Amaryl."

The Elders shared a knowing look. No one in Amaryl had reason to wear armor. To hear of a "hardened tunic" meant the man must have been girded with the attire of an outsider. Yet, somehow, he had not only made it through their foggy borders once, but twice. And he had been unaffected enough to take someone out with him.

Another oddity came in the form of how the woodsman described Lada's abduction.

Everyone in Amaryl knew of Lada. The Elders knew her personally. Lada of Flora Master's Hall would not venture beyond the border without express permission from The Elders. Nor would she interact with an outsider. That the outsider had carried her out meant she had been overpowered.

The outsider may not know, but if anyone else on the other side of the border understood Amaryl, they would certainly recognize Lada's job should she mention it. Should this outsider mean to sell her, he could no doubt bring in a hefty price for her head.

"What shall we do?" another Elder asked.

The old, wise Elder rested his hands around the carved walking stick he cherished. Stories wrapped from the bottom to the knob on the top, all etched by his own hands. One in particular caught his eye, somewhere in the middle of the wooden staff. He remembered listening to the war stories as he carved them there. And, above them, he remembered listening to the oldest and wisest Elder of his time speak out about what should be done.

This time, should they fight or retreat? The old man shook his head slowly. Though Lada of Flora Master's Hall was important to the function of Tribe Amaryl, they could not know what lay ahead for her outside their borders. How did one plan a rescue if they did not understand their enemy?

"Find a brave and capable Guardsman," The Elder decided. "And send him to watch over Lada of Flora Master's Hall. Until we know where she has been taken and why... we will stay our hands."

"But, sir—" the woodsman argued.

The elder held up a hand to stop him. "We know not our enemy yet."

"Lada won't be able to—"

"Lada is special."

The three words silenced everyone in the room. Not because they refused to argue the point, but because they all knew the words rang true. Lada had always been special. An eternal optimist, and something else no one could place. Lada bore the spirit of their forest within her bones. Fate would not be so cruel to cut her life short when it had only begun.

So they allowed the command to take hold. Until they knew what came against them, they would watch over Lada from afar.

CHAPTER SIX

Wistning

"The Tribute Bride has reached Mesmium," Cadfael announced quietly to his sovereign. "They will remain there to stock up for the journey up the mountain, I'm sure."

"I don't need these updates," Davorin sighed. "Tell me instead when they arrive."

The cawing of a raven outside the window substituted for any answer Cadfael might have given. When Dragon Supreme gave an order, no one dared refute it. Least of all Cadfael, Dragon Supreme's closest confidante. They had been to Hell and back, side by side. None could break the bond they shared. But, neither did Cadfael dare to show any signs of impertinence toward His Lordship.

"What of the Amaryl expedition?"

The question, posed so matter-of-factly, caught Cadfael by surprise. It shouldn't have. Dragon Supreme had thought of little else these days. His desire to conquer and possess ran deep in his royal bones. His father, and his grandfather before that, and his great-grandfather before him, had all been the same. Unsatisfied with leaving things as they were. Could they conquer the whole world, they would.

Cadfael braced his sword between both hands and curtly bent his head. "They set off last evening."

"Without issue?"

Cadfael should have known Dragon Supreme would ask it. Cadfael's own answer had been short, concise. When one tried too hard to skirt around problems, they ended up alerting others to the problems' existence. He had meant to keep the issues to himself. How did one go about bringing up such a thing to a temperamental sovereign?

Dragon Supreme inspected one of his metal claw rings while he waited for the forthcoming answer.

Having known Cadfael since childhood, Davorin could tell a lie and an omission with the seasoned instinct of a hunting hawk. Though things had, in the end, gone as Davorin wanted, blunders had been made in the process. Cadfael's hesitance to speak of it meant only one thing. The issue revolved around a touchy subject. With time, Cadfael would answer diligently.

The hall echoed with the silence of Cadfael's thoughts. Only the *click, click, click* of Dragon Supreme's claw rings and the *tap, tap* of his and Cadfael's boots interrupted.

Cadfael wet his lips with the tip of his tongue. Decision made, he dropped to one knee. "My Lord, the scout asked for Wistning Extract."

Davorin's fingers stilled, two rings bent to touch each other. A huff settled in his chest, unfelt by his throat or lips and unknown to the man kneeling before him.

"Did you give him any?"

"No, Your Lordship." Cadfael kept his head bent, his eyes downcast. To look up meant to challenge the beast before him. "Scouts do not require Wistning Extract. I sent him on without any."

"Well done."

Dragon Supreme moved on without announcement or preamble, his boots pounding over the sharp corridor. His reaction, though unpleasant, did not hold the level of ire Cadfael had anticipated. Especially when it came to the mention of Wistning.

None but the soldiers and nobles knew of it. None dared speak its name outside the walls of Isonpool Palace. A core component of their strength lied within this, Qranbu's secret weapon.

Any intelligent person would realize Qranbu could not have so violently and effortlessly won such a grand war without help. No one would guess the power behind Dragon Tribe's army.

Strong on their own, able to overcome nearly any obstacle in their path, Dragon Tribe's soldiers doubled their strength and efficiency with but a drop of Wistning Extract. It had been the secret to their undefeatable military force for thousands of years. Leader after leader had used the extract to ensure their victory in lands with a different climate than their mountain home.

Sadly, few vials of Wistning Extract remained in the royal treasury. The Wistning Refinery operated with a skeleton crew, none of whom dared to speak a word about the lack. No one dared bring it up. It proved an impossible problem for both the court and the country. Those who understood how the extract was made knew the cause for its demise.

Wistning Vine had died throughout the entire castle. Without a reason or a cause, the vines had simply begun to shrivel. Where they had been lush and leafy before, now they clung to walls and trellises by withered brown roots.

It plagued Dragon Supreme day and night. Never before had anyone had to worry about the Royal Wistning Vines. They had resided within Isonpool Palace for centuries. He had not heard the servants say it, but the air in the palace resounded with the untold rumors.

"Perhaps the Wistning Vines die because they do not recognize Davorin Astrophel as the true Dragon Supreme."

If not for the sacredness of the crawling vines in the people's minds, Davorin would have long ago had the plants cut out and burned. Instead, he found himself seeking ways to fix them.

Not a single horticulturalist in the entire kingdom had been able to discover the cause of their death. Davorin didn't understand it, either.

Now, only one living plant remained. It, too, had begun to show signs of demise. Dragon Supreme kept it tucked away for supervision. He could not have their people's pride dying before his eyes.

Cadfael had trailed his master down the hall, over a thousand pieces of glass and shattered Lava Rock compiling the ancient floor. Both men stopped before a pair of iron doors.

Davorin glanced over his shoulder at his confidante. "I will summon if I need your assistance."

It was a dismissal. Cadfael knew the words well. Beyond that door, he must not go unless specifically ordered by his superior. Beyond that door, only Dragon Supreme had unhindered access. If anyone should dare to cross beyond the threshold, they would be executed, no questions asked.

Cadfael knew better than to test his luck and risk Dragon Supreme's loyalty. He took a step back.

Davorin, on the other hand, knew only to go forward. The iron doors, carved with ancient tales of battles and conquests, swung out away from the hall. Davorin stepped through the space they created.

Like a clap of thunder or the closing of an archaic text, the great iron doors slammed shut behind him.

CHAPTER SEVEN

Welcome to Orafel

utside the borders of Amaryl, the world worked differently. Placed along the valley and nestled beside Amaryl's foothills, The Kingdom of Orafel shone brightly. They were a place of advancement and industry, always seeking ways to better the world around them. And yet, they had only won the Great War in name.

The time of year had come for tribute to be paid to the real victors. Orafel's king shrouded it in celebration and joyous occasion. City by city, the Tribute Parade passed through on its way to Qranbu, where Dragon Tribe resided. Town by town, children ran in the streets to announce the parade's entry.

Cart after cart of Orafel goods filed through the streets of each city in which it arrived, followed by carriage after carriage of Royal Tribute Bearers. This year, a rainbow-painted carriage took up residence in the center of the caravan, containing a lady rumored to be more beautiful than any other Orafel subject.

The last city in which the Tribute Parade stopped, before leaving the Orafel border, went by the name of Mesmium.

Mesmium had been built a few dozen miles from Amaryl's foggy borders. Too far for anyone to accidentally wander into those haunted hills, but close enough for Mesmium to swarm with Hunters and Bounty Seekers.

If one sought an Amaryl slave, to Mesmium they must go. A strange plant, secured from the foothills? Mesmium had those, too. Mesmium could—and would—sell anything. Information. Goods. People. If anyone in Orafel wanted to purchase objects rare or difficult to find, Mesmium became their only choice.

Even Amaryl knew of Mesmium. They knew to avoid it. To run away should anyone mention it. If they set foot inside on their own volition, punishment would follow.

Yet, after leaving her beloved forest, Lada found herself entering Mesmium's gates.

The man had secured Lada inside a cart with planks rising from all sides. It resembled a cage used to house a wounded animal.

In some ways, Lada could be considered a wounded animal. The outsider had incapacitated her, after all, and had made it a point to keep using the paralytic herb dust on her for an entire night and now a full day after. Unlike the animals Lada rehabilitated, she doubted she would be sent back to her habitat when she healed.

Their arrival at the gates of Mesmium confirmed Lada's oddly pessimistic suspicions.

The guards stopped them but a moment before they waved the man through. It was then that Lada got her first glimpse at what life looked like outside of Amaryl.

Banners flew high, their colors demanding attention. Along the street, the jing-a-ling of performers' bells and coins passing hands rose like mist. Instead of trees, buildings soared tall and strong on all sides. Smoke from dozens of street stalls wafted through the air like insects, bringing with it the smell of a thousand foreign delicacies.

Curious onlookers turned from their daily business to stare at the girl in the cart.

Had she been able to move, Lada might have tried to hide from them. She had never witnessed stares such as these. They were not stares of admiration, such as the ones she lavished on her flowers. They did not hold love or kindness. They did not mimic compassion or sympathy. These stares contained feelings and sentiments Lada had never witnessed before.

Why did they gawk at her as though she might turn into a monster? Like them, Lada was human. Was it possible they did not recognize the fact? They must be troubled in their minds. Confusion such as this might be from prolonged exposure to any number of pollens. A soothing tea might help.

As for the passers-by, they had no inclination of the helpful thoughts rolling through Lada's mind. They saw only an odd girl, covered in petals and leaves, staring back at them through red-rimmed eyes. The people of Mesmium had seen countless other beings of her kind. All knew where she had come from. Amarylites all entered Mesmium with that same expression on their face. The look of innocent ignorance. It would soon be lost.

The Slave Hunter who had brought the Amaryl woman from the other side of the border walked tall and proud. Chest puffed out, he greeted each Mesmium resident with a dip of his head. They, in turn, dipped a bow or a curtsy. Everyone knew better than to cross a Slave Hunter.

The sun hung like a crown atop the city wall when the hunter stopped at a raised platform in the middle of the Mesmium Common Grounds. He left Lada lying within the cart in favor of taking the stage himself.

"Gather 'round, gather 'round!" he called, pulling in the onlookers with a dramatic motion of his arms.

Lada begged her arm to move and found her fingers twitched. The herbal dust's paralytic side effects had begun to wear off. It mattered little now. She had neither the height nor the strength to escape the caged cart. But at least she would feel less helpless if she could move.

"Come see!" the man continued, bellowing loudly for anyone in the town commons to hear. "A little forest monster, plucked straight from Amaryl forest!"

Monster? Lada managed to crane her head to see the hunter who had brought her here. What had made him think her a monster? They clearly had a misunderstanding between them. If only she could speak to clear the air.

"I risked my life to snatch a living Amaryl monster," the hunter continued, drawing the crowd in with the story. "Fourteen men lost their lives in the fog, seeking this ferocious creature, but I came out victorious. Come see, come see!"

The crowd buzzed with whispers and rumors, none loud enough to reach Lada's ears.

The Slave Hunter beckoned toward a crowd of children hovering nearby. "Come, come, come. It's alright. I've subdued her. She won't be able to do anything to you."

Of course I won't, Lada thought to herself. *Children are innocent and kind.*

The children ventured closer, each whispering to the others as they approached. One of them pressed himself up against the slats, his bulging eyes staring at the flower-adorned girl before him.

Lada managed to move, enough to prop an arm underneath her side and raise up on it.

The children screeched, all skittering back in fear that Lada might rise up and strike at any moment.

"Be calm, beast!"

A switch flew threw the air, passing between two planks to hit Lada's shoulder. A fiery sting broke on her skin, and Lada knew it would bruise later. Those kinds of injuries always did.

Treating the wound would be easy enough. Understanding why she had been struck came with more difficulty. She had done nothing wrong in saving her friend, the Great White Deer. Need she be punished so harshly for her loyalty?

The crowd had grown, by the time Lada began to process her situation. Men and women, children and adolescents all crowded around the stage in Mesmium Common Grounds. For some, this was their first time seeing an Amaryl slave. For others, the spectacle had become commonplace, but never boring. Mystical beings wandering out of the forest never brought anything but trouble.

A piece at a time, the Slave Hunter laid out a whimsical tale of his harrowing journey into Amaryl forest. One at a time, people pushed in closer, until they had surrounded Lada with stares of fascination and malice.

Lada daren't open her lips to counter the lies falling from this hunter's tongue. He spoke of her ferociousness. Her rabid tendencies. Of the fight he endured, almost dying at the end of her sharp claws.

Though none of it had happened, Lada could tell by the people's faces that they would never believe a second story. He had drawn the fable too grand and exciting for them to want to believe the truth. If only she had with her the pollen of a Confession Lily. Then, perhaps, she could make them understand how she had come to their town.

Someone picked up a stick that had fallen to the ground, using it to reach between the slats to poke at Lada's arm. "Show us these claws, beast."

Now able to move almost fully, Lada shied away from the twig's stabbing, pointed tip.

Sadly, it followed her, along with the man's maniacal laughter, until it had worked a hole in her flesh. Red blood trickled down her arm and snaked over her fingers like a vine.

Lada curled into a corner, aware it would not keep her from the onlookers, but hoping it would make them see her as a human.

No such luck graced her with its presence. The switch came again, this time against her back in quick succession. Each lash created a new line of stinging pain for Lada to bear. She did so with hardly a cry, but she couldn't stop the tears pooling in her eyes or the whimper welling in her throat.

"Such a specimen, this one is!" the Slave Hunter continued, tapping the switch against his palm as he paced. "Never like the other slaves. This one is pure ether, worth a prettier penny than any other, I assure you. Of caliber fit only for something as spectacular as... as... as the Tribute!"

A gasp shuddered through the crowd. To be a part of the Tribute meant they could never afford it. Only royalty and merchants owned anything worth adding to the Tribute.

"The Tribute, you say?" came a voice from the back of the crowd.

Heads turned. Eyes sought a glimpse of the voice's owner. The sea of bodies parted, two at a time, as the man made his way forward.

His clothes alone made others step back and quiet down. Such rich dyes didn't belong to the commonfolk. Only the rich could afford vibrant colors like the blue of his robes. Shimmering silver threads sparkled in the light of a dozen torches anchored around the square, in the absence of the sun's light. A smooth pendant hung from his belt to rest against his leg, below which thick leather boots guarded his feet.

Person by person, heads bowed and lips were sealed, leaving way for the man to weave toward the cart.

The man stopped nearby, studying Lada through the odd shadows cast by the darkening sky and the bright torches around them. "You don't seem to be treating her as a specimen worthy of Tribute."

The hunter pressed his fists together and bent over them, bowing to the nobler man. "It's a wicked and unruly beast," he spun his tales again. "I daresay a few lashes with a switch will do little to calm it."

Lada shot a glare and a pout toward the hunter. Had he no common sense? Why would he treat her thusly? If he needed something, Lada would gladly give whatever she could. He needed only to ask.

"If the creature is truly worthy of Tribute, should you not offer her as such?"

The man's suggestion sounded kind and calm. The crowd around him knew better. For some had recognized him, and such a suggestion from a man of his caliber came not as a help, but as a demand.

The hunter didn't notice. "Why, if the Tribute knew of her, I'd be sure to offer her. As it stands, they don't. Now's the time to get your own hands on such a rare creature."

"Oh, you'd offer her, would you?" The man gave a wry chuckle, his arms folding over his chest. "Why not take her straight to Verity Hall, where the Tribute Parade resides?"

"Isn't it more convenient to display the beast here? I would only be rejected at the doors to Verity Hall."

"You wouldn't know unless you tried."

"I did, I did try!" the Slave Hunter lied. "The guards sent me away immediately, which is why you have such a good opportunity to take the specimen home with you now."

Lada shied away from the man's loud laugh. It didn't quite seem to fit with the conversation, but she couldn't be sure since she only half understood what they spoke of. What was Tribute? Why did it seem to mean so much?

The man in blue raised his chin, his lips parting on a sigh. "It seems you aren't aware of my identity. But, then, I wouldn't be found associating with a liar such as yourself."

For the first time since she had been carried from the forest, Lada found a glimmer of hope sparking in her heart. The man had called the hunter a liar. But how had he known?

A second man came running through the parted crowd, panting as he hobbled near to the man in the blue. "I thought I'd lost you, My Lord. What are you doing here, in the Commons?"

"Nettle," the man in blue addressed the servant, "kindly tell this Slave Hunter who I am."

"He doesn't know?" Nettle stared wide-eyed at the Slave Hunter.

The man in blue gave a push to Nettle's shoulder. "Tell him."

"Oh. Certainly. Of course." Nettle straightened his spine, planted his hands on his hips, and cleared his throat. "How dare you not recognize Lord Kavindra, The Tribute Master!"

The Slave Hunter's face went white, outlined only by the changing light around him. He dropped to one knee, the switch falling to his side when he pressed one fist inside the other.

"My Lord!"

Lord Kavindra perused the situation, one person at a time, before he spoke. "An Amarylite is indeed a fitting addition to the Tribute. They are rare and treasured, worth a pretty price."

"I brought her out from Amaryl forest just yesterday," the Slave Hunter continued. "Worth at least ten mollits of gold, she is."

Lord Kavindra smiled to himself, a cluck of his tongue caught before he continued. Not because he found the Amaryl woman worth less than ten mollits, but because the Slave Hunter could have asked thirty mollits easily. He knew not what he held in the palm of his hand. All the better for Lord Kavindra and the Tribute.

"Nettle, take her to Verity Hall." Lord Kavindra leveled his gaze on the Slave Hunter. "I will settle accounts here."

Lada grasped at one of the planks as the cart shifted, lifted, and moved. Had it so easily been handled, this strange situation of hers? She dared not ask, lest she speak amiss and find herself in bigger trouble. But Lada wondered about this kind stranger.

Perhaps not everyone misunderstood the people of Amaryl. Perhaps someone had a similar heart to Lada's.

Lord Kavindra stayed but a moment longer with the Slave Hunter, only enough time to toss a bag of gold at his feet and to utter one command.

"Never mention that Amaryl creature again."

"Yes, My Lord. Of course, My Lord." The Slave Hunter bent and bowed, making promises he would never keep. For, one day, he would speak of the Amaryl creature again, and it would be the beginning of his end.

CHAPTER EIGHT
Verity Hall

orches lit the courtyard, mimicking daylight. Soldiers stood guard at various points, all looking straight ahead. They barely spared a glance when Nettle pulled the cart into the yard. The strangeness of it all hit Lada with the same sting as the switch.

Soldiers were different from Guardsmen. Lada had known since the first time she saw a soldier.

It had been a mistake, crossing the border into Orafel. Lada had recognized that immediately. The barren fields outside of the thriving Amaryl Forest held nothing but depression and grimness. She had turned back immediately, sure to hide herself, but not before she had spotted a patrol of soldiers.

They had worn hard shells over their tunics, and equally hard shells on their feet. Not one had said a word, too busy mindlessly marching at the exact same pace across the packed dirt. The soldiers here were no different, mere statues set against the walls. Neither human nor stone.

Their non-intrusive presence caused Lada to miss Amaryl that much more. Her home didn't demand lifeless soldiers.

In Amaryl, they trained Guardsmen. Guardsmen, though skilled, didn't succumb to the numb uniformity of a paid soldier. They were alive. They chatted and joked, laughed and cried together. They had families and friends. Each Guardsman sought to protect those under his care, but never did they turn away when odd things happened around them.

A Guardsman wouldn't have ignored the girl in a cage being wheeled into the courtyard. They would have made sure she was okay. Would have set her free.

The soldiers here allowed Nettle to do whatever he would, without a word or a question.

Nettle parked the cart near a covered walkway, close enough for the eaves to shield them, far enough away they would be in no one's way if someone should walk by.

"Now, don't you go trying to make trouble," Nettle warned with a shake of his finger to accentuate his point.

Lada, still curled in her corner, found it better not to say the things on her mind. She might say something amiss, and then what would she do to help herself? Lada knew her own weaknesses. She could complain, but she could not fight. Her arguing fell by the wayside compared to experienced debaters. On top of all that, she found Nettle's attitude similar to those who had surrounded her before. Lada doubted this man would listen to what she had to say.

The two remained there—one standing with his hands on his hips, the other curled up and staring back at him—until the front gate opened once more.

Lord Kavindra sailed over the threshold and down into the courtyard, his shoes beating against the stone path in a soothing rhythmic pattern.

Nettle scurried to the far side of the cart and bent a bow to his master. "Lord Kavindra, you've returned. Where shall we put the addition to Tribute?"

"You haven't released her from her confines?" Lord Kavindra pushed past Nettle, his stride directed toward the cart.

The hope that had been growing in Lada's heart inched nearer to the surface. Lord Kavindra had been the first to see her as precious, something to be cared for. If anyone had her best interests at heart, Lada believed it would be Lord Kavindra.

The Tribute Master fiddled with the lock for a brief moment before it gave way beneath his hand. A seemingly impenetrable metal lock lay in pieces in his palm, docile as a blossom cut from its stem.

The cart's door swung outward, balanced by Lord Kavindra's fingers on its side.

Lada, for the first time, stared at the man who had saved her without a single obstruction between them. He stood as tall and proud as a mighty oak, with eyes hardly visible in the dim light, though she assumed they bore a resemblance to black tea. He had been authoritative when he took over the situation outside, but he bore nothing but a calm demeanor now.

"Won't you come out?" Lord Kavindra enticed, his lips turning up into an expression so congenial that Lada had a difficult time believing he would harm her.

Inch by cautious, painful inch, Lada maneuvered her way to the open door. The cart beneath her rocked and swayed, throwing her off-balance with each step she took.

Lord Kavindra didn't move. He hardly breathed, Lada noted. As if he wanted her to come forth from the cart and feared any misstep on his part would scare her back into her corner.

Torches roared atop their sconces in the cricket-ridden air. The eyes of statuesque soldiers turned to stare.

Lada alighted from the cart, clutching a hand to her aching and oozing arm. Such a wound would surely require a poultice, replete with herbs only found in the forest. How would she ever treat her injuries without the plants from Flora Master's Hall?

"It looks painful," Lord Kavindra noticed kindly. To Nettle, he commanded, "Summon the physician."

Nettle shuffled closer, his shoes scuffing against the courtyard stone beneath him. "My Lord, are you certain you wish to free her like this? The hunter said—"

"I know what he said," Lord Kavindra laughed, a sound so light and so full it made Lada want to smile along.

"Then why...?"

"Think, Nettle." Lord Kavindra poked a finger against the man's forehead. "If fifteen went into Amaryl Forest and the other fourteen died, how did he manage to survive?"

"You mean he lied?"

"Of course he lied." Lord Kavindra waved his fingers through the air, toward the front gate. "Bring a physician. This creature can do nothing to harm me in your absence."

Lada nodded her agreement and, though she didn't know it, her wide and honest eyes shone in the torchlight around her, lending her a look so innocent that none questioned her naivety.

It was this look that comforted Nettle and allowed him to turn and flee for the gate.

Lord Kavindra never said, but he found Lada's silent agreement quite winsome. Upon encountering her in the Common Grounds, Lord Kavindra had deduced she must be harmless. Seeing her tremble on her feet and hold her words lest she be scolded, he found he did not believe she could squash an insect, much less ferociously attack fifteen grown men.

With Nettle gone to fetch the physician, Lord Kavindra swung an arm toward the covered walkway nearby. "Let us retire indoors."

Lada studied him a moment, unsure whether to trust or doubt him. Thus far, Lord Kavindra had been a pleasant enough companion, soft to speak and slow to anger. Lada found, though she didn't know him, she trusted him. More so than the hunter who brought her into the city. This Lord Kavindra had done nothing to bring her harm. Quite the contrary. He had helped her from the moment they met.

The stone and wood kissed Lada's feet with a refreshing coolness. Her toes and soles missed the grasses and leaves of her forest, but at least the materials in the courtyard didn't scrape or burn her feet.

Lord Kavindra led her down the covered walkway, past room after room and corridor after corridor. She had never been in such a mansion, but Lada decided each eave and door must have a purpose. Else, what would one do with them? It seemed wasteful to keep more rooms than were needed.

The maze continued for a long while. Over bridges and across minuscule ponds. Lada would have liked to study the ponds in more depth, but she refused to fall behind. Not only would she never be able to find her way out, but she might anger her savior. Kindness came first, before any curiosity Lada held inside.

Lord Kavindra pushed open a pair of wood-and-paper doors, then stepped back. "Ladies first."

"Oh, I'm not a Lady," Lada spoke, finding it necessary to clarify the situation. She held no such title, and as far as she knew did not come from nobility. "I'm merely an herbalist."

Lord Kavindra kept his laughter in check. Both her comment and the fact that she commented at all delighted him. He had thought that the girl had gone mute out of fright. Now he found she spoke quite well and articulated her point, as guileless as her point may be. If he tried his luck, he might receive a bounty of information.

"If I do not refer to you as 'The Lady', how am I to refer to you?"

Lada blinked her surprise. The hunter hadn't asked for her name. He had simply referred to her as 'creature' or 'beast'. Lada didn't like the way those words rolled off his tongue.

Lord Kavindra seemed a genuine person, so Lada smiled her brightest smile and announced, "I am Lada of Flora Master's Hall."

"Lada." Lord Kavindra confirmed with a nod of his head. "You will use this room during your stay here. Please." He motioned his hand toward the open doors.

This time, Lada followed his silent instruction. Lord Kavindra's understanding and congeniality had quickly solidified Lada's thoughts about his character. He must be a good man, to be so kind to a girl everyone despised. That, or he had never been poisoned by the pollen polluting everyone's minds.

Deciding to trust the man who brought her to the mansion, Lada stepped over the threshold into the room.

Someone had already lit the candles within, lending a bright atmosphere to the chambers. Curtains hung in various patterns, creating a flow of spaces throughout. The room was similar in size to Lada's bedroom in Flora Master's Hall, with enough space to comfortably house a bed and a table.

It was to the table that Lord Kavindra roamed, taking his seat on one of the three stools situated there.

Lada scurried to follow suit, taking a seat on the stool opposite him and placing her hands in her lap. She had best behave while she was there. It would heighten her chances of going home.

Lord Kavindra lifted a kettle from the table's center and poured from it water, into a small porcelain cup. He settled the drink in front of Lada.

Lada accepted the gift with another smile. "Thank you."

Lord Kavindra watched her carefully. Her happiness, despite the pain she must feel. The way she tentatively sipped the liquid proffered. He had made assumptions and each one had proved true, in time.

Which was why Lord Kavindra asked his next question. "Do you understand what Tribute is?"

"No, but I've heard it mentioned," Lada set the cup on the table, grinning at the soft *clink* it made. "Is Tribute Master a very important title?"

Most would have scoffed at Lada's sudden change of subject. Not Lord Kavindra. In all his years residing in Mesmium, Lord Kavindra had never met the likes of Lada of Flora Master's Hall. He held a certain fondness for new, inexplicable things, and thus wanted nothing more than to answer all her questions and learn anything she would teach him.

"Tribute Master is in charge of making sure the contents of the Tribute match the specified inventory. He also takes responsibility for delivering Tribute to its destination safely. If anything goes wrong, it is Tribute Master's fault."

"And you're the Tribute Master?"

Lada didn't mind that blood had begun to crust on her arm and fingers. Nor did she care about the lashes on her shoulder and back. Curiosity took precedence now. Her questions came pouring forth as if this meeting were no difficult or strange thing.

Lord Kavindra, seeing the conversation distracted Lada from her wounds, answered forthwith. "This is my first year bearing the title."

His father had passed it on to Lord Kavindra's older brother, who hadn't wanted the title. In fear of being captured or killed by the fierce Dragon Tribe, he had passed the title down to his younger brother. That didn't change the fact that Lord Kavindra's elder brother found reasons to tell him how to do his job. In deference to the hierarchy of their family, Lord Kavindra often listened to the commands.

"You must do well," Lada encouraged. "If you've been given the responsibility, I am sure your role is well-deserved."

"I wouldn't use that term for it. If I make a mistake, Dra—"

"Don't be silly. It's your first time being Tribute Master. Small mistakes will be given leniency."

Under normal circumstances, Lord Kavindra would have corrected Lada. He might have told her about the purpose of the Tribute he traveled alongside, or the ferocity of Dragon Tribe's monarch. But her simplemindedness had convinced him that he mustn't say anything to shatter her naivete. Such a rare quality must be kept secure. Treasured.

So, Lord Kavindra merely smiled and gave a nod.

Lada had never felt happier than when she managed to help someone, especially after they had helped her. Seeing Lord Kavindra so encouraged by her words gave her a thrill of accomplishment.

Apparently, not only the Amarylites took a liking to her. Those outside could be friends, as well. Lada intended to be as kind to them as she would have been to her family back home. If she couldn't go back, she should make the best of it.

The thought lowered the corners of her lips into a frown.

Not go back? She shouldn't think that way. Especially not when her ailing plants and her friend the Great White Deer were waiting for her return.

Lada's heart ached at the thought of Flora Master's Hall. She had grown up there. Had spent every waking hour learning about the foliage and forest, blossoms and herbs. How could she stay away? No matter what happened, she must go back.

"Is something the matter? Are you hurting somewhere?" Lord Kavindra reached out a hand, but stopped before he touched Lada.

Now that he mentioned it, Lada recognized the pain in her own body. Her arm ached and her back stung, only made worse by every moment she had spent using the muscles therein. A belated groan leaped from her throat.

Lord Kavindra's hand landed lightly atop Lada's fingers. "Be brave, Lada. The physician will arrive soon."

He only hoped Nettle had told the man to hurry. Though, it might not have mattered if he mentioned time or not. A physician summoned to Verity Hall, home of the Tribute Master, would undoubtedly quicken his steps in arriving.

On cue, Nettle came scurrying through the open doors. "The physician, My Lord."

An aged and greying man followed close on Nettle's heels, his wise old eyes taking in the scene before him. With both hands settled around the handle of his medical basket, the old man dipped a bow to Lord Kavindra.

"How may I be of service tonight, Tribute Master?"

Lord Kavindra rose to his feet, one hand stretching out to denote the woman at the table. "She has had a harrowing afternoon. See to her wounds, if you don't mind."

Lada looked up from her introspective moment into a pair of eyes she would have recognized anywhere. They were far too similar to be a coincidence. Lada had seen those eyes as she grew, had witnessed the compassion and the wisdom therein. They were not the same, but they might as well be, for all the old stories existed in his gaze.

"Chief Elder?"

The question fell from Lada's lips unbidden, in a manner so quiet she doubted if anyone heard her. Only the old man's startled step back said he had indeed listened to her words. Nettle and Lord Kavindra didn't understand the cause of the sudden reaction.

The physician cleared his throat. "It is improper for you young men to be in the room while I examine her. Please wait outside."

"Of course."

Lord Kavindra shooed Nettle out the door. He spared only one glance over his shoulder before he, too, left. The doors swished shut behind him.

The physician settled his basket on the table and set to work busily emptying out the things he would need. "I am not your Chief Elder."

Lada tipped her head, studying him. He wasn't tall enough to be Chief Elder, nor did his hair have the speckled qualities that Chief Elder's bore. But his eyes were the same. His bearing exuded the same aura. To be so similar, but so different. Lada didn't believe such a coincidence existed.

"You look like him."

"But I am not him. I will thank you to address me as Physician, if anything."

Lada leaned forward, searching his face for any signs of recognition. "You belong to Amaryl, don't you?"

The physician violently cleared his throat, a not-so-subtle warning to Lada that she shouldn't speak of such matters within the gates of Mesmium.

"I won't tell anyone." Lada pressed a finger to her lips. "It's our secret."

With a sigh, the physician lifted Lada's arm to inspect the wound near her shoulder. "Are you sure to keep such a secret?"

"I'm from Amaryl, as well. I won't tell anyone about you." Lada winced as he probed the crusted wound. "Are you acquainted with Chief Elder?"

"Quite intimately." The physician pulled out an herb from the basket, dropping it into a bowl alongside a flower petal. "But I hardly think a woman in your position should be asking such things."

"In my position?"

"Ignorant. You don't even know where you're going or what Tribute means."

Lada yelped as the physician reopened her wound, only to take a wet cloth and clean her arm. She still managed to work up the courage to ask the most pertinent question burning her tongue.

"What does it mean? Where am I going?"

"You, dear girl, will soon be but a pretty decoration in Isonpool Palace."

"Isonpool Palace?"

Lada had never heard of the place. It must be terrible to deserve such ire from a man who came from Amaryl.

"Home of Dragon Tribe's king, the man who receives Tribute each year." The physician sighed, a long-suffering sound that echoed in his old chest and rattled his bones. "I'm afraid not much can help you, there."

"Can't help me?" Lada watched the man grind a poultice and apply it to her arm.

Only when he had finished did he grant her a spare glance. "Dragon Tribe is full of beasts. A flower like you won't last a week."

Lada had questions, and not nearly enough concerns. She had never before heard of Dragon Tribe's ferociousness, nor their love for war. She didn't know the tortures they had prepared or how she would be treated when she arrived. In Lada's mind, the world was simple. How could she know the depths and intricacies of relationships within Dragon Tribe?

She had just formed her most important question when the physician interrupted her.

"Let's have a look at that back, then."

After that, Lada found silence a better friend than inquisitiveness. Though she wanted to ask, Lada didn't dare.

Later, perhaps, she would regret her decision. But in the moment she cared only that she had found an Amaryl friend. And she had learned her final destination.

CHAPTER NINE
Velimir

Shimmering opal columns braced the vaulted ceiling of Fang-Throne Court. The floor, polished until it shone, reflected the glimmering rays of sunshine which managed to peek through slim windows. The Fang Throne, itself, could easily seat two people though it only ever held one. If that weren't enough to show the lavishness of Dragon Supreme, dozens of enormous, jagged stalagmites rose from behind, pointed outward toward the court. The black rock had been left rough and blemished, with only the tips polished and smooth.

No one dared set foot onto even the first step leading up to the throne, unless they sought immediate death. Only Dragon Supreme had access to such a seat.

The Ministers had arrived early to prepare the affairs of state that must be brought to attention. Davorin Astrophel, Dragon Supreme, put much importance on the affairs of his empire. Almost as much importance as he put on battles. To mishandle anything related to the empire meant serious punishment. Thus, the Ministers did their best to handle everything cautiously, but appropriately.

Having put everything in order, the Ministers now stood at various points along the floor. They needn't raise their voices in a hall such as this, for even the softest whisper would be amplified against the stone columns. It had been built as a place where no secrets could be kept. That had never stopped the Ministers from taking their secrets elsewhere.

Dong. Dong... A low-toned bell rang out the hour. Each minister counted off the tolls until the final, eighth toll faded off into the distance.

Fang-Throne Court's doors opened with a clunk and a groan.

Davorin Astrophel, Dragon Supreme, took his first step into the room, his boots clicking a steady rhythm as he made his way toward his throne.

One by one, each minister fell to their knees, hands pressed over their heart in the phoenix symbol. They remained that way as Dragon Supreme passed, his cloak trailing with a hiss behind him. No one dared rise. Few dared breathe.

Davorin mounted the steps to his throne slowly, enjoying the feeling of control and sovereignty. Only when he had reached his throne and turned to face his ministers did he utter his first words.

"You may rise."

Every minister rose to their feet, bent a bow, and straightened.

Davorin took his seat, perched on the edge of his throne. "Begin."

One of the elder ministers took a step to the middle of the room, a scroll held neatly in his hands. "Your cousin's funeral was held as dictated by his family. Would Your Majesty, Dragon Supreme, like the report?"

"Send it to the library," Davorin decided.

He didn't care what had happened after his cousin defied him. It hadn't been the first time that particular cousin had questioned Davorin's orders, and the rebellion had been getting more serious by the week. Taking care of the problem early was the only way to ensure a coup would never take place. Davorin held no fondness for his cousins, anyway.

The elder minister returned to his position near one of the columns.

Instead, a woman with clothes the color of ice and hair the color of glowing embers took the now-vacated position. Nerys Galashiel. Davorin would recognize her anywhere, not only because she was the sole female minister to grace his court, but also because she had a way of making her presence known.

"My Lord, Dragon Supreme," Nerys began, the picture of respect. "It has come to my attention that you are to be wed."

"What of it?"

He tired of this subject. Had not an order been given? The Treaty stated in no uncertain terms what was expected of both parties involved. Even Davorin Astrophel would not be the first to break such an agreement.

"Forgive my insolence, Your Majesty, Dragon Supreme, but I fear for your safety and the safety of Dragon Tribe."

Curious, Davorin remained silent. He had little idea what the red-headed maiden might say or do, but her attempts at using her wiles amused him. Somewhat.

Nerys took the silence as permission to continue. "Surely Orafel will send a spy. A woman too rooted in her people to be of any use to ours. I fear she may bring harm to My Lord and his household."

"Harm?" A laugh leaped from Davorin's lips, too loud and boisterous to be considered anything but sarcastic. Davorin rose to his feet, sneering down his nose at the female minister. "You think me weak enough to come to harm at the hands of a mere woman?"

"Of course that was not my intention, My Lord." Nerys went down on one knee, her head low and her eyes cast to the ground. "My concern is for the safety of our people's secrets. And for the safety and happiness of our sovereign."

"I will accept the Orafel bride should she arrive safely. No more discussion."

Nerys shut up about it, but Davorin saw the wheels spinning in her overdramatic head. She must have deeper thoughts and concerns about it than she let on.

"Is there nothing else?" Davorin pushed.

Nerys rose to her feet once more. "I would address the seat left vacant by the... *passing*... of your cousin."

"No need. It has been handled according to protocol. Which brings me to my own point of business." Davorin flicked his fingers toward the door, but directed his message to Cadfael. "Hail him."

Cadfael saluted with his sword, took two steps backward, and turned to march to the giant doors. He gave an order to one of the doorkeepers, who in turn spoke with his fellow guard.

The doors swung open again, this time to reveal a tall, dark man who looked suspiciously similar to the dead cousin.

Velimir took in the room before him with a barely-concealed smirk. After his brother's death, he would inherit the position left open, by the grace of Dragon Supreme. His cousin.

Forbearance did not reside in the vocabulary of Dragon Tribe nobles, so to see Velimir at court rose the Ministers' ire.

Velimir had done nothing to deserve the position granted him. He had gained the power he now held in a roundabout and diabolical way. Aside from that, the Ministers would all argue it had been an unwise decision to appoint Velimir, as it had been his dearest older brother who had died at the hands of Dragon Supreme. In a place such as Isonpool Palace, no one could be trusted to forgive their transgressors.

Yet, there he stood, tall and proud in the center of the floor, his chin raised and his hands folded in a salute. Not a single minister said a word, as Velimir had been appointed by Dragon Supreme, personally. To question Velimir's presence would be to question the judgment of Davorin Astrophel. All had seen where that ended. It was, ironically, the entire reason Velimir stood before them now.

With the absence of complaints, Velimir took the opportunity to dip a bow. "Your Majesty, Dragon Supreme. Long may your reign endure."

The greeting, though standard, caused many eyes to roll. Hypocrites existed in any government office, and the court of Qranbu was no exception. They, too, often gave the greeting with sarcasm, but the Ministers found it difficult to stomach when someone else did the same.

Dragon Supreme either didn't notice the sarcasm, or he didn't care. A wave of his hand was all it took to dismiss the pleasantries.

"Welcome to Fang-Throne Court, Velimir," Davorin offered, his own words laced with as much facetiousness as Velimir's had been. "I trust we'll work well together in the future, regardless of... more personal difficulties."

"My brother's insurrection became his downfall. My Lord's decision was wise." Velimir bent another bow, no doubt striving to receive Dragon Supreme's favor. "I will serve you loyally, Your Lordship."

No one needed say a word about the promise. With his brother's death still heavy on his shoulders, Velimir would not be able to serve Dragon Supreme *loyally*. Hidden below the surface of his words and actions, seething rage simmered. His calmness bespoke it.

The Ministers dared not question why Davorin Astrophel allowed Velimir to join the royal court, but all knew one thing for certain. Davorin Astrophel, Dragon Supreme, unquestionably had a reason and an objective. Their ruthless sovereign never made a move without a plan. He couldn't hold his lofty position if he made reckless decisions.

Dragon Supreme dismissed his cousin with a flick of his wrist. His silence said more than his words might have, for Dragon Supreme dearly loved to have the last word in such serious situations. Silence meant he had decided to calculate each move he made, going forward. Silence meant only disaster for his cousin, Velimir. But no one dared to address the issue with Velimir. Most wanted to see him bring disaster upon his own head.

With the problem of the vacant position put to a swift end, Dragon Supreme turned his attention back to the female minister.

"Have I provided a satisfactory answer, Nerys?"

His mention of her name held no affection, yet Nerys smiled as she answered, "My concerns have been appeased, Your Lordship."

"We will move on to other matters. Inform me of the Tribute's path through Qranbu." Davorin sat forward, perched at the very edge of his throne when he uttered the next command. "Make no more mention of the bride."

The minister overseeing the Tribute Parade's path took the floor, cautiously and timidly. The bride was the importance of this year's tribute. To avoid the subject meant reworking one's thought process. A feat the minister admirably accomplished.

"This year, the Tribute Parade will take the shortest route up the mountain. They will stop at five cities along the way, never staying long but passing the nights in safety. Tribute should arrive within a fortnight."

Dragon Supreme gave an affirmative tip of his head. "Send spies to each city, and a troop of guards with them. Ensure nothing—and no one—slips away."

The minister, reading the situation and the room, cleared his throat. "What should happen if something were to go missing from this year's Tribute?"

"I said, *nothing*." Dragon Supreme rose to his feet, trailing a clawed finger along the arm of his throne. "See to it."

As usual, The Ministers had no choice. They would do as they were told or face their sovereign's wrath.

None could have anticipated the consequences of the actions they planned in secret. If they had foreseen what would happen, they might not have taken the first step. But, hindsight showed what foresight did not, and by the time The Ministers realized their mistake, all would be too late.

CHAPTER TEN

The Orafel Princess

Birds chirped overhead, hovering around the windows and overhang outside. The same moving water and rustling leaves from the night before created a similar atmosphere, but now the sun had risen and the hustle and bustle of people running to and fro added a new layer of ambiance.

Lada rose, with difficulty, from the bed she had used. The physician had indeed tended her wounds, but she found them more tender after a night's rest. Her skin itself lamented against any form of movement, but Lada knew she couldn't stay in bed. Not when everyone else had risen and gotten to work. She had never been in such a busy place. Lada desired to understand how these people operated in their daily lives.

Her plants! Lada scrambled to stand, only to remember her plants had not come with her. A shame and sorrow. Who would care for her plants in her absence? Would the elders know enough to send someone? Or had they not found her missing from her place?

Dazed and confused, Lada missed the single step between her bed and the floor and went stumbling forward. No sooner had she found her footing than a knock sounded at her door.

Startled and caught unawares, Lada stared at the wood-and-paper entry like it might burst into flames. Until she finally came to her senses.

"Please come in," Lada called politely.

The doors parted.

Lord Kavindra smiled his widest, sincerest smile at the bed-headed elvin creature. "Good morning, Lada."

"Good morning, Lord Kavindra." Lada folded her hands before herself in an attempt to seem more put-together, oblivious to the state of her hair and dress.

Once more, Lord Kavindra found himself hardly able to contain his chuckle. Having never met a true Amarylite before, Lord Kavindra could not have prepared himself for the ethereal klutz who stood before him now, looking more girl than woman. If not for the public announcement that she would leave along with the Tribute, Lord Kavindra would be tempted to harbor her under the protection of the Tribute Master's household.

As it stood, it would be safer for the impish herbalist to leave the city with the Tribute Parade.

A cough served to both clear his throat and remove the grin from Lord Kavindra's too-happy face. "I've brought some things for you."

"You have?" Lada searched Lord Kavindra's empty hands, her head swinging back and forth in case she had missed something. "Where are they?"

Lord Kavindra turned toward the doors to hide the reemerging smile. Never had he encountered a woman who so brightened the atmosphere of Verity Hall. Lest he take too strong a liking to her, Lord Kavindra distracted himself with other matters.

"Come in now," Lord Kavindra instructed.

At the sound of his command, a string of maids trailed into the room. Each, in their arms, carried a tray laden with various feminine delights. The last to enter held a tray of medicine vials. No doubt to treat Lada's healing injuries. In unison, the maids dipped a curtsy.

"Oh, no need to bow!"

Lada's arms shot forward to straighten the maids. She couldn't accept respect on such a level. She bore no title and had done nothing to merit such subservience. Lada would rather make friends than rule subjects.

Lord Kavindra rested a hand beneath Lada's elbow to draw her to a straighter position, as well. "They've been borrowed from Her Highness's entourage to serve you this morning. When you're put together, you may venture to the front courtyard. We mean to be off before noon."

Off before noon. The words rang in Lada's head, a peal of reality reminding her of her place. A mere decoration in a parade of treasures.

If not for the fact that Lord Kavindra had saved her, tended her wounds, and become her friend, Lada would seek escape at the first available opportunity. Since Lord Kavindra had indeed become her friend, Lada felt it unfair and cruel to run away from him. It would get him in trouble, then pour guilt over her head for the rest of her life, happy or not.

If this were her fate, so be it. Lada would welcome it with open arms and an understanding mindset. But that didn't mean the sharp pang of longing for her own home went away. After all, there were Amarylites who trusted her in their weakest time, when they needed her most. What would they do without an apprentice within Flora Master's Hall?

"Lada?" Lord Kavindra's inquisitive voice brought her back to her senses.

"Hm?"

"Allow the maidservants to treat your wounds and prepare you for the journey. I will be in the courtyard when you are done."

Lord Kavindra had left before Lada could ask the pertinent questions.

The maids descended on her like a swarm of bees. With the Tribute Master gone, they found no reason to remain silent, thus the chattering of half a dozen women began in earnest. Each found the Amaryl woman quite charming in a variety of ways, from how she treated them to how her skin fairly glowed. One even commented on the quality of her dress, though it had been ruined during the past days' excursions.

Hands flew, well-practiced and well-prepared. Medicine touched her skin, delicate but firm, and Lada went still so it did not tear her fragile wounds. Lada's old dress disappeared, more than likely headed to the incineration pile. A new one draped over her shoulders, to the tips of her toes, floating around her like mist.

The same half-dozen pairs of hands managed to push Lada onto a stool, where the real work began. Someone started on Lada's hair. Another took up a makeup brush. Yet a third reached for Lada's hands. The pampering began.

Lada didn't know who to focus on first, as she found every aspect of their service fascinating. Never before had someone so concentratedly paid such attention to her. Lada had always been in charge of her own beauty and hygiene, save for the precious memories of her mother plaiting Lada's hair. No one had doted on her before. Lada found it disconcerting.

Feathery touches to her skin counteracted the stronger tugs to her hair as the maid behind her braided and coiled a graceful style against the crown of Lada's head. The maid with Lada's hands in hers had taken some sort of small brush to the nails, cleaning out the deep-set dirt thereupon.

Their intentions eluded Lada, but she allowed them room to do what they must. After all, they said nothing but nice things as they worked.

"How soft and smooth her hair is," commented the maid working on another coil.

The second maid, now drawing with a brush upon Lada's forehead and the sides of her eyes, gave a joyful giggle. "Her skin is smoother than our lady's."

Anything else they might have said was lost on Lada when one of the freer maids returned with a tray of flowers. The sight of the beautiful petals alone was enough to force a smile onto Lada's lips. She dared not say, as she didn't understand the purpose of the flowers, but the colors reminded her of home and for that she felt nothing but gratitude.

One by one, the maid strung the blossoms into Lada's hair, creating a decorative piece that bespoke Lada's floral heritage.

Then, the maids took a step back and allowed Lada the room to breathe.

"You are beautiful, Lady Lada," one offered cheerily.

"Are you through?" Lada stared at each maid in turn, awaiting a positive answer now that they had released her.

Lord Kavindra had said to meet him in the courtyard. Lada still heard the bustle of humans and wanted nothing more than to explore the source of the sound. If the maids had finished, Lada could follow her curiosity out into the mansion.

"We are finished. Except for—" the maid didn't manage to finish her sentence.

Lada shot to her feet and raced for the door, her hands buried in her billowing skirt to lift it so her bare feet could move freely.

"Lady Lada! Wait!" the maid called after her.

Lada didn't hear. She had already taken to the corridors, running in the general direction of the sounds she wanted to investigate. The maids chased after her, but none were as used to flying as Lada.

That's how the courtyard came to see Lada, lower half of her long hair flying behind her and petals dancing on her head, racing barefoot onto the cobblestones with a host of maids behind her shouting about her shoes.

Unbeknownst to Lada, the spectacular entrance made her look more like a fairy than a woman, and drew the eye of every man escorting Tribute Pieces through the open courtyard. For an infinitesimal second, the world of tribute bearing stopped moving. The bearers forgot even to whisper and gossip about this ethereal woman suddenly found in their midst.

As for Lada, she might have kept running, right into one of the Tribute Bearers, had not a woman draped in blue as bright as the sky stepped into her path. To avoid knocking this new and unannounced woman to the ground, Lada fumbled to a halt.

The woman looked down her nose toward Lada, eyes focused and firm.

Lada regained her footing, stumbling only twice along the way, and presented this woman with her brightest smile. "Good morning."

"Lady Lada! Lady Lada..." one of the maids caught up to her, panting heavily from her forced marathon. "Your shoes, Lady Lada. It's important you wear them."

"Shoes?" Lada lifted her skirt and stared down at her bare feet. "Oh. The shells for my feet. Do I need them?"

"Yes, Lady Lada. A proper woman doesn't go around without her shoes." The maid held up the cream-colored boots with an enticing grin.

Lada stared at the shoes, assessing if she would be able to function with the Orafel shells or not. It seemed rude to turn down their custom just because she would rather be barefoot. Especially when they had been so kind to her.

After spending her whole life in a forest where she did as she pleased, Lada found it excruciating to agree to binding her feet inside something so constricting. But she held out a foot toward the maid.

Relieved, the maid bent to fix the shoes around Lada's delicate feet.

The woman in blue lifted her chin in utmost understanding of the situation playing out before her eyes. "You are the Amaryl addition."

Lada's head snapped up at the mention of her heritage. A smile brighter than the sun itself spread across her lips, pressing her eyes into joyous half-moons.

"You know me?"

"I've been told about you, as my entourage was requested to make you presentable."

Lord Kavindra had mentioned that, Lada realized quickly. A thought back to the morning's events brought his exact words to Lada's mind.

"They've been borrowed from Her Highness's entourage..."

A gasp sprang from Lada's lips. Her foot, half-encased by the boot the maid had been lacing, returned to the ground beneath her. With utmost respect and humility, Lada bent a deep curtsy to the woman before her.

"It's a pleasure to meet you, your highness," Lada offered in a tone so friendly none could refuse its pull.

The Orafel Princess lifted her eyebrows, impressed Lada had deduced her identity so speedily. Surely, no one had explained the princess's part in this Tribute to someone as lowly as an Amaryl servant girl. This floral imp must have deduced it from things she had heard upon her arrival at Verity Hall. As things turned out, Lada of Flora Master's Hall was not as stupid as the princess had been brought to believe.

"I suppose," the princess returned Lada's greeting, unsure what to do with such a spritely and free-spirited woman.

"Your Highness!" Lord Kavindra's voice soared from his perch atop the steps at the main gate.

In a flash, he had descended into the yard, his purposeful march headed straight toward the two women in the middle of everyone's way. Lord Kavindra hadn't meant to introduce them in such a way. Two opposing personalities could combust in such tight quarters. He had meant to gently work the princess into the thought of having an Amarylite tag-along.

Lord Kavindra stopped at a respectable distance to bow to the higher-ranking noble. "Your Highness, my apologies for the interruption. I believe she meant no disrespect."

"I took no offense, Tribute Master." The princess graciously offered Lord Kavindra her attention. "I merely came upon her on my way to fetch my entourage."

"Yes, of course, they should be returned to you." Lord Kavindra shuffled toward the maid, lowering his voice to ask his next question. "How did she arrive so quickly?"

"Her feet have wings, My Lord," the maid answered with a laugh, "but they are sadly lacking of shoes."

"I doubt she wears them where she comes from." The princess offered a limp smile to the creature before her. "Mitsie called you Lada. Is that your name?"

"I am Lada of Flora Master's Hall," Lada explained yet again, as happily as last time she had announced it.

"I am Princess Zohana, daughter of His Highness the Eighth Prince and niece of His Majesty, King Vaibhav." Princess Zohana dipped her head in greeting. "As we share the same fate, may we get along well in the coming days."

Lada froze, her brain processing the information at a rate much slower than she picked up on social cues. In an effort to give a faster answer, she skipped over the familial relations to the Orafel king and focused on the general aura of Princess Zohana's comment.

"You mean..." Lada said slowly, thoughtfully, "you wish for us to be friends?"

Always one to accept friendships, even to her own detriment, Lada stared hopefully at the princess before her. If Princess Zohana agreed to the friendship, it would mean Lada had made not one but two friends in a matter of a day. She felt quite accomplished about such a feat.

Princess Zohana gave a tentative, diplomatic nod.

Forgetting all tact and protocol, Lada launched forward to snatch the princess's hands within her own. She paid no mind to the gasp from the nearby maid, nor did she notice Lord Kavindra's swift lurch forward.

He meant to separate the two, but Princess Zohana shot him a glare so stern that Lord Kavindra could do nothing but stand back and watch.

"I'm so very grateful to be your friend," Lada told the princess in no uncertain terms. "It would be terrible for the two of us, sharing the same fate, to put distance between ourselves along the journey. It would only create unnecessary tension, don't you think?"

To the surprise of every onlooker, Princess Zohana turned her hands in Lada's hold and returned the firm grasp. "I think we will be excellent friends, Lada of Flora Master's Hall."

"May I hug you?" Lada's eyes widened, earnest and begging for physical touch.

Princess Zohana hesitated. A seasoned warrior, Princess Zohana had all but put aside the need for physical interaction. No doubt the offer of a hug made her uncomfortable. However, Lada didn't give her a choice as she threw her arms around the princess and gave a quick squeeze.

"Lada," Lord Kavindra intervened after the span of two seconds. "Go with Mitsie and put your shoes on. Your carriage is all but ready to depart."

Lada, not suspecting anything amiss about the instructions, released the princess to follow the maid to a nearby bench.

Lord Kavindra turned to watch the debacle of trying to put shoes on Lada's ever-moving feet. His words addressed the royal woman at his side.

"Have you made a decision, then?"

"I have." Princess Zohana blew out a breath, clearly puzzled at the little woman's actions. "We should return her to Amaryl. She knows no guile."

Lord Kavindra couldn't be more pleased with the princess's suggestion. To keep Lada away from her forest home would surely ruin the very character that made Lada shine. To preserve it, they would have to return her on their way up the mountain.

"I will arrange the path," Lord Kavindra declared.

Should either have realized how terribly awry such a simple plan could go, they would not have rearranged the Tribute Parade's path. Useless as their plan would become, both Lord Kavindra and Princess Zohana saw no other options for the Amaryl woman. None that would keep her alive. For they both knew the horrors of Qranbu and its Dragon Tribe and neither wished Lada to be subjected to such fear.

Fate had other plans, and by the time they realized this, the moment to escape would have already passed.

"I'm ready!" Lada called, haphazardly clopping her way across the courtyard.

Whereas Orafel children wore their first pair of shoes before their first birthday, Lada gave every appearance of never having worn foot apparel in her entire life. She walked like a toddler, kicking her feet out to the side to avoid tripping over her own ankles and stopping every two steps to rearrange her skirt around her toes.

Lord Kavindra dropped his head into his palm. Never had he seen such a sight. It made him want to either laugh out loud or sob out of consternation. They shouldn't have insisted on Lada wearing shoes, but it was too late to back out now.

Princess Zohana, her face the mask of stoic indifference, turned to go. "I'll leave her to you. Do ensure she alights her carriage without harming herself."

"Yes, Your Highness."

Lord Kavindra had every intention of ensuring Lada's safety. From what he had seen of her, she had quite the danger-prone streak, but he would do his best to tamp it down.

Lada finally arrived at her place beside Lord Kavindra, all good cheer despite her shoe dilemma.

Lord Kavindra offered her his arm. It would help her to fall less and appear more graceful before the Tribute Bearers.

"Shall we depart?"

"Oh, that isn't something I have a say in. You say when we stay or go, as Tribute Master." A pause for her to wrap her fingers around his elbow. "Is it a long journey?"

"Not if we stay on schedule."

Lord Kavindra purposefully left out the part about returning her home. They wouldn't want to get her hopes up if their plan failed.

Lada continued to chatter, from the courtyard all the way to the side of the litter assigned to her, but Lord Kavindra barely heard a word. He was far too preoccupied with how he would manage to leave behind the most cheerful individual he had met in his entire life.

CHAPTER ELEVEN
A Secret Plan

"Welcome home, My Lady," Nerys's chambermaid offered sweetly upon Nerys's return to the Galashiel Mansion.

Nerys paid her no mind, her own thoughts scurrying elsewhere, to other problematic issues.

Her absence during the meeting in the War Room had brought about a sea of things unexpected. If she had been there that day, she could have calmed the situation before it escalated.

Nerys found she rather detested the new minister. Velimir, wasn't it? The younger brother of Dragon Supreme's deceased cousin. Undoubtedly, Velimir must hold a grudge.

To top it all off, Dragon Supreme had refused to listen to her concerns over his new bride. Had he no foresight? Cared he not that a spy would enter his bedchamber?

Oblivious to her lady's inner struggles, the chambermaid scurried after her. "Did court run over, My Lady? Why are you late to return?"

"I walked back," Nerys declared detachedly.

"From Isonpool Palace?!" The chambermaid clasped her hands over her heart, stopping the life-threatening flutter of her most important organ before it began. "What of your guard? And your carriage?"

Nerys flung an arm through the air, a directive meant to silence her chambermaid and allow Nerys time to think.

Though loyal, the chambermaid knew not how to catch a hint, and thus continued on her flabbergasted tirade.

"It's dangerous for a lady to walk alone in Isonpool Fortress. What were you thinking, leaving your guard behind? You might have been caught by ruffians and then what would become of the Galashiel name?"

Nerys spun, her hand flying once more, this time to catch the chambermaid's mouth in her palm. She need not be reminded of the responsibility on her shoulders. Nerys had borne its weight since she was but a girl. Every word she spoke, every move she made, either strengthened or weakened the Galashiel family's hold in court and in Qranbu. She would never bring harm upon her family's name.

That was why Nerys needed to act quickly when it came to her future. No other would steal away that which she had worked so diligently for during all these years.

"I am home and I am safe."

Nerys released the chambermaid's lips. The woman would stop questioning her mistress's decisions so long as Nerys had come to no harm.

Indeed, the chambermaid dropped the subject in favor of listening to Nerys's new demands.

"Seek out a tight-lipped guard and send him to fetch me information."

"Information, My Lady?" the chambermaid blinked her eyes, waiting for the remainder of the instruction.

"On Lord Velimir. Whatever he can find will be helpful."

"Yes, My Lady. Is there anything else?"

"When the servant is dispatched, personally go to the Prime Minister and give him the following message." Nerys took a breath, stilling her rattled nerves and upheaved ire. "Execute the plan as we have discussed. The cost is as we all knew it to be."

If anyone should overhear the message, they would not be able to understand what she meant even if they realized it had been a code.

Nerys knew how to keep secrets and operate in the dark. She had been forced to learn the tactics in order to survive in the court. No one would fault her for taking matters into her own hands, when the well-being of her family's household depended on her own plans going smoothly.

Nerys didn't cherish the malevolent actions she pursued, but she understood the importance of clearing the path for her nation. This would allow Qranbu freedom and cut the chain of interdependency along the way.

The plan she had discussed with the Eight High Nobles would have to come to fruition. They had no other choice but to take matters into their own hands. When they had cleared the way before Dragon Supreme, he would see her worth and offer her all she wanted and more. Of this, Nerys was certain.

She had only to wait for the satisfactory end.

CHAPTER TWELVE
The Tribute Parade

The Tribute Parade departed Mesmium among a throng of celebratory residents. Men, women, and children all turned up to see the splendor and to ogle at the treasures visible from afar.

Streamers flew from the corners of every cart and carriage in the procession, held aloft by sturdy poles fastened to the infrastructure. Only after they had exited Mesmium's gates did the Tribute Bearers lower the streamers, for safety. Should anyone with ill intentions see the colorful banners, the Tribute Parade would become a quick target for their villainy. After all, Orafel's greatest treasures lay within a single-file caravan. Even the threat of Dragon Tribe would do little to overpower the temptation of incomparable riches.

The Tribute Master rode at the front of the procession, high atop a mighty war steed, but on occasion he would slip back to check on the Tribute Pieces following his lead.

Directly behind him, surrounded by a dozen guards of utmost integrity, Princess Zohana's carriage rolled along.

Beyond the carriage, a litter bedecked in a thousand rose petals and led by a single white steed carried Lada of Flora Master's Hall. Lada had opened her windows to survey the passing scenery and, sporadically, stuck her full head out of the window to look up and down the line of Tribute.

None but Tribute Master dared tell her to stay inside her carriage. Even the guards surrounding Princess Zohana only glanced at her antics with wry acceptance.

The hours wore on, one after another after another, all full of Lord Kavindra backtracking to Lada's carriage to remind her that closing her windows and staying inside would keep her safer along their way.

The constant reminders, for the most part, worked. Until the parade turned down the path leading through the outlying forest around Amaryl.

"The forest!" Lada's flower-laden head poked out of her carriage again, whipping back and forth to take in the trees and foliage around them.

Lord Kavindra pulled the reins to slow his horse, this time intent on making Lada see the necessity of staying hidden.

"Lada," Lord Kavindra scolded. "Do you hold no respect for me?"

Lada blinked, her focus suddenly shifting from the greenery to Lord Kavindra's face. "I have the utmost respect for you, Lord Kavindra."

"Then why won't you listen to my warnings? You should remain inside your carriage."

"We're in the forest."

Lada said it like it explained everything, when in actuality it only left Lord Kavindra more confused than ever before.

Though he knew Lada came from the forest, he had not expected her to so adore the environment that she would risk her own safety. Did Lada not know the kinds of bandits and thieves lurking in the deepest brush along this path?

"You needn't worry," Lada continued gently. "All is as it should be on this path, at this moment."

Lord Kavindra shook his head at the naive woman. "And how would you know?"

"I listened." Lada propped her arms upon the windowsill, her chin resting atop them when she closed her eyes and inhaled. "Trees. Leaves. Creatures. A brook. Nothing is out of place along this stretch of path. No harm will come to us."

Once again, Lord Kavindra stood amazed at the content of Lada's innocent head. An experienced tracker by Orafel's standards, Lord Kavindra knew the forest road like he knew the back of his hand. Even he could not tell a genuine bird call from those given as signals by the bandits. Let alone listening to the tiniest sounds of the forest and knowing when one did not fit in.

Could she really tell the difference between leather and leaves, just by listening?

Lest he fall deeper into Lada's enchanting nature, Lord Kavindra changed the subject. "The Amaryl border is nearby."

"Is it?" Lada opened her eyes to look around again. "How closely will we pass by? May I visit the border to send word to my Elders about my situation?"

Lord Kavindra had not the heart to tell Lada of their plans to return her. Not when he couldn't promise if the plan would work. Returning an Amarylite was nearly as difficult as extracting one.

"Probably not," he sufficed.

"I didn't think I'd be allowed. My apologies for making things difficult for you."

They must be a thousand times harder on you, Lord Kavindra mused.

Not once since he met her had Lada complained about her predicament. She had taken the knowledge of her captivity with surprising grace, hardly commenting on the cruel things done unto her. As he knew she was not stupid, Lord Kavindra wondered at the adaptability of this Amaryl woman.

"My Lord!" One of the forward-running scouts returned, shattering the moment of silence.

Lord Kavindra left Lada perched on her carriage's windowsill and turned to the man who arrived at his horse's side. "Speak."

"We won't make Qranbu by nightfall, but we've found a suitable clearing for setting up camp."

"Good. Prepare for our arrival."

The scout gave another bow, turned on his heel, and set off running again.

Lord Kavindra never mentioned that they hadn't planned to reach Qranbu by nightfall. Leaving a little late. Riding a little slow. It had all been part of his and Princess Zohana's plan to return Lada to her homeland.

Princess Zohana may not have a choice about her future, but they both refused to allow Lada to be ruined by a place such as Isonpool

Palace. Lada would trust someone she shouldn't, and it would be the end of her. No one wanted to see her young life sacrificed.

Thus, Lord Kavindra would let her go, though he wanted nothing more than to ask her to stay. Bright spots, in his world, were few and far between. Lada could be useful in lightening Lord Kavindra's heavy load.

A tug on the hem of his tunic brought Lord Kavindra's attention back around to the woman in the litter.

"Are we staying in the forest tonight?"

A genuine, joyous smile radiated from her lips, catching Lord Kavindra unawares.

Once more remembering that he had told Lada nothing of their plans, Lord Kavindra returned the smile with practiced grace. "It appears so."

The hands folded on the windowsill now lifted to pound together in a series of childlike claps. A hearty, girlish laugh leaped from Lada and echoed in the forest air.

"Are you that happy?" Lord Kavindra asked skeptically.

Lada nodded. "I didn't think I would get to spend another night in the forest. I couldn't ask for a better parting present."

So simple, the things that made Lada smile. Lord Kavindra couldn't bear to see her overcome her displacement with joviality anymore. Thus, he took his leave to return to the head of the parade.

Lada didn't mind his departure, as she had plenty of things outside her window to keep her occupied. Despite the rumbling of wheels and calls from riders to horses, Lada heard the forest singing to her. Birds chirped and creatures on the floor chittered and chattered, welcoming her into their midst.

Lada propped her head on her arms, listening to their cries. "I've missed you, too."

She remained like that, communing with the things that had grown up alongside her, until an hour later when the parade came to an abrupt halt in a clearing between two copses of trees.

Camp had been made, tents erected for the women and blankets stacked for Tribute Bearers to use. Every man in the parade would rotate shifts, to watch out in case bandits or robbers arrived. The Princess's guards would be in charge of her security, leaving Lord Kavindra and his men to watch over Lada.

Truth be told, no one cared whether Lada stayed or left the parade. She would hardly be missed by the Princess's guards, too busy watching over their charge to add another. The Tribute Bearers only came to deliver treasures and get paid. An errant Amarylite was none of their business. This clearing, at this time and place, was the easiest solution to saving Lada's life. Lord Kavindra knew as such, and acted upon that knowledge.

His own vigil, he set up beside Lada's tent. She would undoubtedly wish to frolic while the guards prepared the meal, but when nighttime fell he meant to be the one who returned her back to whence she came.

If only he had known how tragically his and the princess's plan would fail them.

CHAPTER THIRTEEN
The Forest Debacle

With the sun set and the fires blazing, the forest took on a whole new atmosphere. Even Amarylites trembled at the thought of traversing the forest at night. The Orafel Tribute Parade wished for nothing more than they wished for morning to come.

Had they known what lurked beyond the fire's glowing circle, they might have shook harder. For deep in the foliage, disguised by leaves and twigs, a passel of blackguards waited for their opportunity to arrive.

Vigilant Lada, though deft at hearing abnormalities in the forest surrounding her, had worn herself out on the journey and—having discerned no trouble earlier—did not think to listen for trouble now. Even if she had thought to listen, the fire-grilled pheasant in front of her would have distracted Lada from those thoughts. Food had a way of deafening her senses and enticing her to focus on nothing else.

Those watching cared nothing for the girl feasting upon a pheasant. Instead, they searched for a more noble woman, one with war in her veins and only Orafel in her mind. Such a woman wouldn't care for pheasant as did the sprite by the fire, nor would she lower herself to eat with the men.

Only one such oddity existed, identified by her silhouette against the side of her tent. Within, she must have quite the royal spread on her table, but her shadowy hands never rushed or shook. This was the kind of woman the night rogues sought, the kind they had been told to pursue.

So still and patiently did the scoundrels sit that not even the most watchful guard noticed their presence. Each of the hidden men knew they had one chance to succeed. If they failed their mission, their lives would end by daybreak.

The camp rustled, men spreading out to take watch over the Tribute or to lie down in the shadows. The fire dimmed. The princess's light went out.

Lord Kavindra, seeing the time had come, rose to his feet and beckoned Lada to do the same.

Lada stumbled over the new shoes, but managed to trail behind Lord Kavindra toward her tent.

"Is something the matter?"

"Nothing." Lord Kavindra peeled back the flap for her. "Lie down and rest, for in a few short hours, I have a surprise for you."

No one would miss Lada, but objections would be raised if Lord Kavindra were to take her into the forest now. He wanted no rumors to fly. Letting Lada go swiftly and wordlessly would make it as though she had been but a pretty dream for the Tribute Parade. That was the ending Lada deserved.

"A surprise?" Lada shuffled closer, breaking the sphere of personal space around Lord Kavindra. "What kind of surprise? May I have a hint?"

Lord Kavindra shook his head, denying her request before he ushered her into the safety of her tent. "Rest first."

Lada didn't ask anything, but oh how she wanted to. Did he expect her to be able to sleep now that he had told her of a surprise? Lada had only received a genuine surprise present twice in her life. Both from her now-deceased mother. To gain a surprise here must mean things would go well in the future.

Therefore, Lada found herself unable to truly sleep. She tossed and turned, rolling over and over until she dozed off uncomfortably.

She woke startled, though Lada couldn't place why. Around her, the sounds of men sleeping and a few patrolling floated to her ears. Those had not been what startled her sensitive reflexes.

Rising from the pile of blankets beneath her, Lada reached for the flap at the front of her tent. She could not determine what had irritated her senses. A peek out into the darkness revealed nothing to be frightened of. Nothing to make her wary. Lada lifted one foot out onto the dirt pathway, then the other.

Still, nothing stirred that shouldn't. Had she dreamed of treachery? Had the past days' stress finally caught up with her?

Fwump. This time, the sound didn't fit.

Lada turned toward the new noise. It had come from Princess Zohana's tent. Lada would like to think Princess Zohana had the same issues sleeping as she did, but the abject silence afterward propelled Lada toward the Princess's door.

One of the guards stirred, only to roll over and go back to sleep when he saw it was Lada.

Lada pulled aside the princess's tent flap, ducked her head inside, and gasped.

Lada had personally seen the princess retire for sleep, but now the tent lay empty, save for a single piece of paper perched in the center of the princess's dinner table. Everything inside Lada told her not to touch a thing, but her curiosity got the better of her. She reached for the paper.

Thirty seconds later, Lada knew. Something dire had happened, and she must tell the others. She started with the princess's lax guards.

"Princess Zohana is missing!" Lada called, jabbing a toe against the sleeping guard's shoulder.

The guard, upon hearing the words, jumped to his feet and pulled his sword.

Lada scuffled aside, unwilling to be the sacrifice the weapon demanded.

The guard checked the tent a second time, coming out with a grim look upon his face. A whistle appeared from beneath his tunic, put to his lips to make the clarion call of danger.

The camp sprang to life.

Lanterns lit. Tribute Bearers came running. The princess's guards set off into the nearby woods.

Lada stood still, allowing the whole ordeal to play out around her. If she moved, she might draw attention to herself, and then what would she do? They might suspect her of things she never would have done. Lada didn't appreciate being suspected.

Lord Kavindra appeared, seemingly out of thin air, and took Lada by the wrist.

"Come with me," he enticed.

"But the princess—" Lada didn't manage to finish her sentence.

Lord Kavindra made use of the chaos to implement his original plan. He pulled Lada into the trees, directing her deeper and deeper into the darkness and the night. Farther and farther from the camp.

Lada gave Lord Kavindra's sleeve a tug. "Where are we going? Are we fleeing?"

"I'm taking you home," Lord Kavindra announced solemnly.

"Home?" Lada stumbled along behind him, until finally it dawned on her what he meant. "To Amaryl?"

"Where else?"

Lada yanked her arm out of his hold. "What of the princess?"

"Don't worry about her. Worry about yourself. You need to go home if you wish to survive."

"Won't you get in trouble if the princess can't be found?" Lada looked up at him with honest eyes, accentuated by the moonbeams shining through the canopy overhead.

Lord Kavindra sighed. If he told her the truth, Lada would undoubtedly offer her help in some form or another. He might need her help, in the long run, but he also wished for her safety and full life.

"We will find her," he answered simply.

"What if you don't?"

"Don't think of us. Think only of yourself."

Lada shook her head, her thoughts racing with all the options of which she could ponder. Lord Kavindra, her friend, would be punished if the princess did not arrive, of this she was certain. And what had happened to Princess Zohana? Her letter, written hastily, left much to be desired in way of explanation. If Lada left them behind, she would forever wonder what had become of them.

"Perhaps... just maybe... I could stay until she's found? I can go home in the morning, after she comes back."

"Lada..." Lord Kavindra's hands landed on her shoulders. "You should go back now, while you can."

"The Amaryl border will still be there come morning," Lada argued softly. "I need to see that my friends are safe before I leave them."

"I told you, don't mind us."

"You may not have noticed, Lord Kavindra." Lada heaved a sigh, lifting his hands along with her shoulders. "I am not the kind of person who can leave her friends behind without a thought for their well-being. Once tendered, my loyalty will not allow me to turn the other way. I am a responsible companion."

Yet another of Lada's many layers lay open and exposed before Lord Kavindra. Her heart to help others rooted deep within her character. Lord Kavindra wanted nothing more than to see Lada safely home, but she had deemed both he and the princess her friends. Lord Kavindra would wager—even if he returned her to the Amaryl border—that Lada would find her way back to camp. Better to stay by her side than allow her to wander the forest unguarded.

Thus, with a sigh, Lord Kavindra gave in. "Alright, but only until we locate Her Highness."

"She left a note." Lada lifted the paper in her hand and retrieved one of Lord Kavindra's hands from her shoulder to press it into his palm. "It's meant to be a farewell letter."

In the darkness, there was no way to read the letter Lada had handed over. Lord Kavindra had not brought a torch with him, and though moonbeams could illuminate a human's path, they were not bright enough to read by.

"You read it?" Lord Kavindra asked.

"Yes."

Lord Kavindra suddenly found the situation odd. In Orafel, few women read. Were the traditions different in Amaryl? His curiosity, as strong as Lada's at least, got the better of him.

"You can read?" Lord Kavindra continued.

Lada laughed, a bright sound that broke the night's stillness. "Of course I can read. I read in four languages, write in two, and I am fluent in apothecary shorthand."

It shouldn't have surprised Lord Kavindra. After all, Lada had told him of her job as an herbalist. To appropriately prescribe medicines and learn new cures, one either had to read them or learn them from a master. In a secluded and isolated place such as Amaryl, bringing masters in from the outside would put everyone in jeopardy. Not so if they only smuggled in books. Perhaps the Amaryl people traveled beyond their borders far more often than they led others to believe.

Lada needn't understand his surprise over her level of education. To her, it must seem natural to read in many languages.

For now, Lord Kavindra dropped the subject. "If we're going back to camp, we should return before anyone misses us."

More questions would be raised if the princess's guards discovered the Tribute Master had run off with a piece of the Tribute, itself. Assumptions might be made. Rumors would fly. Lord Kavindra wished Lada would have taken his advice and returned to Amaryl in the dark of night, but her decision to stay would spare him a thousand more problems. Especially in regards to the disappearance of a princess.

Though he realized Lada knew the forest better than he could imagine, Lord Kavindra took her wrist in his hand and turned back toward the twinkling firelight in the distance. She would not run from him, this he knew, but as an Orafel gentleman, Lord Kavindra could not in good faith trust that nothing would happen if he paid the girl behind him no mind.

Lada asked no further questions. She did not bring up *why* Lord Kavindra wanted to return her to Amaryl. He had thought for her because he had a kind heart, and that was all that mattered to Lada.

With the disappearance of Princess Zohana, Lada found her desire to help her new friends overrode her desire to return to Flora Master's Hall. She would have another opportunity in the future, to return home. Of that she was certain. For now, she would follow this fate that had laid a path before her. It might lead to things far greater than she anticipated.

Lada and Lord Kavindra reentered the camp to much the same scene they had exited.

Now, all the lanterns had been lit, and the clearing shone as brightly as daylight. Tribute Bearers checked on each load on each cart, counting the totals and referring to the list to ensure all remained intact. Princess Zohana's guards scurried to and fro, several having ventured into the forest and the others singling out men they deemed suspicious.

Lord Kavindra released Lada's wrist to venture into the fray. "Has she been found?"

One of the guards stopped to answer the Tribute Master, paying almost as much respect to him as he did to his royal charge. "Her Highness's trail leads into the forest. We will do our best, but it is dark."

"Perhaps this will provide answers." Lord Kavindra held out the letter Lada had given him in the darkness.

The guard received it with a furrow of his brow, which quickly turned to surprise and alarm when he noted the contents. "Where did you get this?"

Lord Kavindra beckoned to Lada, signaling her to join him.

Lada questioned the safety of his plan, but as she had chosen to stay, she should listen to those in charge over the parade. Shuffling over the densely-packed clearing floor, Lada scurried to reach the duo in the center.

"Lada found the missive," Lord Kavindra answered. "For further detail, you should ask her yourself."

"You told us of Her Highness's disappearance, as well," the guard accused. In a flash, his sword swung from its sheath and landed near Lada's neck.

Lada froze, unable even to cry out as her shock turned her into a stone pillar.

Lord Kavindra pushed the sword away from Lada's neck, his face stern as he asked, "You dare to threaten the Tribute?"

"I dare not to threaten the Tribute, but to suspect a cunning witch."

"Lower your sword!" Lord Kavindra demanded. "Lada had no more to do with Her Highness's disappearance than you did. The poor girl won't injure a leaf. How could she plot to disrupt the Tribute?"

Thinking better of his rash actions, or simply realizing he couldn't place all the blame on the woman before him, the guard lowered his sword. Its sheath sang as he replaced the blade.

Lada finally dared breathe, inhaling at once all the oxygen she had been missing.

Swords such as those that Orafel guards carried were not used in Amaryl. Their length and surprising deftness frightened Lada. What if she were to find herself accidentally scratched by one? Lada shuddered at the thought.

"How did you come to discover that Her Highness was not in her tent?" The guard's wary gaze flicked to Lord Kavindra, who still stood sentry in front of Lada.

Lada, trying her best to be brave, kept her spine straight and her chin up when she answered. "I heard a noise that didn't belong. So I went to check and found her gone."

"And this letter?" the guard held up the wrinkled and wadded piece of paper.

"It was on the table in her tent," Lada answered earnestly.

Seeing the guard didn't believe the innocent forest woman, Lord Kavindra took over from there. "What of the letter?"

"It is indeed Her Highness' handwriting," the guard confirmed. "And there are no signs of any struggle within her tent. Only her footsteps lead away from here into the forest."

"Princess Zohana isn't the kind of woman to abandon her duty," Lord Kavindra pointed out. "Not when she has been preparing for this marriage since infancy. To fail her mission now would burn inside of her until it consumed her."

Lada almost spoke up again, to ask how Lord Kavindra knew so much about the princess. She held her tongue only because she wanted no attention to be placed back on her.

It must seem suspicious, her discovery of Princess Zohana's departure. No one in the camp believed Princess Zohana would have done such a thing. Thus, something despicable and truly evil must have happened while they all slept.

"She didn't even say goodbye," Lada muttered.

Lord Kavindra went still, every muscle in his body pausing to ponder the connotations of Lada's observation.

He snatched the letter from the guard's hand. A scan of the contents confirmed his blossoming suspicions, and thus Lord Kavindra heaved a sigh.

"She didn't say goodbye."

The guard stared at him blankly.

Lord Kavindra shook the letter in the air. "Princess Zohana didn't leave a farewell for anyone that mattered. She mentions only her uncle the king. What of her mother? Me? Lada? What of her brothers, who will surely be punished for her insolence?"

The guard clapped his hands, coming around to the purpose behind Lord Kavindra's speech. "She must have been coerced or taken, and the doers wish for the failure of this year's Tribute."

"Precisely."

Devious, the mastermind behind this plan. To plan so far in advance, they must know about both the Treaty and the path that the Tribute Parade would take. Had they known the parade would stop for a night in the forest, instead of entering Qranbu? How close to the heart of this matter did the perpetrator sit? Dare they gloat over their plot's success?

The handful of guards that had run into the forest to track the princess came hastening back into the ring of fire and torchlight. Their troop leader shook his head grimly.

"We lost her trail near the river. I fear nothing more can be done tonight, and it may take days to find her."

"Days we can't spare," Lord Kavindra mused.

"We can't arrive in Qranbu without the princess. We'll be captured or killed on the spot." The worrisome guard paced away from the group, then quickly returned. "We can buy time, perhaps."

No one in the circle quite understood what he insinuated.

Lord Kavindra's hands hovered midair, confused and unable to procure anything to say or do.

Lada stared, wondering how they would fix the problem but more importantly wondering how Princess Zohana fared. She might have been injured in the dark, disconcerting forest. Forest wounds required immediate medical care.

"What do you mean, buy time?" the guard from the forest troop queried.

The first guard spun to face Lada, his hands folded in a salute before him. "Please take Her Highness' place until we locate her."

The plea so astonished Lada that she could not immediately come up with an answer. In truth, she should decline the offer. She bore neither title nor ability to impersonate Princess Zohana.

"I object to this proposal."

Lord Kavindra's stern words were not heeded.

"You will be doing Her Highness a personal favor," the guard continued, "and saving dozens of lives in the process. Refuse me if you will, but if we enter Qranbu without a bride, we will all surely perish."

Perish? Lada could no sooner allow them to perish than she could forget about Flora Master's Hall. Did someone so wish them all dead that they would set them up like this? And what of Lord Kavindra. He had been a friend to her since her arrival at Verity Hall. Lada felt obligated to repay the favor he had bestowed upon her.

"I..." Lada nibbled at her lip, unsure how to phrase her next words but unwilling to leave them all out to shrivel like petals in direct sunlight. "Perhaps... I could occupy her carriage. Until you rescue her. It won't be long, will it?"

The second guard bent into a salute, his hands folded before him. "If the trail is clear enough, not even three days."

"Lada, you cannot..." Lord Kavindra shook his head, his eyes so soft and sad Lada thought he might actually cry.

Finding a smile, Lada shook her head back at him. "It is not that I cannot do it. This is something I should do. Her Highness's guards will undoubtedly locate her in time. Then you can bring me back to Amaryl."

Lord Kavindra planted his hands on Lada's shoulders, ensuring he had her full attention when next he spoke. "Lada, if you do this, you will become a part of the Tribute. You may never return to Amaryl."

"If this is my fate, so be it." Lada landed her hands on Lord Kavindra's wrists, her smile still in place and brighter than ever. "I will think of it as an adventure. Whatever will be, will be. No one knows whether or not I will return to Amaryl, but I am optimistic about the matter."

"You will decorate a castle that will hold no respect for you," Lord Kavindra warned.

"I believe the princess will return in time."

After that, neither spoke a word. Both knew arguing was pointless. Lada had made up her mind and no matter how much Lord Kavindra opposed her decision, she would not back down now. If for her friends, Lord Kavindra thought Lada may be able to walk through fire or swim an ocean. He hated to think what she could be convinced to suffer for the sake of her family.

"I will do as you have requested," Lada announced to the guards.

The Royal Guards bent a bow toward their fake princess. "Thank you for your kindness."

It wouldn't be easy, for certain. Lada knew none of the etiquettes instilled in Princess Zohana. Her bright character counteracted the deadliness of a Mission Marriage. Even the maids would have a difficult time convincing Lada how to act in the presence of strangers. The Amaryl woman could try, but she could never be an Orafel princess.

Lord Kavindra had only one thing he could do for Lada, in this situation. From a pocket in his sleeve, Lord Kavindra produced a small, carefully embroidered pouch. He balanced it in his palm, weighing the emptiness before he held it out toward her.

"I believe this is yours. One of the maids rescued it from the incineration pile."

Lada, recognizing the pouch at once, snatched it up and clutched it to her chest. "I had thought it gone forever! Thank you, friend."

And there went that smile, once more bright in the direst of situations. Would she never understand the pressure of danger or the price of consequences? If only it were possible for Lada to keep on smiling, no matter what happened. Lord Kavindra knew of many terrible things that would wipe away her radiance. He prayed she never need discover what kinds of things would bring her demise.

CHAPTER FOURTEEN
Into Dragon Tribe

ada's litter was left behind for the princess, and Lada found herself in the princess's carriage, seated alongside three of the maids who had attended her at Verity Hall.

If not for their stoic expressions and the gravity of the situation the Tribute Parade found itself in, Lada would have enjoyed the day's journey. Instead, every second reminded her that her friend might be in danger. Lada could only help by sitting in her friend's carriage and pretending to be someone she would never be able to impersonate.

The sun crept up, higher and higher in the sky. The forest gave way to a sparsely-wooded, winding path. A lonely path, spiraling upward as the mountain greeted them with hostility.

Patrolling border guards stopped to stare, but each knew the Tribute Parade's streamers and they dared not stop its progress. Dragon Supreme had been waiting patiently for its arrival. Now that it had passed onto Qranbu lands, the Tribute Parade would not be touched by bandit or thief. No one dared to offend Davorin Astrophel.

Even so, Lord Kavindra and the Royal Guards kept their eyes open for danger. Qranbu, feared for their ferociousness and their wars, could never be trusted.

Lada, however, didn't quite believe that no one in Dragon Tribe could be trusted. She listened to the world passing by, and though she knew little of the barrenness around them, she heard nothing but their own parade. Until proven otherwise, Lada was remiss to believe all Dragon Tribe people were bad.

The landscape around them lay still and silent. Until it didn't.

Outside the gates of the first city they encountered, a throng of excited children raced out to meet them. They bore strange markings and wore even stranger baubles, yet each child reminded Lada of the children in Amaryl. The ones who had come to her for advice or for a story, depending on the day. In these children's faces, Lada saw home. But she dare not speak it out, for fear of being found out.

Other Dragon Tribe subjects greeted them, but Lada never saw them. The maids took care to close the curtains and keep them that way. The fewer who saw the woman in the princess's carriage, the fewer who would notice when they switched the women later.

Lord Kavindra, as well, took great care when settling Lada in the accommodations prepared for them. Between his vigilance and the Royal Guards' trickery, no one saw a single hair of Lada's head.

And thus continued their careful journey the next day.

The promised three days passed, and yet no word of Princess Zohana came to the Tribute Parade. Without a choice, they pressed on another night. And yet another.

Hundreds of Dragon Tribe citizens throughout five cities greeted the Tribute with honor and glee. Not one managed to catch a glimpse of the bride.

But the Tribute Bearers had run out of time to hide.

On this, the final night before entering Isonpool Fortress, none would sleep. Concerns lay before them, on a number of levels they dare not mention.

Lord Kavindra, especially, found himself at a loss. Without Princess Zohana, he had no choice but to send Lada in her place. However, to do such a thing would be as good as signing Lada's order of execution. She would never be able to survive a place such as Isonpool Palace. Nor would she be able to fool Davorin Astrophel, Dragon Supreme for long.

The Royal Guards had a matter of hours to return the princess to her rightful place, or Lada would become the sacrifice to save the rest. Lord Kavindra hesitated to allow it. Sacrificing one for the good of all had never been something of which he desired to be a part.

Those were the sufferings that brought him to Lada's room at an hour too late to be considered proper. Only the presence of Her Highness's maids saved the duo from beginning rumors intense enough to kill them.

Lada had taken up a stance on the bed, her knees tucked to her chest and her arms wrapped around her legs. She knew the weight of the evening's potential.

Lord Kavindra took up residence at the room's table. He had now poured himself too many cups of tea to count them. The pot had been refilled at least twice. Surely the kitchen would question how one woman devoured such an amount of tea at this hour. Hopefully they would not ask.

The hours drew on, through the night and toward the morning, and Lord Kavindra knew he would have to discuss the day's plans with Lada. He could wait no longer.

"Are you afraid?" It seemed the most logical question to ask the woman curled on the bed.

Lada shook her head. "It's cold here, that's all."

But the petals atop her hair trembled in her place. Of course she should be frightened. Impersonating a princess came at a heavy cost, and impersonating a Tribute Bride wreaked more havoc than Lada could imagine. Lord Kavindra didn't want to consider what Dragon Tribe would do when they discovered her true identity. When the lies became clear and inescapable.

"You're cold?" Lord Kavindra stood to his feet, willing to take the excuse to avoid the real problems. "Shall I retrieve another blanket?"

Once more, Lada shook her head. "It's not that I won't be alright, it's just that I don't like the cold."

In truth, the room's warmth wrapped around her as snugly as the blanket on her shoulders. Only because she knew about the chill in the air outside did Lada shiver.

That, and because deep down she knew. Princess Zohana had not yet been found and would not be coming to take her rightful place. Come morning, Lada would be the one to enter Isonpool Fortress.

Both Lada and Lord Kavindra knew the outcome of their charade, but neither dared to voice it. Neither dared to address the necessary topics at all.

Until, finally, Lord Kavindra worked up the courage. "If you wish to flee, now is the time."

Flee? Of what use would fleeing be now? They had come too far to turn back, had deceived too many to apologize. To flee would bring certain death for all. At least the lie would save the Tribute Bearers and, perhaps, the Tribute Master.

"I said I would take Her Highness's place." Lada stuck to her decision, not because she wasn't anxious but because she had made a promise. She dared not back out now.

Some might call her foolish, but Lada's principles held true. The Amaryl Elders would approve of her decision. Amaryl valued lives and loyalty above all. To abandon innocent people in their time of need would be the true disgrace. Lada would never give up on saving her new friends, not even if a thousand flaming arrows came flying her way.

"You could be killed if you enter Isonpool Fortress tomorrow."

The reminder did little to dissuade Lada. She merely smiled against the fear. "I have ways to protect myself."

Lord Kavindra dared not ask what she meant. He had grown up in Orafel, where Amarylites were both highly scorned and highly feared. He had seen Amaryl slaves use strange tactics and peculiar herbs to escape their masters. An Amarylite protecting herself? He didn't doubt Lada could do it, but he worried what it would entail.

Had he known the lengths Lada would go to, to protect herself from harm, Lord Kavindra might not have let the subject drop so easily. At the time, he thought only for the safety of his men and the life of Princess Zohana.

Allowing Lada to sacrifice herself pained his heart, but Lord Kavindra couldn't have convinced her otherwise. He had given thorough warning. And, thus, he allowed her to press on, oblivious what his one moment of weakness would bring.

CHAPTER FIFTEEN
Receiving Tribute

unk. The doors to Fang-Throne Court complained upon their forced opening.

Cadfael sailed down the length of the hall, majestic in scaled armor and billowing cape. The ceremonial armor had been granted to him upon his successful termination of a rebel faction. Cadfael only wore it when he needed to show off, or when he accompanied Dragon Supreme to a special occasion.

Today, indeed, qualified as a special occasion.

A single sentence from Cadfael's lips confirmed it. "Tribute has arrived at Isonpool Fortress. They await Your Majesty, Dragon Supreme's presence at the palace gates."

All according to plan. All running as smoothly as Davorin anticipated.

Davorin rose from his throne, his shimmering black cape cascading over his arms, wrapping around his torso, and pooling around his feet. He had dressed for the show. Accepting an Orafel princess into his household? No. Davorin knew better. Today, he would meet an intimate spy. His fiancée would not be like other women, of this Davorin was certain. Because he had checked.

The Ministers all thought Davorin had accepted the Orafel princess blindly. That there would be no way to know her true intentions. Those Ministers didn't have a clear enough view of the future, nor did they place enough importance on the past.

Davorin need not say a word in response to Cadfael's announcement. He need only move.

Boots clicked against the stone floor. The swish of his cape whispered like wind in the air. Davorin descended each step, from his throne to the middle of the court.

One by one, Ministers fell in line behind him. For their Dragon Supreme to meet his bride, this day had indeed been blessed by Heaven. Few dared to miss this auspicious occasion. Some had, nonetheless. Davorin took note of all the missing Ministers' names carefully. He would need someone to keep an eye on them.

Cadfael fell in line two steps behind his master. He leaned in close to update him. "They've been standing with the carts and carriages for a long while. Should we not hasten?"

"Let them wait."

Davorin, in fact, slowed his steps. Catering to those in a lower status than his own would present a front of weakness. Dragon Tribe had never been weak, nor would they begin now. In all things, Davorin kept the advantage. Only by being in the seat of superiority could one truly rule.

The ministers, of course, whispered and gossiped as they trailed Dragon Supreme. None dared speak loud enough for him to hear.

No one could ever tell what might enrage him. None would take a chance to find out.

Servants they encountered in the halls scurried to allow their sovereign to pass. Though they might stare at or whisper about the ministers, none said a word about Davorin Astrophel, Dragon Supreme.

Finally, Dragon Supreme and his entourage burst forth into the light of day. The Entry Courtyard remained as quiet and demure as the palace's interior, not a rock out of place or an insect brave enough to sing.

The guards awaiting the presence of the Dragon Tribe nobles rushed to open Isonpool Palace's main gates.

The announcement of, "His Majesty, Dragon Supreme, arrives," went up.

Davorin crossed over the gated threshold and stopped atop the tiers of stairs leading up from the road.

A perusal of the Tribute Parade didn't impress him. Just a host of tactless colored ribbons and timid Orafel servants. The treasures would lie in the Royal Treasury, perhaps for the remainder of his rule. There was no reason to get worked up over petty baubles.

Having seen what could be seen of the carts, Davorin's gaze swung to the carriage. Specifically, to the new Tribute Master.

The young man wasn't older than Davorin himself, undoubtedly thrust upon such duties through familial connection. In the younger face, Davorin saw many details he knew from the old man who had come the year prior. This new Tribute Master's eyes reflected the same trepidatious wisdom as his predecessor. A pity, that the old man had passed on, but a blessing his son had taken on the responsibility.

A son was sure to understand what the job entailed. Davorin hated to train a new Tribute Master if it were not required.

This well-trained Tribute Master bent forward in a forty-degree bow, his hands folded over his heart in the traditional Dragon Tribe phoenix symbol. "Your Majesty, Dragon Supreme."

He said nothing more. Clever of him, really, waiting to be asked questions before explaining. This young Tribute Master had confidence in himself. Surely he had done his job well. Mistakes were not tolerated in Isonpool Palace. The Tribute Master, no matter how new and inexperienced, would be well aware of the fact. Failure meant death.

Cadfael stepped forward, knowing his master's preferences when it came to conversing with strangers. "We have been anticipating Her Highness, Princess Zohana."

"It is my duty to deliver what I have been entrusted." The Tribute Master bent a little farther forward before straightening to motion to the woman beside the carriage behind him.

Davorin stared, examining every inch of the prepared bride.

A comely woman, her figure hidden beneath the dress and skirts engulfing her in a voluminous pile of yellow and pink. Half her hair piled prettily atop her head, adorned with white flower petals but no headdress. Every inch of her demeanor screamed her reservedness. From what news had been brought, Dragon Supreme had rather expected someone tall, brash, and grim. Looks could be deceiving.

Dragon Supreme tilted his head, tossing Cadfael a silent symbol to continue.

A brief pause from the guard at Davorin's side. Then, "Her Highness may enter via her carriage. We will take care of her arrangements."

A ripple of discontent stirred the Orafel servants gathered around the princess's carriage. Dare they rebel against Dragon Supreme? The whole of Dragon Tribe's court held their breath, waiting for the coup that would last mere seconds.

It never came. Despite their whispers and hesitation, the servants went into motion, surging forward to take the little princess by her arms and turn her back toward the carriage.

The woman in question bent her head near to one servant's ear to ask a question. Then she stumbled over her own two feet. If not for the servants holding onto her, she might have landed on her face in the dirt.

Dragon Supreme, ever observant, made note of the blunder and turned again to his most trusted guard. An inspection of his claw rings and a raise of his eyebrows were enough to put Cadfael into motion.

Cadfael gave a nod, already knowing what his sovereign had seen and how he would want to proceed. He extended a hand in greeting to the Tribute Master. "Our servants will take the Tribute from here. Your Tribute Bearers can return. We will welcome you inside for refreshment and a night's stay. Please leave any weapons outside the gate."

"It is quite generous of you," the Tribute Master replied.

As if he could have said no to the offer. Until they sent him away, Tribute Master served at the leisure of Dragon Supreme. No matter that his loyalty and citizenship lay in Orafel. He stood on Dragon Tribe soil now. They would treat him well, as he had accomplished his job. It would take half a day to assimilate the Tribute into its rightful place. Tribute Master would stay until they had finished, at least.

Having achieved his goal in this place, Davorin Astrophel beckoned the Tribute Master to follow as he turned back into Isonpool Palace.

Of course, the ministers fawned over the young Tribute Master in hopes of winning favor in court. Their attention distracted the Tribute Master from attempting conversation with Dragon Supreme. A fact used to its full advantage by Cadfael, who stuck to his king's side like metal to magnet.

"What shall we do with the woman?" Cadfael asked quietly.

Davorin weighed his options, found many lacking in ingenuity, and decided, "Take her to the quarters prepared for her."

"You've... taken a liking?" Cadfael, had he not been such a loyal guard, would have reached out to check on Dragon Supreme's temperature. Never before had he shown leniency to a spy.

"I'm intrigued," Davorin clarified.

Intrigued that the Tribute Master had so quickly shown his true colors. That he had thought this would get past Davorin Astrophel's keen eyes.

"By her looks?" Cadfael tried, still, to discern his master's intention. "Or her status as princess?"

Davorin shook his head at his guard. How oblivious, to think trivial matters such as those would attract Dragon Supreme's attention. Lest Cadfael continue to interrogate him, Davorin Astrophel found it in his best interests to explain. Just one sentence to expound on his findings.

"I don't know who she is, but she isn't a princess."

CHAPTER SIXTEEN

Entertaining Guests

parkling crystal candelabras offered an extra haze of light to the Dining Hall. Dragon Tribe had spent days outfitting the Dining Hall with intricate tapestries and silken tablecloths. Subordinates or not, Orafel would judge Dragon Tribe based on their experience inside the borders of Qranbu. Let it not be said that Dragon Tribe consisted of barbarous neanderthals. They entertained guests as dutifully as any other palace.

At Nerys's suggestion, dancing girls had been summoned from Ingot Inn. Along with a carefully selected troupe of minstrels, they spun and twirled in the middle of the room, sure to catch anyone's eye. After all, the art of attention-stealing had been taught to them from the time they were young.

Running down the middle of long tables and set up as a buffet around the room's edges, delicacies of all kinds sat steaming. Dragon Tribe hadn't spared any expense when it came to food. If their guests didn't leave full to the brim, it meant Dragon Tribe had underplayed their hand and underexposed their wealth. Dragon Supreme had left specific instructions for the evening. He wanted Orafel to speak of this Tribute Feast for years to come.

Under the guise of a feast and a celebration, any number of secret agendas lay hidden. For Dragon Tribe, it served as a covert way to misdirect their possible enemies. Orafel need not realize Dragon Tribe knew the only purpose for Tribute was to establish dominion.

For the Tribute Master, it managed to hide his indecision and anxiety. If he made it through the formalities, he would leave with his head perched safely atop his shoulders.

In an unprecedented display of congeniality, Davorin Astrophel reserved the seat nearest his own dais for the young Tribute Master. Lord Kavindra, he had been told, had inherited the position the eldest son of the family wanted not. To show a bit of esteem for the responsible youngest son would harm no one. It might loosen Lord Kavindra's lips.

By no means could Lord Kavindra read the mind of Dragon Tribe's leader, but he knew better than to trust the kind welcome he had been given. Dragon Tribe, notoriously, played with their conquests before they betrayed them. Their extravagant party lent credence to Lord Kavindra's resolve to keep Lada's name off his own lips. Should he worry for her, someone would take notice of his interest and chase down the cause.

He had not stopped her from traversing this dark and sodden path, but Lord Kavindra would not add any more hardships to her suffering.

In the custom of any Dragon Tribe festivity, all remained standing until Dragon Supreme sank into his gilded chair. Then, and only then, did the party-goers take their own seats and reach for the nearest pastry, soup, or meat within their grasp.

Lord Kavindra followed suit. Dragon Tribe would not harm him during this auspicious occasion. In essence, this feast served to celebrate a long-standing engagement and a forthcoming wedding. No such serious endeavor would be met with wrath and treachery. That, if it came to fruition, would wait until after the Tribute's manifest had been thoroughly checked.

Davorin Astrophel found he respected the young Tribute Master for taking up the job, yet he didn't trust him. The furtive glances and silent conversations that had occurred in the courtyard were enough to set anyone on edge. Clearly, Lord Kavindra thought to trick the mightiest strategist in Dragon Tribe. Determined Davorin would not allow Lord Kavindra's chicanery to last.

With Cadfael settled in behind him, staring out into the crowd in search of danger, Davorin Astrophel found he rather wanted to test the Tribute Master sitting at the nearby table. How much pressure would it take to make him crack?

With narrowed eyes and raised suspicions, Dragon Supreme held aloft his goblet to allow the nearby servant girl to fill it. She did so with speed and ease, having served the great lord long enough to know how to please him.

His cup now full and his observation only just begun, Davorin Astrophel raised his goblet toward Lord Kavindra's seat. "To thank you for your service, I will raise this toast."

Lord Kavindra, left without a servant to tend him, scrambled to raise his goblet toward the Qranbu's reigning king. He bent his head in respect, buying him time to swallow the food in his mouth before he spoke.

"I am honored, Your Majesty, Dragon Supreme. May you enjoy the tribute spoils to the full content of your heart."

Though he did not let it show on his face or in his voice, saying the words pained Lord Kavindra. After all, the tribute spoils included Lada. All involved had made their choice, without a thought of turning back, but Lord Kavindra detested the thought of Davorin Astrophel and Lada of Flora Master's Hall living in the same space. Lord Kavindra served Dragon Supreme as Tribute Master, but he held no fondness for the man or his people.

Davorin downed the entirety of his drink in one go. A silent motion toward Lord Kavindra encouraged him to do the same. If a little pressure didn't loosen the man's tongue, a few drinks would. The previous Tribute Master, despite his old age, had been a lightweight. Davorin wondered if it were a familial trait.

Lord Kavindra took heed of the order, but he also took note of the sinister tone simmering beneath the exterior. This Dragon Supreme would not be trifled with. All the more reason to avoid the subject Lord Kavindra knew would give him away.

Dragon Supreme, on the other hand, had different ideas. He had done nothing wrong in the grand scheme of this Tribute Parade, nor had he displeased Orafel in any way, save their long-standing grudge against his kingdom. Dragon Supreme could afford to ask whatever he wanted, in any way he wished.

He began with uncomfortable questions.

"You and... Princess Zohana, wasn't it?"

In a satisfactory turn of events, Lord Kavindra choked on a piece of meat. If not for the flustered way he sought a kerchief to dab at his lips, Dragon Supreme might have written it off as coincidence.

But Davorin knew better. "The two of you seemed close."

"Your Majesty—" a cough interrupted anything Lord Kavindra intended to say. He cleared his throat before he went on. "Your Lordship, I dare not assume what your words mean. The Tribute Parade has traveled far. Of course camaraderie is forged along the way."

The answer didn't satisfy Dragon Supreme, but he understood Lord Kavindra's attempt to appease any anger that may appear. After all, the woman was to be Davorin's bride. To be close to her could mean death. If Davorin deigned to care about that sort of thing.

Truth be told, Davorin cared not whether she lived or died, much less who she loved. A single glance had been enough to convince him a creature like that would never survive Isonpool Palace. Davorin would wait to see how long she lasted before her inevitable demise.

Lord Kavindra, on the other hand, was too concerned about the woman's well-being. Judging by the way he had stared at her during their arrival, he held feelings of some kind. Feelings were only a weakness, especially for the already weak Orafel nation.

If indeed Lord Kavindra sought the woman for his own, allowing him to stay on any longer than necessary presented a problem. No telling what Lord Kavindra would do if Davorin allowed him to stay, with the way he looked after the woman. Having received the year's tribute and with all his people in high spirits about the marriage, Davorin had no mood to kill the new Tribute Master.

Willing or unwilling, it didn't matter how Davorin felt about the wedding. It had to commence. If Lord Kavindra stayed, he might make an attempt to take the woman away with him. Men had risked their lives for less.

"Your father," Dragon Supreme changed the subject, "was an excellent Tribute Master during his time. He served me well."

"My father carried his responsibilities heavy on his shoulders," Lord Kavindra confirmed. Sometimes to the detriment of his own family, the former Tribute Master had carried out his duties.

Dragon Supreme gave a thoughtful nod. "I expect you will do the same."

"I will not fail Your Lordship."

This time, Lord Kavindra's bow—indeed, all of his respect—felt more forced than it had before. He had heard the threat beneath the kind words. Any sane man, anyone who knew the kind of person reigning in Dragon Tribe, would understand the meaning underneath the compliment.

"I trust you won't." Davorin leaned back in his seat, for the first time allowing himself to enjoy the atmosphere around the room. "Enjoy yourself this evening, Tribute Master. I will send you on your way come morning."

Lord Kavindra heard the real intention behind the words. It appeared, despite his claims to the contrary, Dragon Supreme didn't trust his Tribute Master. Not nearly as much as he would lead Lord Kavindra to believe he did. Sending the Tribute Master away so swiftly meant Dragon Supreme wanted him gone, unable to present any more obstacles.

Lord Kavindra would agree wholeheartedly, if not for Lada. Every fiber of his being wanted to take her away with him, but he knew a stupid decision when he saw one. He could no longer assist Lada to flee from her troubles. From here on out, she would have to face them alone.

CHAPTER SEVENTEEN
Acclimating

The carriage took the long way into Isonpool Palace, a smooth but echoing stone path winding around to a gate better suited for wheeled vehicles. Lada dared not peek her head out of the window, even if she wanted to see. Tripping over the new shoes had been bad enough. To break any more etiquette would undoubtedly put her under heavy suspicion. She must hold on, at least until Lord Kavindra left.

The kind maids who had helped her in Verity Hall shared the carriage with her, as much a part of Tribute as Lada herself. Despite their quick etiquette lessons along the journey, they and Lada all knew she would never pass as Princess Zohana.

Worried about that exact issue, Lada leaned closer to the nearest maid. "Do you think they noticed my clumsiness?"

With the way Lada tripped over her shoes, the Dragon Tribe onlookers would have to be blind to have not seen her fumble. Try as she might, Lada had not yet learned the art of walking in shoes. For a girl who had spent her life barefoot in the moss and grass, this progress came as a miracle. None blamed her for her lack of ability. She had been thrust into this as they had.

"Such a small mistake will be overlooked," the maid lied.

Everyone knew their time within Isonpool Palace would end before it began. Not a soul would tell Lada. To do so would destroy her bright personality and her innocent view of the world around her. They didn't dare to touch such invaluable things.

Trustful Lada took the words as truth. After all, who would lie about such a thing? It involved all their lives.

Thunk, clunk. The carriage wheels stopped abruptly.

Lada's hands shot out, bracing against the carriage walls to hold her steady. If not for her quick reaction, she might have gone rolling on the floor. What a sight that would have made.

The stop was as abrupt and cold as the rest of Dragon Tribe's lands, at least what Lada had seen of them. A whisper of icy wind tickled the curtains hanging over the carriage's door and windows. It carried with it the voice of a single, impassive servant.

"It is time for Her Highness to alight the carriage."

Alight the carriage. A harrowing ordeal. Knowing not where they had come nor if it would be safe, one could not possibly obey the order directly. Alongside all the foreboding and all the unknowns, another grand problem obstructed Lada's path to convincing them of her identity.

"May I leave the shoes behind?" Lada checked with the nearest maid, in a voice low enough no one outside the carriage would be able to hear.

With a wry smile, the maid shook her head. Even if it were allowed in proper etiquette to run around with bare feet, none could be sure Lada wouldn't injure herself. Any number of things could attack her in a place such as this. Lada no longer resided in a soft and forgiving forest. They now bowed to the whims of cruel palace politics.

Lada sighed, but she did not complain. The maids had quickly come to realize Lada never complained. Her optimism and bright personality curried Lada favor with whoever stood before her. They only hoped it would do the same for her in this fierce and brutal Dragon Tribe.

The kind maid that had been guiding Lada for the past days exited the carriage first. If Lada should fall over her own feet again, someone should catch her. Every maid attending Lada knew it would not be a Dragon Tribe guard who did the catching. In this new environment, no one cared for Lada's safety. Only those who knew that Lada had never been meant to arrive at Isonpool Palace understood how to care for the girl.

Following the instructions, Lada picked her way out of the carriage and down one step to the ground. A merciful twist of fate allowed her to keep her balance the entire way down.

It was from that position, standing alongside her carriage with a dozen Dragon Tribe guards watching her every move, that Lada gained her first real glimpse at the palace.

Sconces lined the walls, barely illuminating the gray alley they had traveled. Overhead, equally gloomy clouds hung too close to the earth. Distant thunder rumbled, but a moving guard drew Lada's attention to an iron gate nearby. The design thereupon leaped out as if it might take flight; mythical eyes, staring out from a dragon's head, glowed in the torchlight. With a groan, the doors began to move.

Despite the frisson of fear crawling up her spine, Lada tiptoed her way forward to follow the guard through the doors.

The princess's attendants huddled close, one clutching each of Lada's arms. Another pressed up against her back. Lada shivered, but the attendants trembled. If only she had a decent calming tea to offer them. Lada hated to see anyone in pain, physical or emotional.

Suspicious, prying stares followed Lada across a small inner courtyard. The eyes belonged to guards, stationed at intervals so close together they must have been able to hear each other breathe.

The courtyard served only as an avenue between the palace's exterior and interior. Yet another layer between the outside world and the heart of Isonpool Palace. Did those who worked inside the walls ever interact with those who existed beyond their little world? Or did they hide away like ants avoiding the rain under tree bark? Did fear or loyalty keep them inside these impenetrable walls?

The guard leading Lada and her attendants stopped inside this next set of doors, also iron. Before him, a half dozen royal maids bent their knees in a curtsy lacking any respect.

"These attendants will take you to your quarters," the guard announced.

The cluster created by Lada and her Orafel entourage came to a stuttering standstill, all staring at the scene before them with the same expression. Everyone had warned Lada about the fierce Dragon Tribe, but she had not prepared herself to be ripped away from everything that had become comfortable along the journey. To take the attendants she had first met in Verity Hall meant taking away her backup plan. What would she do if she broke protocol horrendously in their absence?

"What of my attendants?" Lada dared ask, thinking it better to know than to worry.

One of the Dragon Tribe maids stepped forward. "Etiquette is different here. They will be given an orientation. You may see them when they have integrated into the palace."

A collective breath of relief went up from the maids surrounding Lada. As long as the servant girl kept her words, they would not perish or disappear into the Isonpool Palace dungeons.

"Come with us, Your Highness," the Dragon Tribe servant ordered.

Lada bit her tongue to avoid pointing out she held no such title and she would rather they refer to her as Lada, or Lada of Flora Master's Hall. Much as she enjoyed making friends, such a blunder would get them all beheaded before they had a chance to return the missing princess. Lada had a sneaking suspicion that Princess Zohana would encourage her to do whatever she could to remain alive.

Thus, Lada worked to extricate her arms from the vise grip of her maids. Hopefully, no one had reopened the wound on her bicep. If she bled, the servants would no doubt have to check on her safety. Then she would have to craft a lie to pile on top of all the other fibs she had told thus far. If avoidable, Lada sought to avoid lying again.

The maids all protested with hushed tones and pointed looks, but Lada doubted if Dragon Tribe left room for negotiation. Given the brashness of Isonpool Palace, negotiations must be frowned upon in this place.

"I will be fine," Lada promised. "Come to me as soon as you can."

But no one believed the words Lada said. How could she be fine when she could barely walk in the shoes they had given her? What about other minute etiquettes she would surely botch? If they left her, the maids knew Lada would be unable to continue on. She depended on them, as strongly as they doted on her.

The Dragon Tribe servant girl took Lada—by her good arm, thankfully—and dragged her into the midst of a half-dozen attendants waiting to relocate her. Reluctantly, and with little faith they would ever see Lada again, the Orafel maids scampered off on the trail of the guard guiding them.

It couldn't be helped that Lada tripped over her own feet several times during the journey down strange and winding halls. Even the Orafel maids couldn't stop Lada's clumsiness. These unhelpful Dragon Tribe servants wouldn't care to assist Lada. Their presence was a cage around her, meant to keep her imprisoned until they reached their destination.

Sadly, due to the swarm around her, no satisfaction came for Lada's curiosity about the palace's inner workings. Enclosed as she was, Lada saw nothing aside from servants' backs and the occasional glow of a torch on the walls.

Too focused on trying to observe her surroundings, Lada didn't note the path they took. In hindsight, she should have observed and memorized the turns and twists, the direction of her forward motion.

At the end of a particularly long hall, Lada found herself shoved through yet another pair of iron doors. These bore no stories, only a clean slate waiting to be engraved.

The clean slate slammed behind her.

As quickly as they had encircled her, the Dragon Tribe servants broke away, leaving Lada to stumble into the center of a rather haunting chamber. For such a large space, the room lacked furnishings. A dark curtain at the far end hinted at a bed beyond. A few old and dusty rugs were scattered haphazardly on the ground. The entertaining table leaned as if a leg had broken.

"You must be tired from your journey," one of the Dragon Tribe maids intoned. "Allow us to help you into something more comfortable."

"I can do it my—" Lada cut herself off before she finished her sentence.

She doubted the offer had come as an option, and a princess must require help to do anything. That's what the other maids had told her. Thus, if she were to keep Princess Zohana's place, Lada must remember to act as Princess Zohana would act.

Even if Lada had finished her words, the royal maids wouldn't have listened. They had been given specific instructions and far be it from them to alter the plan that Dragon Supreme had set in motion.

Skilled but frigid hands deftly assisted Lada out of the frothy pink-and-yellow dress. Still more hands helped to remove her shoes and jewelry. The dress and shoes found a home hanging on a nearby rack, while the jewelry went onto a warped and dilapidated vanity table.

"This way, Your Highness," enticed the Dragon Tribe servant in charge of the whole ordeal.

Lada, left without a choice, tiptoed after her toward the dark and ominous curtain. A whistle of wind managed to sneak in around a covered window and rustle the curtain, adding to the sinister ambiance.

The Dragon Tribe servant parted the curtain to reveal a wooden bed, adorned with two round pillows and a single blanket. Hardly the expected luxury of a princess, but Lada had never been picky about such things. As long as she laid down her head and warmed her cold body, she would be content.

It never occurred to Lada that everything the royal maids did to her might be part of a test. Nor did she think to ask for warmer blankets and better accommodations. To Lada, who had slept alone in the forest more than once, the bedchamber's grandeur already exceeded her expectations. How dare she ask for more than that which was given to her?

Lada curled up on the bed and pulled the blanket over her shoulders. Had she known her identity had been exposed, she might not have rested at all.

As for the Dragon Tribe servants, they had instructions to follow. Torches were put out, curtains drawn, and as they left doors were locked. The guards would take care of the rest, and all they had to do was to observe the fake Orafel princess.

Oblivious to all the dangers escalating around her, Lada huddled under the blanket all night, not warm enough but accepting of the fate she had chosen for herself. Perhaps she would never be warm enough again. Lada could bear the cold. For a while.

She only hoped her presence didn't put strain on the Dragon Tribe's servants. They were only there to do their jobs, and Lada didn't want to make their lives any more difficult than they must be in this cold and ungenerous place.

CHAPTER EIGHTEEN

Acclimating

he night passed swiftly, too calmly to ease Tribute Master's anxiety. Exchanging Lada and Princess Zohana had gone too smoothly. None had uttered a word about Lada's odd behavior. Dragon Supreme, himself, hadn't questioned her identity. For such a suspicious tribe, it seemed out of place for them to fall for the trick.

Yet, here stood Lord Kavindra, healthy and free, waiting for his horse to be brought round so he might leave Qranbu. The accountant had consulted with him earlier in the morning, asking only a few brief questions about the Tribute's manifest before he confirmed all had arrived as specified. For another year, Orafel would be safe under Dragon Tribe's protection.

If only Lord Kavindra could say as much about Lada of Flora Master's Hall.

Upon asking to say his farewells, he had been given the royal runaround. The accountant, of course, had no say in what went on in the palace, and thus had offered to pass on the message to those who could help. Those who could help had been no help at all.

First, they had given excuses. Her Highness had yet to awaken. Her Highness was indisposed. Dragon Supreme would like to see the Tribute Master off, and he had matters of state later in the day.

Due to the last excuse, Lord Kavindra had given up trying to see Lada before his departure. It would sadden her, that he did not say goodbye, but in this circumstance he had no choice.

Seeing Lada, for that matter, would only pour salt into his festering wounds. He had chosen the coward's way out, substituting one woman for another only to save his own skin. He had pushed Lada into an ocean of predators. A better man would have accepted the consequences no matter their cost.

If Lord Kavindra went back and did it again, he would choose a different path. He would send Lada back home instead of accepting her nonsensical help.

The rustle of fabric and the cadence of a dozen pairs of feet announced the arrival of Davorin Astrophel, Dragon Supreme.

Against all his better judgment and every instinct in his body, Lord Kavindra turned toward the commotion to dip a bow. For any chance to save Lada in the future, he first had to make it out of Qranbu alive.

Dragon Supreme looked beyond Lord Kavindra toward the open gate. There, the road stood empty, devoid of horse or carriage to return the Tribute Master to his own residence. The servants had been becoming more lax in their duties when it came to the Tribute Bearers. A detail someone at court would undoubtedly address later.

For now, Davorin Astrophel raised a hand to hail the nearest guard.

A guard who came running forthwith to serve his master. "My Lord."

"Check on the progress of Tribute Master's steed," Davorin commanded.

The sooner he expelled the Tribute Master, the better for everyone. Tribute Master need not stay beyond his welcome, or the Ministers would complain again. Davorin held no sympathy or compassion for complaints.

The guard hastened away to do as he had been told, leaving Lord Kavindra standing awkwardly beside Dragon Supreme and his ministers.

"Our deepest apologies. Her Highness was unable to send you off," one of the ministers piped up, speaking on Dragon Supreme's behalf.

A probe or a sincere apology, the Tribute Master dared not guess. Either way, he would do his utmost to keep Lada of Flora Master's Hall as safe as he could leave her.

Despite the ache near his heart, Lord Kavindra pasted on a smile to send toward the minister. "I am of no importance. It would have been a great honor should she have graced my departure with her presence."

Lord Kavindra knew better than to believe it had been Lada's decision to stay away. She had entered Isonpool Palace as the Tribute Bride, and it appeared Dragon Tribe now wanted to ostracize and control her. Sweet, naive Lada would fall directly into their clutches and never speak an ill word. Yet another reason he should have found a way to take her away with him. Now, the time for plots and intrigues had passed. From here on out, Lada would be on her own.

How had she spent the first night in this strange place? Would she last a week at their hands? Could something have been done to save her? All questions that swam in Lord Kavindra's mind. All their answers frightened him. Therefore, he pondered them not.

The impatient Dragon Supreme surveyed the courtyard, glared at one of the minister's whispers, and turned back to the Tribute Master. "You have done your job well, Lord Kavindra."

"It is my honor to serve." Another lie, but nonetheless it must be said.

"I expect next year's Tribute will run as smoothly as this year's." Dragon Supreme inhaled a breath of chilly wind before he let his next words float like bees. "I will be sure to invite your household to the wedding, when it takes place, so as not to put you in a bad position with your king."

The wedding. A wedding that would take place with the wrong bride, or never take place at all. Lord Kavindra hated to imagine what Dragon Tribe might do when they discovered they had been tricked. The marriage that should have saved everyone could easily turn to disaster and death. Such was the precipice it teetered upon.

So as not to incite Dragon Supreme's suspicion or wrath, Lord Kavindra accepted the offer with another gracious bow. "You are too kind, Your Majesty."

Kind? Both men knew Dragon Supreme's offer had not been *kind*. He had meant to remind Lord Kavindra that mistakes and lies could come back upon the blunderer's head. Dragon Tribe may not know Lada stood in for the princess, but the Orafel king would undoubtedly recognize the face of his own niece. Should it not be his niece at the wedding, explanations and interrogations would ensue forthwith.

It wasn't that Lord Kavindra didn't know fear. Only that he had people who worked beneath him and depended upon him for their safety and health. He would not let them perish prematurely. When the time came, he would take upon himself all the responsibility for this trickery.

Clip, clop, clip, clop. The sound of horseshoes against stone rang behind Lord Kavindra. The time had come. Leave, he must.

"It has been a pleasure, Your Majesty, Dragon Supreme. Ministers." Lord Kavindra greeted all with one final bow. "I shall be taking my leave, with your blessing."

Wordless, emotionless, Davorin Astrophel whisked a single hand toward the waiting horse. Without a purpose, Dragon Supreme didn't make conversation. Especially not with those who would see their own demise in due time. The Tribute Master had done well, for his first time, but there were things to be learned in a job such as this.

Lord Kavindra turned his horse to leave, sparing only a single glance back at Isonpool Palace. A single glance, and a prayer for Lada to find a way to protect herself from the evil within those walls.

Dragon Supreme didn't watch Lord Kavindra leave. He knew the Tribute Master would eagerly return to whence he came. Dragon Supreme turned back to the castle, prepared not for the first time to play a little game of cat and mouse.

CHAPTER NINETEEN
Locked-In Lada

o one had bothered to light the sconces. What little light filtered through the window Lada had opened brought with it the cold of mountain air. From what she had been told about Dragon Tribe, Lada might have expected such treatment for the Orafel princess. Their plan to disconcert the princess wouldn't have done much other than inconvenience Princess Zohana. Too bad the girl currently curled up in Princess Zohana's bed had come from Amaryl.

In truth, Lada might have taken things better if she hadn't frozen for the majority of the night. The quilt left behind by the impudent servants held little stuffing and less warmth. Without sconces or brazier to provide fire's heat, the stone room had quickly chilled to an unnatural temperature. Having lived her life in Flora Master's Hall, where a steady amount of heat and humidity were pertinent for healing ill plants, Lada detested the cold.

Unused to the chill, Lada had not slept most of the night and had tossed about for the remainder. On top of that, she had been offered no food and now her stomach grumbled its complaint. Clearly, neither nation desired this marriage. Only one nation decided to make that fact known.

Another gust of howling wind swirled in through the open window.

With a startled cry, Lada threw the blanket over her head and tucked it under her feet, as well. Even if it provided little warmth, it created a wonderful hidey-hole. Lada remained there until the breeze stopped shrieking. Then she allowed herself to peek her head out of the self-made tent.

The room around her remained as dark, cold, and empty as it had been since the servants left. The scent of sconce oil mixed with the smell of dust and decay assaulted Lada's nostrils, as it had all night. If she had a flint, she could light the fires. Alas, she had none and had not been able to find one, either. Not that she had searched far. Lada couldn't stand being outside the blanket for long.

The clip-clop of horse hooves echoed up through the open window from somewhere below.

Lada scrambled to see, her curiosity motivating her more than the noise itself.

Her room sat at an angle from which she could see the main road, though she could not access it. High enough to present a danger if she should jump, her window overlooked the path the Tribute Parade had taken to reach the main gate of Isonpool Palace. A path that sported a single rider as he departed Isonpool Palace's gates. Lada could tell, more by the color of his robes than actual details, it must be Lord Kavindra.

She had known, of course, that he would leave her. He had no other choice and she did not blame him. It only hurt that she had not been given the privilege of bidding farewell to her new friend. Whether she lived or died in this palace, Lada suspected she would never be able to see him again. If fate decreed it, so be it, but Lada didn't agree with the turn of events.

Lord Kavindra didn't look back, from the time he exited the outer palace gates to the time he disappeared over the horizon.

Alright. Fine. She had completed her mission and allowed everyone to leave safely, except the maids in orientation. Lada shuffled away from the window and into the center of the room. She should get to know her new surroundings, no matter how glum and gray they were.

Wrapping the blanket tightly around her shoulders, Lada padded first to the doors she had entered the evening prior. A gentle shove satisfied her curiosity and answered her question. They had been locked, and she had no key.

How cruel, to lock a woman up without food or water in such a terrible place. A seed of discontent settled in Lada's heart, amplified by her lack of sleep and longing for home. This room held not a single leaf or blossom. How would she survive without food, water, or flowers?

Lada took a deep breath, reminding herself to seek the brightness in any situation.

Very well. There were other nooks and crannies to explore.

Traveling first to the clothing rack near the bed, Lada risked shucking the blanket aside in favor of pulling on her dress. Mucking around in her underclothes would do her no good. Wearing the dress, despite its open shoulders, would keep her warmer. As quickly as she had tossed it aside, Lada retrieved the blanket and snuggled back in.

The vanity and table held little except the things she had brought in with her and a half-empty teapot. Lada poured herself a cup of cold tea while she surveyed the rest of the room.

Doors, locked, as she had already confirmed. Furniture, in desperate need of refurbishing or overhaul. Floors, solid stone. Window, open and still freezing her. The only solid, secure thing about the room were the curtains hanging from the top of the vaulted ceiling to conceal the bed in the corner.

Since they had locked her in and left her alone, Lada decided she must find a way to create more warmth. The walls here were made of stone, as were her flints back in Flora Master's Hall. Creative Lada suddenly found use for her icy confines. The disastrous state of the walls may be a help, rather than a hindrance.

Lada scurried to the nearest broken corner and searched the ground for a piece of stone large enough to be used. None there, but the second corner turned up a stone almost as wide as Lada's hands. Perfect. Now, if only she had something made of iron.

Bit by bit, Lada's head turned to stare at the giant doors locking her in. Doors made of iron. With a newfound hope, Lada dashed about gathering a candle, her stone, and some ratted pieces of fabric from the bed covering. It may not work, she may be subjected to the dark and cold, but the least she could do was try.

Taking up residence on the floor inside the door, Lada scooped her skirts out of the way and set to work placing the ratted fabric at the door's base. Creating any sparks at all came at a slim possibility. Lighting the fabric may never occur. But try she would, if only to pass the time.

"Please, please work," Lada appealed to the inanimate objects before her.

At first, nothing happened. Not a single spark, no reaction from anything save a loud thunk from the door. Still, Lada pressed on. If not now, perhaps later the instruments would work with her. Again and again, Lada struck the door with her makeshift flint stone. On occasion, a spark spit off, but never toward the kindling she had placed.

Lada's arms grew sore. Her resolve wavered. The lack of sleep caught up to her and amplified her frustration tenfold. With a final thrust, Lada struck the door so hard it quivered on its hinges.

A spark flew from the contact between metal and stone, landing on the dusty and dry rags.

With a gasp, Lada pressed closer to the floor, blowing oxygen into the fledgling fire until it strengthened and held. With a giggle of glee, she pressed the candle's wick into the flame. The candle sputtered, but accepted the flame nonetheless.

Amazed and relieved that the trick had worked, Lada shot to her feet and pranced a circle.

Impossible, for Dragon Tribe to forget her existence. Someone would come to check on her. She would be fed and clothed.

With those optimistic delusions singing in her head, Lada skipped to light the other candles and a sconce or two, should she be able to reach them. It may still be cold and she may still feel hunger, but at least now she could dance in the glow of candlelight.

CHAPTER TWENTY
Princess Zohana's Fate

Days of rain gave way to morning sun, bright but veiled by the treetops. Forest creatures scurried about, birds called and insects chirped, but none dared go near the figure laying limp at the side of their favorite stream. Outsiders were not welcomed in their habitat, but were feared by all. Even the scavengers would not near the mess of fabric and hair to see if it had died.

Cautious as they were, it could not be overlooked that the forest creatures held an interest in a specific area of the stream. Someone was sure to take notice.

Had creatures or human, alike, taken a vote or wagered a bet, none would have anticipated the Guardsman who came upon the stream first. Valor of Champion's Post did not often visit the streams and rivers. He guarded elsewhere, in places where his specialties and skills were needed. Rivers and streams usually sported only forest creatures and the occasional herbalist. None dared use them to enter the borders. His brothers-in-arms could handle those positions.

Truth be told, Valor wasn't quite certain why he chose to seek out the animals' interest on that wet but sunny morning. Something about how the birds flitted nervously. Or the way the creatures on the forest floor stopped to stare. Whatever the case, Valor only knew disruptions in the flow of the forest meant bad tidings had arrived.

Valor, at first, approached the animals, listening to their chatter for worries or fears. They remained surprisingly at peace, just curious. For this reason only did Valor relax his defenses against the intrusion.

Leaves rustled and branches cracked as Valor stepped out of the forest and into the stream's clearing. Though the trees hung in a canopy overhead, they dared not grow too close to the water. Their kindness granted a natural opening for the use of animals and humans alike.

Valor's ears told him that nothing broke the woods' serenity. His eyes told him a different story. For there, on the bank, face-down in mud created by the last days' rain, a peculiar figure lay motionless.

A woman, Valor surmised, from the skirts wound around her legs and the pieces of jewelry placed in her hair. Hair that spread out around her in every possible direction, caked in moss and mud. She did not belong in this forest. No one from Amaryl dressed such as this, not even the elders and their families.

An errant, curious chipmunk flitted around Valor's feet as he ventured closer. The whisper of Valor's scythe leaving its sheath sent the creature bounding for the nearest tree trunk.

The figure on the bank could be dead. Most who turned up in this way had either been thrown in the river to drown or had succumbed to the Border Fog. On the off chance this woman had survived her journey, Valor wanted to be sure he had the upper hand. To under-estimate an outsider—especially when all had heard of how an outsider had taken Lada of Flora Master's Hall—could mean death. Or worse.

Valor knelt near the woman's head, taking note of each detail before he made a move. Her hands lay palms-down near her cheeks, half covered in her hair but revealing enough for Valor to make out scratches and marks. Discoloration around her wrists. This woman had been in a scuffle of some sort, bound by something heavy enough to bruise her.

It could be a ploy, or it could mean she had come without intent to harm anyone. Valor would not risk guessing which one it may be.

Using the flat of his blade, Valor lifted her hair out of her face and flicked it over her shoulder-blades. Like the rest of her, the woman's face bore mud and angry red scratches. She must have fought with all her might, to thus injure her lovely features.

Valor reached out a hand, settling his fingers beneath her nose to check for breath. Though faint, warm air graced his fingertips. Some-how, in the midst of turmoil and foggy conditions out of her control, this woman had survived and appeared alongside one of Amaryl's most prized streams. A spy, perhaps? She looked half-dead, and that's how Valor should have left her. For dead. Alone. After all, on close inspection the insignia on her headpiece belonged to Orafel.

But those long lashes of hers fluttered. A pained groan slipped from her pretty lips. And she uttered a word that would have made any Amaryl Guardsman take notice.

"Lada..."

Valor paused, half-risen to his feet but in dire need of answers to his now pending questions. "What did you say?"

"Lada..." the woman breathed the word, her fingers twitching against the ground. "I... help..." And again, she went still.

The spy sent to monitor Lada had sent word of her departure in the Tribute Parade. For this woman to know of Lada, she must have been a part of that parade. He knew little of the exchanges between Orafel and Dragon Tribe, but Valor knew this woman must have met Lada personally. She may carry information that would help them. Or she may only know the name and, when she woke, would betray them all.

Not able to predict which she would choose, Valor took stock of his own situation and pondered how telling the Elders would affect all of Amaryl.

This woman required medical attention. Lots of it. Within the stream, she would have passed through Border Fog. Those symptoms would be tricky to treat, let alone the wounds from her fight that would cause complications.

For now, Valor decided, he should do right by her.

Thinking no more of how it would affect the nation or what she might do to him and his kinsmen, Valor sheathed his scythe, secured his feet beneath him, and hauled the dying woman into his arms. For now, he would take charge of her. They would discuss other matters if she woke.

CHAPTER TWENTY-ONE
Attempted

Another day passed. One by one, the candles around Lada's bed melted into puddles. The cold, tasteless tea on the table ran out. Lada's poor excuses about Dragon Tribe not being able to forget the princess came to an end. Without food, Lada found herself both tired and weak. The candles had been her only blossom of hope in an otherwise gloomy imprisonment. Now that they had gone, she had nothing left to look forward to.

Lada stumbled to the door, giving it a knock before she ventured to speak. "May I have more tea, at least?"

She could survive the hunger if she didn't go thirsty.

Minutes passed. A muted conversation outside the door didn't last long enough for Lada to make out what they had said.

A key turned in the lock.

A maid slipped into the room, carrying a pot of tea and a cup on a tray. So, someone had listened.

"Thank you," Lada offered the maid.

The maid didn't answer Lada's gratitude. She simply poured a cup of the hot tea and held it out toward Lada.

Lada shuffled over and took the warm cup in her hands. The heat seeped into her bones. Finally, she felt as if she could live. Lada lifted the cup to inhale its scent. Ginger, cinnamon and...

Lada froze, the cup poised at her lips. The third, final scent registered in her mind like the pealing of warning bells.

Pelidon berries. A rare, highly effective poison.

If not for her upbringing as an herbalist, Lada might not have thought twice about the foreign scent. By brewing Pelidon Berries into her tea, they were telling her to die. Though Lada had been prepared to sacrifice herself for her new friends, she suddenly found she didn't want to die.

She wanted to survive.

Lada gripped the cup tighter, inhaled one more courageous breath, and threw the cup's contents at the maid's face.

The maid screeched, stumbling backward in her attempt to avoid the searing liquid.

Guards came running to check on the commotion.

And Lada ran. She dodged around the two guards, darted out the open door, and set her feet to flying.

Boots chased after her, resounding around the stone halls in an ominous echo meant to send shivers down Lada's spine. The trick would have worked, if Lada hadn't been prepared to do whatever it took to ensure she stayed alive.

Now knowing she should have paid attention to the pattern of hallways taken when she arrived, Lada stopped briefly at a crossroads to make a plan. A split second decision sent her sprinting into an indoor courtyard and hiding behind a screen of dead vines. They would see her, eventually, but it bought her time.

Lord Kavindra had returned to her an embroidered sachet that he believed to be empty. Lada knew better. She had saved the sachet for such a situation, and would use it now to ensure her fate. Amarylites knew how to protect themselves in the worst of times. This seemed to count as the worst time, and thus Lada felt little shame in the trick she would now use.

From the sachet, Lada pulled two long needles, taken from the center of the harvested Mirror Flower. One needle, covered in pollen. The other, nearly bare and almost invisible to the naked eye.

Lada braced the tip of the first needle against a vein in her arm. Took a deep breath. And gave it a shove through her skin.

"She's here!" came a call too close for comfort.

Lada spun toward the guards breaking into her hiding spot, tucked the second needle between two fingers, and accidentally dropped the sachet to the ground. It wouldn't matter. The sachet held little importance in the game she had chosen to play.

One of the brash Dragon Tribe guards took hold of Lada's arm.

Lada cried out as her barely-healed wound tore open. They need not manhandle her, but then again they had allowed an assassin into her room without a question. Needless tasks were their strong suit.

A second guard grabbed hold of Lada's other arm, and between the two they pulled her to an uncomfortable but upright position.

"This's the runaway, sir," the first guard announced to a third guard. "Shall we send her off to dungeon or gallows?"

The third guard perused Lada from head to foot, making assumptions and creating plans. He knew the inner palace workings better than the others. Had seen more and knew whom they should never manipulate.

This girl, breathless and with fire in her eyes, belonged to only one person in Isonpool Palace. Thinking of what would happen should they unilaterally pass judgment on her, he grimaced and shook his head.

"We have no say over her fate," the third guard mused.

The other two didn't relax their grip, but their faces turned into disappointed confusion. They were used to getting their way when it came to punishments. After all, that was the use of a good system of guards.

Their lack of hospitality said many things about the running of this palace. Lada, unimpressed, returned her gaze to the third guard. At least he had demonstrated common sense.

The third guard circled a hand in the air. "Take her to Dragon Supreme immediately."

Not for the first time, Lada wished to be anywhere except where she stood. She did not regret her place in the Tribute Parade's plan, but perhaps it would have been better had she returned to Amaryl. Facing Dragon Supreme not only frightened Lada, it petrified her to the point of muteness.

"Dragon Tribe is full of beasts. A flower like you won't last a week." The Physician's words rang in her head, mocking her frail attempt at survival.

Any sane person would remind Lada that a nation full of beasts must be run by a beast, as well. Lada might have listened to them. Perhaps His Majesty, Dragon Supreme, did come from a line of beasts. But those sane people overlooked one fact that Lada clung to with endless optimism.

Lada had a knack for befriending beasts.

CHAPTER TWENTY-TWO
Survival Plan

ourt had been adjourned hours ago, but now Davorin Astrophel, Dragon Supreme, once again sat perched on his Fang Throne. The cat-and-mouse game had been boring thus far, without a single attempt made by the princess to see him or negotiate terms. But, then, she had always been a fraud.

Days had passed and now Dragon Supreme had summoned those from whom he wished information.

Kneeling before him now, in the empty Fang-Throne Court, three of his finest Shadows awaited their cue to speak. All had been sent to find information about the fake princess, in the simplest way possible. They had been the maids assigned to her by Dragon Tribe. More loyal than anyone, Davorin's Shadows would not let him down, even if it meant their lives.

Dragon Supreme rested an elbow on his knee and waved a hand through the air, encouraging them to offer what they had gathered.

The first Shadow pressed her hands over her heart in the typical phoenix symbol. "My Lord, Dragon Supreme. It is as you foresaw. The Tribute Bride is clumsy and uncoordinated. She asked for nothing more than the room's contents. Even the unstuffed quilt and shoddy pillows satisfied her."

He had suspected that would be the case. If not a princess, one would not think to press their boundaries. Princesses were known for their spoiled natures. This Tribute Bride was far too docile to be the actual Orafel princess. Somewhere along the line, something had gone wrong.

"What of her demeanor afterward? What has she done these days aside from starve and freeze?"

Dragon Supreme asked it not because he was curious, but because he needed to understand the kind of tactics she would use to slay him. Orafel would not substitute a warrior such as Princess Zohana with someone who could do no damage.

The three Shadows glanced to each other in silent conversation. How to tell their sovereign what had taken place in the room over the last few days? How did one phrase it to make sense when it sounded nonsensical?

"Spit it out," Dragon Supreme commanded.

The third shadow bent forward, her hands over her heart. "My Lord, she lit candles for herself, then..."

Dragon Supreme sat forward, suddenly interested to hear what his Shadows had to say. They had never hesitated before. Had never tried to hold back any information. To lie meant death and to hesitate often meant they had considered lying.

"Then... *what*?"

The third Shadow moistened her lips with the tip of her tongue. "She... danced."

"Danced?" The word took Dragon Supreme by surprise.

"Yes, Your Lordship. After lighting candles, the woman sang and danced. She seemed quite content. Happy, even."

What kind of convoluted pastimes did the imposter have? Who in their right mind sand and danced while they were starving and freezing? Did she have no sense of self-preservation? Or, perhaps, Orafel had sent a lunatic who might turn feral at any moment. That sounded like something Dragon Supreme's least favorite protectorate would do, just to spite him.

"Also, Your Majesty—" his third Shadow's words were cut off by another, louder cry from the open throne room doors.

"Reporting!"

A roll of his eyes and a heavy sigh did little to express Dragon Supreme's distaste at being interrupted. The guards knew he hated intrusion, however, and would not put themselves in the path of Dragon Supreme's anger unless absolutely necessary. Thus, Davorin Astrophel leveled his dark gaze at the frazzled guard at the door.

"Enter."

The guard came scurrying down the length of the court, his boots clacking against the polished stone. Beside the Shadows, the guard took a knee and saluted his master.

"My Lord, Dragon Supreme. Her Highness fled from her room and was apprehended by two of my subordinates. As she is under orders to remain in her quarters, and has disobeyed your decree, we have brought her here posthaste for punishment."

What an intriguing turn of events. She dared disobey the arrangements made for her? And, on top of that, had not attempted to slay a few detestable Dragon Tribe guards in the name of her country, but had fled instead? What an excellent spy Orafel had sent, unable to create the smallest disturbance in the correct way.

"Bring her to me."

The guard rose, bowed, and turned to summon his brothers-in-arms.

Dragon Supreme looked to his Shadows. "Make yourselves scarce."

The third Shadow lifted her gaze insolently, then lowered it again. "But, My Lord..."

He held up a hand to stop her. "Anything that needs to be said can be said after I handle this."

The Shadows all rose to their feet. Each knew their sovereign held no tolerance for disobedience. Not even theirs. Especially not the disobedience of an Orafel princess. It appeared the game would come to a close sooner rather than later. No doubt, for her bad behavior, the princess would die. Or be punished so severely she wished for death.

Wanting not that end for themselves, the Shadows disappeared from Fang-Throne Court.

Two guards marched into the room on the tail of their superior. Between them, flower petals now wilting in her hair and a few days' worth of soot on her clothing and skin, a weak imposter fought their manhandling.

She would never be able to escape them. Not when they could easily overpower her. She especially couldn't escape when she required sustenance to return to her the strength she had possessed to begin with.

Unceremoniously, the guards dropped Lada to the ground in the center of the court.

Lada didn't bother to attempt to get up or move. Anything she did or said could be taken the wrong way, but that wasn't her motivation. Lada hadn't slept peacefully in two nights, she had grown tired of the cold, and she wanted to leave. Remaining still and glaring at Dragon Supreme were the only petty acts of rebellion she could afford. For the moment.

Dragon Supreme didn't seem all that grand, after closer inspection. He wore dramatic, draping black robes, but the gold coronet on his head stuck out like antlers on a deer. Lada's friend the Great White Deer was better looking, and had a better temperament too. If she were braver, Lada would tell him as much.

As for Davorin Astrophel, he had no intention of letting this game play out any longer. She had grossly disappointed his expectations of a spy, and thus he had grown tired of keeping her. Flogging her or executing her were the correct punishments for disobeying the will of Dragon Supreme and he meant to choose one and send her to her fate.

But, first, Dragon Supreme had a few questions requiring answers.

"Who are you, really?"

Satisfaction purred in Davorin's chest when the little fraud's eyes turned from fire to clay. He had caught her and she knew it. Thus, she must answer him with great detail.

Lada, not knowing any of the thoughts racing through Davorin Astrophel's mind, found it in her best interests to remain silent. If she answered, they would have reason to kill her on the spot. She needed to buy more time. She needed Dragon Supreme to come closer. If he came close, her plan for survival had a higher chance of success.

Lada may not have intended it, but her silence irked Dragon Supreme. When asked a question, one should answer. Had she no sense of impending disaster? Knew she not that with a flick of his fingers, Dragon Supreme could put a swift end to her life?

Davorin rose from his seat, taking a step closer to the defiant woman before him. "Will you not answer me?"

Lada shook her head.

"Where is Princess Zohana?" Dragon Supreme tried next.

Surely, the imp before him would give an answer. She could not have been heartless enough to accept this suicide mission without knowing the terms. She would answer if she wanted to save herself.

Answer she did, but not with anything Dragon Supreme wished to hear.

"I do not know."

If asking earnestly would do nothing, he would change tactics. Dragon Supreme knew quite a few tactics that opened lips quicker than torture or threat. The mind was a mysterious weapon, once one walked into it. Since the woman didn't bend to force, he should try his hand at cunning.

One step at a time, allowing each click of his boots to echo up into the rafters, Dragon Supreme descended from the Fang Throne to the floor of the court. With each step toward her, the creature winced, but never did she break eye contact or try to flee.

Davorin silently commended her for her idiotic bravado.

"There are rules and regulations in this Palace." Dragon Supreme paced a step closer to her with each word. "Are you not aware?"

"No one told me the rules," Lada answered honestly.

Honesty had served her well. She only found herself in this terrible situation because she had lied. If they had told the truth from the beginning, things would be different now. Certainly she would not be sitting on a hard stone floor explaining others' blunders to Qranbu's reigning sovereign.

"Ah." Dragon Supreme clicked his tongue. "A lapse in execution on our part. No excuse."

Dragon Supreme circled past her shoulder, his cape brushing her skirts. A whisper of his fingers against her shoulder, met with a flinch that stiffened her whole body, cleared away the woman's hair long enough for him to spot the switch marks healing upon her skin. Not a noble, then. Nobles didn't bear scars. An oozing reopened wound on her other arm confirmed his suspicion.

"I gave specific instructions for how to treat you, with only the stipulation that you were not allowed out of your quarters. Punishment for disobeying Dragon Supreme is severe." Davorin stopped in front of her, reached down with one hand to tuck a finger under her chin. "And yet you tried to escape."

Something inside of Lada, built up from all the horrible things she had endured the past days, came crashing down in the form of tears. Once the first fell from her eye, the others swiftly followed. Her words went sailing, carried out like a ship on the waterfall of her sobs.

"Of *course* I tried to escape!" she burst, jerking her chin out of Dragon Supreme's grasp. "I came here because I didn't believe the rumors that *all* Dragon Tribe people are bad, but they're turning out to be truer than I thought. The room was cold and dark and I hate both the cold and the dark, and though I tried to endure it you starved me and when I thought it might be over you sent Pelidon Berries in the tea. There isn't a leaf, limb, or blossom to be found in my quarters so I'm lonely and the vines you do have are all wilted and dying, not like the forest at all. I don't want to stay here. I want to go home to Flora Master's—"

Lada pulled up short, but it was too late. She knew her blunder. Had heard the words come out of her mouth but had been unable to stop them.

Davorin Astrophel paused, taking in her tirade with a practiced calculation of every word. When she snapped her lips closed, he knew. He knew exactly what kind of person Orafel had sent in their princess's place.

"You're from Amaryl?" Dragon Supreme asked, in a tone dangerously low and slow.

Lada pressed her lips together, the tears still flowing but her words run out.

Amaryl, the nation which he had set his sights on overcoming. The heavens indeed worked in his favor, to send an Amarylite into his palace under such a guise. A guide such as this came as a once-in-a-lifetime chance. To be sure she could indeed guide his quest, Dragon Supreme need only confirm his supposition. Yet she remained close-mouthed.

His domination so close that Dragon Supreme tasted it, he held no tolerance for her silent tongue. She must speak, or her use here would end.

Impatient and at the end of his rope, Dragon Supreme's hand clamped around the little forest imp's throat. "Amaryl is your home?"

Still, she didn't answer, instead hiccupping another sob.

Dragon Supreme's hold tightened, pressing down on Lada's windpipe as he dragged her to her feet. She would speak, or she would die.

Lada's hands wrapped around his wrist in a silent plea for him to release her. If he released her, she wouldn't have to employ the means of trickery she had set out to use to save herself. If he showed leniency, they could be friends without peril.

Dragon Supreme only squeezed tighter. His voice rose, his shout echoing not only in the court but down the halls and through the palace, frightening everyone who knew his temper. "TELL ME!"

He meant to slay her, and Lada knew it. She had hoped for the best, but he would not release her without a push. Lada hated having to hurt others, but this Dragon Supreme left her no choice if she wanted her life.

Lada's fingertips slipped to Davorin's pulse point, just shown at the bottom of his sleeve. They lingered there, finding a vein though her vision went hazy. Positioning the second Mirror Needle at the top of a vein, Lada executed her plan.

Her palm slammed against Dragon Supreme's wrist, sending the needle through his skin.

A sharp stinging pain ended Davorin's hold on the woman. She collapsed to the ground in a heap of dingy pink and yellow fabric, a series of coughs escaping her throat like invalid prisoners.

The pain did not cease, but continued on, starting at Davorin's wrist... working its way up his arm and through his body... Until it pierced his very heart. Dragon Supreme went down on one knee, a hand clutched to his heart as if it would end his suffering.

"My Lord!"

"Your Lordship!"

Guards—and Cadfael—came running from all corners of the court. The two who had escorted Lada in bent to pick her up.

Their superior appeared from behind a pillar, his arm raised with a sword in it. The sword landed at Lada's neck, close enough to nick the flesh.

She went still, but her eyes remained on the man she had been forced to injure in order to survive. Nothing too harmful. A bit of mischief, really. Those were the things Lada told herself to make it better.

"What have you done?" Dragon Supreme growled at the annoying, scheming woman before him.

Waves of pain, a thousand fire ants pinpricking his internal organs, rolled through Davorin. They stole his strength and then returned it, as if parasites had taken up residence inside of his blood. As if he found himself at the mercy of things he didn't understand.

"I'm sorry," Lada apologized, her words gruff from the harsh treatment of her throat. "It had to be done, or you would have killed me. I'm truly sorry."

"I am stronger than you give me credit for." Davorin took a few deep breaths, sighing when the stinging subsided and ebbed away.

It would take more than a foolish woman's blunder to do him in. However, she had injured his person and that could not be tolerated. His own family were not allowed to produce a scratch or a mark on his body. This outsider had dared to insert a foreign object into his veins.

"Death is sweeter than the punishment you deserve. You dislike the dark and cold? Fine."

It had been meant to terrify her and make her plead for forgiveness and mercy. Instead, Dragon Supreme found he saw only pity and sympathy in her expressive eyes. An odd reaction, but she had been odd since her arrival. Little did she know. Davorin meant not to kill her. Not yet. She had made the game interesting again, and he needed information she possessed. From this moment on, Dragon Supreme would do whatever it took to see to it that the unnamed Amaryl woman found no comfort in his palace.

One inch at a time, Dragon Supreme rose to his full imposing height and pointed an accusing finger at the Amarylite at his feet. "Drag her to the dungeons."

CHAPTER TWENTY-THREE
The Dungeons

Dark, damp tunnels spiraled under Isonpool Palace, winding like snakes into the heart of the mountain. Insects crawled along the walls, following streams of water into the earth's core and then out. The scent of dirt and human filth filled the air, an unpleasant sensation that would repulse the lowliest of individuals.

Lada's tears had dried on her face, as no one offered to wipe them for her. To be expected, as she had insulted their reigning monarch. In Amaryl, any weeping woman would be given comfort. At the least, her fears would be abated and her health looked after.

Yet, the guards holding Lada continued on, unaffected by the groans and screams of prisoners deep inside the prison. Unyielding to the clink and clack of chains and locks. They held no mercy for her.

Not yet. Not until someone discovered what she had done. Then, Lada would have to explain and interpret many things.

That time had yet to come.

This time—this present moment that Lada existed within—brought her to a cave where men lay chained to enormous stalagmites. At various intervals, trails led off to deeper parts of the dungeon, presumably to cells where the hardened criminals were locked away properly.

Prison guards sat playing cards at a ramshackle table in the corner, their armor askew and some with their helmets cast aside. Here in the dungeons, they cared little for decorum or ceremony. Dungeon Guards held nothing but animosity and brutality. How else would they survive? Only by removing the basest level of their heart and emotions could prison guards perform their jobs properly.

"Delivery," one of the Royal Guards holding Lada announced. If he had remained silent, the Dungeon Guards may have never looked up from their game.

A big, bulky man with jagged teeth and a mole near his eye raised his head to glare. A glare that let up considerably when his confusion overwhelmed him.

The dungeons had seen many a woman come through their gates, but never one covered in soot and wilted flowers, with tears staining her cheeks. A peculiar creature, indeed, this new addition to their dank cave. Women such as her rarely appeared anywhere in Qranbu, let alone in a place like this.

"What have we here?" another guard asked, his cards forgotten.

Lada gave a sniff, clearing her throat and sinuses so she may answer anything asked of her when the time came.

"This one displeased His Majesty, Dragon Supreme."

"A little thing such as this? Hardly believable."

The Dungeon Guards all laughed. All except the bulky one in the corner. He had seen a thing or two in his years belowground. He may work in the dungeons, but the Head Dungeon Guard better understood the outside world because of his position.

The sprite hadn't come from Dragon Tribe, else she would be fighting tooth and nail to leave this godforsaken place. She had displeased Dragon Supreme. That meant she had to have been inside Isonpool Palace and close enough to Dragon Supreme, himself, to have done something worth imprisonment.

The Head Dungeon Guard, having made his deductions, clucked his tongue at his subordinates. "I'd keep a distance, were I you. To touch her is akin to raiding the Royal Treasury."

"Royal Treasury? That girl?" Another insubordinate underling burst out laughing as he rose to his feet. Clearly, his knowledge of palace workings needed updating.

Caring not whether his employee managed to lose his head or keep it, the Head Dungeon Guard leveled his stare at the harmless-looking woman between two Royal Guards. "What instructions from His Majesty, Dragon Supreme?"

"Nothing special." One of the guards at Lada's side brushed off the ignorant Dungeon Guard who had approached. "Just ensure she stays alive."

"Put her in the cell." Leaving such a creature out in the open would wreak havoc on his well-running prison, The Head Dungeon Guard decided. If she had done enough to irk Dragon Supreme, perhaps keeping her locked safely away would be a better choice. Moving on to other matters, he addressed the disobedient subordinate. "Ivo, fetch the meal for the prisoners."

"But, sir—"

"Do as I say and you may see that pretty kitchen maid you've had your eye on." The Head Dungeon Guard knew how to manipulate and subjugate those beneath him. Ivo was no exception.

The promise of seeing the girl he had taken a liking to sent Ivo scrambling for the exit. The walk to the kitchens would take him a while, and when he got back they would have tucked this little Tribute Treasure away.

"Take her to the cell," the Head Dungeon Guard reiterated in no uncertain terms. He turned back to the game before him.

Lada, who had watched the whole exchange quietly, found she liked this burly man. Rough and gruff, yes, but he had a sense of honor and knew where his place lied. He had also made a quick decision concerning her identity, and had guessed correctly. Lada appreciated those with smarts as well as muscle, much like the Guardsmen of Amaryl.

Aside from all that, whether he had been aware of it or not, Lada felt this Dungeon Guard had saved her from unpleasantries at the hand of the other guard. For that, she would consider this man an acquaintance, not an enemy.

As the Royal Guards urged her toward a lonesome hall, Lada turned her head back toward the table of prison guards and addressed the bulky man with a single phrase.

"Thank you."

The Head Dungeon Guard snorted. Never before had anyone thanked him for locking them away. The Head Dungeon Guard had seen many strange things over the years. This took the trophy for the oddest event to happen in his prison. This woman had no sense of self-preservation. If she survived her stay, it would be a miracle. But, for that matter, most came here to die, anyway.

Unaware of the effect she had on the Head Dungeon Guard's racing mind, Lada found herself dragged through a barred door at the end of a tunnel. Instantly, she regretted thanking anyone for putting her there. Wet cold seeped up through her bare feet and into her bones. A single candle outside the door did nothing to brighten the room's black interior.

Lada stiffened in the grasp of the two guards. It should only be a short while in this place, but she didn't want to stay at all. The darkness had never been her friend, only a nemesis she couldn't avoid. Exhausted as she was, Lada wanted nothing more than to avoid it.

Lada shied closer to one of the guards, pressed up against his side as though it would save her. "Are you positive a sincere apology won't change His Majesty's mind?"

The guard knew better than to allow a Tribute Piece to touch him in such a close and intimate manner. He immediately scurried to the side, leaving the girl stumbling over her own two feet for a moment before she righted herself. A deep breath did little to still his nerves.

Had Davorin Astrophel, Dragon Supreme, seen the girl touch the guard, there was no telling the outcome. Perhaps the woman knew and had used it to her advantage, but she didn't appear intelligent enough to have thought it through.

"His Lordship, Dragon Supreme, doesn't accept apologies."

"That's what I thought," Lada sighed, resigned to her fate.

The Royal Guards, knowing they could not stay and should not linger around this odd and conniving woman, closed and locked the door on their way out. Such an unprecedented series of events led to nothing but trouble. Neither would stay to see what kind of problems arose. In Isonpool Palace, one lived longer when one minded their own business.

Lada felt her way forward, until she encountered the stone ledge meant as a bed. Stone didn't hold heat that didn't exist. The room in Isonpool Palace had been a blessing in disguise. There had been sconces and fire there, at least.

She never should have mentioned hating the dark and the cold. This Dragon Supreme of theirs had seemed unreasonable for as long as she had been in his presence. Lada should have known he would act out in a petty way when she pricked him. A Mirror Needle didn't warrant this kind of behavior, did it?

Then again, she had injured a king. Lada understood the protocol that went with that, even if she had never had to adhere to it before. It wouldn't matter in a while, anyway.

Unreasonable, he had been, but he held himself as an intelligent man would. She believed this Dragon Supreme to be quick-witted enough to deduce what had happened, yet she may have to be in harm's way before it dawned on him. He must figure out what she had done, or their ends would come in a catastrophic parallel.

Lada curled her knees to her chest and tucked the hem of her skirts beneath her soles. She wouldn't dwell on it. She would wait to survive this dungeon first. It couldn't be so bad. She may be cold and scared, but here they would offer her food. A basic courtesy that had not been given her in Isonpool Palace.

Leaning against the wall reminded her that the rough guards had reopened her wound. Lada wished for a poultice to mend it. She would not be given one. She only hoped it mended itself, or she might end up in dire straights.

CHAPTER TWENTY-FOUR
Rationale Returning

For hours after the woman left, Davorin Astrophel, Dragon Supreme, remained in Fang-Throne Court alone. Or, rather, as alone as a Dragon Supreme could get.

Cadfael, always dutiful, remained a ghost along the outer wall, ready to intervene or appear whenever his lord and master required it. To leave his post or abandon his sovereign would not only sentence Cadfael to death, but would tear his loyal heart into a thousand pieces. No fate could be worse than betrayal, toward him or from him.

Whereas the Royal Guards who had appeared before cared only about the traitorous female in their midst, Cadfael turned his attention to Dragon Supreme. Few had the ability to so outrage Davorin Astrophel, to make him lose restraint over his carefully calculated emotions. The Amaryl girl had managed to destroy his control in a matter of minutes. Perhaps precisely because of the fact that she came from Amaryl.

Dragon Supreme did not deign to quarrel with many, but he had indeed started the fight when it came to that imp. Cadfael knew, beyond a shadow of a doubt, Davorin Astrophel wanted Amaryl for his own. None could fathom Dragon Supreme's reasoning, but Cadfael knew Dragon Supreme had walked into the notion understanding full well what it would entail. The Amarylite would be their way in to the isolated tribe, if they played their cards correctly.

Cadfael knew it, and indeed Davorin had mulled over the same issues, but now Dragon Supreme had cooled his boiling wrath and found more than one thing amiss.

"Cadfael."

Cadfael appeared in a thin beam of sunlight from a high window. He had been waiting only to hear his name mentioned.

His hands folded around his sword, held aloft before him in a salute. "My Lord."

Davorin beckoned his guard with one hand. "Come here. I wish not for the guards to have more to gossip about."

The Isonpool Palace rumor mill had been given enough fodder for the day. Come nightfall, the entire palace would undoubtedly hear of the fake princess's real identity. If not for her station as a Tribute piece, Davorin would have had to lower himself to issue a royal decree of protection. Thankfully, his people knew better than to interfere with Dragon Supreme's handling of Tribute.

Cadfael, with permission granted, ascended the steps to the very top and bowed before the Fang Throne and the Dragon Supreme. "My Lord."

"You heard the things the woman said, yes?"

Cadfael nodded his head once. Like his master, he disliked using words when it could be helped.

"Tell me," Davorin commanded, his fingers drumming against the arms of the throne. "What were my instructions for the treatment of Her Highness?"

Without hesitation, Cadfael recited the instructions given to the three Shadows and the other ladies' maids that had been sent to Princess Zohana's chambers. The ones who had inadvertently been put in charge of the Amaryl woman.

"She was to be left alone, given nothing but water and tea for a number of days. They were not to touch her or interfere with her in any other way. My Lord wished to know how she would answer being treated as a lowly individual."

"Not to touch her or interfere with her in any other way..." Dragon Supreme mused.

Yes, those were the words plaguing him. The ones which clarified the suspicions and doubts swirling in his mind. The maids were told not to touch her. Not to interfere in *any other way*.

"The Amaryl girl," Davorin went on, now placing the puzzle pieces together. "Her diatribe... did you hear the things she mentioned had set her to flight?"

With his rationale returning, resurfacing after his bout of rage, Davorin found quite a few things out of place beside the little woman. He would start with the obvious, the things she had revealed herself. The secret things would reveal themselves with time.

"Cold. Darkness. Starvation. And..." Cadfael, though respectful, found he could not keep staring at the ground when realization smacked him in the face. His gaze found Davorin's and held.

Davorin arched his brows, knowing his most trusted guard understood exactly what he had heard in the woman's speech. "Pelidon Berries."

They had overlooked the mention of the rare poison in their frenzy. Dragon Supreme had been so caught up in sentencing the Amaryl woman he had overlooked the important things. Like Pelidon Berries. An Orafel princess might have missed their presence in her tea. If Lada had truly been Princess Zohana, a war might have already broken out over the corpse of a beloved royal.

"Someone's playing tricks," Davorin growled, put out by the fact someone had disobeyed his commands and put poison in the woman's teapot. "I want to know who has the audacity to cross me."

Cadfael, of course, cared that Dragon Supreme found those who acted against his orders, but raising his eyes had alerted him to a disturbing fact about Davorin Astrophel's current situation.

"My Lord, are you injured?" Cadfael blurted out the question before he thought better of it.

Davorin stared down his favorite guard, mind spinning with the possibilities and connotations of Cadfael's query. Had the man not witnessed all that had happened? Certainly, Cadfael had come running and thus must have understood all.

"The Amaryl women violated me. Have you lost your reason?" Davorin shot back at Cadfael.

"Oh, no, My Lord." Cadfael quickly reassessed how he had phrased his question. He should have been more specific with his curiosity. "Your throat, My Lord." Cadfael pressed two fingers to the joint of his own neck and shoulder, at the approximate point he had spotted a drop of scarlet marring Davorin's flesh.

Dragon Supreme lifted his own fingers to touch the skin showing above the collar of his robes. A lightning-quick pang shot through his neck and shoulder. It dissipated in the same second. Davorin Astrophel's expression never changed. He never flinched. Not for such a small thing as a scratch.

"Perhaps I injured myself during training," Davorin blew off his guard's concern.

Had Dragon Supreme been injured during training, Cadfael surely would have noticed. After all, who but Cadfael sparred against such a powerful and domineering opponent? Minute by minute, Cadfael replayed the morning's match in his head. He came to only one conclusion.

"My Lord, I dare not draw any weapon to your throat, lest an accident occur and I foolishly take your head." Cadfael bent his own head, showing the respect his annoyed master deserved. "I assure you, the injury is not from your training. Indeed, it seems quite fresh."

The gentle reminder was meant to open Dragon Supreme's eyes to the sudden wound's strangeness. Cadfael found, though he had observed his master closely all day, he could not remember anything sharp coming near Dragon Supreme at all. The Amaryl woman had kept her clutches far from Davorin's throat. In Cadfael's opinion, she was more apt to play tricks than do any real harm.

Deduction brought no answers to the dilemma set before him. How did one acquire an injury that had never existed in the first place?

"It matters not," Davorin insisted. "I am more concerned with the perpetrator who thought to poison Princess Zohana's tea."

A pointed look in Cadfael's direction originated out of pure impatience. Someone in *his* palace, under *his* rule, had dared to plot behind his back. Treason wouldn't be tolerated in Isonpool Palace.

"Issue an order to locate the maid who gave the Amaryl woman tea."

A straightforward approach was the best approach, if used wisely. In this situation, using a bare-bones tactic would undoubtedly draw out the mastermind behind the ploy. No mere maid would have the kind of mettle it took to diagram and execute such a plan. Someone had ordered her to do it, and Dragon Supreme meant to find them sooner rather than later.

They would pay for defying him. Just as everyone who had defied him before them.

Cadfael rose to his feet, prepared to deliver the order as swiftly as possible. He stopped only when his master held up a hand to signal him to wait.

"Have the maids stoke the braziers."

Davorin couldn't remember the last time he noticed the cold, but he felt definitively colder than usual. Stoking the braziers would hold no meaning for the maids, anyway. They were swift to do as Dragon Supreme ordered. A mere fire? It wouldn't require a second thought.

One thing alone bothered Dragon Supreme about his own command, even as Cadfael left to deliver the words. Cold hadn't bothered him in decades. Why did he feel it now?

CHAPTER TWENTY-FIVE
Report to Nerys

hat do you mean, the woman who entered Isonpool Palace isn't Princess Zohana?"

The returning spy bent his head to the ground. "I've traveled a long way to tell you. Your bandits lost Princess Zohana at the Amaryl border. By no means did she enter our realm with the Tribute Parade."

Nerys had assumed, of course, that the hired assassins had botched the job when they didn't return to report their success. It had been a mistake to hire them based on their word alone, though the other Ministers hadn't agreed with Nerys's opinion. Nerys had assumed they hadn't been able to snatch the princess at all. That they had allowed her to take her place as the Tribute Bride. Else, why would they stay so far away from those who hired them? Her assumption that Princess Zohana had made it into Isonpool Palace appeared to be wrong.

A less rational woman would have flown to reveal the information, to take action against the imposter. Nerys knew better than to act on her emotions. She hadn't come this far by being quick to action and slow to thought.

"My lady, what are your orders?"

Nerys drummed her fingers on the arm of her chair, waiting for the perfect solution. Revealing too early that she had known about the imposter meant she might draw suspicion upon herself, but being first to discuss the information with Dragon Supreme might spare her life.

A second servant came scuttling into the room, dropping desperately to her knees. "My lady! His Lordship, Dragon Supreme, has issued an order to locate the maid who put poison in Her Highness's tea."

"It isn't Her Highness," the other servant muttered testily.

Nerys shot out of her chair, too unsettled to remain seated. The plan had been shoddy, but not shoddy enough to warrant this.

Who had overlooked their part of the grand cover-up? It hadn't been anyone in her household. They all knew better than to leave evidence. Orafel wouldn't know about Pelidon Berries. Who had left evidence of poison behind? How had the fraud escaped the poison in the first place?

Now, most importantly, Nerys needed to avoid suspicion. To act as she would have acted, had she not in fact been the mastermind behind the princess's disappearance and the poison in the tea. No one could blame her for not revealing Princess Zohana's whereabouts, as Nerys didn't know them herself. The poison, however, had the possibility to taint her reputation. She would have to handle it carefully, despite the identity of the almost-assassinated woman.

Who cared that Nerys had sent poison to a fake? Who was to say it had not been delivered by the order of Dragon Supreme? A lie the imposter might believe, should she be gullible enough, but one which Dragon Supreme would never tolerate. Nerys needed to be on his good side. Only then would she receive all her heart desired.

First, she should be conservative about her actions for a while.

Nerys leveled her gaze at the female servant kneeling before her. "What of the maid who carried the tea?"

"She is still in the palace, my lady," the servant girl answered.

Nerys couldn't very well storm Isonpool Palace and take the maid away, but she could easily pay a visit. As long as the conditions were correct.

"Is she trustworthy?"

"My lady, she has been a Galashiel spy within the palace since young. She will not betray you."

"Can you be certain?"

Spies turned on their masters when faced with dire straights. The maid's circumstances were certainly not ideal for keeping secrets. Dragon Tribe, as a whole, was known for its cruelty and violence. Should they catch her, she would see no end to the tactics they would use for interrogation. The best spy might be tempted to crack under such pressure.

"She would give her life for you, my lady," the servant girl assured.

Even so, Nerys found she couldn't rest at ease. If they extracted the maid from Isonpool Palace, Nerys would feel more assured. Dragon Supreme would use dire methods to eliminate his enemies, and Nerys had no foothold by which to request mercy for her transgression.

Only two options were left to her. Retrieve the errant spy, or make sure she never mentioned Galashiel Mansion.

"You," Nerys pointed a finger at the man who had come to tell her of the bandits' failure. "Return to your brethren and let them heed my words. Without proof of Princess Zohana's death, I will not pay them one more coin than they have already received."

Knowing it had been a mercy for Nerys Galashiel to bestow such minimal punishment for the failure, the manservant bent one last bow before he scurried off to relay the news. Surely the lack of funds would allow them all to work faster and harder to rectify the botched mission.

"You," Nerys turned her finger toward the maidservant. "Prepare to enter Isonpool Palace. We must find the poisoner before His Lordship does."

What a mess had been made of the whole ordeal. Could nothing be done correctly without Nerys's personal intervention? She could not be the only Dragon Tribe Minister wise enough to see the end of a plan coming. They all had their secrets. They couldn't have kept them if they were careless.

Entering Isonpool Palace was a risk, but staying away practically announced her involvement in the plot. Nerys would rather take the chance than sit around waiting to be investigated.

Her decisiveness had made her into a woman who demanded respect. Nerys would not back down this time, even for Dragon Supreme. She would see her plan through to the end.

Yet, Nerys didn't plan to have to wait to enter Isonpool Palace's gates. Nor did she account for the things that would happen within the palace walls. For though spies existed in the dark, other villains thrived in the blackest depths of night.

CHAPTER TWENTY-SIX

Isonpool's Gates

Twenty-four hours passed from the time of poisoning. The maid who had sought to poison Lada, elusive as they came, had managed to hide away in a crack or crevice as yet undiscovered. Not a few wondered how the escaped assassin knew Isonpool Palace well enough to hide from the Royal Guards.

Due to the maid's knowledge and Dragon Supreme's own suspicions, Isonpool Palace's gates were closed even to Ministers. Not only did he mean to buy time to weed out the assassin, Dragon Supreme understood mind games better than others. If the mastermind could not enter the palace to clean up their mess, they must be fretting terribly outside the gates.

If he had realized how true his suspicions were, Dragon Supreme might have laughed. In this small thing, he had managed to outwit his Ministers' intentions.

Indeed, the Ministers now gathered outside Isonpool Palace's main gates, gossiping about the purpose behind their exile. Outside the gates, the wind blew strong and cold, whispering doom into the ears of each minister and stirring up unease within the minister who knew what had happened within.

She, of course, said nothing to the others. They would sooner put all the blame on her than to help her spy escape.

Within the palace walls, blazing braziers lit and warmed every room and hall. And still, Dragon Supreme found he could not feel the heat. In fact, the longer it wore on, the harder he shivered. He had tried everything, and yet the chill in his bones remained. Perhaps a side effect of the pressure he put on himself. Perhaps an illness brought on by any number of things. Whatever the case, Dragon Supreme had no intention of bringing it up until they had found the woman who had used Pelidon Berries.

No one dared disobey orders given by Dragon Supreme, and he would not allow a meager kitchen maid to rebel. Dragon Supreme had raised a command, and this time it would be heeded.

Guards scurried to and fro, bringing in every maid from every corner of the palace to Fang-Throne Court. Most were immediately pardoned and excused for having never been near Princess Zohana's quarters or because they feared their supreme master.

Only a handful remained secluded, tucked in a corner beside guards with swords drawn to keep them there. And on it went.

Beyond the gates, covered in furs and wool to keep warm, Nerys worried away the hours.

Like slow leaks in a breaking dam, news reached the Ministers from inside Isonpool Palace.

An assassination attempt.

The culprit at large.

Braziers burning hot and Dragon Supreme's temper running hotter.

All to be expected, in Nerys's book. After all, who would sit idly by and allow such blatant treason in his own castle? The spy's plan only worked if Dragon Supreme never knew such a spy existed. In failing to complete her mission, this girl had failed Nerys in all aspects.

"My lady, shall we—"

"We wait," Nerys instructed her maid.

They had yet to find the spy, and thus Nerys would wait where she stood. To flee would only give Dragon Supreme reason to catch her.

She needed his trust. Trust was the foundation of all mutually beneficial relationships. Dragon Supreme would have to trust her for her grand plan to succeed. She didn't mind being used for political gain, so long as trust tied her to the man who mattered.

Thus, wait they did, alongside every other minister murmuring about treason and consequences.

Hour upon hour, the Ministers waited. Hour upon hour, the guards brought in more and more maids to Fang-Throne Court. By evening, every corner of Isonpool Palace had been cleared.

Dragon Supreme surveyed the pond of quivering maidens, not placing any one as an active threat. "This is all?"

"Yes, Your Lordship." One of the investigating guards folded his hands into the phoenix salute over his heart. "Only these have unknown whereabouts, uncorroborated by witnesses, at the time mentioned."

Cadfael, near the shadows at the side of the room, gave a single nod of affirmation.

For that reason, Dragon Supreme believed the investigator. Cadfael did not lie, and he always did his due diligence when it came to such matters. The gaggle of maids gathered in the corner contained their culprit, and he was prepared to lay down a heavy hand of punishment.

Tired, weak, and frozen, Davorin Astrophel gave the command to open Isonpool Palace's gates.

CHAPTER TWENTY-SEVEN
Unhealthy

In the darkness of cavernous dungeons, time didn't flow as it did in the open forest. Without sunlight, wind, or moonbeams to tell the hour, Lada existed in a black night that knew no passing. Only a song in her heart and the Mirror Needle in her veins kept her lucid and optimistic.

The Head Dungeon Guard had personally brought her no less than three meals, all meager but filling enough to satisfy.

If not for the dark and cold, enveloping her like icy blankets, Lada would have no complaints about their treatment of her. But the stone beneath her was hard and chilly. The walls seeped water and the candle outside the door granted only a small circle of light.

Despite now being fed, Lada found herself weaker than she had been within Isonpool Palace. Shivers and shakes wracked her frame, rattling her bones with frigidity. Try as she might, Lada couldn't get warm. She wanted nothing more than sleep, but she feared if she slept she may never awaken.

In her sorry state, sleep-deprived and desperate, Lada held on to only two bits of hope. The first: her knowledge of Mirror Needles' abilities. They had saved many an Amaryl Herbalist in the past. The second: the rays of light radiating out around the candle.

Lada had long ago given up on the stone bed in the dark corner. It granted her no peace and offered nothing but suffering. Instead, she chose to curl up inside the barred door, her bleary eyes fixed on the candle above her head. If she listened closely, Lada could hear the drip-drop-drip of wax as it melted and ran down the girandole. The path of sap through a tree made a similar sound. For a moment, listening to it, Lada imagined she had returned home.

Home waited for her, Lada knew. Her recovering plants. The areas of the forest that needed tending. Her friend the Great White Deer must have noticed her absence. Without an herbalist, how would Amaryl survive? How would children attend their wounds or parents heal their diseases?

If she had been in Flora Master's Hall, someone would have been able to diagnose this illness of hers. Here, Lada doubted anyone cared. They wouldn't, until her illness touched them, as well. By now, someone should have noticed. Dragon Supreme should be on his way to have a word with her.

Or, perhaps, that was her wishful thinking. Perhaps he would never come, too stubborn to investigate, and they would perish together.

Dizzy and disoriented, Lada scrambled to get her feet beneath her. It should be almost time for food now, judging by the candle's diminishing, and she would hate for the Head Dungeon Guard to see her shriveled up like a dying flower. Better to stay in the dark corner until he left, so as not to further distress her acquaintance. He could do no more than his job, and he had been told to keep her here. Lada couldn't blame him.

One step. Two. Lada stopped to press a hand to her head. It ached and swelled, feeling too heavy for her body. Her arm ached, as well, where her wound had reopened. In fact, her whole body complained about its existence.

A third step. Lada fumbled. Her balance skewed, tossing her to and fro like a leaf in a storm. And then she crumbled, unable to fight any longer. Lada never felt her head hit the floor.

As expected, the Head Dungeon Guard came with Lada's dinner not long after. He didn't trust Ivo to keep his hands to himself, despite the fact a Tribute Piece sat in their dungeon. Ivo had a way of torturing everyone, including his colleagues. Try as he might to put it aside, the Head Dungeon Guard wouldn't allow Ivo to torture this imp and end up at the gallows for it. In his own way, Ivo had use down there in the prison.

"Meal's here," the Head Dungeon Guard called into the dark cell.

The girl inside rarely came forward to retrieve her meal, but she always had a pleasant word of thanks to offer. Not a single time since her imprisonment had she forgotten to show her gratitude. Thus, it struck the Head Dungeon Guard as odd when no tinkering feminine voice greeted the announcement.

Perhaps she hadn't heard him or had fallen asleep. The Head Dungeon Guard cleared his throat and raised the volume with which he declared, "Get up. Time to eat, little lady."

Surely that would bring her around. The last time he called her *little lady*, she had been quick to correct him and assure him she held no such title. A girl such as this would correct him again.

Except she didn't. Not a sound echoed in the dark chamber. Not even the drip of water from the walls. As if the whole world around her had ceased to move.

The Head Dungeon Guard reached for the keys on his belt, kneeling as he did to set the food tray on the ground. It could be a trap. Others had tried to escape in such a way. It was the still silence that made him wary to believe it.

Calloused and heartless as he had become, the Head Dungeon Guard had been given strict instructions to keep this girl alive. If something had happened, it would be on his head. And she had thanked him when they brought her down.

For those reasons, the Head Dungeon Guard unlocked the barred door, reached for the lantern he carried, and stepped into the cell.

A heap of fabric, hair, and dead petals lay shivering in the center of the room. Knowing not what to do with the fact, the Head Dungeon Guard bent beside her to check on the Amaryl girl's state.

Her eyes had closed, as surely as her arms had wrapped around herself to provide warmth.

The Head Dungeon Guard checked first her breathing, which warmed his hand but not her body. So she hadn't died, but she wasn't fully alive.

He would do well not to touch her, the Head Dungeon Guard knew, but how did he discern her problem if he didn't touch? Call a royal physician? He didn't have the authority to direct physicians. His authority extended only within the walls of this prison.

"Just ensure she stays alive."

If he let her die, the Head Dungeon Guard knew the consequences. They would charge him with treason. At the very least, they would take his job. Then what would he do with his life?

Against his better judgment, the Head Dungeon Guard reached out to lift the girl's head from the cold floor onto his knee. Like fire, her skin flamed against his touch. In the lantern-light he couldn't be sure, but the Head Dungeon Guard had an inkling the dark spot on her temple belonged to a burgeoning bruise. If she had fainted, she might have hit her head.

Those kind eyes of hers fluttered open, but he doubted they saw anything.

"Take me... to His Majesty..." she managed to mutter before she went limp.

"*...she stays alive.*"

"Ivo!" the Head Dungeon Guard couldn't sit by and let her die. Like it or not, she needed help.

Ivo came jogging down the hall, his hands raised as if there might be a battle.

"Bring some blankets," the Head Dungeon Guard directed. "And you might as well inform the Royal Guards of her condition in case anyone cares."

Ivo, feeling neither sorry for the poor waif nor wanting to do his job, went grumbling off with a mutter of his superior's name on his lips. If he knew how to curse a man, the Head Dungeon Guard would be his first target.

As for the Head Dungeon Guard, he trusted Ivo would do as he was told. They had been informed in no uncertain terms that she had to stay alive. Maybe someone cared about her life. The Head Dungeon Guard would call it a miracle if such a thing happened, but miracles occurred every once in a red moon. This girl could be an exception.

Though he doubted she would last the night, the Head Dungeon Guard did his duty to ensure she had a chance. One day, in the future, it might save his life or earn him a promotion.

If only he had known how true those unspoken thoughts would become.

CHAPTER TWENTY-EIGHT
Delayed Discovery

uffled sobs rose up from the far corner of Fang-Throne Court, along with the occasional query of "what will happen to us?" The majority, of course, knew what would happen should they be discovered guilty of treason. Only a select few remained blissfully oblivious to their fates.

One by one, each as cautious as the first, Ministers filtered into the hall now that the gates had been opened to them. Not a single minister missed his—or her—chance to glance to the gathering of maids in the corner. No doubt the news had leaked out to them, as Davorin had given specific instructions to make sure the Ministers heard the goings-on within Isonpool Palace. He wanted them sweating. The squirming would come later.

The thought of outmaneuvering his Ministers brought Davorin great joy. Sadly, he could not enjoy the moment with his head pounding as it was. It had gotten worse over the day, and now felt as if it might explode, but Davorin refused to let his ill state show. If he did, the Ministers would make quick work of sending him off to rest and all his efforts thus far would go to waste.

Bit by bit, the Ministers fell into line in their usual places. Not one looked upon their sovereign, for fear his wrath would far overpower his rationality. Indeed, none dared to utter a sound, not even breathe, save one particularly nonchalant minister. A new appointee who clearly hadn't learned his place.

In actuality, Velimir did not care to fret over what might happen to him, as he knew he had not been a part of this disaster. He observed with a chuckle, awaiting which maid and minister might be dragged to their demise. A twisted but entertaining tale, this episode of villainy.

Dragon Supreme leaned back on his throne, completely at ease in front of a sea of discontent. "My Ministers."

"Your Majesty, Dragon Supreme."

As a chorus the Ministers echoed Davorin's title, followed by a rippling of bows from front to back. They had unanimously decided to follow the protocol to the letter on this, the oddest of days in Fang-Throne Court. To step out of line, even by a fraction of a centimeter, meant death or banishment.

A lesser man would ask forgiveness for making them wait. Davorin had no intention, especially feeling as terrible as he did, to put forth any form of apology. "I fear you have heard the bad tidings in Isonpool Palace."

One of the elder ministers stepped into the center of the floor, saluting with the phoenix symbol over his heart. "Devastating news, Your Lordship. We have stood heartbroken and anxious in the cold and wind, awaiting word that you have captured the culprit of this uprising."

Heartbroken. Anxious. Uprising. All words selected carefully to play to Dragon Supreme's sense of crisis. To convince Dragon Supreme they were with him in this time of confusion and need. To show they meant not to harm him or cross him.

Despite their efforts, Dragon Supreme was remiss to believe the sugar-coated words. Chances were, one of his Ministers lay behind the scheme, waiting to see the outcome. Davorin had allowed them all to enter for that very purpose. To watch them sweat and squirm before him as he wheedled out the spy among Isonpool Palace's maids.

Head pounding and eyes bleary, Davorin waved Cadfael closer to deliver his first order.

Cadfael saluted his sovereign, eyes carefully downcast but not unaware of the sweat beading on Davorin's brow or the way his fingers trembled against his throne. "My Lord."

"Bring me the girl."

"Yes, My Lord." Cadfael spun on his heel, marched to the nearest guard, and passed on the order.

Ministers stirred, unable to stand still after the announcement. They, of course, had heard the rumors about the woman abiding in Her Highness, Princess Zohana's rooms. Who hadn't heard the tale of how a fraudulent princess had stood up to the Dragon Supreme? The guards had spread the story far and wide within the palace, and thus the Ministers' spies had told them. The slave had not died at the poisoner's hands, and therefore must have seen and remembered the assassin in detail. If Dragon Supreme summoned her to Fang-Throne Court, he meant to allow her to identify the spy.

Feet shuffled and throats cleared. Ministers with a clear conscience suddenly found themselves nervous. What if they should discover the assassin, but she lied about her master's identity? In this dilemma existed the perfect opportunity for the real mastermind to frame their minister of choice. Whose demise would follow this unfortunate circumstance?

Davorin studied his Ministers one by one, recognizing fear in many eyes and practiced indifference in others. Time slowed, weaving through the court like a snake through the grass. At long last, Davorin deigned to speak.

"If anyone wishes to admit their mistake before we proceed, now is the best time."

Dragon Supreme didn't expect any of the Ministers to come forward and admit to the crime. He wished only to give them a chance to act remorseful, to apply more pressure that would break them given the right circumstances. No one fooled Dragon Supreme and got away with it, especially not when it pertained to Davorin Astrophel's personal matters.

The Ministers remained still and silent, unwilling to do anything but breathe. A misplaced whisper could see them executed on the spot. None dared cross Dragon Supreme when his temper ran this hot.

The guard who had exited to fetch the imposter came marching back in, alone. He paused to murmur something indistinguishable to Cadfael, who in turn strode to Dragon Supreme's side.

"Head Dungeon Guard has brought the woman, himself, but it seems she has fallen ill. Severely."

Discreetly, Davorin raised a hand to rub his fingers against a decisively more throbbing temple. How one half of his head held more pain than the other, he could never fathom, but it did. Davorin's own discomfort gave him no time to consider the words before he answered.

"Bring her anyway."

Cadfael spoke not his concerns, nor did he try to explain what ailed the Amaryl woman. In a good mood, Dragon Supreme would not heed excuses or complaints. Dour as he had been all day, even the suggestion of excuses or complaints would bring punishment on everyone's head. Thus, Cadfael faced the Fang-Throne Court's enormous iron doors, cleared his throat, and sent out the directive.

"Bring her before His Lordship, Dragon Supreme."

Having realized they held none other than a Tribute Treasure in their prison, no subordinate—save Ivo—had been willing to lay a finger on a single hair from Lada's head. Tribute belonged to Dragon Supreme, alone. When the directive had come, the Head Dungeon Guard had been the only man willing and capable enough to deliver the Amaryl woman from her cell to Fang-Throne Court.

He entered cautiously, cradling his precious cargo within his arms.

Ministers turned to stare. Some snorted or gawked.

Davorin Astrophel, Dragon Supreme, took particular notice of the woman's incapacitated state. Had she been able to walk on her own, the Head Dungeon Guard certainly wouldn't carry her in his arms as he would a child. No less than three blankets wrapped around the woman's form, encompassing her in a shell that hid her from those who wished to see her.

The Head Dungeon Guard laid the bundle in his arms at the foot of the grand dais. If not for the breath raising and lowering her shoulders like moss covering a fountain, Dragon Supreme might have thought her dead. Death clearly sat on her shoulders, awaiting its time to take her. Davorin could not have that.

"What is wrong with her?" Dragon Supreme spat at the Head Dungeon Guard.

The guard took a knee beside the bundle of blanketed woman, his head lowered respectfully. "Your Lordship. The Royal Guards brought this woman to the dungeons with instructions to keep her alive. I am failing. Please punish me."

The Head Dungeon Guard no more wanted punishment than he did a beheading. He used the tactic only to secure the status quo in the room. Dragon Supreme reigned over all. The Head Dungeon Guard had no authority to do anything but punish those in his prison. Calling a physician to examine the Tribute Treasure had not been an option for him.

"Is she lucid?"

Dragon Supreme needed her lucidity to make his plan work. If the Amaryl woman couldn't identify her assailant, he should give up his own ruse immediately.

The Head Dungeon Guard dared not move, and when he did speak, each word had been carefully calculated. "Her high fever causes her to sleep, but she has woken several times. She is ill, but can be of use to Your Lordship."

Velimir, stationed to the side of the hall, rolled his eyes so heavily it drew his cousin's attention.

"What is it?" Davorin demanded, rising to his feet in his agitation.

Velimir shrugged his shoulders, then raised his hands to press them over his heart in the phoenix symbol. "Why not get rid of her? She is merely a treasure."

"*My* treasure," Davorin pointed out heatedly. "I shall say what becomes of her."

Though he had been angry when he sent the woman to the dungeons, Dragon Supreme understood his need for her. An opportunity to invade Amaryl didn't arrive every day. The woman had to stay alive to be able to guide them. And guide them, she would. Davorin would convince her to do it one way or another, whatever it took.

Velimir said no more, which managed to keep his head atop his shoulders for another day. Unlike his beloved older brother, Velimir understood what lines should not be crossed.

"Wake her," Dragon Supreme ordered in Cadfael's general direction. He would not step down from his throne for such a trivial matter. Anyone could wake the poor creature, regardless of rank or merit. He need not do it himself.

Cadfael crossed the court under the scrutiny of dozens of Ministers. One misstep or misplaced emotion would create a weakness for them to exploit. One twitch of an eyebrow or tightening of his lips could mean revealing his inner thoughts, or the thoughts he shared with Dragon Supreme. Cadfael cautiously bent beside the Amaryl woman.

Beneath the blankets, her entire body shook. Dirt and soot covered her face, neck, and shoulders, but despite that Cadfael managed to make out a red and swelling area on her left temple. It could not be confirmed, in this state, if she had developed a fever or if she had been beaten. But, Cadfael had his orders. Thus, he removed his sheath from his belt and used the tip to give her shoulder a shove.

The woman whined, her body convulsing through another shiver as her eyes fluttered open. A nearby minister flinched during the split second she stared at him.

With great pains, focusing intently the whole way to ensure she remained conscious, Lada turned her head away from the Ministers and toward the Fang Throne. Her lips quivered, parted, and gasped words so weak Cadfael barely made them out.

"Your Majesty."

Her head craned, searching for the subject of her attention. The blankets lost their grip on her shoulders.

It was then Cadfael saw it. Perched gracefully at the joint of her throat and shoulder, an angry red scratch.

Cadfael tore his gaze from the girl at his feet to look back at his sovereign and master. "Your Lordship..."

"What is it now?"

Usually limitless with his patience during a plan, Davorin Astrophel turned into a cross monster when uncomfortable or in pain. If not for the educated guess and the sad hunch growing in Cadfael's mind, he would not have dared to bring it up. Especially not in front of the Ministers. Yet... His Lordship deserved to know.

Cadfael spun, putting both knees beneath his body and saluting his master reverently. "I have woken her, but I fear her voice is far too weak for Your Lordship to hear from this distance. Please allow me to bring her nearer the Fang Throne."

Dragon Supreme tipped his head, considering the words his loyal guard had said and how he had given them. On his knees. Bent and begging. Like his master, Cadfael never begged. Most in the palace thought of Cadfael as Davorin's loyal dog, but those words didn't ring true. Cadfael, if anything, was the closest person Davorin Astrophel had to a friend.

Now, this almost-friend asked for something so ludicrous and ridiculous Davorin could do nothing but consider granting the request. The Ministers could not fault him for granting it, yet they had begun to whisper and murmur. They all knew the only solid evidence to convict the assassin lied in the form of the woman's testimony.

Cadfael knelt waiting, and with every second that passed Davorin became assured there was more to the story than Cadfael could say in front of the court. If such was the case, Dragon Supreme intended to find out.

"Permission granted," Dragon Supreme lifted a hand to motion Cadfael to rise. "Bring her to me."

Cadfael returned his sheathed sword to his belt, securing it before he scooped up the bundle of blankets and hastened up the stairs. As quickly as he had moved her, Cadfael laid her at Dragon Supreme's feet.

"My Lord..." Cadfael nodded his head toward the girl's exposed throat, knowing his master to be intelligent enough to see what he saw.

Davorin peered down his nose, for all intents and purposes sneering at the girl who had insulted him, but in reality observing the Amaryl girl's illness. A fever, so high it shook her bones and tinted her lips. An area on her left temple swelling and bruising. An injury to her neck, joining her shoulder and throat.

All of her injuries and illnesses were present in the things Davorin had been feeling all day.

The Amaryl imp tipped her head back to take a shaky breath. "I'm sorry," she whimpered, seeming sincere.

The Forest Mystics, Amaryl citizens had been deemed following the Great War won by Davorin's father. Nothing anyone in Amaryl did made sense, but it always benefited their personal interests in one way or another. This creature had exposed him to things far beyond his comprehension, but in that lied the very reason he believed Cadfael's silent assumptions. Coincidence existed, but not to this extent.

Intrigued by her apology and curious as to her methods, Davorin bent to better see the woman struggling to stay alive.

She rolled to her side, managing to angle her head to allow her to gaze on Davorin's visage. All the better. She would remember his ire and know her place.

Davorin, on the other hand, studied each soot-sullied inch of her face, its smooth contours and regal lines. Every wince that clenched her muscles as the shivers continued to rock her in time to his own hidden trembling.

At last she made eye contact, sorrowfully staring at him as if her sympathy had been real all along. Davorin thought otherwise. He would rather see her rot, but he now doubted he had that chance.

Davorin bent near, his face but a whisper away from hers, to ask a simple question. "What have you done to me?"

The girl managed to get an elbow beneath her in order to maintain her propped-up angle. "My pain," she muttered, her voice barely a breath, "is now your pain, as well."

As if she had accomplished all she had set out to do, the woman collapsed into the heap of blankets around her.

Davorin dared not wince at the shooting pain in his skull, presumably delivered thanks to the bruise on her temple.

Amaryl had played its tricks on him, if only to spite his desire to own them. Thinking this creature could do nothing to him had been a gross oversight. She may be lying, but Davorin wouldn't bet on his life. In that lied the rub. To secure his own health and strength, he might have to secure hers, as well.

What a vicious little guide.

Davorin, seeing they would gain no help from her now, rose to his feet. "Cadfael, return her to her chambers and summon the royal physician."

"Yes, My Lord." Cadfael, having missed nothing, need not ask why Dragon Supreme had suddenly changed his mind. If the imp had connected her own ailments to His Lordship, they would indeed need to care for her.

Cadfael hefted the bundle into his arms and scurried from Fang-Throne Court.

Nerys Galashiel, bane of Davorin's diplomatic existence, took a step to the center of the court. "Your Lordship, allow me to take Her Highness home to treat her."

"Are you saying your physicians are better than mine?" Dragon Supreme spat at the redheaded courtier. Did she not know to question his decision meant endless pain?

Nerys bent her head. "No, My Lord. But she is a woman and—"

"She is part of my tribute, Nerys. She will remain at the palace, as shall you, following my order. Hear this." To the court, Davorin showed only his fiercest and most impressive authority. "Those under suspicion will be locked away in the dungeons until such a time as the woman can identify her assailant. My Ministers will be given their own quarters within Isonpool Palace. Inform your homes that you will not be returning soon."

Not a single minister misunderstood the intent of Dragon Supreme's decree. If they left Isonpool Palace, there would be time to cover evidence or line up their stories. He meant to keep them as prisoners in luxury until the matter had settled. It could be days, or it could last for weeks. No matter the cause, they would be unable to reach the outside world unless Dragon Supreme commanded it. Isolation, the oldest trick in the book, worked most effectively.

The Head Dungeon Guard, hearing the command within the decree, rallied the Royal Guards and the maids in their care before leading them out of Fang-Throne Court.

The Palace Administrator appeared out of thin air, no doubt summoned as soon as Dragon Supreme mentioned allowing the Ministers to stay on. With a bustling movement of his arms and a bow at his waist, the Palace Administrator greeted Dragon Supreme.

"How may I be of service, Your Lordship?"

"Lead the Ministers to their rooms. Assign each a servant to see to their needs." Davorin scoped his Ministers, searching for signs of nervousness or duress. All had learned efficiently how to hide their inner opinions. Fine. They would play the game the hard way. "Dismissed!"

Every minister, adhering strictly to protocol, pressed their hands over their hearts and chorused, "Long live Dragon Supreme. Long may your reign endure."

To the beat of his Ministers' anxious and troubled hearts, they turned and fled, following the Palace Administrator. When the last minister turned down the hall outside, Davorin glanced to the dark recesses beside the Fang Throne's magnificent dais.

"Show yourself."

One of Davorin's Shadows, quick-witted and willing to risk all for his sovereign, stepped into the light. He need not say anything. Dragon Supreme would direct him at will.

"Bring the Orafel maids to Her Highness's quarters. Posthaste."

As silently as he had appeared, the Shadow slipped back into the darkness to adhere to his master's bidding.

Davorin, still aching but now aware of the cause, folded his hands neatly behind his back. For now, he would tamp down his ire and see to the well-being of a woman he needed for many purposes. They could work out any other problems later, so long as the royal physician healed her.

Davorin would position himself in her chambers nonetheless. When she woke, she would answer to him alone.

CHAPTER TWENTY-NINE
Goading Nerys

Davorin Astrophel, Dragon Supreme, had dared to put all his Ministers under house arrest within Isonpool Palace. While staying within palace walls might sound beneficial to some, Nerys wasn't dense enough to overlook the blatant threat to life and limb. Remaining within Isonpool Palace meant there existed no chance to extract the spy. Indeed, the spy had assuredly been within the quarantined maids in the corner of Fang-Throne Court.

These were all reasons Nerys created extra plans to back up the plans that may change or fail. Now, knowing her own inadequacies within palace walls, Nerys would have to dream up another way to cover her own tracks. The assassination of the Orafel princess could never be tied to Galashiel Mansion.

Lord Velimir, who had chosen to saunter down the halls nearby Nerys for reasons unbeknownst to her, now fell in line by her side.

It irked Nerys, that all this had happened before she gathered any decent information about Velimir. Cousin to Dragon Supreme, she knew. Younger brother of the cousin Davorin had slain. Velimir must have grown up rich and spoiled. No one in the Supreme Family lacked for anything. Beyond that, Nerys knew little.

Velimir had done nothing to harm her or insult her, yet she didn't like him. Nerys found she would rather avoid him than have any dealings with him. Strange, considering her own ambitions. But, perhaps, her subconscious meant to warn her.

"Quite brave, you are," Velimir mused quietly.

Nerys rolled her eyes, but didn't allow him to see the action. Velimir wasn't the type to take kindly to sarcasm aimed his way.

Nerys had no desire to converse with him. However, Nerys had a reputation to uphold at court. She meant to remain in everyone's mind as the kind but capable Galashiel heir. Until she rose to a position of higher rank.

Nerys turned that sweet smile of hers to Velimir. "Pray tell, Lord Velimir, whatever do you mean?"

"Manipulating His Lordship? Quite brave, indeed."

Manipulating Dragon Supreme, as per the words from Velimir's lips, brought with it a hefty price to pay. Never mind that Nerys had indeed manipulated the entire situation for her own gain. To say it aloud would see the sword brought down on her neck before she had a chance to remedy the situation.

In which case, she should dissuade Velimir's suspicions.

"I fear you overestimate me."

"I fear you overestimate yourself." Velimir leaned closer, conspiratorially entering Nerys's sphere of personal space. "My cousin,

Dragon Supreme, is not one to be trifled with. Manipulating him will get you nowhere."

"I have done nothing that isn't in His Lordship's best interests."

A true statement. Davorin Astrophel deserved a better, more loyal woman than an Orafel spy or an imposter. The Dragon Queen should match his abilities and prowess.

Velimir giggled like a young girl gossiping about the man she had fallen for. "Oh, so it's love that motivates your rash actions. How quaint."

"I have never acted inappropriately toward His Lordship. How dare I hold feelings toward Dragon Supreme when he has shown no interest in me?"

Quick to assess the situation, Nerys had always been. She had said nothing untoward and had, indeed, kept a far distance from Dragon Supreme, yet Velimir knew the points of pressure it would take to overcome her firm foothold in Fang-Throne Court. Nerys knew when a new minister wanted power beyond his capabilities. Velimir had clearly set his sights on winning Dragon Supreme's utmost favor. She would tell him nothing of her ambitions.

Unbeknownst to Nerys, Velimir had his own ambitions in Fang-Throne Court. None of them included keeping favor. He came to Nerys only to sort out the situation unfolding around him. As he hadn't had a hand in this rebellion, no blame would fall on his head. Clever Ministers knew a new addition to the court couldn't be attacked before one clearly understood his intentions.

Velimir hadn't meant to stumble onto the knowledge that Nerys wanted more than Dragon Supreme's favor. She wanted his heart. And she was the most likely candidate to receive it after the Tribute Bride's disappearance.

Yet, this could not be addressed in the palace's halls. Not if he wanted to use it to his advantage.

Velimir walked two fingertips along the back of Nerys's shoulder, just to goad her further. "You shouldn't pretend you weren't staring at a particular maid in the pack." A dodge to avoid Nerys's hand flying, then Velimir leveled his lips near her ear. "I saw you."

Nerys's heart raced at the words, but allowing Velimir to see her panic meant giving up her authority and position in court. Willing participant or not, Nerys needed to keep her firm hold in order to rise higher. Court games were akin to climbing a cliff's face. Once one lost their grip, they fell to their death.

"Saw what?" Nerys laughed, too loud and forced.

How else should she respond when her most feared nemesis threatened to reveal her secrets? Long and hard, she had worked to keep the hidden things hidden, to put up a front of perfection that would take her to the ultimate heights. Velimir would not interrupt her plans now. Not when she could taste success.

As for Velimir, he loved nothing as dearly as he loved a good intrigue. To know the secrets and keep them. In that lied the true thrill of living.

"Don't act coy with me." Velimir gazed around nonchalantly, uncaring how others may hear if he raised his voice but a fraction. "I know what I saw, but don't worry. I'm no tattle-tale."

Offering a truce or currying an owed favor, Nerys knew not. But she didn't trust Velimir enough to allow either. Even if he had seen her as she sought the spy and found her, he could prove nothing. Nerys need not fear he would hold her accountable when she had left nothing to trace back to the Galashiel family.

Thus, Nerys ignored Velimir's probe for information, gave a stomp of her foot, and trudged ahead without him.

"I'll help end this torture for you. You wait and see," Velimir hummed after her.

Nerys did not understand the true intentions behind his offer, nor did she vocally accept. Sincerely, she hoped he would not cause more troubles for her, nor interfere with the circumstances. At the moment, every breath was calculated. If a third party chose to wreak havoc, all would be out of Nerys's control. All lost in a matter of moments. Therefore, she prayed he would keep to himself.

Velimir, of course, had no such plans.

CHAPTER THIRTY
First Curiosities

The scent of sconce oil could not overpower the aroma of herbal incense, burning around the room to encourage a healing atmosphere. Windows had been shuttered, drapes hung, and candles lit. A new quilt had been brought to add to the blankets covering feverish Lada, this one stuffed and sewn properly. Now the bed, appropriately lit and deliciously warm, welcomed an unconscious Amarylite into its embrace. By her side perched a man dressed in green, with a pointed physician's hat atop his head.

The creak of leather and clang of metal as the guards outside the door straightened hailed the arrival of a guest most important. Through the iron doors, exerting little energy to shove them aside, Dragon Supreme entered. Cadfael, stationed outside the curtains separating the bed from the rest of the room, turned and bowed.

Davorin waved him off, allowing him to return to his relaxed vigil. Outside of Fang-Throne Court, Davorin saw no need to adhere to formalities with Cadfael. They had grown up alongside one another and spent all their days together. To remain formal would ruin their interdependent relationship.

Normally impatient, Dragon Supreme had no choice but to wait until the physician had finished his examination. Long ago, on a battlefield to which Davorin never wished to return, he had learned. To interrupt a physician could mean a man's life. Physicians held the power to heal or destroy without a trace. Even stubborn, domineering Davorin Astrophel had to respect them.

Thankfully, a new interest arose to keep Davorin occupied while he waited.

Having been separated from their charge for the better part of three days, the Orafel maids came scuttling in as though the world might cave in if they couldn't see her. One almost lost a shoe in her haste. Another cried out and flung herself against the bed's frame. A third, more logical maid assessed the situation before her, studied the physician, and dropped to her knees before Davorin.

"Your Majesty, please save our lady. Do not leave her to die. She's already so pitiful."

"Why do you all call me that?" Dragon Supreme mused loudly enough for the maid to hear. "It is not the proper address."

The maid fell prostrate on the ground, her head on her hands. "Forgive me, Your Majesty."

"My Lord," Davorin corrected. "Your Lordship. His Majesty, Dragon Supreme. If you are to be a Dragon Tribe servant, especially in my palace, you shall use the proper forms of address. If you must address me as Your Majesty, add my title to it."

"My apologies. It is a habit from my own country."

"That's just it," Dragon Supreme snarled. "You are in *my* country now. We use such terms as 'My Lord' to show our allegiance. To remind ourselves how personal it is to serve a master. A sovereign. You will be allegiant to me while you are in my residence. Is that understood?"

"Yes, Your Majesty. Dragon Supreme."

"Good." Davorin, having settled the trivial and annoying matter, sank onto a stool at the dilapidated tea table. "Summon your peers here. I wish to speak with you all."

The maid rose to her knees, keeping her eyes downcast in a proper and educated manner. At least she had the decency to follow what protocol she knew. "Yes, My Lord."

For Lada's sake, the Orafel maids would do anything. Changing a form of address ranked low on the list of problems for them. They had been servants since young. Swearing allegiance to a different master would make no difference.

Only Lada's unhappiness or discontent would weigh on their hearts, as they had all been sent to ensure her well-being. If Lada found no happiness, when it took so little to appease her, they would have failed their jobs.

The maid lifted from her knees to her feet, hastening to collect the other two from their positions of concern. It took no effort to convince them to follow her. Now that Lada had fallen ill, it was their responsibility to ensure her safety until she awakened. None would allow Lada to come to harm on their watch.

Mere moments after the instruction had been given, not one but three Orafel maids knelt before their new sovereign, eyes downcast and hands folded neatly in their laps.

As relaxed as he could be with a throbbing head and cold sweat breaking out over his body, Davorin surveyed the sight before him. All three Orafel maids knew he held the power to end their existence with a flick of his finger. He didn't have to point it out. Thus, they would answer him if they valued their lives.

"Tell me of your mistress," Davorin commanded.

No good could come of such a powerful man asking about Lady Lada. All three maids hesitated to answer without a more specified field of curiosity from Dragon Supreme. A look exchanged between them was sure to garner his ire, but each maid silently resolved to remain as loyal to Lada as she had been to them.

"I've known of her Amaryl descent for days now," Davorin continued. "Tell me all you know of her. Not only will it spare your heads, it will spare her life."

The maids, of course, had no way of knowing that Davorin Astrophel had no plans to kill Lada. He needed her for other matters, but not a single maid would understand that for some time to come. Davorin had a knack for keeping strategic secrets. He found it useful in every situation. More so when dealing with women.

"Her name is Lada," one of the maids offered, then clamped her lips shut.

Davorin leveled his icy stare at the trio. They would soon start spouting as much information as he required. A well-timed, cold stare could open the tightest of lips.

A second maid wrung her hands together, twisting her skirt between her thumbs as a distraction. "Lord Kavindra purchased her from a Slave Hunter the evening before our departure from Mesmium."

"Are you aware what position she held before her arrival in

Mesmium?"

The maids shared another look, a few shrugs, and a silent conversation.

It was the one who had given the woman's name who answered. "On the journey, she mentioned apprenticing as an herbalist."

"She's very kind," the third maid threw in.

Davorin snorted in deprecation. Kind? Bringing bodily harm to her lord and master did not lend itself to kindness. Years had told him kindness existed not in those who sought their own survival. Neither did kindness flow from Amaryl Mystics who claimed they wanted peace but did nothing to assist.

Just Davorin's luck to run into an herbalist for help. Surely she had done something that would cause him distress in the future. She must be a trickster devil.

The maids, too, knew the legends preceding Amaryl Herbalists. As revered as physicians and as tricky as snakes, able to treat any illness so long as they knew of its existence. Able to turn any tide in their favor with the use of a few mysterious plants. Amaryl heralded them as Orafel heralded its royalty. Amaryl Herbalists, the legends said, were below only the tribe's Elders.

"She's also very honest," the third maid continued, ignoring the things they all knew about herbalists. "And quite loyal. She only took Her Highness's place to save us all from execution."

Loyal? Davorin would have liked to ask what she had done to make these Orafel maids see her as more than an Amaryl slave. What she had said to incite their loyalty toward her.

He might have voiced his concerns, if the Royal Physician had not at that moment risen from Lada's bedside.

Davorin rose to greet the physician. He need not ask about the patient lying beneath a mound of blankets. In his own time, the Royal Physician would tell all.

The physician spared but a glance at the women kneeling nearby. They were of little importance when Dragon Supreme waited for a comprehensive analysis of the patient's condition.

"Your Majesty, Dragon Supreme." The Royal Physician bowed to his monarch. "The girl has contracted an infection in a reopened wound on her shoulder. It has caused chills and fever. I have lanced the wound to remove the infectious pus and will prescribe a medicinal tonic. She must take it three times a day for a week."

Davorin observed the maids on the floor to see if they heard and understood. They did not disappoint him.

"She is also starved and dehydrated," the physician went on. "Someone should feed her small bowls of porridge to fill her stomach and should ensure she ingests water or tea."

"Someone will see to it," Davorin assured. "Cadfael, see the physician out."

Cadfael appeared from his shadowy corner to escort the physician into the hall.

Davorin, on the other hand, turned back to the weepy and concerned maids. "A reopened wound, he said. Where did this wound come from?"

He had, of course, seen it oozing that day in Fang-Throne Court. Davorin simply hadn't cared to mention it or discover its origin. Now that it involved him, as well, he should investigate the full story.

"Your Majesty, Dragon Supreme." The first maid he had talked to dropped into another prostrate bow, after which she rose to her knees. "Lady Lada came to us with this wound. Lord Kavindra had a physician treat it the night she arrived. We know not where it came from, only that it appeared. I assume the Slave Trader had something to do with it."

Davorin had no involvement with Slave Traders, and hadn't been aware the lengths they went to in order to torture their victims. Such things didn't surprise him, however. Slaves needed to be subservient to their masters.

Amaryl, notoriously tricky and stubborn, would not give up their people easily. Nor would their people give in without a push. No doubt such tortures were allowed in order to break the slaves' spirits. Davorin, should he take up such a menial job, could conjure up much worse to bestow upon the newly captured slaves.

This maid had impressed him with the clever spin in her words. Since her tongue first spun, she had been absolving her mistress of sins, catering to the superiority of Qranbu's throne, and passing blame onto those unrelated to her lady's chamber. All of it had been done with such subtlety that Davorin almost missed her purposes. Such loyal protection no doubt merited quite a few rewards. None of which Davorin had the mood to give her.

None but one.

"The three of you will care for this... *Lady* Lada of yours. See to it you follow the physician's instructions." Davorin glared down his nose at the clever maid. His next decree would keep her awake all night. "Notify me the moment she wakes."

The maid bent her head again, this time in a manner so slow it might have been taken sarcastically. "As you desire, My Lord."

She picked up on things quickly. A trait that Dragon Supreme respected. He still trusted no one in the chamber intended for Princess Zohana. None had proved their trustworthiness.

"Cadfael," Dragon Supreme called.

Cadfael broke away from his station and fell in line behind Dragon Supreme as they exited. Only when the iron doors had shut and the sound of scurrying maids had begun did Davorin turn to Cadfael to dictate further instructions.

"Watch over them closely. I want no unauthorized servants to so much as breathe upon these doors."

"Yes, My Lord."

"The Shadows will see to the medicine and food. You are here strictly for her safety."

"Yes, My Lord."

"And Cadfael..."

Cadfael waited patiently, his sword sheathed but at the ready in his hands, as Dragon Supreme turned to stare at the plain iron doors.

Davorin heaved a sigh so great it could have destroyed a village. "If my guide dies, I will have a difficult time forgiving you."

Cadfael accepted the threat for what it was, a directive to keep the impish woman alive and healthy. Given what appeared to be a trick of dire proportions, Cadfael would sacrifice life and limb to see to it. Dragon Supreme required answers, and far be it from Cadfael to prohibit him from receiving them.

"I will remain alert, My Lord."

"Good." Davorin clapped a hand against Cadfael's shoulder, firm and commanding, before he turned away.

He did not care for the imposter, but he did need her. Perhaps more than he knew. Davorin Astrophel had never needed someone before, not even his own parents, and the knowledge settled oddly in his gut. If this guide died, he could find another, but where would he find one more perfectly suited to his cause?

Davorin might have been less inclined to protect her if not for two things. First, he desired to understand the trick she had played on him, the turning point in a far-too-easy game. Secondly, someone had tried to poison her. If his Ministers wanted her dead, Davorin would see to it she survived.

CHAPTER THIRTY-ONE
Back in the Forest

A scream pierced through the treetops and radiated against the ground, sending forest creatures scattering to their respective holes to hide.

Valor of Champion's Post shot into the clearing that housed his humble abode.

Champion's Post had been built as a single family home and had never housed more than two Guardsmen at a time. Currently, Valor lived alone, save the Orafel woman he had brought back from the stream. Her cries meant either she had woken or she suffered from nightmares. Neither boded well for her healing.

The wooden doors of Champion's Post clattered as Valor threw them open.

Facing him, wobbly from all that had happened, the Orafel woman held a candlestick aloft as a club.

Valor paid little mind to the weapon in her hands. In her state, he doubted she could do much harm. He did, however, give special attention to the state of the woman herself. Her eyes, though open, refused to focus. Instead, they peered right through him, to the ground behind his feet.

That's how Valor knew. She had neither woken, nor did she sleep. Somewhere between the two, this woman found herself. Memories like ghosts played through her mind and her vision now. Try as he might, Valor could not stop this. She would have to overcome it herself.

"I'll tell my father," the woman muttered, and Valor noted the blue tint around the edges of her lips.

"What will you tell him?" Valor asked quietly, hoping to direct her hallucinations through the use of quiet companionship. If not, they were in for a bumpy ride.

An unearthly giggle leaped from the woman's throat, chilling the air as though winter had found them early. "You can't kill me. This is treason."

Valor took in each sentence with careful calculation of every word. Should he provoke her, he had no doubt this woman would attack. Hallucinations were powerful things, and if she thought herself in danger she would react accordingly.

"I'm not here to kill you," Valor attempted. "I'm—"

"Get out."

"Listen to me. I—"

"Get out now!"

The woman launched herself at Valor, swinging the candlestick. Where Valor had assumed she would use it as a club, the woman wielded it as a sword aimed at Valor's throat.

Valor dodged the weapon, allowing the woman past him toward the door.

Much as he would like to allow her to run to her heart's content, Valor knew she could not leave his residence. Not only would she be captured if the other Guardsmen found her, but she might inadvertently run into the fog again. She wouldn't survive a second time.

Having taken the responsibility of seeing to her health and safety, Valor lunged forward and caught her by her slim waist before she had time to escape.

The woman struggled in his hold, twisting and turning until she managed to halfway face him. The candlestick made a reappearance, this time aimed at his head. Valor loosed one hand to snag it out of her grasp.

A mistake, in hindsight.

No sooner had he laid hold of the candlestick than her teeth sunk into his ear, digging deep and probably drawing blood.

Surprised and in pain, Valor released the woman.

Though Valor still held her candlestick, the woman managed to get her hands around one of Valor's scythes. A much more deadly weapon than the one she had been holding before.

"Die!" she bellowed, her voice both hurt and ferocious.

Thankfully, Valor had trained with his fellow Guardsmen for years. He could avoid a scythe and had learned tactics to overpower those who held the stronger weapon. But he did not want to do anything to harm the poor woman before him. The fog's side effects were to blame, not her personality or her temper. Valor could no more fault her than he could fault himself.

The first swing of the scythe shattered a vase on the wall. With the second swing, Valor found his opportunity. In one smooth movement, Valor tackled the woman to the ground, using his knee to pin down her kicking legs and one hand to secure her wrists on the ground above her head. With his free hand, he removed the scythe and tossed it aside.

The woman writhed and screamed, trying her best to escape Valor's grasp. But she would not be capable of breaking his hold. Fierce she may be, but she had no strength. Valor did not use half his own strength to pin her down.

"Shh. Calm down," Valor enticed, though he knew it would not work.

Somewhere in the forest nearby, someone struck up a tune on their flute.

Miraculously, the woman's fight became weaker. Slower. Calmer. Her eyelids fluttered, shut then open. Her screams silenced.

If he had been a lesser man, Valor might have written it off as coincidence. However, Valor belonged to Amaryl. He had seen stranger things before his fifth birth celebration. A flute calming a woman's hallucinations? He would believe it within the span of a heartbeat. Music cured a multitude of illnesses, Lada of Flora Mas-ter's Hall had once told him.

Along with the flute's voice, Valor raised his own to sing. A lullaby taught him by his mother before the Slave Traders caught her. A piece of his childhood precious to Valor in ways he could not explain.

Bit by bit, lulled by flute and song, the Orafel woman went lax in Valor's hold.

Valor released her, inch by inch in hopes she had truly fallen back into her blessed slumber. When she did not stir, he took it as a good omen. Still singing, each word resonating through the cottage and greeting the animals who had come out to listen, Valor scooped the woman from his floor and returned her to the bed. Covered her with a quilt so white it shone. And, finally, Valor rested a palm against her forehead, both to check on her condition and to bless her dreams.

May they not have to fight again. May the hallucinations cease. May she live to see the dawn and the birth of all things new.

CHAPTER THIRTY-TWO
Recovering Lada

Sleeplessness marked the passing of an entire night, along with the dimming and brightening of sconces on Isonpool Palace's walls. The Ministers dared not sleep, lest events take a turn that would require their attention. Cadfael and the Orafel maids dared not miss a second in case Lada should wake. Yet, she slept soundly the whole night, only moved by the maids to feed her the prescribed medicine.

Through the darkness, the Orafel maids scurried about, tending to their charge as if she were indeed a princess. If they could not protect someone as simple and kind as Lada of Flora Master's Hall, they no longer deserved their posts as attendants. Each, in her own heart, vowed to do all in her power to restore Lada's health. However long it took them, they would see her up and cheerful again.

Dawn broke over the mountain and, with it, Lada's fever. Still, the maidservants scuttled, refilling a basin of water and rinsing the sweat bursting upon Lada's skin. As fragile as Lada seemed, her weak and small body had managed to push out the heat of a fever. They all counted it as a good omen of Lada's swift recovery.

Another three sets of medicinal decoction marked the passage of a full day and, finally, Lada began to stir.

Mitsie—the Orafel maid who had helped Lada put on her first pair of shoes and also the maid who had spoken most directly to His Majesty, Dragon Supreme—rose to her feet to obey the order given her by her Dragon Tribe master. After all, should they obey him as he wanted, Dragon Supreme might be more lenient toward their mistress.

Mitsie had not made it halfway across the room before the iron doors swung inward. Waiting in the abscess, tall and regal and wearing nothing but ominous midnight black, stood none other than Davorin Astrophel, Dragon Supreme.

Thinking quickly for the safety of herself and her mistress, Mitsie dropped to her knees before the frightening monarch. "Your Majesty, Dragon Supreme. I had promised you to report when My Lady awoke. To what do we owe this honor?"

"I had a premonition."

Dragon Supreme, as used to doling out instructions and issuing decrees as he was used to breathing, did not take time to explain himself. If such a thing as explanations existed within his limited habits, Davorin would spend all his time talking and none of it doing what should be done.

Mitsie, knowing none of that and not caring about it anyway, shuffled aside to allow the owner of this palace to pass. Better to allow him a look at Lady Lada now, while she remained asleep. He may see beauty in her, or at least calm his anger toward her. The

Orafel maids knew not what Lada had done to deserve such wrath, but none thought her actions could have been harmful. Lada had been unable to harm the smallest insect and had volunteered to take Princess Zohana's place, knowing it could mean death. She was incapable of malicious behavior.

"Her fever broke," Dragon Supreme mused.

He had felt the cold leave his body and, somehow, had known. When the little Amaryl woman said her pain was his, she had meant it quite literally. Whatever the case, whatever she had done, Davorin feared they were bound by more than ill fate. When this woman ached, he ached, and for that alone Dragon Supreme wished retribution.

Mitsie turned on her knees, as she hadn't been granted the ability to rise. "She shows signs of waking."

A reply did not come, but Mitsie knew Dragon Tribe's monarch had heard her full well. People like him, arrogant and pretentious, had a way of brushing off those they deemed less important. A servant, though required for a noble lifestyle to exist, could not measure up even to a horse from the Royal Military in their eyes. Mitsie had never expected him to acknowledge her information. She had done her part and would leave the rest to fate.

A whimpered groan from Lada brought all three Orafel maids to their feet, hastening to her bedside.

"Lady Lada!"

"Are you awake now?"

"How do you feel?"

Their words tumbled over each other, one lost in the concern of the next. The women, themselves, bustled about pulling up blankets, rearranging pillows, and checking the state of Lada's condition.

Lada, upon opening her eyes, found herself surrounded by anxious acquaintances, their eyes full of worry and their lips moving as quickly as crickets through the grass. Hardly could she focus, yet she knew something important must have happened, as she no longer lay in a cold and dark prison cell.

Lada recounted what she could remember.

The kind Head Dungeon Guard had brought her food during her stay, though it had done little to dispel her chills. She had been watching the candle burn down outside the barred door... Things became fuzzy after that.

She had desperately wanted to tell His Majesty, Dragon Supreme, what she had done to him. Had she dreamed the part where she accomplished her goal? Lada decided she must have, or someone would have things to say about it.

Then again, maybe they had and she had not listened attentively enough to understand them.

"What is it you have done to me?"

The growled intonation came from behind the maids within Lada's vision, leaving room for discussion on who might have asked it. The voice, however, left nothing to be assumed. Lada had heard the voice before and wagered she would again. He never sounded pleased. Not even, she dare say, did he sound congenial. If he treated everyone in this way, he must have few friends.

But, after all, he held a title too noble to care about such things as friends. Lada knew she should respect him, if only for his title.

Lada wiggled until she got her elbow beneath her. The first attempt at sitting resembled a fawn learning to stand. So awkward and gawky did she portray herself that the maids leaped to help, moving pillows to support her and tucking the blankets around her shoulders lest she catch cold again.

Dragon Supreme allowed them to fuss. He needed the women docile to turn this situation in his own favor. Answers were more freely given when coaxed, especially from the likes of *her*. As torture had failed him last time, and imprisonment had led to this, Dragon Supreme found himself with nothing but a light-handed approach to gain him answers.

He detested being light-handed.

Lada, now resting in a semi-upright position with blankets encasing her in a cocoon, dipped her head in what he expected had been meant as a proper bow. The least of their worries at this point, etiquette. Given how she had attacked him with such a mysterious object in his own court, Dragon Supreme doubted all of this woman's sincerity.

"What trick have you played?" Davorin asked, knowing his tone rang harshly but not caring. Seeing her at all fueled the anger in his veins.

"I did apologize for it at the time," Lada returned, unsure what she had done to frustrate Dragon Supreme.

Yes, she had played a bit of mischief, but he had meant to kill her. She had no options at the time and she had regretted it as she had done it. What more did he want from her?

Dragon Supreme clenched a fist around the inside of his cloak, silently begging for this all to end. How could he play soft with a woman who didn't admit her mistakes? If he didn't need her alive, he would slay her where she sat. Deceit. Insolence. Defiance. All were crimes punishable by death in his empire. Why should she be excused from paying for her crimes?

"It was only a Mirror Needle," Lada continued. "I don't see why you must be so upset over it."

Finally, something to work with. Dragon Supreme loomed a step closer. "What, pray tell, is a Mirror Needle?"

"Part of a rare and sensitive plant."

"And what does it do?"

This gave Lada only a moment of pause. Mirror Flower's secret belonged solely to Amaryl, but rules and regulations in Flora Master's Hall permitted one to tell about Mirror Needle to the one on which it had been used. Not all were intelligent enough to understand the purpose behind such a trick. Fewer discovered what had been done to them without having a proper explanation given.

"Mirror Needle strives to be with its twin."

No reaction registered on Dragon Supreme's face, but given his attitude thus far Lada hadn't expected it. She only looked in case she managed to shock him.

"One twin in your veins." Lada extracted her hand from the blanket and held up her wrist. "One twin in my veins."

This elicited an arch of Davorin's eyebrows. This woman had gone so far to see his demise. To the point of injuring herself. Why hadn't she said as much before he had her dragged off to the dungeons? It would have served her purposes better.

"What do the twins affect?"

He had suspicions, yet Davorin couldn't be sure without her telling him. He had never heard of a Mirror Needle and had no reference for what kind of magic it entailed.

"Oh. That." Lada covered a cough, then snuggled her arm back under the warmth of the blankets. "As they strive to be together,

naturally the younger twin will strive to exist in the same environment as the elder. Thus, when they communicate, the younger will
change its environment to be likened to the elder."

"Summarize in simple terms." Davorin's head ached from trying to
follow the explanation.

"If I am injured, you receive the same injury."

"Why did you fall unconscious while I remained awake and
lucid?"

A pout pursed Lada's lips. "Mirror Needle can't help it that you
have a higher pain tolerance and better stamina than I."

"What if I had been the one injured?"

"Then it would have only been you who incurred the injury."

As he had suspected. She had dragged him down and meant to do
away with him. Only an Amaryl pest could begin to consider such
outright treason. Dragon Supreme shot forward, meaning to clamp
his hands around her throat.

The Orafel maids dropped to the ground, on their knees, creating a
barrier between Dragon Supreme and his intended prey.

"Show leniency, Your Majesty!" one cried, dropping to touch her
forehead to the floor. "Lady Lada is from Amaryl and knows not the
proper etiquette of a royal court."

"Yet she manages to humiliate me in front of my Royal Guards, so
the whole palace speaks of my misery."

"I am certain she meant no harm."

"Meant no harm?" Dragon Supreme scoffed, arms flailing through
the air like windmills. "She has made me weak!"

"I didn't intend to!" Lada lifted her chin, allowing her own
frustrated tears to pool in her eyes. Defiant she may be, but she had

never wanted to harm anyone. "You forced my hand, do you not see? If I hadn't defended myself, I would be dead by now."

"You would be better off dead." Dragon Supreme kicked at the maids, forcing them aside to step right up to the edge of Lada's bed. "Now that you've tied yourself to me, did you think I would go easy on you?"

"I never expected that." Lada stared him down, despite her desire to curl into a ball and cry until her tears made a new river. "I wanted only to survive."

"Survive, you will, for I wish not to be harmed any further. But survival does not mean I will not torture you until you can bear no more. Hear this, Little Florist." Davorin reached down and took her chin in his hand, forcing her glare to remain pointed at his face lest she try to back out now. "You'd best keep up your bravado. If I see any signs of wavering in your passion, I will not hesitate to use your weak nature to my advantage."

Davorin's fingers slipped from Lada's chin as quickly as they had snatched it up. If he stayed longer in this insolent woman's room, he knew not what he would do to her. If her injuries indeed became his own, he had no choice but to see to her protection. That didn't mean he had to enjoy it. Nor would he tolerate all her antics. He would make life difficult for her, if only to appease his own rage.

Throwing open the doors, Dragon Supreme lifted his own chin and bellowed one order. "Guards! Bring the Little Florist along to Fang-Throne Court. Summon the Ministers and the suspects."

Healed or not, Lada could function well enough to identify her attacker. Davorin didn't care to wait another moment to end the charade. She would go along with it or she would suffer the consequences. Dragon Supreme was not known for his kindness.

Lada collapsed back onto her bed. Since she met Dragon Supreme, he had only been angry and upset. Someone or something must have hurt him terribly to make him this way. Still, he could have at least had the decency to use her own title appropriately.

Lada snuggled back into the pillows, waiting for those who would carry her off to the court, with only one thought gracing her lips for the briefest moment.

"I'm an herbalist. Not a florist."

CHAPTER THIRTY-THREE
The Accused

Seeing the Ministers tremble before the Fang Throne served to ease a portion of Davorin's anger. Their sweat trickled down to drop against the polished stone beneath them. Their shivering and sniveling echoed nearly audibly. At least they had the decency to be afraid for their lives. Unlike other palace guests who thought only of their own safety above their actions.

Dragon Supreme shook off his annoyance in favor of glowering toward the hall's inhabitants. Anything could have happened in twenty-four hours. A full day. The Ministers could have selected a scapegoat or collectively decided to accuse someone. Some must have struck a deal between themselves. All had a propensity to seek only their own benefit.

Dragon Supreme had no intention of allowing them to skirt around the issues. No scapegoats or sacrificial lambs for them to fall back on. Someone had gathered the gall to usurp him in his own palace. No ruler would allow such treason when he had been alerted to its existence.

Head by head, Davorin Astrophel counted his Ministers and checked them off the list inside his mind. All, indeed, stood before him, awaiting their demise. All, perfectly in line, lifted their chins as if no guilt rested atop their head. Someone in their midst lied, and Davorin would discover their identity. One way or another, he would shatter their shadowy mask of innocence.

One of the elder Ministers dared to step forward, saluting Dragon Supreme before he spoke. "Your Lordship has confined us in Isonpool Palace for more than a day. Pray tell, for what have we now gathered here?"

"No need to ask him," Velimir interrupted before Davorin answered. "It is obvious to us all. Since we've been summoned, that means the girl has awoken. Am I correct, cousin?"

As much as Davorin thrilled to see his ministers fear him, so too did Velimir revel in the anticipation of an intriguing game. What a sight to see, the ministers who scrambled for a solution when they had done no wrong. Such fear in their eyes, and for what? Because an impetuous boy had become a powerful man? Need they fear one so familiar with death? Or should they all seek his advice to grow stronger in their own right?

Velimir preferred the latter option. Trembling in fear would get him nowhere. Much rather would he stand proudly alongside his own decisions. The weak didn't survive in Fang-Throne Court.

Davorin's eyes took in every twitch of his cousin's robes. Every brush of hair against his shoulders. He had known, upon appointing Velimir to the court, he would not easily be controlled. He had mistakenly expected Velimir to have learned from his elder brother's insolence.

Because it was not the worst of his worries, Davorin let the interruption slide.

Cadfael pushed open the doors of Fang-Throne Court and breezed his way down the center, through the rows of ministers as if they were nothing but statues alongside his path. One of his knees hit the ground before the grand dais, his sword poised in front of him in a salute.

"She has arrived in Court Hall, My Lord."

Cadfael's omission of the Little Florist's name and status said he understood the situation at large. A dramatic reveal of Lada's identity would be useful for Davorin. Keeping the secret intact, for the most part, would assist their dealings henceforth.

"Proceed," Davorin instructed.

Cadfael dipped his head, rose to his feet, and turned to the open hall doors. "Bring her in."

Held upright by the assistance of two Orafel maids, swathed in blankets, and wobbling more than walking, Lada of Flora Master's Hall entered the court.

Or, rather, Lada and her bustling attendants entered the court. None could accuse the Orafel maids of neglecting the safety of their charge. The two holding her supported Lada's slight weight, while the other hastened before them to give instructions to her ailing mistress.

"Careful, My Lady, there's a threshold," the free-floating maid muttered. Followed by, "the floors are slippery here, My Lady. Walk carefully."

Davorin doubted she knew the entire Fang-Throne Court heard her slightest whisper. Her attention, so rapt toward her mistress, didn't allow her to make such assumptions. If not for the incident upon their arrival in which Lada tripped over her own feet, Dragon Supreme would question the necessity of such cautious oversight. However, their hovering made the Little Florist appear that much more pitiful, and pity was something he could very well use to his advantage.

The comedic quartet, oblivious to the stares and sneers sent their way, picked their way through the middle of the court until they found themselves standing beside Cadfael.

To her credit, and despite her recovering state, the Little Florist dipped a rather graceful curtsy. "Your Majesty."

Though he could give her the same speech he had given the Orafel maid, Dragon Supreme decided against the scolding in favor of reaching his ultimate goal. The sooner he weeded out the spy, the sooner he could focus on other schemes.

"Bring them forward," Dragon Supreme commanded the guards in the corner.

Cries and requests for mercy echoed in the room as the suspected maids were herded like sheep into the center of the court. One at a time, each with a gruff hand on their shoulder from one of the guards, the suspects went to their knees in the center of Fang-Throne Court.

"I gave everyone involved ample time for confession," Dragon Supreme reminded all, his eyes never leaving the Little Florist facing him with a look of grim determination on her face. "I am rarely lenient, but I will say this one last time. If those behind the assassination step forward, I will show grace."

A long, poignant pause settled over the room. Voices went silent, heads bowed to the ground like weighted branches. Only the braziers and a few soft sniffles interrupted the court's decision of silence.

Seeing he would get nowhere by being generous, Dragon Supreme heaved a sigh toward Lada of Flora Master's Hall. "Do you remember the woman who served you poison?"

"Clearly," Lada answered, her voice as determined as it would get in her current state.

Lada sought to be kind to all people, but she never took assassins lightly. If they had attempted to slay once, they wouldn't hesitate to attempt a second time. If she could save more people, Lada would do anything.

"Tell me, is she within the maids before us?" Davorin raised a hand to denote the herd of kneeling maids, beckoning Lada to turn and study closely.

With the assistance of the Orafel maids, Lada shuffled in a circle to see the suspects kneeling before her. Some cowered, others begged with only their eyes for mercy from the newest addition to Isonpool Palace. All belonged to Dragon Tribe, and thus believed the woman before them would be cruel in her dealings with them.

As for Lada, she had no such thoughts. Seeking only the one who sought her harm, Lada forced herself to focus on studying each face in the crowd.

Many, she had never seen before. Others had assisted her on her way into the palace. But only one stood out, stern and menacing among the sea of her peers. Lada would recognize the look in her eyes anywhere. It had been the same stare that had silently commanded Lada's death.

Heart racing and fingers trembling, lest the maidservant attempt yet another assassination, Lada wiggled a hand out of the blankets surrounding her and pointed the tip of one finger toward the woman in the crowd's center.

Lada swallowed, fear for her safety once again rearing its head. No one here would care if she lived or died. Perhaps not even the one who would perish with her, should the unthinkable happen.

But he had guaranteed she would live.

Lada chose to trust his words. "The one in green, in the middle."

Guards moved swiftly. Cadfael moved quicker. One hand clamped around the collar at the base of the woman's neck, hoisting her forward from the pack. Unceremoniously, Cadfael dropped her to the polished floor at the base of the Fang Throne Dais.

Dragon Supreme peered down his nose at the woman, watching as she wrinkled her nose in outrage. As her fingers clenched against the stone beneath her, waiting for their opportunity. Had she thought she would get away with this? Had she been led to believe Dragon Supreme could do nothing to ensure his decrees were heeded?

If not for the delay between her capture and this moment, Dragon Supreme would not worry that she may have acquired a weapon. Seeing as how she had been left alone, he now found himself requiring preventative measures. After all, the maid knelt close enough to the Little Florist that she could attack if given opportunity. Knowing what he now knew, Davorin couldn't allow any mistakes.

Lada chose that moment to hack a chesty cough and heave a shiver. Her eyelids drooping, she teetered on the spot, stumbled sideways, and only came back to her senses when one of the maids caught her.

Davorin surveyed her failing alertness and came to a decision. His

Ministers would better accept this maid's fate if they took pity on the Little Florist. Or, perhaps, if they saw *he* took pity on her.

"Assist your mistress to sit on the Fang Throne steps," Dragon Supreme commanded the Orafel maids.

On the steps, the assassin would be less likely to manage an attack, therefore keeping both Dragon Supreme and his Amaryl guide safe. Not even an assassin would dare to touch Dragon Supreme, if she held any loyalty to Dragon Tribe.

As instructed, the Orafel maids ushered Lada to the bottom-most step of the grand dais, positioning her in a seated position thereupon. The blankets wrapped around her as a cocoon once more, lifting from her feet and ankles, and now all could tell the Orafel maids had swathed Lada's feet in thick cotton socks. No wonder they had warned her of slipping.

Seeing his new weakness would be safe where she rested, Dragon Supreme turned back to his court. "Who gave the order to kill?"

The question had been addressed to the maid quivering in rage before him, but Dragon Supreme would gladly accept an explanation from his ministers. Dragon Supreme would find nothing but disappointment for all his ministers if someone did not take the initiative to complicate the matter. They were, after all, so talented at espousing doubt in any situation.

The maid, trained as she had been, did not open her lips to speak. Nothing she said would clear her name. If she spoke, she would only implicate herself further.

Such was not the case for the so-called righteous ministers.

"Your Lordship." One of the testier ministers took a step to the middle of the hall. "How can we be sure this woman tried to poison

Her Highness? I implore you to consider this might be Orafel's plot to cause division within our ranks."

"How quaint a theory," Dragon Supreme bit out. "The victim, herself, told me of the attempt on her life. The pot of tea contained the poison specified."

"I have been told she referenced Pelidon Berries," the minister continued. "Of course this is suspicious. Orafel has no knowledge of Pelidon. How could Her Highness recognize it without a glimpse of it? Perhaps she placed the poison herself. I beg of you to investigate this thoroughly, Your Lordship."

"Investigate?" Davorin chuckled at the impudence displayed before him.

Did they not see the wrathful waif scathing at the foot of the Fang Throne? They couldn't possibly believe that no assassination attempt had been made. This meager, flimsy plot to discredit the victim, had it been all they thought of in their time spent confined? Davorin had thought more highly of their abilities than that.

"Why would I poison myself?" The Little Florist piped up weakly from her seat on the steps.

Lada hadn't meant to interrupt. The question leaped from her lips in an action so unbidden that she startled herself.

Once more, her curiosity had gotten the better of her. Asking to investigate if someone would serve themselves deadly poison? Would anyone take such drastic measures? What if it went wrong and they killed themselves? Both unintelligent and clumsy, this plan they proposed she had made.

"With all due respect, young lady, it is a common court plot." The minister sneered at her, clearly looking down on her intelligence and assuming she had been behind the whole plot.

Yet, Dragon Supreme said not a word. She had surprised him with her simple yet effective question. Either she had not thought such a trick existed, or she had been intelligent enough to play dumb. Whichever were the truth, Dragon Supreme wanted to see how she handled his persistent ministers.

Lada, seeking only pure and honest answers to her questions, didn't get angry at the slight or try to assert herself as higher than the man questioning her. She merely stated the facts exactly as they existed.

"I am not part of the court. Therefore, I never would have thought this possible."

A ripple of shock and dissatisfaction spread through the ministers like a wave upon the shore.

"Not part of the court?" the flabbergasted minister burst. "But you are a princess!"

"You ask how she knew of Pelidon Berries. Very well." Dragon Supreme took a step forward, glowering at his own court like a manic prince. After all, that's what he had been, once upon a time. "I shall tell you."

Any ministers who had dared to begin a line of gossip in the last moments shut their mouths. All turned their attention to Dragon Supreme. All but Velimir, who had taken a sudden and unusual fascination to the hem of his sleeve. No matter. Velimir wouldn't have been stupid enough to attempt this feat, anyway.

"You have heard the rumors. The woman before you is not, in fact, Her Royal Highness Princess Zohana."

Once more, murmurs went up around the room. Many had heard the rumors involving a missing princess and a replacement imposter. They hadn't taken them to heart. Now, the tales proved true. Plans that had been in place for decades came crashing down around them. Dragon Supreme would certainly hear about political vying later.

For now, he relished the surprise on their faces. Especially the insufferable Nerys Galashiel, who had gone white as a sheet at the announcement.

"Allow me to introduce you." Dragon Supreme flicked an open hand toward the girl on the steps. "This is a piece of my Tribute. Lada of Flora Master's Hall. An Amarylite. Does anyone have more questions about how she knew Pelidon Berries by smell alone?"

The following silence rang in his ears, the sweetest symphony. Only the voice of a battered and angered spy interrupted his reverie.

"All the more reason she should have died when I gave her the chance."

Velimir's head popped up, his interest reawakened with the sound of dissension in the air. A trouble-seeker, he had always been.

"I gave specific instructions that she was to remain alive," Dragon Supreme threw the accusation at the maid like stones at a sinner. "Who ordered you to kill?"

"I'll never say," the maid leaned forward, lifting her head to stare her sovereign straight in the eye. "You'll never know."

The woman lifted a wrist to her lips, biting at one of the beads on a bracelet hanging there until it broke in her mouth.

"Stop her!" Dragon Supreme ordered, but it was too late.

The woman collapsed, convulsing and foaming at the mouth.

Lada—who had almost tuned out due to the sheer amount of politics and condemnations being discussed—focused in on one fact. Someone before her was dying.

Casting aside the blankets without a thought for her own decency,

Lada scrambled forward to the dying assassin's side.

"Leave her," Dragon Supreme commanded.

Lada shook her head, her hair flying. The girl's pulse was thready, but salvageable if they acted quickly. The poison taken would be effective for her purposes, but Pelidon Berries would have been swifter. This choice had clearly allowed time to bring her back.

"I can save her," Lada informed Dragon Supreme, though she could not use the force she wanted to use.

Dragon Supreme shook his head, just once. "What's the use? She will not speak of her master even if we do save her."

"But she's dying!" Lada met his gaze, wondering at the cold indifference behind his eyes. Who had wronged him to elicit this behavior toward human lives?

"I said, leave her."

"No. I won't." Lada reached for the woman's wrist, meaning to inspect the poison she had eaten. "Someone call the physicians. I can save her life."

"She will die anyway," Dragon Supreme spat the words, hoping his vexation would speak to the fool woman trying to rescue the one who had attempted to poison her. "Leave her."

"I must do something."

"Cadfael," Dragon Supreme bellowed. "Take Lada back to her quarters and keep watch over her. I will finish here."

"Yes, My Lord."

Cadfael reached down to snag Lada's arm in his hand.

Lada glared at Dragon Supreme for the first time since entering Isonpool Palace. She had not thought him cruel before. Lada had done her best to see the good in him, to be optimistic about her situation. Had she bound herself to a man who would never care for life as she did? Even a criminal deserved a chance to repent.

"Lady Lada," Cadfael enticed.

Lada didn't want to move. Blood and bodily fluids didn't bother her. The ill and dying had never caused her stomach to churn. The only thing Lada couldn't stomach—more than disloyalty—was the lack of concern over a human life. Life could not so easily be tossed aside.

"Take her out," Dragon Supreme commanded again.

Cadfael must have retrieved the blanket from the Orafel maids, because he wrapped it around Lada's shoulders now. Using it to keep her still and secure, Cadfael hoisted Lada into his arms and hastened to return her to whence his master commanded.

Lada, though she did not complain aloud, silently reminded herself of all the things she could have done to spare the maid who had hurt her. If she had been given the opportunity, the maid might have come around to apologizing.

With Cadfael, the Amaryl girl, and the Orafel maids all rushed off, Davorin's ministers could only stand there in silence and confusion. Had Lada of Flora Master's Hall known she wore nothing more than a thin under-dress? Uncouth, it had been, for her to expose herself in the presence of strangers. Then again, Amaryl had never been known for its couth behavior.

Dragon Supreme waited until the odd cluster of people had left before he deigned to give his ministers their last warning.

"You've seen what happens to those who betray me. Ensure you never meet this fate."

As confused as his ministers about why an Amaryl trickster would want to save the one who hurt her, Davorin Astrophel descended his throne and stormed out of the hall. Those left would see to the cleanup.

CHAPTER THIRTY-FOUR

Up & About

For days, Lada wondered why she hadn't been allowed to save the dying spy. It would have benefited everyone. Who was to say, should they have saved her, that she would not tell them the name of her master? The maid need not have died to save face for those involved. Had they been in Amaryl, Lada would not have hesitated to give the order to take the girl back to Flora Master's Hall.

But they were not in Amaryl. Here, Lada held no power except that bestowed to her by His Majesty, Dragon Supreme. Status, she did not have. A title, if asked for one, she could not give.

No one knew to tell her that His Lordship, Dragon Supreme, found himself in much the same mental dilemma as she. Never had he heard of anyone desiring to help those who brought harm upon their head. A trickier woman he had never met. Could not she have spared him the sufferance of her mischief by the same line of thinking? If one could be kind to their enemy, what had he done to merit such abuse?

A contradictory battle of dissatisfied wills had begun that day, at the foot of the Fang Throne. Neither of those involved realized it. One thought the other stupid, while the the other thought the first brutal and unkind. Neither had tolerance for the bad things they saw in their counterpart's disposition.

Over the following days, bedridden Lada had only been able to stew over the injustice. Meanwhile, Dragon Supreme did not deign to lower himself to check on her condition. She meant no more to him than the other Tribute Pieces and he would not act as if she did, even for the sake of his own well-being. She could not do much to harm him while locked away.

What Dragon Supreme failed to realize was that Lada, day by day, began to heal. With her fever gone, she spent more time awake. The infection from her festering wound slowly left her body. By the end of the week, the kitchen began to deliver food more substantial than the porridge prescribed to soothe her angry and malnourished stomach. Bit by bit, Lada began to recover in earnest.

Davorin Astrophel, Dragon Supreme, thought not of how much better he felt. The Little Florist owed it to him, after all she had done.

Davorin Astrophel also failed to remember that Lada was a human being, and not just a puppet in his grand scheme. Underestimation had the potential to sabotage one's own plans, and often led to the demise of whole countries. Dragon Supreme, well-versed in wartime strategies as he was, did not pause to think that a small and weak Amaryl woman would be a hindrance to all he desired.

In a cruel twist of fate, Davorin Astrophel began to forget the trick Lada had used on him. Who would remember such a thing, when it appeared to hold no sway over their daily routine?

Then, one day, Lada rose from her bed.

"My Lady," Mitsie scolded, reaching to steer the imp back to her resting place. "You are still recovering. You mustn't run about."

"I've been recovering for so long." Lada's arms sprang forward, snatching Mitsie's sleeve and giving a series of tugs to urge her closer. "I want to do one thing. Just one." She held up a single finger, her wide eyes begging to be understood.

However hard they tried, not a one of the Orafel maids could say no to Lada. Not when she asked her favor so sincerely. Lada had never asked them for anything before, except the permission to shuck her shoes aside. Why, now, would they refuse a request coming from a mistress who had nearly died because she had wanted to save them all?

With a sigh, Mitsie relented. "What is it you wish?"

Lada, who had been fully expecting the maids to put her back to bed, beamed at the sudden change of heart. "Take me to the kitchens so I can make herbal pastries."

"The... kitchen?" Mitsie wrinkled her brow, trying to decide what kind of thoughts had led Lada to this decision. "Herbal pastries? What are those?"

"Orafel doesn't have herbal pastries?" Lada's eyes went wider, her shock so evident it pained Mitsie to admit she did not know of the so-called delicacies.

Yet, how could she lie to the mistress she served? "I've never heard of them."

"You must try them. All of you must!" Lada grinned at the other two Orafel maids as she addressed them. "They are both sweet and healthy, an excellent way to ward off sickness caused by damp, cold places."

"Ah." Mitsie nodded, catching a string from the web of Lada's thoughts. "You wish to make them so you will recover more quickly."

"Oh, no, I would never. Herbals pastries aren't made for oneself." Lada shook her head, her whole expression changing to express her disgust at such a thought. "No, no. I thought to send them to Head Dungeon Guard. He was kind to me while I stayed there. I should repay the favor, don't you think?"

Honestly speaking, not a soul within the room would have thought to thank a man who held them prisoner within the dungeon. No one would see kindness where there had been none. No one except peculiar, naive Lada. But they would not say that. They cherished Lada's innocence far too much to speak a word that might ruin it.

"You may not be allowed to go there, my lady," one of the other maids intoned.

Enni, by name, erred to the cautious side. Better to remain alive and breathing than to recklessly plunge forth into destruction. As a maid, she had learned early on to calculate each move before she made it. Serving Lady Lada came with new complications that placed a yoke of stress atop her shoulders. Yet, she wouldn't change Lady Lada. Even if offered the world on a silver platter.

Lada had never cared for obstructions or restrictions. Herbalists in Amaryl enjoyed almost unlimited freedom. Never had the forest shut her out or the creatures therein disallowed her access to any part of their home. Dragon Supreme could not be worse than wild animals.

"The kitchens are so far away, My Lady. Won't we all be tired by the time we arrive?" The third maid, Sina, laid a neatly-folded quilt at the end of Lada's bed.

The chamber had never gotten any brighter, but the blankets at least had been replaced. Try as they might, neither Lada nor her maids enjoyed the chamber. It offered nothing worth praising. Then again, neither would the kitchens, should they choose to traverse all the way to their doors.

"We should at least try," Lada encouraged.

Since her arrival at Isonpool Palace, she had been confined to one room or another. Always watched, always caged. Lada had tolerated it in the place of her friend Princess Zohana, but now that the palace knew her identity as Lada of Flora Master's Hall, she no longer had to accept the treatment given to an Orafel bride. Surely His Majesty, Dragon Supreme, would understand their bond enough to allow Lada free rein inside his castle. She didn't ask for escape, not yet. Lada asked only for the room to breathe.

Reluctant to dampen Lada's high spirits any more, the three Orafel maids exchanged a silent agreement before they continued.

Mitsie reached for a thinner blanket lying nearby Lada's bed. "Wrap this around your shoulders, at least. If we leave the room with you in such indecent clothing, we'll bring shame upon our own heads."

Lada, of course, saw nothing wrong with what she wore. A basic white under-dress covered everything of importance and offered more than enough warmth for a kitchen. She had never been in the habit of tying up her hair every day, so allowing it to hang loose around her shoulders presented no problem. Still, she would not deny the Orafel maids their one condition.

Lada snatched the blanket from Mitsie's hands, wrapped it around her shoulders, and clutched the front closed with her fists. "Now may we leave?"

"We might as well," Sina muttered, seeing she would get nowhere if she sought to argue. Lady Lada had made up her mind.

With a squeal of glee, Lada shuffled to the door, sneaked one hand out of her blanket, and gave the iron barricade a firm tug. It complained, but swung inward nonetheless. Being small, Lada didn't require a fully open portal to slip out. She made do with a halfway open door. A fact which assisted her in her haste to exit.

Only, a guard's sheathed sword appeared in front of her to bar her progress.

Lada pouted at the offending object, then turned her best pleading face up to one of the men beside her door. "Why are you stopping me?"

"You are to recover in your chamber. Rest well."

"I have rested well," Lada shot back. "You'll have to give a better excuse than that."

These Dragon Tribe Guards had never dealt with the likes of Lada and had no idea what their boundaries were in dealing with her, anyway. Dragon Supreme wanted her healthy and whole, thus they dared not use force in the case that it might defy his wishes. They also dared not allow this Amaryl woman out of sight, lest they lose their heads for allowing her escape.

"Where are you going?" the second guard asked, a more level-headed thinker than his counterpart.

Lada spun, sending him her brightest and most exuberant smile. "To the kitchens."

"You aren't allowed to leave our protection," the first guard reminded both the woman and his colleague.

Lada, unwilling to keep tossing her head back and forth, instead chose to stare straight forward at the sconce across the hall. A sconce made of gold, with scales hand-carved into its conical shape. Lada hadn't had time to notice the details before. Not even had she noticed the brown and drying vine barely clinging to the hallway wall.

But that was for another time.

"Come with us, then!" Lada decided unilaterally. "I daresay I won't be able to escape the two of you, as you have swords and strength I do not possess."

Neither guard dared to bring up how Lada had outrun everyone who chased her last time, and had almost managed to hide until they passed. They could not allow the same to happen this time, and her offering of allowing them to escort her seemed the best course of action. Especially if they wanted to remain in the favor of their sovereign, Dragon Supreme. If they chose to escort Lada to the kitchens and back, she would technically never leave their charge. Above all, they would not have to resort to force and risk their own lives.

The second guard, seeing their opportunity clearly, spun on his heel and motioned down the hall. "After you."

Lada leaned sideways, pressing as close to the guard's shoulder as she dared, her head tilted back so he could hear her next question. "Is that the way to the kitchens?"

Both guards, now realizing their odd protectee knew not a single passage of the castle, exchanged a glance of relief. She would much less likely get away from them if she did not know where to flee.

"It is, My Lady," Mitsie stepped up to take the lead. "I will show you the way."

Enni and Sina scurried to Lada's side, both pulling her away from the guard and pushing her down the hall. Neither knew the punishment for touching a Dragon Tribe guard. Nor did they care to find out if one existed. Lada had been through enough trouble. They couldn't risk yet another visit to the dungeons when she had barely recovered from the last.

The Orafel maids' orientation into Isonpool Palace had been full of impediments and persecution, but they had at least been taught the paths through Isonpool's halls.

On occasion, they still found themselves lost or confused, but Lada's illness had forced them to learn the path between the chambers and the kitchens. After all, they could not be sure if anyone would attempt another assassination. They dared not serve Lada food or drink if they had not observed its creation personally. Now that Lada wanted to visit the kitchens, herself, they found their new knowledge quite useful.

And, thus, an odd group of misfits and outcasts picked their way through Isonpool Palace. A maid in the front, two more sandwiching Lada in the center, and a pair of Dragon Tribe Royal Guards bringing up the rear. Only this fearsome sight sent palace servants scurrying out of the way. One did not disturb Royal Guards on a mission. To do so meant punishment.

That was the sole reason no one disturbed the Amaryl woman and her Orafel maids, not even once, on their journey to the kitchens.

The whole group stopped outside the kitchen doors, in the open courtyard air.

Lada, already shivering in the cool mountain wind, tugged the blanket tighter around her shoulders. The forest never allowed her to feel such discomfort. Wind in Qranbu's mountain nation strangled her like a vine and pierced her skin like sparks off a fire. How cold could burn, Lada would never understand.

Mitsie pushed aside the woven mat covering the door's opening. Lada stepped inside, her bare feet finding warmth against the wooden floor.

Kitchen hands from all directions stopped work to stare at the strange creature entering their domain. Swathed in a blanket, only a hint of a white skirt showing beneath, and her hair swaddling her like fur. None had ever seen a fairy of her caliber before. None dared to guess who had brought her or why she had come.

All desired to kick her out. Fairies were mischievous beings, and had one appeared in their kitchen it must mean disaster.

The Kitchen Master, a versatile servant known for his quick temper and high standards, snatched a broom from the corner. Fairies and nymphs were notoriously stubborn, but no one could stand being beaten with a broom.

"You dare invade this, the royal kitchens?" Kitchen Master raised the broom to swat at the girl.

In a flash, he found himself incapacitated by one of the burliest Royal Guards he had ever laid eyes on. What powers did the tiny imp possess to require such a brute to protect her?

"This is Lada of Flora Master's Hall," the guard introduced him. "A Tribute Piece."

The statement alone made Kitchen Master rear back in fear. Dragon Supreme was notoriously jealous over his Tribute Pieces, to the point that staring at a piece of his treasure for long might incite him to decree heavy-handed punishment.

Kitchen Master may not understand why this girl had been given as Tribute, but he realized the importance of staying away. The tale of this girl's near-death had been passed along the halls like a forbidden fruit. Even a Dragon Tribe servant had been shown no mercy, on this woman's behalf.

"What—" A squeak interrupted his sentence before it began. The Kitchen Master cleared his throat, willing his voice to return to its original octave. "What brings the lady to our humble domain?"

"I want to make herbal pastries!" Lada took a step forward, purely out of excitement.

Her single movement forced every Dragon Tribe servant in the room to take a step back.

Lada's face fell, from gleeful animation to wounded confusion. She had come only to make pastries, and had not anticipated her presence would disrupt the entire kitchen. In her whole life, no one had looked at her with such fright in their eyes. She must have done something terribly wrong to elicit such a reaction.

The Orafel maids had blessedly received the opportunity to meet Lada under calm and acceptable circumstances. They knew well of her character. Lada had no distrust within her and wanted, the most, for everyone to get along as friends. Having anticipated how Lada would react should she discover the palace servants now feared her, the three Orafel maids sprang into action to remedy the situation.

Mitsie shuffled around Lada and bent a bow toward the Kitchen Master. "My Lady wishes to bake some pastries as a thank you to those who have helped her. Is this too much to ask?"

"No, not at all!" The Kitchen Master would rather die than go against Dragon Supreme. Death, at least, would be quick. "Come, come, I will clear a station for you. What ingredients will you be needing? I will send someone to fetch them if they aren't in the kitchen proper."

The guards, seeing Lada and her retinue would be fine in the Kitchen Master's capable hands, quietly took up their posts outside the kitchen doors.

Lada flew forward, unable to wait any longer to begin her adventure. If only she had realized sooner the differences she would have to overcome to handle a Dragon Tribe kitchen, as opposed to the setup she had grown used to in Amaryl Forest.

CHAPTER THIRTY-FIVE
Royal Problems

"A letter from the border," Cadfael announced, holding out a sheet of leathery paper toward his master.

Letters from the border came rarely and, because of their scarcity, demanded attention from the highest level of nobility. Border letters contained news of battles won or lost. The inconclusiveness inspired by the unopened letter left most feeling trepidatious.

Such had never been the case for Dragon Supreme. Since young, he had seen battles and wars on a scale others hoped they would never encounter. A border battle hardly mattered when one had witnessed the things Davorin Astrophel had witnessed. It meant only an update on the security of his nation's boundaries. If the battle had been won, rewards would go to the victors. If it had been lost, reinforcements would march to expel the rebels from Qranbu.

All the same, Davorin Astrophel, Dragon Supreme, would never have the gall to take lightly a letter from his Border Officials.

Davorin accepted the missive with a firm hand and wasted no time in opening the seal.

To his surprise, it was not a Border Official requesting rewards, but one of his father's most trusted young generals. Though he could no longer be described as young, he served the country well at the border. Davorin had no complaints about him, as the general took his post more seriously than winning favor with Dragon Supreme. For him to have written, something must have indeed happened.

The report, given concisely, offered only the details necessary for Dragon Supreme to make a decision regarding what to do. Every word counted. Every sentence told a tale of rebellion and uprising. Beshotan had invaded Qranbu's borders again and, for the first time in thirty years, they had won the scuffle.

Davorin scanned the contents a second time, paying close attention to the battle's details. Judging by the curt descriptions, Dragon Tribe had fought their fiercest and with their cleverest strategies. Power in Beshotan must have changed. The old regime would not have been able to outsmart the border generals.

In the past, Beshotan had come the closest to overpowering Dragon Tribe. Davorin Astrophel would not allow them to overthrow Dragon Tribe's legacy now.

A quick, sharp spasm in Davorin's hand sent the letter floating to the ground. Atop his skin, round and growing redder by the second, a mark appeared. Davorin would not complain of its sting, as he had suffered far worse in battle. He did, however, sneer at its existence, a reminder of the creature who had tied herself to him.

"The Border requires reinforcements," Dragon Supreme continued on without a second thought to the new injury atop the dorsal aspect of his hand. "Bring a soldier to carry my order and prepare ten thousand cavalrymen to assist the border generals."

"Yes, My Lord." Cadfael, heedful of the letter lying on the floor instead of the desk, said nothing about Dragon Supreme's odd behavior.

Davorin, focused solely on his kingly duties, laid out a fresh scroll and reached for a quill to inscribe his order thereupon. Scarcely had he written half of his decree when the forefront of his head took up an invisible beating. One quick pound that set the rest of his head to throbbing. By the time he reached the end of his writing, three more spots had appeared on his hands and a bruise had begun to form around his wrist.

The last straw came in the form of a heavy, persistent throbbing located in the center of his foot.

Try as he might to be tolerant, to have patience while he discovered a way out of the ill woman's trap, Dragon Supreme found his determination faltering quickly. Over the past days of her recovery, the Little Florist hadn't caused him much trouble at all. Why now—today of all days—did she indulge herself in pain and suffering?

A angry flourish scrawled out his signature on the decree. An equally outraged stamp of his seal finished the task.

Dragon Supreme rolled the scroll closed, tied it, and rose to his feet.

"Deliver this to a trusted soldier, then come with me to see the Little Florist." Davorin shook the decree toward Cadfael, encouraging him to get a move on.

Cadfael, seeing his master's dilemma and not wanting to add to Dragon Supreme's wrath, accepted the scroll and took off jogging out the doors.

For centuries, Dragon Tribe had been careful calculators in battle, the gods of patient strategies. It had won more than a dozen wars. Yet, here and now, Davorin Astrophel found in himself not a smidgen of patience left. Not a crumb large enough to entice him to wait for Cadfael's return.

Ire rising once more, Davorin stomped out of his study door and turned down the hall leading to his intended destination.

She had become the bane of his existence, but the Little Florist had never left a question unanswered. Davorin intended to ask her quite a few when he saw her. Never mind that she had only just recovered. What could she possibly be doing to deliver such blows to his body? It made no sense to Davorin, how easily this woman injured herself.

Guards saluted and servants bowed as Dragon Supreme charged through Isonpool Palace's halls in pursuit of the only chamber that currently mattered. None dared to stand in his way, nor did they presume to ask what ailed his mind. Dragon Supreme wouldn't lower himself to converse with the help. More likely, he would punish any who questioned him.

Had anyone been presumptuous enough to speak out, Dragon Supreme would not have hesitated to lash out his anger toward them. As they did not, he bottled it all inside and set its aim for a specific florist who vexed him indeed.

The hall outside her chambers rang with emptiness and silence, causing Dragon Supreme to stop in his tracks to take inventory of the situation.

The floor remained burnished, without signs of struggle or battle. Flames still danced in the sconces on the walls, proclaiming the unlikelihood of an ill-intentioned brawl. The chamber door sat ajar, open just enough for a thief to sneak through. That fact alone stole all of Dragon Supreme's attention.

Seasoned in battle and suspicious by nature, Dragon Supreme refused to believe all was well in the quiet hall. Men had died for their lack of wariness. He would not be the next to fall for such a trap. With all his training and every tactic he had learned swirling in his head, Dragon Supreme took a cautious step toward the open door.

A push too forceful sent the door swinging. It landed against the inner wall with a *clang*.

No one rushed to attack. Nothing moved, save a flame catching the wind from the door's opening.

Suspiciously void of Orafel maids, the room remained untouched otherwise. For those reasons, Dragon Supreme ventured further within, toward the curtain obscuring the florist's sickbed.

Though no assassin worth their weight in gold would attempt to take a life twice in such a condensed period of time, Dragon Supreme would rule nothing out. Whoever had instructed Pelidon Berries to be used to rid the palace of the imposter princess would not easily step aside and allow this to pass. Dragon Supreme cared not if the imposter princess perished, but he cared a great deal for the only Amaryl guide he had found. If his plan came to ruin because of this grudge, someone would pay dearly.

A sweep of his hand set the curtain sailing, blown aside in the powerful gust of wind to reveal an empty bed.

Dragon Supreme wrinkled his nose disdainfully, suddenly disappointed. Not because he had hoped her dead, but because he had wanted to give a good tongue-lashing. Any other lashing would only harm himself.

"My Lord?" Cadfael stepped through the open door as cautiously as his master had, alert for any signs of danger or turmoil. He had served by Davorin Astrophel's side for too long to believe any situation came with a simple solution.

Davorin turned from the curtain, his feet already taking him back to the center of the empty chamber. He need not ask the words on his mind, for Cadfael had anticipated the coming inquiry.

Cadfael, prepared and waiting to assist, bent forward in a bow. "It seems your Amaryl guide has taken her guards with her and wandered off."

Lada had been so obedient to stay in the room during her first few days at Isonpool Palace that Dragon Supreme hadn't been inclined to believe she would want to wander away. Her behavior during those early days had been strange, but she had not presented herself as the uncontrollable type. Then again, he wouldn't have assumed she would spear him with a forest weapon, either. The Little Florist, for all her idiosyncrasies, was not the woman he originally imagined her to be.

As if in retaliation to his scathing thoughts, a burning sensation sizzled on his right forearm. Since the attempted poisoning, she had been nothing but troublesome.

Dragon Supreme struggled to keep his annoyance controlled. "Where has she gone, taking my Royal Guards with her?"

"They were seen leaving their station, My Lord." Cadfael, trying his best to appease his master's rage, kept his tone firmly in check. Lada's disappearance amused him, but he would not want Dragon Supreme to see how entertaining he found their circumstance. "If we follow their trail, I am certain it will lead us to Lady Lada."

"*Lady* Lada?" Davorin sneered at the title.

Cadfael, nothing if not honest, answered dutifully. "It is how the Orafel maids refer to her. Others have begun to use it in reference to your guide."

Pointing out Dragon Supreme's ownership over the impish woman was meant to calm him. Over the years, through battles and bonding, Cadfael had learned the ways of his superior. Dragon Supreme's anger soared higher and hotter when he lost control of things. Reminding him that he did, indeed, control everything would surely cool some of the heat within him.

Dragon Supreme waived the explanation with a slice of his hand through the cool air. "Lead the way."

In truth, not a single word from Cadfael's lips had dissuaded Dragon Supreme's anger. Learning the Little Florist had wandered off only raised his ire by tenfold. She had yet to fully recover and had no right to wander his palace's halls and rooms without his permission. If left unpunished, Dragon Supreme had no doubt this *Lady Lada* would take advantage of his leniency toward her to act in a spoiled, pretentious way. For the sake of rules and regulations, let alone his reputation, Dragon Supreme would not have that kind of behavior running rampant within Isonpool Palace.

Following the trail left behind by an odd assembly of maids, guards, and Tribute, Cadfael made quick work of tracking down their location. Had Dragon Supreme not heard the answers to Cadfael's continued question of, "have you seen the Tribute Woman?", he would never have believed where the path took them.

Yet, there they stood, staring across a courtyard at the two Royal Guards who had been assigned to watch The Little Florist. Now, the guards stood stationed outside the open doors of Isonpool Palace's kitchens. At least they had not slacked in their vigilance, a saving grace for them, though they did not know it. Their presence here could have been described as a dereliction of duty, if Dragon Supreme did not fully believe they had escorted Lada here and taken up watch while she took up residence inside.

Dragon Supreme turned to his bodyguard and aide, narrowing his eyes in disbelief over the whole ordeal.

Cadfael merely shrugged. He had done his job in a way most suitable. Dragon Supreme had demanded he find Lady Lada, and now here they stood before the doors that would lead them to her.

If there were any chance of Cadfael being wrong about The Little Florist's whereabouts, Davorin would have threatened him with punishment. Alas, Davorin had seen for himself the guards stationed without the kitchens and could not fathom a more fitting reason than their accompaniment of Lada of Flora Master's Hall.

But, on the off chance those guards had betrayed him, Davorin offered an agitated empty threat, anyway.

"If you are wrong, I will demote you to Private First Class and strip you of your privileges."

"As My Lord wishes." Cadfael bent a bow meant to be deferential. It appeared more sarcastic than anything else, as he knew His Lordship, Dragon Supreme, did not mean the words he uttered. The threat had been made more than a dozen times over the years.

Unsatisfied with the result, but content to have made the threat anyway, Davorin turned on his heel, squared his shoulders in the regal manner befitting his rank, and marched forward into the courtyard.

The guards, keeping their attentiveness since they had charge of a Tribute Piece, spotted Dragon Supreme's approach immediately. They could not, by any means, miss it. Black silk shimmered on his person like waves of heat in a desert, his eyes stern and his march set in a firm line directly toward them. What Royal Guard, of any caliber, would dare to overlook such an advance?

Working solely on rote muscle memory, the two royal guards faced each other from either side of the kitchen entrance and bent forward. They remained that way until Dragon Supreme and his guard flew by them.

The rattan mats, hanging inside the door to keep out pests and wind, clattered aside at the shove of Dragon Supreme's palms.

Each member of the kitchen staff looked up angrily, aware someone had invaded their space but unaware of their identity. One by one, each staff member recognized the intruder. One by one, they fell to their knees, the standard phoenix-symbol salute perched over their hearts. Work ceased. Only the crackling of fire and bubbling of mixtures boiling on the stoves remained.

The Orafel maids turned to see, put aside their work, and bent their heads respectfully. They did not have the luxury of ignoring Dragon Tribe's supreme master.

Lada didn't seem to notice the newcomer at all. Yet, he stood in the center of the kitchens and stared at her alone.

And, oh, what a sight to behold! Lada wore nothing more than a single layer of white under-dress, the sleeves rolled up to her elbows and flour scattered across the length of it. Flour marred her cheeks and forehead, as well, sticking to her like paint. Hair hung around her like a blanket. Her actual blanket had been long cast aside. Somehow, and unbeknownst to the waif, she had managed to procure several pieces of straw atop her head, each sticking out in a different direction and bobbing in time to her flitting around the kitchen.

Focused solely on her creations, Lada skipped to the oven, using a towel to reach in and procure the baked pastries.

"Ah! Hot, hot, hot, hot, hot!" Lada fumbled the pan onto her counter space, dropped the towel nearby, and scowled down at her red and burning hands.

Davorin, silently, turned his palm upward and sighed as it, too, grew a concerning shade of red.

So, she had been cooking. As a woman, Davorin would have expected her to possess a more delicate skill set in the kitchen. It appeared this Little Florist, when it came to kitchens, did not know her way around. A groan escaped his lips before he could stop it, solely out of anger and frustration.

Lada raised her head, her scowl disappearing in favor of a smile so bright it burned Dragon Supreme as badly as his injured hands. How dare this nemesis of his smile at him? Did she not fear him in the slightest?

What he did not understand was Lada's mindset. Though Dragon Supreme had been harsh and unfeeling toward her, Lada never wasted an opportunity to make a friend. Even where there had never been anything but animosity before.

"Your Majesty!" Lada squealed the title. She had it all wrong as she didn't complete it with *Dragon Supreme.* "I'm glad you came. I'm making pastries and could use a taste tester. No one here will do it."

Of course no one would test her pastries. The job held no benefit. They might die for interfering with a Tribute Piece or, perhaps, just as easily die from whatever black cuisine the Amaryl imp had cooked up. Dragon Supreme held no interest in assisting her, either. He had come solely to stop her from doing the things she had been doing. A fact which he hesitated to state aloud with his subjects in the room.

Lada's fingers shook and trembled, recovering from the pan's heat, but she snatched a cooled pastry nonetheless and sprang out from behind her station.

Having not paid attention to her before, Davorin hadn't realized that Lada of Flora Master's Hall did not walk as a normal human being. She skipped. In the mind of a man who took everything seriously, nothing grated on his nerves as quickly as a giggly, skipping woman.

Regardless of Davorin's feelings, Lada skipped her way over from her station to the center of the floor and stopped before Dragon Supreme. Her head tilted back, neck craning to see his haughty face. The hand containing the pastry lifted, rising higher and higher to offer the delicacy to the man before her.

"I made Herbal Pastries," Lada announced guilelessly. "But I don't know if I did it correctly. Will you taste one for me, Your Majesty? I assure you, they're quite beneficial to your health."

Beneficial or not, Dragon Supreme couldn't have an Amaryl slave disrespecting him in his own domain. Nor could he have her thinking he wouldn't retaliate for all the injuries she caused him in the past hours. At this rate, the slightest inconvenience would kill her. She couldn't even manage to avoid hot pans.

Dragon Supreme swatted her hand away, too violently, which sent the pastry thereupon flying. It splattered across the floor, its pieces skidding into corners and crannies.

"Everyone out!" Dragon Supreme bellowed.

Scuffle, scuttle, shoo. Every member of the kitchen staff scurried out the door as if the room had caught on fire. It very well might, were Lada given any more time to do as she wished.

Lada took everything in stride. Her eyes followed the pastry to where it landed on the floor. Her attention lingered there, sizing up the damage before she opened her mouth to speak.

"Irregardless of your status, Your Majesty, it is very rude to waste food." Lada took a breath, the smile returning to her lips as quickly as it had wavered. "But don't worry. I have a different kind, as well. I spent time to fry them in oil instead of baking them. I think you'll find them perfectly delicious."

Lada spun to retrieve a different pastry, but forgot to factor in how close she stood to Davorin.

Unwilling to let her have her way any longer, and with his rage running high and mighty, Davorin snatched her wrist in one hand and gave a tug. He would say what he wished, and she would not interrupt if she knew what was good for her.

Lada came stumbling back toward him, narrowly stopping herself before she collided with his chest.

"Is this what you have been doing all day?" Dragon Supreme gave Lada's arm a shake to denote the oil burns on her hand and the oven burns on her arm. "Do you not know when you have been injured?"

"It's not a problem to be injured when one is making something to help others." Lada leaned closer, inspecting her own hand for a moment before she mused, "Oh, that one's new."

Dragon Supreme's patience came to an abrupt end. As quickly as he had snatched her wrist, he shoved it away, leaving Lada reeling before him as he took in her shoddy state.

"Help others? You can't even help yourself."

"I don't need to help myself. I trust I will be fine as long as I think of others first."

"Think of others first?" Dragon Supreme scoffed at her philosophy. "You should have thought of me, then, when you went around burning yourself and by proxy, me."

"Oh." Lada blinked, realization settling in her eyes as she thought of all the things that must have hurt him. The burns. Hitting her head on a beam. Dropping an iron pan on her foot. "I'm sorry, Your Majesty. Are you alright? Does it hurt?"

Lada reached out to check, startling Davorin into motion. He pushed her away, taking his own step back to regain both his footing and the status quo. He wouldn't allow her to lie to him. Lada clearly didn't care about him at all. Fine. If she didn't care about him, he wouldn't care about her.

"What of my reputation? Why should I allow you to run around my palace looking like... this?" Davorin waved a hand to denote Lada's messy state. "You don't even have a proper dress on, and you expect me to allow you free rein? Did you ask permission to leave your chambers?"

"I have to ask permission for that?" Lada frowned at him, distraught by how tightly he wished to rein her in. "I've never asked permission for something as simple as freedom. Couldn't Your Majesty make an exception and allow me to roam your palace freely?"

"This is no time to negotiate!" Dragon Supreme stepped forward, forcing Lada back by steps as he invaded her personal bubble. "Return to your room and there you will stay until I say otherwise."

"Then I'll hang myself from the rafters," Lada answered resolutely, knowing he wouldn't allow her death.

"Don't test me, Little Florist," Davorin spat back. "Your threats won't work against me, regardless of my own safety."

Lada hated when anyone misremembered her occupation, as she had been raised to be proud of it. The title of Herbalist had been the last gift left to her by her mother. If Dragon Supreme had a single ounce of respect for what Lada did to help others, he would refer to her as such.

Stubborn anger welling in Lada's throat, and her eyes shooting daggers at the man before her, she mustered up the courage to act as rebelliously as she could imagine.

"I'm not a florist, I'm an herbalist!" Lada raised a bare foot, struck forward, and stomped on Dragon Supreme's boot.

It wouldn't hurt him or faze him, but Lada found it necessary to use extreme tactics with a man such as him. A man who didn't care to listen and treated others without respect.

With a flip of her hair that still didn't manage to displace the straw on her head, Lada marched around him and out the door.

She stopped only to turn and offer one last order to her maids. "Mitsie, you take the pastries to Head Dungeon Guard on my behalf!"

Davorin Astrophel, Dragon Supreme, rolled his neck to loose the kinks tightening in his muscles. As impossible as Lada of Flora Master's Hall had become, he would need a solid plan to control her. For now, he overlooked the pastries in favor of the more pressing issues of decency.

"Cadfael, find the girl some garments to wear in the case she should escape again."

"Yes, My Lord."

"Tell the guards to keep her in her chambers until I speak with her."

"Yes, My Lord."

Dragon Supreme inhaled a deep breath of hot kitchen air, waiting for it to soothe him and growling when it did not.

One little woman, as unobtrusive as they came, had nearly brought him to his knees. He would not be allowing himself a full surrender to her wiles, but clearly they must negotiate their terms. If he were to stay well and she were to stay alive, a compromise must be reached sooner rather than later.

CHAPTER THIRTY-SIX
The Forest Couple

orning birds chirped their happy song, waking Valor of Champions Post from his fitful slumber. The rising sun had yet to penetrate the forest canopy, but hues of dawn had begun to waken in the moss and leaves nearby. Mist and dew covered the ground, a haze that would soon lift with the coming of a new day.

Valor rose from his makeshift bed.

A glance spared for the Orafel woman assured Valor she still slept, as content as a newborn fawn. As opposed to the previous days, now the fog did not affect her as much. The obstacles in her mind appeared to be things of the past. Her memories did not seek to take her life or the lives of those around her. After such a purge, after all the days she had lied there healing, hope glimmered on the horizon alongside the sun.

And thus, Valor's day began the same as every day had begun these past weeks.

Champion's Post had a reputation to uphold, a duty to fulfill. Valor could not bring himself to neglect his life's mission, even for a weak and ailing woman such as the one in his care. The Border Fog's aftereffects had kept her unconscious. Valor, though optimistic about her condition, thought not that she would awaken before his return.

Forest creatures greeted him in their usual way as he set out, skittering to and fro around his ankles. Others, loping along nearby, dared not approach. Wind swept through the leaves overhead. Valor took a deep breath of the aromas he had loved since infancy.

Protecting Amaryl Forest had long been a dream of his, instilled in him since his childhood. In those days, peril had found Amaryl from all directions. Plague and hunters had diminished their population and taken with them Valor's mother and father. It had been then, weeping at the foot of their graves, that Valor had decided. If others would not protect that which he held dear, he would do the job himself.

His resolute nature forced Valor to take his tasks seriously. To focus wholeheartedly on each mission set before him. How else would he have risen to inhabit Champion's Post?

The creatures avoided the Border Fog as often as not, and thus Valor found himself alone during his morning patrol. Hunters rarely entered Amaryl Forest nowadays, but Valor would never let his guard down. Not when he had sworn to protect the forest at all costs.

Like most days, the border remained quiet. Few hunters dared to challenge the Border Fog and, if they did find the courage, even fewer survived to set foot on Amaryl's soil. Valor guarded against only those select few, for the dangers that would cause Amaryl to fall into the wrong hands. His loyalty belonged to his country, his tribe, and his elders.

Having seen to his duty and made note of the border's safety, Valor returned to Champion's Post by the time the sun had reached the height of the sky. The small creatures returned, dancing around him until Valor tossed them a handful of seed-and-berry mix he kept for them to feast upon. Thoroughly distracted by food, the animals ran away as fast as they had come.

Valor stirred a pot that had been simmering over the fire overnight, ladled out a bowlful of the medicinal mixture, and carried it inside with him. Fresh water, he retrieved into a basin from a rain barrel he had rolled inside after it had filled. He had seen to his duties, and would now turn his focus to the woman he had been nursing back to health.

Due to her hallucinations and lucid dreams, the wounds she had incurred before her arrival in Amaryl had not yet healed. They could not heal when she kept reopening them in scuffles and tantrums. Aside from that, the woman had deeply scraped her arm only the day prior during one of her episodes.

Valor set the basin of water and bowl of medicine on a small table, then gingerly seated himself upon the bed beside the sleeping woman. His fingers, deft from years of forestry, lifted her arm out from under the blanket and settled it upon his lap. Taking up a piece of cloth which he had boiled to disinfect, Valor dipped it in the fresh water and wrung it out.

Carefully, humming the lullaby that had soothed her before, Valor wiped clean the wounds on her arm.

To the tune of a lullaby and the tender care of a stranger, Princess Zohana opened her eyes. Had she been in her right mind, or had an ounce of the strength she usually possessed, Princess Zohana might have attacked him immediately. Instead, she found she could not move or speak. Bound to the bed in a way she did not understand, Princess Zohana could only stare wearily.

Valor was no fool. He noted her waking by the shifting of her person and the flutter of her lashes. By his calculations, he had anticipated her awakening to be in the coming days. Her sudden coherence did not startle him.

He feared, however, that it startled the woman in his bed.

"You're finally awake," Valor stated simply, in the kindest voice he could muster. Few had heard such a tone from him, but wounded things must be caressed.

Princess Zohana, her tongue numb and her brain mush, narrowed her eyes to glare at this strange man. He did not speak as a captor would. Nor did he attempt anything other than another soft brush of wet rag over her chafed skin. In an attempt to speak, a guttural and unladylike sound flew from Princess Zohana's throat.

"Be calm now. You will have to heal further before your tongue works."

Leaving out the part where he had needed to sedate her with paralytic herbs was the smarter course of action. Valor doubted she would take kindly to the fact. For now, he needed her compliant so he could assess the extent of her internal injuries.

Valor set the rag aside, laid the woman's arm back under the blanket, and shifted to lean her upright against his chest and shoulder.

Princess Zohana protested at the touch of his arm behind her shoulders, lifting her.

Valor clucked his tongue at her. "You've been here almost a fortnight. If I wanted to do something untoward, I would have done so by now, don't you think?"

Whether it was his words or his tone that calmed Princess Zohana, neither knew. But in a desperate moment of weakness, Zohana allowed Valor to lift her torso off the bed and rest her head against his shoulder. A firm chest, warm through layers of tunic, supported her back.

"Now, it's time for your medicine." Valor retrieved the bowl of medicinal concoction. It had sat there long enough to be cool enough to drink. "It's bitter, but it will heal the effects of Border Fog. Be a good girl and drink up."

Princess Zohana couldn't have argued if she wanted to, but she found she didn't mind the way this man soothed her.

Last she remembered, she had run from those who would see her dead. The river had been an accident but her last and only hope of escape. If she had stayed in the camp with the monsters who had chained and beat her, Princess Zohana would have failed all the expectations of her family and her people.

Valor ensured the woman swallowed each bit of medicine that he spooned into her mouth. Her unconscious processes seemed to all work. Healing external wounds would be easier than fixing internal problems. Valor knew only enough herbalism to get by. If Lada were housed within Flora Master's Hall, they would need not worry about any ailments at all. Truly, Amaryl felt the absence of their favorite herbalist.

When the woman had finished her last sip of medicine, Valor laid her back down on her pillows. This was the first time she had been lucid enough to react normally to his handling of her. A good sign, indeed. Valor had grown oddly attached to her during her stay, finding her more curious than troublesome, despite her outbursts. The Orafel woman had no control over what Border Fog did to her mind. Valor wouldn't hold it against her. So long as she had no intention to betray his kindness, they might become friends.

"You must have many questions," Valor pointed out as he secured the blanket around her. "I promise to answer them as soon as you can ask them aloud. For now, sleep. Your body needs rest."

The same melody he had been humming when Princess Zohana awoke sprang once again from his lips.

Unexpectedly, Princess Zohana found she could not resist the song's sweet pull. As if her body knew its own needs and desires, Princess Zohana's eyes closed and sleep pulled her back into its warm embrace.

CHAPTER THIRTY-SEVEN

Thieves and Fire

The arrival of a black-and-gold trunk caused quite the ruckus in Lady Lada's chambers. Since her arrival, and ever since the Orafel maids remembered, there had not been a gift given. Lada had done nothing but give to others, and hadn't received anything except medicine to cure her infection.

The Orafel maids, of course, muttered about it often. One could not hate Lada no matter how hard one tried, and thus the selfishness and disdain shown by Davorin Astrophel, Dragon Supreme, became characteristics the maids thoroughly scorned.

Again and again, he had set himself against Lada, as though he despised her existence. The Orafel maids simply didn't understand why he would keep Lada in his palace if he didn't want her company. It would be easier to send her home and forget she had ever existed.

Lada, of course, knew he would not acquiesce to either option. Having tried her best to be his friend, she had learned a thing or two.

Since she had tied herself to him, for the sake of his own well-being he would not easily let go of her. Every plan had its flaws, and this was the flaw in Lada's plan. Originally, the Mirror Needle had been meant to buy time for Lada to escape. Now, she had realized her error.

Dead or alive, attaching herself to Dragon Supreme in such a way would not assist in her escape at all. She had not thought of how it would affect the other person subjected to Mirror Needle's trickery. His Majesty, Dragon Supreme, would not lead a peaceful life anymore, because of her stupidity.

Those reasons alone were enough to plant seeds of suspicion about the gift Lady Lada's chambers received. More so did the maids suspect foul play when Cadfael arrived with the trunk. Dragon Supreme would never send his personal bodyguard into Lady Lada's chambers without a purpose.

"Lady Lada." Cadfael dipped his head.

Every instinct in his body wanted to bow his respect toward Lada of Flora Master's Hall, but he would not. Not now. Dragon Supreme would frown upon anyone bowing to the Amaryl addition to Isonpool Palace. Lada, herself, would correct his protocol. Cadfael had seen her refuse such treatment from more than one Dragon Tribe maid or guard. Lada did not believe herself worthy of such high respect. Indeed, she may not hold a title deserving of it, but in Cadfael's estimations, Lada had far surpassed nobles and ministers alike. Not every woman could hold her own when contesting Davorin Astrophel.

"I bear no such title. Please call me Lada." Lada abandoned the trunk being settled on the floor in favor of shuffling over to Cadfael's side. "Why are you here?"

"To escort the gift to its rightful owner," Cadfael answered simply.

Dragon Supreme had not labeled it a gift, nor had he had any intention of flattering the young woman to whom it had been sent, but Cadfael knew an opportunity when he saw one. If Lada began to think good things about Dragon Supreme, she would be more likely to help their expedition into Amaryl later. Force never achieved everything. Sometimes a gentle hand worked miracles.

"Is it truly a gift?" Lada craned her neck, peering up at Cadfael's face in suspicion.

Cadfael had never lied to her before, but he did work for His Majesty, Dragon Supreme. Lying might be an option.

Lada knew she had utterly and completely offended His Majesty. She had apologized for it many times, yet he never forgave her. It went against all Lada had been taught since childhood.

Forgiveness, loyalty, sincerity. All were needed to live a prosperous life. Why did Dragon Supreme fight against them?

Cadfael, for his part, took everything in stride. Lada's suspicion had its foundation in cold, hard facts. Dragon Supreme had not treated her with respect, nor had he seen her as a human. Then, there was that threat Dragon Supreme had made about torturing her. Of course Lada should be suspicious of this kindness.

Yet, Cadfael also knew her forgiving nature.

"It is, indeed, a gift. Dragon Supreme ordered it brought, himself."

"Truly?"

"Truly."

With a grin, Lada unglued herself from Cadfael's side and hustled back to the trunk in the middle of the chamber.

Click, clack, went the clasps holding it closed. *Thunk*, went the lid as Lada threw it open. A squeal leaped from Lada's throat and bounced around the vaulted ceiling overhead.

The Orafel maids, distracted from their bustling by their mistress's cry, hastened to peer over Lada's shoulder.

"They're beautiful!" Lada exclaimed.

Piece by piece, each one floating through the air as Lada shook them out, a passel of dresses emerged into the light.

Dragon Supreme had ordered Cadfael to find the woman some dresses. Cadfael, in the hopes of garnering favor with the fairy-woman, had scoured the town to locate garments to suit both her taste and Dragon Supreme's miserly budget. It had taken hours to acquire the dresses now being thrown around like sacks of flour.

"This is Beshotan silk." One of the maids held up a pink dress that had been a reject from one of the finer silk sellers in Isonpool Fortress. Dragon Tribe women did not often select pink as their color of choice.

Cadfael didn't mention that part of the story.

Another maid pulled a blue overdress from the trunk's depths. "This should be Orafel-made. Her Highness had a similar dress in her adolescent years."

Lada, oblivious to the conversation going on at the trunk, spun around the room humming a song of her own. A pale yellow dress swung in her arms, clutched tightly to her chest like a much-cherished childhood toy.

"See to it your mistress is fully outfitted from now on. If she requires more garments, you may alert Dragon Supreme."

"Wait!" Lada stopped spinning, stumbling to catch her balance. "I would like to thank His Majesty for the gift. May I?"

"My Lord, Dragon Supreme, cares little for compliments." Cadfael offered a wry smile, hoping it would appease her though he knew differently.

Lada of Flora Master's Hall may appear stupid, but her tenacity could outlast seasoned generals.

"It's the first and only gift he has given me since my arrival," Lada pointed out. "I'm certain His Majesty would not object to my gratitude. Where is he? I'll go thank him personally."

Seeing that he could not stop her, nor force her to stay in her room any longer, Cadfael took the risk of his plan failing. "His Majesty is out training with the soldiers. He will return via the back courtyard. By now, I have no doubt your attendants know the way."

If only for their own safety, the Orafel maids had indeed learned quite a few exits. As foreigners in a strange land, they could not expect everyone to welcome them. In fact, some had been hostile toward them sheerly for being from Orafel. The back courtyard was a standard entrance and exit for Ministers. It had also been the path they had used to enter upon their arrival in Qranbu.

"I will deny divulging this information if Dragon Supreme should ask." Cadfael saluted, his sword held out tip-to-ground and his hands folded around it. "I will take my leave."

With her mind now on a single track toward her next goal, Lada didn't bother to hold Cadfael back or to tell him goodbye. He came and went as a shadow. An undeniable fact, that she would see him again. More pressing issues took her time and efforts.

Lada wiggled into the pale yellow dress, finding the fit too large and her shoulders exposed through the slashing on the arms. The high neck kept it in place and she could lift the skirts so as not to trip over them. At least with their length, no one would notice she didn't wear shoes beneath.

Mitsie glanced up from folding the other dresses back into the trunk. "You changed quickly. Are you really going to run out and thank His Majesty, Dragon Supreme?"

"Of course!" Lada spun a circle, giggling at the way the dress flowed like water around her ankles and against the floor. "His Majesty offered such nice things. It's only right to thank him for his kindness, to promote more acts of kindness in the future."

"His Lordship, Dragon Supreme, isn't a nice man, My Lady," Sina tried to explain.

Lada shook her head. "I believe, deep inside, everyone has a root of kindness. It need only be exposed to the proper conditions to grow the most beautiful blossoms."

None dared argue with Lada's reasoning, skewed as they found it. Thus, they changed the subject.

Or, rather, Enni changed the subject. "Why do you not refer to Dragon Supreme as 'His Lordship' or 'My Lord' as we've been instructed?"

"He isn't my lord," Lada threw the explanation with a shrug, then raced for the iron doors. "I'm going to find him with or without you!"

The three maids exchanged a look of utter dismay, but none deigned to command Lada to remain indoors. As free as a bird—and as flighty—Lada could not be forced to remain inside this cold and gilded cage.

"I'll go with her," Enni offered quietly.

"Be careful," Mitsie returned with a sigh.

Lada did not understand that Dragon Tribe held no fondness toward the false princess and her attendants. They would sooner see them dead than help them live. Each time any of them left the room, they walked into a dangerous, treacherous place.

Yet, for Lada, Enni scurried into the hall and trailed her toward the back courtyard.

Only the knowledge of Lada's identity as a Tribute Piece kept others at bay. Enni, on the other hand, received every ill-intentioned stare with a growing sense of dread. She had no guarantee that they would not hurt Lada. She held a certainty that, given opportunity, they would harm her readily.

Oblivious to the glares thrown from all sides, Lada sprinted her way down hall after hall, until she burst through two familiar iron doors into a courtyard filled with gravel paths. At her arrival, Lada hadn't noticed how intricately the ground had been patterned. The hands that had made such paths had been skilled, indeed. Craftsmen held a dear spot in Lada's heart. To see their masterpiece splayed out before her warmed Lada from the inside out.

A warmth that was not to last.

Lada had barely stepped foot onto the gravel path before her when the doors she had come through burst open once more. The clang of iron against stone paled in comparison to the shouts and threats that echoed out of the inside hall.

Something—or some*one*—shot out of the open doors and into the courtyard.

Enni wrapped her hands around Lada's arm and tugged.

Lada went stumbling behind a pillar.

Anyone looking on would not have noticed the hidden Amaryl girl. They were intent on chasing down the other woman.

Indeed, the culprit was a woman, a fact evident to everyone on her tail. Her hair had been skillfully plaited atop her head and concealed beneath a man's bonnet, her body shielded by layer upon layer of loose cloth. But none missed her fragile feminine features, nor the small hands clutching a paper-wrapped parcel to her chest.

"Help! Thief!" shrieked a maid chasing her down.

A guard took notice, then, and sent a bolted arrow sailing toward the fleeing woman. The bolt embedded itself in the rock near the woman's foot, causing her to lose her balance. She recovered quickly, racing toward the outer doors with a ferocity born of sheer desperation.

Whomp. Crack! The edge of a bullwhip smacked against the woman's leg, sending her rolling on the ground.

From a side hall Lada hadn't seen, a form emerged. Red hair, brushed until it shone like the deadliest forest fire, fell from the crown of her head and trailed down her back like lava. The whip swung in her hands, more like a venomous snake than a tool.

"A simple thief managed to get this far in Isonpool Palace?" Nerys scolded the maids and guards nearby.

No one had a decent answer for her. The famous temper of Nerys Galashiel knew no bounds. Should they say anything to her disliking, they might be the next to encounter the sting of her whip.

"And you," Nerys addressed the woman struggling to get her legs beneath her. "You dare to steal from Dragon Supreme? Do you openly seek death?"

Standing did not come easily to the woman in the courtyard, but she managed to climb onto her knees. Palms pressed together, head down but eyes lifting, she offered an earnest plea.

"Please, My Lady, spare me. I meant no harm to anyone."

"Thieves all say the same. The punishment for theft remains the same, as well."

"I only took the medicine I need. I dare not take anything else." The woman pressed her fingertips to her forehead, shaking her folded hands to show her sincerity. "Please spare me, this once. My mother... she needs these herbs. She'll die without them. Have mercy."

"Theft is theft." Nerys raised the whip, preparing to swing another time. "You know the price for your actions. Don't blame me for enacting the law."

Thwap... thwap... The circling of the whip sent a heinous cry into the air.

Nerys reared back her arm to strike.

A flash of pale yellow darted across the courtyard and wrapped around the woman's trembling form.

Cra-splat! The whip found its mark, except it wasn't the intended target at all.

Lada, the thief engulfed in her embrace, took the brunt of the blow. The reeds and switches back in Mesmium had hurt. They had stung. But they had been nothing compared to the burn of a whip's mark. Fire sprung upon the skin of Lada's back and shoulders, flaming hotter with every passing second. The horrendous pain reminded Lada only of why she had leapt forward to help.

"Who are you to interrupt a thief's punishment?" Nerys shot at the intruder.

Lada, refusing to release the woman in her hold—lest Nerys whip her again—lifted her head to stare the female minister down. "Who are you to punish her without trial?"

Lada didn't know Qranbu's laws, but she knew what she had been taught in Amaryl. To punish a crime, one needed evidence or testimony. Even then, punishment could only be doled to the extent the criminal had erred. If anyone could indiscriminately punish anyone, at any time, wouldn't chaos overtake them all?

Nerys had never been talked down to in such a way before. Those who served Isonpool Palace knew her face and name, she had seen to it. Anyone in the palace knew her status and station. They dared not cross her for fear of crossing Dragon Supreme himself.

Nerys had spent years setting herself up as the woman for whom Davorin Astrophel cared. She couldn't let an ignorant imbecile threaten the power she had gained.

Judging by her lack of knowledge and the way she threw herself around as if the palace owed her, this must be the Amaryl woman. Nerys gave her a once-over, sneering at the differences between the feverish, disheveled woman who identified the spy and this bathed and pampered girl now in her way.

"This is my business," Nerys bit out. "Move."

Lada stared back at her, eyes all-seeing as she sized up the woman before her.

"Uncontrollable rage is sometimes a symptom of unconsolidated inner heat." Lada mused aloud. "Should I make you a cooling potion?"

Nerys, oblivious to Lada's ways of helping, took a menacing step toward the bleeding girl and the thief in her hold. "I *said*, move! Unless you wish to be punished for this girl's mistakes."

Enni, realizing things were about to get out of hand, came skidding across the gravel to fall to her knees beside Lada. "We're terribly sorry to have interrupted. We won't do it again."

Enni reached for Lada's arm, which Lada promptly tugged out of her hold. A hiss of air through Lada's lips was the only thing to denote the pain still blazing through her body.

"We mustn't interrupt, My Lady," Enni instructed quietly.

"I won't budge," Lada confirmed.

Though tears misted in her eyes and she wanted nothing more than to allow the pain to drag her under, Lada refused to allow someone who might be innocent to incur more punishment than they were due. Her own suffering was already too much for her to handle. How could she sit by and allow someone else to go through such pain?

The thief in Lada's hold didn't try to argue, bargain, or move. She was safest where she sat, leg throbbing but clear of the whip's aggression. Why run when she would only be caught?

"I will say it one last time. Move!"

"My Lady, please, no," Enni entreated.

Lada curled tighter around the thief, willing to take the punishment.

Crack! went the whip, blossoming a second crimson line across Lada's back and shoulders.

"Get up!" Nerys shrieked, her hand pulling back to send the whip sailing again.

"You *dare* to touch what belongs to me?"

Time froze within the courtyard's confines. The great iron gates rattled as they hit the stone walls. A bird of prey landed with a squawk atop a corner section of the roof. The whip that had been meant to burn Lada went limp in Nerys's hold.

Davorin Astrophel, Dragon Supreme, stepped over the threshold into the courtyard. Braids contained both sides of his hair, sweeping it back from his face in a way that made his eyes look fiercer than usual. His trailing robes had been replaced by a tunic built specifically for military tactics.

Yet, Lada found she could not focus on any of that. Her vision went hazy as she set her sights on Davorin's black leather boots.

Davorin, of course, had known the moment the first strike had landed against Lada's back. The second strike had raised his ire and his suspicions. Now, he found the sight before him as deplorable as he had feared.

"My Lord." Nerys bent a curtsy, finally coming back to her senses.

Davorin, knowing it would be the best chastisement, ignored Nerys' greeting altogether. His own back aching as if he had fought a dozen battles, Davorin bent to be nearer the whole scene.

"Your Majesty..." Lada gasped the words, each syllable displacing beads of sweat on her brow.

Impressive, that a fragile florist such as she had survived not one, but two stripes at Nerys's hand.

Davorin encased the back of Lada's neck in his palm, turning her head until she had no choice but to make eye contact with him. "Did I not command you to remain in your chambers until I said otherwise?"

"She sneaked out?" Nerys scoffed at the shaking woman, her own hand raising with the whip in her hold. "I should punish you justly for disobedience to Dragon Supreme."

"Whose house is this, Nerys?" Dragon Supreme spat over his shoulder, temper ablaze and patience thin for the way she ordered around his servants.

Nerys, for all her ill intentions and inherent flaws, knew when to shut up. Should she push the matter further, Dragon Supreme would surely shun her.

With the testy redhead silenced, Davorin turned back to the Little Florist in his grip. "Tell me. Why are you here? Did you mean to escape?"

"I wanted... to thank you." Lada's eyes, red and teary, shone with her sincerity. "For the gift."

By the way she said it, alone, Davorin could tell how Cadfael had presented it. All for the better. Allowing her to believe he had generously gifted gowns had softened the Little Florist toward him. Cadfael had known what he had done.

Davorin held no conscious affinity toward the Little Florist, but in a roundabout way her presence in the courtyard had assisted him in dealing with Nerys Galashiel. Nerys had always been arrogant, but lately her unconcealed disdain for protocol had far exceeded Dragon Supreme's limits. It was time to teach her a lesson: she could not always have what she so desperately desired.

"You had no right to leave your chambers, and have been punished for such behavior." Dragon Supreme didn't care how limp the Little Florist felt in his hold. He released her and rose to his feet. "Cadfael."

Having just arrived on the scene, Cadfael jogged from the interior hallway to his lord and master's side. "Yes, My Lord?"

"Take the thief to the dungeons."

"My Lord, Dragon Supreme." The thief scrambled out of Lada's hold, bowing low before the country's sovereign. "I care not if I am punished, but don't punish anyone who doesn't deserve it. These herbs.... please have someone take the herbs to my home."

"Take her away," Dragon Supreme instructed, caring not for her reasons.

Thieves were as thieves did. He need not care what would happen to her. They would interrogate her properly. When they had gained all they could from her, he would bestow punishment.

Cadfael shot into action, pulling the girl from the ground and turning toward the hall that would take them to the dungeons.

Dragon Supreme lifted his hand, hailing two guards without a word. "Return Lada of Flora Master's Hall to her chambers."

The guards, under the careful scrutiny of Enni's instructions, lifted Lada and—careful of her oozing wounds—carried her toward the door.

Lada turned back, staring at the steely face of Davorin Astrophel for a moment. A moment long enough to see the light catch in his eyes, turning them a strangely beautiful shade of gold. Impossible, with the dark depths usually found there. Lada attributed it to her own failing eyesight.

"If that is all, I will take my leave," Nerys offered politely.

Dragon Supreme rolled his shoulders and winced at the pain coursing through his back. He couldn't let her off so easily for such a transgression. "Nerys Galashiel will kneel in Fang-Throne Court until I address her offenses personally."

"But I—"

"The Royal Guards shall escort her there and see to her safety."

Both Nerys and Dragon Supreme knew he didn't send the guards to see to her safety. He sent them to ensure she did as she had been directed. Nerys had a bad habit of skipping her punishments or pretending they hadn't been given at all. Seeing as how she was a girl, Davorin had gone easy on her in the past. No more. As a competent woman, Nerys should know what she had done wrong.

Davorin did not spare another moment for the woman who had disrupted the peace in his palace. As a minister, she should understand how dearly he despised the scuffles between women. It had been avoidable, but now it had escalated. Sadly, this time, only Davorin and Lada paid the price for Nerys's stupidity.

CHAPTER THIRTY-EIGHT
Velimir's Advice

neel in the Fang-Throne Court... Nerys had never been made to kneel for punishment in her entire life. Since her appointment as Minister Galashiel, Dragon Supreme had not deigned to subject her to such humiliation. Whether because of her reputation or her devotion, Dragon Supreme knew better than to cross her.

The only thing that had stopped Dragon Supreme from engaging himself to Nerys had been the Orafel bride. In Nerys's mind, she had cleared his path for him, opened up the possibility for greatness. Yet, he chose to shame her over a mere disagreement? Nerys could not have seen it coming. Even if Dragon Supreme needed to keep his reputation as a just ruler, he could have found forms of punishment better than indefinite kneeling.

Fang-Throne Court had not been built to make its inhabitants comfortable. Torches along the walls did not brighten the enclosed interior, especially when the tapestries over the high windows had been pulled shut. Floodwaters of cold, wet wind glided along the stone floor, making Nerys's kneeling task more difficult.

These things and more, Velimir knew as he sashayed into the grand hall.

The story written by the tip of Nerys's whip had spread like a mudslide through Isonpool Palace. Maids told other maids, who spread the news to the kitchen staff. By then, anyone receiving a meal from the kitchen had undoubtedly heard. Gossip mills spread news faster than messengers by far. Velimir had merely overheard what everyone already said.

He happened to know more of the story behind it all.

"Oh, dear. Look at you." Velimir clicked his tongue as he approached Nerys from behind. "Kneeling here obediently with no hope of respite from your struggle."

"I am not in the mood to indulge your nonsense, Lord Velimir," Nerys spat at him.

Neither cared how the other felt. Both wanted only their own gain. Alone in Fang-Throne Court seemed a fitting time to have such conversations. The walls might have ears, but both Velimir and Nerys had done their fair share of rat-trapping.

"Are you not the least bit curious as to why you can't get closer to my cousin?"

"It seems to me, you speak defiantly of your cousin's personal life."

"Your plans fail because you're emotional." Velimir circled around Nerys and spun to face her. "You want him too badly, and that's why you fail to plan in advance."

"You shouldn't be offering advice when your own cousin still distrusts you."

"Did I say anything about him distrusting me?" Velimir folded his hands behind his back and bent forward to better see Nerys' eyes. "Do you want him to trust you?"

Nerys lifted her gaze, meeting Velimir tit for tat in this queer battle of wits. "He does trust me. I've never betrayed him or interfered in his affairs."

"Well." Velimir laughed. "You and I both know that's a lie."

Whereas they both, indeed, knew the lie in Nerys's words, Nerys would never admit to such a fault. Her interference had never involved Dragon Supreme directly. She existed on the fringes of his plans, exacting her own battles when necessity demanded.

"I'll care for my own affairs. You care for yours." Nerys arched her brows at Dragon Supreme's cousin, looking him up and down in an unimpressed manner. "If he ever trusts you, I'll listen to your words."

Velimir straightened his spine, stretching his arms as if the bent posture had tightened his muscles. "It must be so uncomfortable, kneeling there waiting."

"I have survived worse," Nerys lied.

Velimir spun a circle, dropping a heavy sigh into the atmosphere as he did. "You're too direct. Helping him without expecting anything in return. Obeying every order he gives. Waiting *so patiently* for him to see you. To love you."

Nerys said nothing. How could she refute the facts? It had been years. She had done everything for Dragon Supreme, anticipating he would choose her once his greatest rival disappeared. Yet, another had taken her place. A mercy, that Davorin Astrophel would never love a weak woman such as the Amaryl spy.

"I feel bad for you, truly." Velimir turned back to Nerys, his voice dropping conspiratorially. "Your emotions. Rein them in. Control them. There's only one obstacle between you and power now. You've eliminated many over the years. What's one more?"

"Do you not know that girl is a Tribute Piece? No one can touch her."

"No one can touch her, physically." Velimir squatted down to be at Nerys's level. "This will be my final advice. You don't have to make your rivals disappear. You only have to ensure they will never... ever... love him."

For a moment, Nerys and Velimir stared at one another, both forming questions and suggestions they dare not say aloud. On a subconscious, primal level, both knew they played games no one ever imagined. And yet, somehow, they both found they understood the inner workings of the other's mind.

Velimir broke eye contact first, rising back to his feet and scuffing a toe against the stone floor. "I've said all I came to say. I hope you are allowed to rise soon."

Nerys didn't believe him, but she refused to say as much. Velimir, behind all his flamboyant exterior, held a cunningness Nerys had witnessed within very few. He was not as he appeared, this new minister, and more dangerous than she had calculated.

Regardless, his advice made sense.

"I do hope we get along in the future," Nerys offered, by way of leaving herself a chance of escape later.

Velimir chuckled as he headed back toward the Fang-Throne Court's doors. No more words, no more actions. Just a lingering laugh that could mean anything.

Nerys didn't know if the next shiver came from cold or dread.

CHAPTER THIRTY-NINE
Heartfelt Talk

Pada's chambers had become a familiar place to Davorin Astrophel, Dragon Supreme. Illness after injury had brought him seeking her out to check on the severity. A thankless task he neither liked nor desired to pursue. Yet, despite all his complaints and all his attempts to stay away, Dragon Supreme found himself entering those accursed chambers once more.

In the bustle and hustle of maids leaving and entering—in the stark formality of guards changing shifts—the imposing figure dressed in braids and military uniform did little to impress. Subservient subjects bowed quickly on their way to procure the things they had been ordered to fetch. The iron doors swung open and shut, open and shut, creaking against one another with each pass. None desired to raise Dragon Supreme's legendary ire, and thus went about their business with the knowledge that failure would be met with fatal punishment.

Disobedience and disloyalty, Dragon Supreme would never tolerate, but he did not go so far as to steal all the attention for himself. The Little Florist had bled, beaten with the length of a whip, and according to his guards had passed out on her way back to her rooms. In such an instance, if he had any hope of keeping his Amaryl guide, Dragon Supreme would certainly not interrupt those who sought to heal her.

Inside the chambers, braziers had been lit and stoked, ensuring no cold would seep into Lada's open wounds. Floor-to-ceiling curtains, usually tied aside, now hung as a barrier between Lada's bed and the rest of the room. Beyond them, weak but conscious, Lada lay on her stomach on the bed in question, the now-ruined yellow dress cut aside to reveal the extent of her injuries. The Royal Physician sat alongside her, prescribing medicines and reaching for salve.

Even impatient and easily angered Dragon Supreme would not break etiquette to the point of seeing a lady's undressed skin. Thus, with the mirrored wounds on his skin burning and pulling in a constant reminder, Davorin Astrophel lowered himself onto a stool at the ramshackle table in the center of the room.

The Orafel maids skirted around him in as wide a berth as they could manage. One would think, after his saving of their mistress, that the maids would show a nature more friendly than hostile. One would be wrong. They suspected him of more nefarious purposes. He had done nothing but harm Lada, yet had now decided to show a kinder side.

Dragon Supreme would have scolded their behavior, had he not been focused on his own wounds. Had not Cadfael arrived at that moment, stern-faced and knowledgeable of the situation.

"My Lord, should I...?" Cadfael glanced around to ensure that someone who need not know would not discover the secret.

A small, pained voice, not as firm as her previous arguments had been, spoke up from beyond the dark wall of curtains. "Treat your wounds, Your Majesty."

Lada had not thought through her actions when she had jumped in front of the whip. With an ill-treated woman before her and endless compassion backing her up, she had leapt before she calculated the cost. No one in Dragon Tribe would care about her health and well-being, but Lada could not easily sit by and see others punished. Especially not anyone as pitiful as that woman.

"Treat your own wounds before you give me orders, Little Florist," Dragon Supreme bit back. Pain and suffering did not inspire patience or grace in Davorin Astrophel. In fact, wounds and injuries brought out his worst nature.

Little Florist. The words had been carefully selected to force Lada of Flora Master's Hall to quiet down. Dragon Supreme did not have the energy to argue their situation's finer points.

Yet, to everyone's surprise, Lada did not take offense or quiet down. Instead, she offered only one more plea to the man who had sent her dresses and stopped the whip.

"Don't be in pain."

The most hardhearted tyrant would sway toward those words, said in such a forlorn tone. Only a true fool thought about another when they had suffered such injustice. Yet, tied together as they were, Lada had no choice but to consider Davorin's suffering. Davorin had no right to call Lada a fool. Even if they both wanted to be stubborn, they couldn't afford it.

Dragon Supreme couldn't refuse her when she begged so delicately.

"Bring the best Celeron from the infirmary," Dragon Supreme directed Cadfael.

"No, wait!"

Lada got her arms underneath her, prepared to rush over and reprimand the misinformation. Her movement managed only to reopen the wounds across her back. Lada cried out, a pitiful, pained wail, and collapsed back onto the bed.

Dragon Supreme shook his head, tiring of her antics. "Bring the Celeron."

"You can't put Celeron on such an open wound," Lada sobbed. "It will make the pain worse."

"I'm a warrior. I don't need to be coddled."

Celeron, an expensive and effective battle medicine, had been used for decades within Isonpool Palace. Since childhood, Davorin had been enduring the pain to heal his wounds. Now, it came second nature to him, repairing pain with Celeron's fire.

"I told you I'm an herbalist!" Lada's outburst, followed by yet another distressed whimper, lacked the punch she intended. "Celeron is used to increase blood flow."

"Stop talking, Little Florist, you're only making yourself suffer."

"You need to heal the tissues, not increase blood flow." Lada buried her head in her pillow, letting her next cry of pain be muffled so she could continue professionally. "Use Denbrec. Denbrec will heal it faster."

If this argument continued, it would hinder the Little Florist's healing. She squirmed much when upset and angry.

Denbrec had never been used to treat a wound in Qranbu, but Amaryl had become known as Mystics. Their herbal knowledge dwarfed the knowledge in Dragon Tribe. If he relented, Lada of Flora Master's Hall would favor him more. His reputation may enlarge in her estimation.

"Bring both," Davorin acquiesced. The one who told him not to be in pain would cause herself more pain if she continued with this agitation.

Cadfael jogged out the door. His return would be swift, as the infirmary sat no farther from Lada's chambers than the kitchens. A few minutes would be all it took.

Lada went still and silent, closing her eyes to recuperate from the outburst. Dragon Tribe had no reason to trust her knowledge. No reason to understand that Lada wanted nothing more than the ease and peace of her patients. Any injured person within her sight, regardless of status or enmity, became her patient. Dragon Tribe thought she would bring harm to their monarch. Lada would never stoop so low.

Allowing Lada time to rest and regain her bearings, Dragon Supreme unbuckled his tunic belt and shucked the tunic, itself, onto a nearby stool. The open air, though warm, did not compare to the cocooning heat of his military wear. Thus, his flesh prickled in the cooler atmosphere. The whip marks, open and angry on his back, blazed hotter than the braziers themselves.

Yet, Dragon Supreme made no complaint.

"Did you deliver the herbs as she requested?" Lada asked weakly.

The herbs? Davorin mused. Piecing together Lada's mental journey to arrive at the topic, he decided she must be referring to the thief's final plea.

Davorin didn't dare answer the question, as he hadn't decided what to do with the thief yet. Without information, he would make no promises, even if the promise would secure him an Amaryl guide's help.

"You should think of yourself before others. Look at the state of you."

Yet, somehow, Davorin knew the fool wouldn't listen to his advice. He had misjudged her selfishness during their first meeting. It had been an act of survival, not malicious intent. She had apologized too many times afterward, and her actions now spoke of her true nature. His entire plan needed to be rethought.

"I should have let you use Celeron," Lada muttered, thinking Davorin couldn't hear her.

"Lie still," the physician chastised softly.

Davorin snorted derogatorily. Even injured, the fool couldn't manage to cooperate. True to her nature, indeed.

Cadfael returned, shutting the doors behind himself. "My Lord. I've brought the medicine."

"Apply it for me," Dragon Supreme commanded. "The Denbrec."

If using a different medicine made the Amaryl guide trust him, Dragon Supreme wouldn't hesitate to listen to her. Sitting there, in the Little Florist's parlor, with his tunic tossed aside and his bare torso exposed had been a conscious act to force her to trust him. Bit by bit, he would steal her trust and achieve his goal. That had been the plan, after all.

Cadfael unloaded an apothecary bowl and set to work mixing the Denbrec with oil. Like a salve, Cadfael applied the paste over Dragon Supreme's injuries, one inch at a time. And for the first time in

Davorin's life, the medicine soothed instead of torturing. The Little Florist did, indeed, know her herbs.

Lada let forth a cry, as pitiful as a dying lamb. Tears followed. She could do nothing to stop them. Her pain dictated she cry, so cry she did. In her whole life, Lada had never felt such fire alight on her flesh.

Davorin, somewhat softer now that he knew Lada hadn't tricked him, scowled in the physician's general direction. "Take care."

"Yes, My Lord," the physician returned, his touch lightening upon Lada's skin. He cared little for Amaryl Mystics who sought to steal his job, but he dared not offend Dragon Supreme.

Dragon Supreme, realizing he had too harshly chastised his own Royal Physician, turned his outrage on Lada. "You shouldn't attempt to rescue thieves. It's liable to kill you."

Lada paused, thoughtfully piecing together what she should say to such a comment. Davorin Astrophel, Dragon Supreme, had never been reasonable before. However... he had sent her a gift. He had saved her from an angry noblewoman. He had taken her advice on how to treat his wounds. The wounds she had given him.

Honesty had always served her best, so that was the route Lada chose.

"She didn't want to steal."

"Are you saying she was forced?" Davorin shot a glare over his shoulder as Cadfael pressed firmly on one of the lash marks.

Cadfael sent back an apologetic look, but daren't say a word to interrupt the first cordial exchange the Amaryl girl and Dragon Supreme had managed.

Lada sighed, the exhaustion of injury and treatment beginning to blur her eyesight. "She just wanted her mother to live."

One sentence, delivered so innocently it sickened Dragon Supreme, brought memories cascading in like shooting stars.

Blood. Laughter. Tears. And the end of it all.

For a moment, both Davorin's torso and his fearful heart lay bare and exposed before Lada of Flora Master's Hall. The curtains hid Davorin's skin, as his position of power hid all the scars upon his hardened heart.

Lada had no way of knowing the wounds her words had reopened. Lo and behold, she had lost consciousness again before she could witness Dragon Supreme's reaction.

Lada's true colors, in this circumstance of ill repute, had shown through to the man who despised her the most. Only someone with a clear understanding of loss could utter the sentence in such a tone.

Beyond the thread of Mirror Needle's binding, Davorin sensed the weaving of a new thread. A thread of mutual understanding. Few understood the trauma of losing a mother, yet in this fool girl Davorin had found a piece of kindred spirit.

"Cadfael." Dragon Supreme turned his attention to his guard.

"Yes, My Liege." Cadfael set aside the medicine.

"Deliver the herbs as the thief requested. Investigate her thoroughly."

"As My Lord wishes." Cadfael stepped in front of Davorin to offer a bow. "Will that be all?"

Dragon Supreme, not wishing to converse any longer, waved a hand in dismissal.

The injured sovereign sat still even after Cadfael left to do his bidding, thinking of things to come. Lada of Flora Master's hall was more trouble than she was worth, klutzy and unruly. But she was his only chance at a guide. He would use her and discard her. Any other bonds were completely coincidental.

Yet, there sat Dragon Supreme, unwavering and unmoving, until the Royal Physician stepped out from behind the curtains and gave his final words.

"The young lady needs her rest. She may get up and walk around when she feels able, but I would not suggest it for several days following. I've sent her prescription with her maids."

"Check on her daily, in case her condition changes." Satisfied his guide would live, Dragon Supreme reached for his tunic.

The physician bowed his way out the door, medicine box held so tightly the handle may break.

With a wry grin and a wince of pain, Davorin secured his military wear on his person. There was a culprit to handle, and having seen Lada's condition, Dragon Supreme meant to take full advantage of the situation at hand.

CHAPTER FORTY
Punished Nerys

ours went by, none of which lent warmth or comfort to the Fang-Throne Court. Midday light gave way to evening shadows, and with it the cawing of black birds. Their ominous cries echoed from the top of the chamber, a cacophony of anger and frustration mirroring Nerys's growing impatience.

The guards stationed to watch the female minister whispered among themselves. Hours upon a stone floor would make any able-bodied person's legs go numb. Much longer and Nerys Galashiel ran the chance of never recovering. A kneeling punishment could cripple soldiers, let alone a noblewoman.

Already, Isonpool Palace walls told the story of powerful Nerys Galashiel's assault on Dragon Supreme's Amaryl Tribute. An unprecedented tale of kindness winning over rage. Once more, the rarely-seen Amaryl woman had surprised Dragon Tribe with her way of interfering. No one from Dragon Tribe would think to protect a thief. Thievery would be punished, no matter the reasons. One should allow the perpetrator to accept their fate.

Yet, Lada of Flora Master's Hall kept intruding on the natural order of things.

Now, Minister Galashiel knelt in punishment, though all knew her close relationship to Dragon Supreme. The gossiping guards could not forthrightly make a decision on which woman they would stake their money.

Nerys and her attending maid knew the conversations that went on behind their backs. In such a position, humiliated as she was, Nerys had no power to stop it. Until the decree came from Dragon Supreme, himself, Nerys could do nothing but kneel where she had been told to kneel. Any form of demand might be seen as rebellion. Any luxury might be misconstrued as taking her punishment lightly.

Indeed, the maidservant had brought back a meal for Nerys, but Nerys would not eat. If she indulged in such comforts now, news would reach Dragon Supreme's ear. For her own safety, as well as the sincerity of her argument, Nerys would do nothing except wait.

Still outfitted in military attire, Dragon Supreme stormed through the open Fang-Throne Court doors. As if his presence commanded them, the black birds ceased their squalling.

Agitated, cold, and angry, Nerys did not make any attempt to rise from her perch. She would do nothing to make her punishment worse. As Lord Velimir had pointed out, she had played this game too directly. A mistake she would remedy.

"My Lord, Dragon Supreme." Nerys bent her torso just enough to count as a bow. Any farther and she might have tipped over.

Davorin Astrophel, Dragon Supreme, did not stop to greet Nerys. He had tolerated her insolence long enough to recognize when to draw a line and how to make her obey. What she wanted, he doubted he would ever desire to give to her.

Sitting again would agitate the wounds on his back. Thus, Dragon Supreme stopped at the bottom step of his grand dais and turned to stare at the woman before him. "Have you reflected upon your actions?"

"Your Lordship says I was wrong, and therefore I am at fault." Nerys dipped another shaky bow, this one purposely pitiful.

Having come from a room containing a truly pitiful girl, Dragon Supreme held no tolerance for Nerys's ploy. "I see you have not reflected."

"I see not what I have done wrong. I meant to punish a thief. A girl got in my way. Should I then allow the thief to escape?" Nerys kept her eyes downcast, but every embittered word leaped from her throat with the sting of a thousand wasps.

"To punish the innocent for the wrongdoings of another is not what a minister should do," Dragon Supreme clarified. "Much less when the interruption belongs to *me*."

Dragon Supreme leveled a glare at Nerys at the same moment she raised her head to glare at him. Their eyes met, sending invisible sparks of inner fire careening toward the ceiling.

In Dragon Supreme's words, Nerys found both his reasons and her fears. Going forward, she should choose each word carefully, to weed out the information she wanted without igniting Dragon Supreme's rage.

"How was I to know her identity?" Nerys tipped her head petulantly. "She is but an object in your treasury, but you have not shown her to anyone for us to recognize her face."

"You know how I hate it when anyone mars the treasures in my storehouse." Dragon Supreme bit out each word with the ferocity of an awakened beast. "An object, she may be, but she comes from Amaryl. I will not stand for anyone souring my plans."

A frisson of exuberance shot through Nerys's veins, prickling her skin and sending a shiver of anticipation up her spine. Dragon Supreme's anger had not been out of affection, but possession. Nerys need not worry about his taking a liking to the Amaryl girl. A strong Dragon Tribe man such as Davorin Astrophel would never hold affection for a woman as small and fragile as Lada of Flora Master's Hall. Not unless he had been beguiled or seduced.

"My sincerest apologies, My Lord." Nerys saluted, her hands in the phoenix symbol over her heart. "My emotions got the better of me. I meant no disrespect to your treasure house."

"Then what did you mean?"

Both Nerys and Dragon Supreme fell silent, each waiting for the other to continue. A question had been asked that both knew the answer to, but neither dared tell.

In the end, Nerys spoke first. "I meant to catch the thief. I wanted to impress Your Lordship."

Such verbal territory should not be entered, but Nerys said it as a way to test the waters, not as a confession of her undying affection. That would come later, when Dragon Supreme understood all she had done for him.

For now, Dragon Supreme's eyes offered nothing but cold indifference. "You are not authorized to run my household, Minister Galashiel. If something has gone wrong within my home, I will handle it myself."

Nerys bent her head again, retreating from the verbal joust in order to win the battles yet to come. One day, he would see.

As for Dragon Supreme, he wanted nothing more than to put an unruly minister in her place. To teach an impertinent woman her position. And, thus, he offered the cruelest punishment he could give her.

"You will be confined to your home for three days. No one in, no one out. Is this understood?"

Nerys, knowing it would take days to process her humiliation and recover from her kneeling punishment, gave a single nod of agreement.

"And," Dragon Supreme continued, "you will apologize to both the imprisoned thief and Lada of Flora Master's Hall. Nothing less than a completely sincere apology will do."

"Yes, My Lord," Nerys agreed too quickly.

Without a word, without imploring her to stand or offering to send a physician to check on her, Dragon Supreme marched off to deal with other matters. His day had been wasted. He would spare no more time on a woman who couldn't separate personal and public affairs.

Dragon Supreme never saw the sly smile spread over Nerys's prideful face.

CHAPTER FORTY-ONE
Cadfael's Investigation

Isonpool Fortress, home to Isonpool Palace and a host of rich and famous nobles. Mansions sprouted along every road. Merchants bartered their wares to the fortunate and unfortunate, alike.

Yet, for all its glamour and splendor, every city had its hidden poverty. Isonpool Fortress was no exception to this rule. The homeless and destitute found their ways to survive, be it an honest job, stealing, or begging. To those who didn't care, corner communities and box houses were things to be glanced over. Cadfael, more than most, knew how to navigate those poor and overlooked areas.

It was in one of those communities, struggling but homey, that Cadfael found the address given by Isonpool Palace's resident thief. The buildings around him, as he traversed ever forward, grew more and more decayed. Those hovering in doorways or venturing out for provision, more ramshackle and beggarly.

An old, rickety door at the far end of the dilapidated alley greeted Cadfael with a groan. Appropriate, this kind of dwelling for a lowly thief, but not inasmuch appropriate for a filial daughter. If indeed the woman had told the truth.

A spy knew better than to alert his enemies to his presence. Thus, the bulky man standing outside the wind-shattered door wore nothing to identify himself. No gold or jewels. No fine silks or delicate brocades. Any emblem which could tie him to Isonpool Palace had been left behind. The streets in these desolate corners were known dangers. One who could manage to survive them dared not bring any trifles to define his station.

The very air in this godforsaken vestibule complained with the rap of knuckles against the door.

A bird of prey squawked in protest of an interrupted meal.

Cadfael beat his palm against the door once more, twice in succession.

"She can't come to answer," a gruff young boy shouted from the alley's opposite side.

Cadfael spun to watch the child carefully. In this part of town, even children had plans to pickpocket or gaslight. Like burrowing moles, poor children tunneled into the finer streets and markets, seeking only to take what didn't belong to them.

The boy had no such intentions, having noticed the sword hung at the large man's side. Cunning as children in the desolate corners could be, they were no match for those who practiced the art of war. The boy had seen enough soldiers to tell the difference between a curious nobleman and a trained fighter. One day, he hoped to join the military and learn to fight as one of the strongest and bravest Dragon Tribe Warriors.

"You'll have to go in on your own," the boy finished. As quickly as he had appeared, he dissolved into the smoggy, smoky air.

The street offered nothing more of interest, only dirty children playing ball, oblivious to the presence of a palace servant. Beady eyes stared out from holes in the walls, but none would chance an encounter with the dangerous, cloaked intruder. Weaklings and cowards hid and watched. The brave ones, the ones who ran gangs and stole often, had not returned from their daily search for prospects.

When a stranger offered advice in a place such as this, it could mean many things. Inside the shaky entry, other strangers might lie in wait for a gullible man to enter. Yet, within the community of this alley, a stranger had offered advice without asking for anything in return.

Training and battles had taught Cadfael lessons, most importantly that caution could be taken without a retreat. Orders from Dragon Supreme were not to be delayed or discarded.

Taking the boy's advice at face value, Cadfael gave the door a push. It nearly swung off its hinges, creaking in a pitch so high it echoed through the alley like a scream.

The inner courtyard housed a mess of failing amenities. A washing tub with a crack down the side rested beneath the only standing pole of a simple clothesline. A fire pit lay cold and dormant. Along the far wall, a pile of half-woven straw shoes perched under a makeshift canopy of leaves.

Across the way, only one leaning building occupied the rest of the space. From within came a barking cough.

Cadfael had heard such a sound before. A deep, wracking hack that threatened to destroy one's lungs with every breath. The Death

Cough had haunted him since his first battle expedition. Strange, that he would hear it again here and now. The thief hadn't lied about needing the herbs to save a life.

Step by silent step, Cadfael crossed the courtyard to the thief's home. On a mission or not, no Dragon Tribe man would barge into an elderly woman's home without adhering to etiquette first. Elders were respected in Qranbu, more so when they were the center of an investigation.

Careful not to break or bend the wood before him, Cadfael knocked upon the door separating him from answers.

The bark of a woman's cough greeted him harshly, followed by a wheezing breath so loud it made Cadfael shudder.

"I got no money to steal and no possessions to take," a gruff voice rasped.

"I'm not here for either of those things." Cadfael checked over his shoulder, in case of an ambush. "May I enter?"

"I don't see why not. But I'll warn you, if you're here to kill me, you're wasting your time. I'm a dead woman already."

Her brusque words forced up the corner of Cadfael's lips. A pessimist, this woman.

Had she not been bedridden by the Death Cough, she would have chased him off with a broom or blade. In her younger years, she had been a formidable foe in the back alley streets. Now, illness took the strength she had spent years to build.

She did not know Cadfael brought a solution to her ailment. Nor could she have guessed from whence he came to deliver it.

Just as Cadfael could not have known she would lift a sword toward him as soon as he stepped through the door. But that's what she did.

The old woman's sword had been made of the finest materials. Once upon a time, she had loved and lost. The sword, her means of protection, was the only thing left by which to remember her love. Now, decades later, his gift protected her as if he still stood by her side.

Cadfael stopped with the door half-shielding him, staring cautiously at the weapon in her quivering hand. Poor as she was, the old woman had no way to eat healthily enough to regain her strength. Not with her illness so prevalent and persistent.

"I will not harm you," Cadfael promised solemnly.

The old woman eyed him, taking in what was visible to her. He could pass as a street thug, except for a few minor details. The hair on his head laid too neatly. His posture stood too proudly. And, beneath the perfect mask of a tattered cloak, the hilt of a plain-but-expensive sword shone in a ray of sunlight from outside.

"No, you wouldn't be here to steal or slay." Inch by excruciating inch, the woman rose to her feet, using her old sword to hold her aloft. "What's your business here, then?"

The woman tried to bite back her next cough, but it wouldn't be shuttered. Hacks and wheezes splurted from her lips as fiercely as a death toll.

Cadfael wrapped a hand around the old woman's free arm, using his leverage to steer her back toward the bed. "Sit down, grandmother. I've come at the behest of your daughter."

"Daughter?" The old woman hacked again, her shoulders shaking with the force of it. Her coughing fit caused her more pain than standing, thus she easily fell back into bed as directed.

"She sent me with an herbal prescription for your illness." Cadfael released her, pulled the bag of herbs off of his belt, and held it up. "So you will recover."

"Ah. The girl." The old woman nodded in understanding. "She said she'd send medicine to repay me."

That was the moment Cadfael's interest piqued. It was also the moment that would change a thief's life forever. Good or bad, no one could say. Not even those who did the changing.

CHAPTER FORTY-TWO
A Loaded Apology

Time ticked by, not by hours, but by the healing of a pair of lash wounds. Three days of peace gave way to the day of judgment.

Gossipmongers roaming the halls made sure to tell everyone they saw. Nerys Galashiel was coming. Her three days of house arrest had ended. Now, the real punishment began.

Almost more famous than Dragon Supreme's temper, was Nerys Galashiel's pride and arrogance. Yet she had been told to apologize. Not only to a woman who had become oddly close with Dragon Supreme, but also to a lowly, imprisoned thief.

Dragon Supreme had sent a message, loudly and clearly, said the gossip mill. Nerys did not hold as high a position as she thought, nor did she have what she desired. Everyone in the palace knew she pined for Davorin Astrophel, Dragon Supreme. Yet, he had commanded her to lower herself before a prisoner and a tribute. No one cared for

Nerys within the walls of Isonpool Palace, no matter how badly she wished it.

Dragon Supreme remained in his private chambers, shut off from the rest of the world and from any plea Nerys might make. No one dared pass through his private doors, under penalty of death. None had seen Davorin's private chambers, save Cadfael and a single cleaning maid. The maid no longer lived.

In another corner of the palace, Lada's attendants scrambled to see to their mistress's needs. Not because Lada demanded it, but because she had been bedridden these three days and they sought to make her comfortable regardless of her physical pain. Lada had never complained, not even after she lay crying in bed for a full evening. Each Orafel maid wished Lada would look after her own well-being, just once, but alas Lada did not have such habits.

The guards outside Lada's doors had begun to pay attention, to have empathy toward the woman inside. For she treated them kindly and cared about their well-being despite their station.

The guards had not failed to notice Dragon Supreme's protective care over her, either. Though Lada of Flora Master's Hall had been a fake bride, she had been sent as Dragon Supreme's bride, nonetheless. No one could guess what would happen now that Orafel had failed their part of the treaty. Only the leaders of the two countries knew the terms and conditions in the pact.

Regardless of terms, the guards were under strict orders. Should Nerys try to bring any more harm to the Amaryl girl, they were to inform Dragon Supreme personally. It was why they kept their ears and eyes open. Why they listened to each rumored report floating through the halls.

Rumors that said Nerys had come. She had visited the dungeons. She would soon arrive within the palace proper.

Lada's guards did not miss the significance of the fact that Nerys had visited the imprisoned thief before she deigned to visit Lada of Flora Master's Hall.

Lada, of course, knew nothing of the commands given while she slept. She knew only that His Majesty had forced upon Nerys the task of apologizing. Though Lada had already forgiven the temperamental minister, she understood Davorin Astrophel's purpose. When one had done something wrong, such as harming innocent bystanders, they should apologize for their wrongdoing.

A smile worked its way onto Lada's face. How strange, that in this she and His Majesty would find a topic to agree upon.

"Only fools smile in such dire circumstances," a sharp woman's voice echoed against the vaulted ceiling.

The bed complained and her bandages stretched as Lada sat forward. Unaware of her own tragic state, Lada stared at the red-headed minister who elegantly trudged into the chambers.

"His Majesty called me a fool, as well," Lada confessed. "I suppose he didn't support my decision to help the woman."

"He shouldn't." Nerys stopped her advance near the curtains that had obscured the bed from view only nights before. "Yet, for all his condemnation, here you sit in such comfort."

"His Majesty is very kind to allow me to stay on in Princess Zohana's chambers."

Lada didn't enjoy lying, but she realized when things should remain unsaid. She would tell no one about the bond between her and Dragon Supreme. They might not be as lenient as His Majesty had been toward the bit of mischief Lada had played. Nerys had come into the room in bad spirits. Lada had no desire to see her leave in a worse mood.

"I suppose you expect me to kneel or grovel, as I have been commanded to apologize to you." Nerys raised her chin like a fox guarding its den. "I will do no such thing. Put it out of your mind immediately."

"Oh, no!" Lada held up her hands, waving them to ward off Nerys's assumptions. "I would never ask you to kneel or grovel. I don't hold a position high enough to warrant that kind of behavior and forcing someone to submit hardly encourages friendliness."

Nerys's eyebrows raised, her hackles settling as she took in the sight before her. The girl was a flower, unused to any climate but sunlight and notwithstanding of heavy rains or violent storms.

Lada of Flora Master's Hall had every right to be angry toward Nerys. After all, Nerys had whipped her. Yet there she sat, injured but unwilling to speak out her true thoughts. Unless, of course, she had no true thoughts at all. Weaklings like this one never lasted in Isonpool Palace. Nerys would barely need to lift a hand to get rid of her.

"I do apologize," Nerys continued sweetly. "There was no need to whip *you*. I lost my temper."

"Thank you for your apology. It must have been difficult for you."

Hardly the reaction Nerys expected, but the only one Lada was capable of giving. Thinking of other people's emotions came second nature to Lada, after being raised in Flora Master's Hall. To apologize sincerely, especially when one's pride had been hurt, must be excruciating for someone such as Nerys.

"You have *no* idea," Nerys muttered, more to herself than to the woman on the bed.

"Since you have apologized and I have forgiven you..." Lada scrambled onto her knees, earnestly imploring Nerys with both her posture and expression. "Does that mean we can be friends now?"

Friends? Nerys wanted nothing more than to expel Lada of Flora Master's Hall from the palace. Yet, this forest woman thought they could be friends? How naive of her to trust one who had not hesitated to break open her flesh. Yet, in this situation, it would be wise to work smarter, not harder.

"I suppose... since you are one of the only females within Isonpool Palace and I dislike the ministers as much as any others..." Nerys heaved a sigh. "Begrudgingly, we could be called upon as friends."

Lada's eyes sparkled with the force of her smile. "Truly?"

Of course not. But Nerys turned her lips up into a pained and awkward expression. "Truly."

"Then you must come visit me regularly. It will be refreshing to have someone to speak with other than the maids." Lada cupped her hands around her mouth, as if it would keep the Orafel maids from hearing her. "They're sweet, but they fuss too much."

Nerys could hardly believe the foolhardiness of this woman. Had she no guardedness at all? At this rate, she would believe it if Nerys told her that she had descended from a line of Mountain Spirits.

"His Majesty, Dragon Supreme, will not tolerate our close proximity."

"Why not? He's kind enough, really. You just have to look past his cold exterior."

Nerys snorted a laugh. "Dragon Supreme is not a kind person. Not at all. He would not wish me to tell you, and therefore will try to keep us apart."

"What do you mean he isn't kind?" Lada pouted, sitting back on her heels and letting her fists drop into her lap. "He gave me gifts and brought someone to tend to my wounds—"

"If he's being kind to you, it means he wants something from you." Nerys, knowing she could push her luck no further, gave a soft sigh. "Be wary of him, please. His kindness means your demise."

Lada couldn't fathom what Nerys meant, and she didn't have time to ask. Nerys spun on her heel and left the room without another word.

It must be how Nerys dealt with everyone, that abrupt nature of hers. Lada took no offense to it. Nerys had promised to be her friend, albeit begrudgingly. Therefore, Lada had every intention of making Nerys a close and intimate friend. The feisty redheaded minister looked like she needed someone to confide in. Lada wanted to be that for her, even if it took effort to make her open up.

The Orafel maids, who had been listening in from dark and concealed corners, knew better than to trust the peace offering. Lada may never suspect someone who said they wished her friendship. The Orafel maids knew better than to believe in anything a Dragon Tribe Minister said. Especially one with the reputation of Nerys Galashiel. If Lada couldn't protect herself from the wiles of her enemy, the Orafel maids had every intention of doing it for her.

If only they had known the disaster and destruction that would befall Lada despite their efforts to protect her.

CHAPTER FORTY-THREE
A Plot Within Isonpool

alls had ears. Doors had mouths. Regardless of location or station, secrets spoken aloud were never kept for long. Workers, thieves, spies. All the parts of a functioning fortress had mouths and ears. All the parts of a bustling city, if they were indeed human, had a price for using those appendages.

Loyal and fierce Dragon Tribe had dissenters, those who were unsatisfied with their monarch or their country. Enemies and friends, alike, took advantage of weak links.

Every country had to trade with other countries if they wished to flourish. More so the strongest country, the victor of the Great War. In caravans and trade treaties, outsiders found their chance to sneak in to Isonpool Fortress. A few scouts, to secure the information that would make their own country victorious. More than that would surely draw attention and suspicion.

Hidden within shops and markets, elites searched diligently for those who would offer up information, even if they did not realize it.

Ministers, unfortunately, had loose tongues around their servants. Those servants had looser tongues when it came to complaints about their masters. Tidbits of useful information could be gleaned in any corner of Isonpool Fortress, if a minister's servant frequented the establishment. More details could be purchased from others after the foundation had been laid.

Rumors ran rampant in the city, based on facts unchangeable. The Orafel bride had never arrived, sending an imposter in her stead. Dragon Supreme had punished his only female minister because of the imposter. Now, he would lay plans to conquer Amaryl.

In a dark shop, one particular spy mulled over the information bit by bit. Seemingly, it all revolved around a single person. But, in the wealth of information lay a clever and convenient omission.

If they, the spies, had so easily infiltrated Isonpool Fortress, there must be a counterspy keeping the important information from them. This man's job, as the leader, was to locate and eliminate those who stood in their path.

His fingers tapped against the counter, his eyes staring at everything and nothing all at once. So stern was his expression that honest, paying customers dared not step foot too close.

Thankfully, the man caught his own wandering thoughts and returned to his present façade. "Have you found all you seek?"

"Your Beshotan silk is of the highest quality here," the woman beamed, dropping three bolts onto the counter. "I'll take all of this."

Excessive. Greedy. But if she paid for it, the man would not bother to point out those facts. The less attention he drew to himself, the better. In this place, he was no more than a common store clerk. No matter his station in his own country, he could be nothing more in Qranbu.

"They left so suddenly," continued the woman before him to her companion, "The regiment didn't give us time to say a prayer for them or make them new armor. The whole camp, gone overnight. I couldn't even say goodbye to my son."

"That's the military for you," the companion answered testily. "Trust them with your men and you'll end up a widow."

The man packaging their fabric never glanced up, but drew assumptions from the facts he had been told. The timing was suspicious. The movement of an entire military camp more so.

Thus, the whispers were heard by ears that should never have listened.

If only those ears had known that eyes watched them in preparation for a plan that could coincide or contradict their own.

CHAPTER FORTY-FOUR
Exploration

It had been almost a week since her injuries had been incurred. They didn't hurt as badly anymore. His Majesty must feel better, as well.

A smile worked its way onto Lada's lips. He had been kind to her since she revealed her trick, and thus she felt better knowing he would overcome the injury she had given him. Never before had Lada repaid evil for kindness.

"If he's being kind to you, it means he wants something from you. His kindness means your demise." Nerys's words didn't make sense, and were laced with bitterness, but they haunted Lada.

Never had she happened upon anyone who used kindness as a sword. True kindness could not be faked, Lada firmly believed. True kindness came from the depths of one's heart and spread out to touch those nearby.

For the sake of kindness, Lada remained within Isonpool Palace, her prison. For the sake of kindness, Lada forgave His Majesty for the things he had done before she had saved herself at his expense. That, alone, left her feeling guilty. She had done it to save herself, but it had harmed His Majesty. Lada disliked using others for her own gain.

"His Majesty Davorin Astrophel, Dragon Supreme, sends an edict." The Palace Administrator announced from outside Lada's chamber door.

Lada scrambled to the edge of her bed but dared not step foot off of it. Mitsie had warned her twice now that if she left the bed, the maids would be cross. Lada didn't understand the connection, but they must be looking out for her safety. Yet, staying in bed hadn't stopped her from tumbling headfirst to the floor a number of times in the past days.

Enni pulled open the iron doors, hiding behind them so as not to be an intrusion on the Palace Administrator's task.

Like a brightly feathered bird stalking out over a high tree limb, the Palace Administrator paraded into the room. Typical robes, worn by all palace servants, appeared elegant and expensive draped over his thin frame. In his hands, accentuated by a golden knob on each end, an intricate scroll hung loosely. Within the missive, the edict resided.

Curious Lada, unbeknownst to the girl herself, appeared all too eager to receive the edict. With hair flowing over her shoulders like moss around a tree and eyes sparkling like the night sky, oblivious onlookers might see a woman in love, rather than a prisoner resigned to her fate.

The Palace Administrator saw a girl anticipating a letter from her beloved. So, too, would other Dragon Tribe servants swear that His Majesty, Dragon Supreme, treated her differently than he had ever treated another woman. Dragon Supreme and an Amaryl Mystic?

None condoned the match. None would express their displeasure, either.

Especially not the Palace Administrator.

With a huff and a clearing of his throat, the Palace Administrator opened the scroll and read. "By order of His Majesty Davorin Astrophel, Dragon Supreme. Lada of Flora Master's Hall is benevolent and gracious. Her just actions have pleased Dragon Supreme. Because she has proven herself compassionate and useful, Lada of Flora Master's Hall is hereby granted permission to enter any public space within Isonpool Palace, with the exception of those outside the walls. None should prohibit her within the Palace."

The Palace Administrator folded the scroll in half, stepped forward, and held it aloft toward Lada.

Lada clapped her hands together, already planning all the ways she would explore. "He truly means it?"

"Do you think I would deliver a false edict?" The Palace Administrator answered testily.

Generous? Benevolent? Compassionate? The girl before him barely had a brain. How she had managed to seduce Dragon Supreme, no one could say. Least of all the Palace Administrator. If Dragon Supreme knew what was good for him—for the kingdom— he would put her aside and marry someone more worthy of the title Dragon Queen.

"I can explore anywhere in the palace?" Ecstatic Lada didn't notice the sarcasm emanating from the Palace Administrator's every pore.

"Except the private areas such as other residents' chambers." The Palace Administrator jutted his chin toward the edict hovering in his hands midair. "Are you going to accept His Majesty's orders?"

"Oh. Yes!" Lada snatched the edict and clutched it to her chest, as she might cradle a baby bird with a broken wing. "Thank you."

The Palace Administrator forewent the bow he usually gave to the recipient of an edict. Lada of Flora Master's Hall was nothing more than a piece of Tribute. Posing as the Orafel Bride should have earned her the death penalty. Instead, Dragon Supreme had offered her access to the palace. Lest he question his sovereign monarch, the Palace Administrator ended his inner complaints there.

Lada may not have paid any mind to the crusty man with a chip on his shoulder, but the Orafel maids were less likely to trust those around Lada. As they always did, Mitsie, Sina, and Enni shared a silence each understood to mean they would discuss it later. Lady Lada didn't take kindly to discussing others in a negative light, even when they deserved the criticism. It was part of her charm, something the Orafel maids wouldn't taint for the world. A naivete that must be sheltered lest it crumble and break the woman holding onto it.

"Mitsie?" Lada held out the edict as an explanation. "May we go exploring now?"

Since Lada had been given permission to be out and about, Mitsie saw no real reason to keep her cooped up in the room. As always, Lada had never complained, but the Orafel maids saw the dissatisfaction in her features. Lada had been raised in a forest. To imprison her within four walls seemed cruel, especially to those who knew her love of freedom.

"We will have to dress you, first," Mitsie conceded.

Lada threw her arms wide, ready to allow anything if it meant leaving the room. "Finish your tasks quickly, then."

A squirming, wiggling Lada did not make for an easy completion of the morning's preparations. Excitement bubbled out of her like a spring from the ground, bursting forth with all the fanfare of a fountain. Like a caged bird finally able to breathe freedom again, Lada could hardly sit still for Sina to apply medicine to her healing back.

With delicate handling and a few soft scoldings, the Orafel maids eventually managed to treat Lada's wounds, fasten her hair with simple combs, and pull a dress over her head.

Mitsie pulled the last corset lacing tight and tied the ribbons.

Lada shot toward the door without another moment's hesitation.

Shoes? Forgotten as always. Lada didn't care what others thought of her, a mindset not a single maid understood. In a place such as Isonpool Palace, it mattered what others thought. Their thoughts would determine their actions. If Lada wanted to survive, someone had to watch over her. The Orafel maids were convinced it would never be His Majesty, Dragon Supreme, doing the protecting. Thus, they took the responsibility upon their own shoulders.

Lada stopped briefly in the hall, debating which direction she wanted to flee.

In the end, it was the word "flee" itself that made her decision for her. The curiosity that had rested dormant in her mind sprang forward with the force of a storm's wind. Her course set, Lada skipped down the hall in the general direction of the indoor courtyard.

Enni, the only maid without her hands full, hastened after Lada. She knew not Lada's plan, nor if Lada even had a plan, but she intended to keep an eye on her lest something happen. Their history with the Dragon Tribe servants did not bode well for Lada's excursion.

This time, the halls didn't seem as ominous, nor the servants as murderous. A royal edict had been passed down. They may dislike Lada of Flora Master's Hall, but the servants would not disobey Dragon Supreme.

Even if someone dared, Lada's guards had taken it upon themselves to keep an eye on her location. Not because Dragon Supreme had asked it, but because they had witnessed firsthand the innocence of their charge. Unbelievable as it seemed, Lada of Flora Master's Hall treated everyone in the same way. Her nature would not abide well within Dragon Tribe, but her safety must be kept. Their jobs and their lives depended on it. Therefore, the guards assigned to her door followed the Amarylite and her cautious Orafel maid down the halls.

To outsiders, the group's sporadic timing would have appeared coincidental. To those watching closely, the intent was obvious. The servants who noticed kept a wide berth, skirting around Lada of Flora Master's Hall as if she carried a plague into their midst. Those who didn't notice her entourage sufficed with sneers and whispers, lest they be accused of disobeying Dragon Supreme's wishes.

Lada, intent on finding her way, tuned out every stare she received. Instead, she focused on remembering. She had run in a panic that day, but that didn't mean she couldn't remember what had happened. Lada had been blessed with a superior memory. This time proved no different, as she managed to direct herself to the crossroads she had stopped at before. If she remembered correctly...

A screech from down the hall momentarily distracted Lada from her mission.

An untrained ear would certainly hear the cries of a woman who had encountered trouble and sought help. To a more experienced ear such as Lada's, that possibility didn't exist. Only a bird made such a cry, too high and tinny to be human. Lada hadn't seen a single woodland creature since arriving on the mountain.

Thrilled, but hesitant to believe what she had heard, Lada turned in the sound's direction.

In a fortuitous turn of events, the hall opened into the same courtyard she had visited on the night of her escape. In the brighter light of daytime, Lada made out more details of the room.

Like the fountain in the center. The sparkling tile adorning the floor. The painted glass windows telling stories high above her head.

Another screech jerked Lada's attention to the climbing vines that should have housed leaves and flowers. Instead, all that remained were brown ropes clinging to the walls as their last hope of revival. And, from atop them, another screech warbled to the ground.

Lada craned her neck to see the creature, unlike any she had experienced in her forest. A bird, indeed, but void of the vibrant colors found in Amaryl Forest. This screeching bird sported only black, save for the blood red eyes glaring down at the servant girl near the dead wall of vines.

"Come down!" the servant girl commanded, giving a tug to the leather string in her hand.

The bird screeched again, lifting one foot to strike the end of the leather string tied around its other foot.

"Now!" the servant girl shrieked back at it. "I swear, if you were my bird, I would as soon kill you as go through this torture." This time, the tug she gave sent the bird careening off the vine and flying across the room.

Only Lada saw the way the leather string wrapped around a portion of vines and hauled the bird back in.

"Stop." Lada scurried across the courtyard before the servant girl made another mistake.

"It's none of your business," the girl shot back, raising her hand to give another tug.

Lada reached out and swatted at her hand, as a mother would reprimand a child. The leather string gave way, falling out of the servant girl's fingers and out of her reach as the bird flitted higher.

"You can't treat him like that," Lada admonished.

"I'll treat him how he ought to be treated. I'm in charge of Dragon Supreme's hunting bird, not you." The servant girl looked down at her hand as though Lada had committed a grave sin. "Who are you to strike me? I should—"

The servant girl raised the same hand to strike.

Enni threw herself in front of Lada, intending to take the blow.

A guard from Lada's door caught the servant girl's arm before she could lash out. "I suggest you stop as you were told."

"Why should I? I've never seen her before in my life. She's disrespecting my appointment as an Aviary—"

"This is Lada of Flora Master's Hall," the guard intoned.

The magic words silenced the entire courtyard. Servants who had arrived to check the commotion now turned and fled as if a disease had arrived. A woman capable of garnering Dragon Supreme's protection could do far more damage than a loosed bird. That knowledge did not stop a select few from hovering in the nearby halls. A fight had been picked, between Lada and the Aviary Mistress. No one in Dragon Tribe could resist a good fight.

The aviary servant sneered at the small woman before her. "I don't care who you are, you are not allowed to interfere with my work. You aren't the Dragon Queen."

"Your work, as you call it, is about to maim the poor creature." Lada pouted up toward the bird, caring little for the servant girl who thought she knew everything.

"You don't get a say in it." The servant girl folded her arms across her chest. "This bird belongs to Dragon Supreme and I was specially assigned to look after it. Will you face his wrath for loosing the bird?"

"Will you face his wrath for disfiguring it?" Lada shot it back without much thought, her full attention up at the top of the winding brown vines.

The black bird had stopped it's screeching, in part helped by the lack of screaming from below. Now it sat still, save the flapping of its wings and the fidgeting of its foot in an attempt to remove the leather string.

"Wrath or no wrath, the bird is loose now and unlikely to be recaptured when it sits so high." The servant girl tossed her head haughtily. "Take responsibility for your actions."

Lada didn't reply, busy studying the structure of the dying vines before her.

Instead, Enni took a step toward the servant. "You mustn't speak to Lady Lada like that. Mind your tone."

"My rank is higher than a Tribute Piece, surely. Let her mind her own tone and take the responsibility she owes. Tell Dragon Supreme it was your doing."

"No need to fret," Lada assured gently. "I will free the bird for you."

"He's at the top of the wall. How do you propose to bring him down? Poke him with a stick?"

"Climb the vines, of course."

"Climb? You want me to *climb* the sacred Wistning vines?"

Lada nodded. "It's the only way to free him."

Oblivious to the servant girl's growing ire, Lada's mind thought only of how to rescue the creature tied up in leather constraints. Had Lada taken the time to give the servant girl a secondary thought, she might have noticed the red of her face or the anger in her eyes. If not for the guards attending Lada, the servant girl might have lashed out.

Instead, the servant girl saw the opportunity for the intrusive woman to seal her own demise.

The servant girl's wave toward the vines invited innocent Lada to proceed. "If it can be done, do it."

To Lada, this was the best option. The servant girl had been tasked with the bird, but she didn't seem to like him. Birds were sensitive creatures, responding to their handlers' moods in dramatic fashion. To treat the creature thusly out of her own frustration had been a selfish and ill-thought action on the servant girl's part.

The dying vines before her appeared sturdy enough. Lada had climbed plenty of things in the forest. Without much thought, Lada stepped forward, tucking her skirt into her waistband.

"Lady Lada, you cannot!" Enni leaped forward, grasping Lada's arm to stop her mistake.

The Orafel maids had heard of the Wistning vines since their arrival. Few had permission to touch them. Fewer had the audacity. The vines belonged to the Supreme Family and without their permission, it could be seen as a rebellious act to touch them.

Lada, on the other hand, cared not about rebellions or permission. A bird danced anxiously atop the Wistning vines. If she did not assist the poor creature, Lada would be rejecting her own inherent traits. In her forest, not a single piece of moss would be left alone when it struggled to survive. She could not let the bird be in pain or agony, no matter the protocols surrounding Isonpool Palace.

Lada gently put aside Enni's hand, offering but a smile and a few reassuring words. "He will not harm me."

She could be referring to anyone and anything, but Lada knew Enni's fear. The Orafel Maids all lived in fear of Dragon Supreme's rage. Mitsie had all but begged Lada to stop antagonizing His Majesty, though Lada had no idea how she had antagonized him, to begin with.

Despite all their trepidation, Lada knew one thing to be true. Dragon Supreme would not harm her. He couldn't, if he wanted to remain healthy himself. The effects would not last forever, and Lada should begin to consider returning to her homeland, but for now those things would wait. For now, she would be safe.

Before anyone else stopped her, Lada latched onto the vines, set a bare foot between two branches, and pulled upward. Metal and leather clanked and creaked as the guards from her door took startled steps forward, but Lada paid them no mind. If they dragged her away, she would find a reason to return to help the bird.

A broken piece of vine accosted Lada's wrist as she progressed upward. It broke through her skin and stung like a wasp, yet Lada continued her climb. Up, up the wall. Foot over foot and hand over hand, until she reached the height of the magnificent stained-glass windows near the ceiling.

The bird squawked at her, snapping his bill testily.

Lada found her footing, wrapped an arm around the vines to steady herself, and relaxed. "Good morning to you, too."

Another squawk, this one with a shake of the poor bird's captured talon.

"Yes, it must be terribly uncomfortable," Lada sympathized. "It's heartless of your handler to be angry at you, when your own entrapment may not be your fault."

The bird ruffled his feathers, but made no more obnoxious or angry noises.

"Oh, my deepest apologies." Lada swung on the vine to better position herself for a bow of her head. "I forgot to make introductions. My name is Lada. I don't come from your tribe, but I've been acquainted with my fair share of birds over the years. If I may say, you are quite majestic, kind friend."

Man or beast, none below could fathom why a girl would speak in such a way to a bird. Birds could not be understood, only tamed. If speaking to the bird had a chance of bringing it down, they would have solved their problems long ago. Complimenting the creature had nothing to do with retrieving it from its perch. If they had changed their minds and considered the possibility of communicating with the bird, perhaps those below would have possessed Lada's confidence about freeing it.

Heedless to those watching, Lada lifted her free hand to show it to the black bird. Its red eyes studied her fingers with an intensity she had only seen from Dragon Supreme.

"I think it's time to loose you, don't you?" Lada reached for the tangled leather string. "I'll be gentle, but please remain still. If you move, it might make it worse."

An understanding squawk echoed against the vaulted ceiling.

Lada leaned closer, inspecting the knot closely before she made her first move. Knots weren't difficult to untangle, so long as one took the time to understand how they had been created.

Slip, pull, tug. Lada one-handedly worked out the knot in the leather string, in the process untying it from the bird's foot. The leather string, itself, she looped around the back of her neck.

"You're free. Shall we go down now?"

Lada took firm hold of the vines again, loosened one foot, and started back the way she had come. In a surprising twist of fate, at least for those observing, the bird followed her. One branch at a time, he hopped down the vines alongside Lada. From the top, to the middle.

"Where is she?" came the demand from one of the entryways into the courtyard.

Lada, recognizing the voice immediately, leaned back to better see his entrance. "Hello, Your Majesty!"

As always, Dragon Supreme remained emotionless despite the situation. His coming had little to do with coincidence and much more to do with the scratch that had appeared around his wrist. Having wondered what possible dangers Lada encountered within the first two hours of her permitted exploring, Dragon Supreme had come investigating. Just in case.

He hadn't expected to find her halfway down the Wistning vines, which meant at some point she had been at the top. The headache beginning at the base of his skull had nothing to do with the bond between him and the Little Florist.

"Please be careful, My Lady," Enni entreated from below.

The guards on either side of her echoed the sentiment with anxious nods.

"They're just vines," Lada laughed.

As if they had heard her and taken offense to what she said, the vines shifted beneath her. Lada, skilled climber that she was, lost her footing and handhold all together. With a screech echoed by the bird following her, Lada went tumbling toward the stone floor. She expected to hit the ground and injure herself.

What she expected never happened.

Oh, Lada landed below, but beneath her palms sat something pliable yet firm. Her fingers took hold of something decidedly fabric, her face buried against the same. Inch by inch, Lada raised her eyes to stare up at the visage of a disinterested but perturbed Dragon Supreme.

"You caught me?" her voice came out small and uncertain, as it always did when he took her by surprise.

Dragon Supreme raised his brows. "I can't have you dying."

Lada knew the words to be fact, but she took pride in knowing Dragon Supreme himself had cared enough to stop her fall. If he hadn't cared, the guards would have stepped in. He didn't have to make it personal.

A flutter of Lada's heart went unnoticed by the woman, herself. It would be much later that she remembered the beginning of her feelings. In the moment, she knew nothing.

With one arm firmly cradling Lada's waist and the other supporting her legs, Dragon Supreme turned to the group of servants and guards standing around. "Who allowed her to climb the vines?"

"Begging My Lord's pardon," Enni spoke up hesitantly, "but we couldn't have stopped her if we tried."

"I doubt that." Dragon Supreme set Lada on her feet, noticing the way her fingers slowly released their grip on his robes. The way her balance wobbled before she stood straight. Knowing he wouldn't get a straight answer from Lada, Dragon Supreme continued to question the servants. "Why did she climb them?"

"The bird wouldn't come down, My Lord," one of the guards answered.

"Bird?"

In response, the black bird circled above Dragon Supreme and came to rest on the monarch's shoulder.

Dragon Supreme inspected his bird for a moment before he finally understood the situation. "Who was in charge?"

The servant girl timidly lifted a hand.

"Oh, it isn't her fault," Lada insisted suddenly. "The bird had gotten this twisted around the vines." Quickly, Lada retrieved the leather string from around her neck and held it out.

"As an Aviary Mistress, you should have climbed the vines yourself instead of letting a Tribute Treasure do your work." Dragon Supreme snatched the leather string and threw it at the servant girl. "Dismissed. I will return him to his coop."

"Yes, My Lord." The servant girl went scuttling out, thankful she had not been more severely punished.

Dragon Supreme turned his attention to the Amarylite before him. "This is Belu, my scouting bird. I suppose I owe you thanks for saving my trusted battle companion."

"Belu." Lada rose up on tiptoe, craning her neck to be closer to Belu. "It's very nice to meet you, Belu."

Lada had no idea the consequences to her actions. Dragon

Supreme, stoic on the outside, found himself studying her closely for the first time. Lada was not ugly, nor ungraceful. She simply focused too intently on one thing, which often led to her own clumsiness. Davorin had never met someone like her before, and it confounded him how she still acted this way after all he had done to her. Her kindness would be the death of her, one day.

Belu abandoned Dragon Supreme's shoulder in favor of Lada's. Davorin would have stopped the bird, but Lada accepted its company with such familiarity that he wanted nothing more than to understand how she had become friends with the creature so quickly. He dared not ask aloud, lest he sound interested. Lada of Flora Master's Hall would be his guide into Amaryl. Then he would put her aside. He had already made such a decision.

Lada, having not the talent of reading minds, cooed and coddled Belu before she turned back to Dragon Supreme. "Thank you for saving me."

Dragon Supreme signaled his bird, which obediently flew back to him. "As I said, I cannot have you dying."

Then, both Dragon Supreme and Lada at a loss for words, the two turned separate ways to resume their day. Neither saw the other look back in bewilderment. If they had, perhaps the future would have looked a bit brighter.

CHAPTER FORTY-FIVE

Firesbreadth Hall

ash wounds healed better when one listened to the mystic herbalist, Davorin found. Her prescription gave him great relief from the usual pain of his skin knitting itself back together. A blessing in disguise, which had come only because she had mentioned mothers. Davorin knew the pain of losing one's mother, and a brief glimpse of compassion had stirred in his long-dead heart.

However, with the news of a lost battle circulating and the end-of-year festivities closing in, Davorin Astrophel found he had no time to worry about the bond lingering between him and Lada. Such denial and avoidance only lasted until briefly after Nerys's apology.

As the first period of peace had fled, so too did this one. Lada of Flora Master's Hall could only be peaceful when bedridden. The moment she exited her bed, her clumsiness began. Which, in turn, triggered Davorin's annoyance.

Her first few tumbles were merely headaches, in the literal sense. Davorin disliked the throbbing of various points on his skull, but having handled far worse he ignored it. Then came the inevitable.

Dragon Supreme realized the edict setting her loose within the palace was a risky ploy. He had calculated the dangers when he sent the order. Unfortunately, he hadn't foreseen into what level of danger Lada would thrust herself.

Davorin had, mercifully, been alone in the library when the scratch appeared. If not for his knowledge of the bond between he and Lada, he might have thought the book in his hands had reached out to cut him. On closer inspection, Davorin found familiar markings along the ridge of opened skin. He had injured himself on the vines enough times to know their fury.

Dragon Supreme hadn't expected to find Lada saving his Battle Scout, nor had he expected her to be pleased to see him. In all his years, Davorin hadn't seen a woman climb the vines, but Lada had always surprised him.

Just as surprising was how the feeling of her weight in his arms and her head buried in his chest awoke something that Davorin dared not look into. Such weaknesses could not be afforded. For those reasons, and for the purpose of keeping his distance, Davorin parted ways uncomfortably.

He regretted not doing anything about Lada's klutzy tendencies. Calm always came before the fiercest storms.

At times when Dragon Supreme had nearly forgotten the bond, Lada chose kitchen excursions. Burns and abrasions lit upon Davorin's skin like a pox, each worse than the one before. Always, he reached the end of his patience, resulting in the simple question of, "Where is she?"

Cadfael never failed to understand what he meant, nor did he fail to answer accordingly.

"Where is she?" Davorin asked after he gifted Lada a box of inexpensive jewels.

She had spilled the box and promptly tripped herself up. A sprained wrist and ankle, as well as a variety of cuts and scratches on her palms and cheek had promptly appeared on Dragon Supreme's body.

On a particularly rainy day, she had ventured to the outer court-yard, knocked over a boulder, and nearly crushed herself to death. The question had been more panicked that day.

Weeks went on. Davorin and Lada fell into a sort of routine. Separate during the day, dinner in the evening.

Bit by bit, Dragon Supreme learned tidbits of information about Amaryl. About the fog that kept outsiders away. About the rituals of daily life in Flora Master's Hall. Lada always seemed sad after speaking of Amaryl. Dragon Supreme cared little so long as he received what he sought from his guide.

And, bit by bit, he did receive what he sought. The gifts Cadfael insisted on giving worked wonders on the girl, when mixed with her kind nature. It appeared Lada of Flora Master's Hall took kindness for granted, believed it came out of good intentions.

Dragon Supreme merely failed to mention that he saw things a different way. His kindness came out of necessity and deep-rooted trickery. Or so he told himself.

Perhaps because of this very lie, Dragon Supreme deserved the pain that went shooting through the soles of his feet during a late after-noon court session. A pain so intense that Dragon Supreme clenched his fingers around the edge of his throne in an effort to keep the surprise and agony from his features.

The ministers, preoccupied by their petitions and agendas, did not notice. Why would they, when all stared at Dragon Supreme's face to try to determine how he would answer?

"Beshotan has repeatedly advanced upon not only our borders, but the borders of outlying nations," an older minister continued his speech. "I think it may be best that Your Majesty, Dragon Supreme, pays the borders a visit of his own."

An important topic, but not a topic Dragon Supreme wished to focus on. Forming words at all, when given the state of his throbbing feet, would be difficult. Making such a decision would require more mental stamina than he could muster.

Thus, Dragon Supreme used his most diplomatic approach. "A visit to the borders, made by Dragon Supreme himself. What a... *unique* idea. I will consider this carefully. Is that all?"

Please, let that be all, rang the entreaty from the depths of Dragon Supreme's soul. So loudly did it ring that the ministers realized the meeting had come to a close, with or without their permission.

Dragon Supreme gave them no more time to tarry. "Dismissed," he growled.

Slowly and hesitantly, the Ministers filed out of Fang-Throne Court. Not a word did Dragon Supreme utter nor a movement did he make until the last minister had crossed over the threshold and disappeared down the outer hall. Only then did he duck his head and intake a breath so sharply it caught Cadfael's attention.

"My Lord?" Cadfael stepped closer, suddenly aware of the situation.

Dragon Supreme clenched his fingers tighter around the throne's edge. "*Where... is she?*"

"I will ask the Shadows immediately." Cadfael turned on his heel and went racing toward the door.

At Cadfael's command, backed by Dragon Supreme, a unique and silent network of spies went to work to compile their report on the tribute woman's whereabouts. It took no time at all, as the network of Shadows constantly had an eye on Lada of Flora Master's Hall. They had been given an order. Only death would stop their following through.

Yet another sharp pain tore through the soles of Dragon Supreme's feet. The agony of torn flesh brought a gasp from Dragon Supreme's lips. Such suffering, and yet it continued? The Little Florist sought to antagonize him.

"My Lord, Dragon Supreme." Cadfael returned, bowing respectfully from his position at the bottom of the dais. "The Shadows saw Lady Lada venturing toward Firesbreadth Hall."

Cadfael and Dragon Supreme, both, realized Cadfael had taken up the form of address that the Orafel maids used for Lada. Neither bothered to speak of it, both preoccupied with the danger at hand.

Dragon Supreme rose from his throne, bent and hobbling. It had been years since any had inflicted such harm upon him.

"Take me to her."

Cadfael need not lead the way. Dragon Supreme knew the halls of his palace by heart. They had, after all, been his home for decades. What child of Isonpool Palace would need a guard to guide him through his own house? Dragon Supreme took Cadfael along as a countermeasure, lest he lose his temper once more in regards to the Little Florist.

Lately, the entire palace knew that Dragon Supreme and Lada of Flora Master's Hall had been tolerating each other quite well. Though Dragon Supreme showed no favoritism for the spritely woman, neither had he put her in danger or threatened to have her head. In the eyes of the Dragon Tribe people and servants, Dragon Supreme could show no greater kindness.

Little did they know the truce resided in a tentative state, at best. Lada had come to trust Dragon Supreme over the past weeks, seeing in him a kindness that no one else saw.

Dragon Supreme knew how to present himself as others wanted him to be. Lada responded to kindness, and the bond remained between them. Thus, Dragon Supreme treated her well in hopes of accomplishing his own goal.

No one anticipated the snapping of all the ties that had been carefully crafted between the two.

Especially not Dragon Supreme, as he hastened through doorways and porticoes, seeking the imp that haunted his home.

They found her where the Shadows had said she would be.

Firesbreadth Hall had only two reasons for existing. The first, to provide passage to the castle's farthest reaches. The second, to house the entrance to Davorin's personal quarters.

The corridor's importance stood out from others. As such, its floor had been carefully crafted from the finest lava rock extracted from the center of the mountain. Within the rock, ferociously embedded, a billion shards of shimmering glass created a sea of destruction, should one not wear shoes blessed with a proper leather sole. And there, in the middle of it all, a spirited hobgoblin ran her fingers over brown and dying vines as if her touch alone could heal them.

Davorin stopped to stare, not because he found her in the hall outside his door, but because of what she wore.

Only once before had he seen the outfit in such a decent condition. Lada of Flora Master's Hall had arrived at his palace wearing the godawful cloud of yellow and pink. The dress's volume stood out twice as wide as Lada, making her appear more fairy fallen to earth than devil ready to annihilate Dragon Tribe. Davorin had thought the dress ruined after Lada's excursion to the dungeons. The Orafel maids could work miracles with the laundry, if it remained in such pristine condition. Dragon Supreme made a note to force them to throw it out.

Regaining his composure, Dragon Supreme took stock of the rest of the situation. Lada of Flora Master's Hall appeared unscathed, at first glance. Until Davorin noted the hem of the dress he hated. A hem that tore against the lava rock and glass. A hem that bore a suspicious red-brown color in its tatters.

Knowledge dawned on him like the sun crowning the mountain's peak. Furious and, admittedly, concerned, Davorin stormed forward into the shadowy corridor.

Lada looked over at the sound of boots and anger, her lips turning up into a courteous smile. "Your Majesty, what brings you to—"

Ignoring her earnest attempt to spark conversation, Dragon Supreme squatted beside her and wrapped a hand in the light-but-cumbersome layers of fabric near Lada's legs. A tug lifted it high enough to see the problem. As always, Lada of Flora Master's Hall had refused to wear her shoes.

Davorin used his free hand to lift Lada's foot from the floor. As he suspected, it was covered in gashes and welts, all covered in the brown and red of Lada's own lifeblood.

"Fool girl," Davorin muttered, meaning to keep it to himself. Yet he had words to say to her, a crossness that required him to make it known to Lada. "Do you never think of the wounds you inflict upon yourself?"

Davorin, of course, had no way of knowing how his actions made Lada's heart flutter. Nor of how his clear concern for her safety changed Lada's opinion of him, ever so slightly. No longer was Dragon Supreme a selfish and twisted monster in Lada's eyes, for she had seen him capable of kindness. She meant to encourage such behavior in the future. If indeed a future existed between them.

Lada knew not how to tell Davorin Astrophel, Dragon Supreme, that she had not felt her feet breaking apart upon the rock and glass beneath them. So intent had she been on following the trail of the vines, nothing else had registered.

Even if she had found the words to explain, Lada would never have had time.

Dragon Supreme rose to his full height, dropping Lada's skirt in favor of scooping her up into his arms.

With a gasp, Lada reached out her hands to seek a handhold. One landed around the collar of Dragon Supreme's robe, the other buried into his sleeve.

Dragon Supreme, unimpressed and mostly unaffected by the slight woman in his arms, gave a single heft to resituate her, turned on his heel, and marched out of Firesbreadth Hall.

None saw the Shadow creeping along behind them, keeping an eye on the woman under their care. None noticed Cadfael, either, as he went ahead to prepare bandages and salve.

The grander sight, foreign to even those who had worked in Isonpool Palace for many years, was the sight of Dragon Supreme effortlessly carrying a woman in his arms. With a posture so excellent and his regal head held high, Dragon Supreme had no idea the image he portrayed was one of a lover caring for his beloved. The thought never crossed his mind.

But it crossed the minds of every servant who saw the duo traipsing through the halls. In a matter of minutes, the rumor had started. The Amaryl Mystic had bewitched their sovereign. When she injured herself, their monarch had lowered himself to the role of a servant to see to her needs.

Lada fidgeted, aware of the servants glaring at her, but she knew better than most she could not escape Dragon Supreme's hold. Strength had always been an advantage of Dragon Tribe. Lada wondered if Dragon Supreme knew his own.

In truth, Davorin had acted without thinking. A deep, lost instinct within him had taken over and commanded he not allow Lada any further suffering.

Davorin covered the instinct with the excuse of his own feet. He told himself that after the bond had been destroyed, he would get rid of the Amarylite maiden. But none, not even Dragon Supreme, knew if he would be able to discard her.

By the time the couple reached Lada's chambers and allowed the iron door to slam shut, the damage had been done. If the previous rumors weren't enough to start a war among the servants, this one would certainly do the trick.

Surprisingly, not a maid appeared to welcome them into Lada's chambers.

The Orafel maids had duties, all of which had been laid aside in favor of searching out their missing lady. If only they had known how far she had gone, they wouldn't have needed to search so diligently in her usual haunts.

Davorin bypassed Cadfael, who had arrived with bandages, to set Lada on the edge of her bed. The friction between her skirt and the blankets caused a rustling of fabric that echoed overhead. Davorin ignored it in favor of taking a knee beside Lada and reaching for the heinous skirt covering her abused feet.

"Your Majesty," Lada began, "are you—"

Davorin gave the skirt a yank, tearing it through the middle.

"—angry?" The final word came out in a sheepish whisper.

Lada hadn't meant to upset Dragon Supreme. He so rarely appeared when she went exploring. She had thought he wouldn't know she had left her room. If all had gone according to plan, she meant to gift him a way to save the vines when she saw him at dinner. Nothing had gone according to plan.

In her effort to please him, Lada had unknowingly angered him instead.

Davorin took stock of Lada's feet, bruised and battered from their ordeal in Firesbreadth Hall. Removing his shoes to check his own wounds would be futile. Davorin knew they would mirror those upon Lada's feet.

"Little Florist, are you determined to use the bond to inflict pain upon me?"

Of course, with Lada's personality, she hadn't thought that far ahead. Her entire focus had been on the vines. "I didn't mean to harm you."

"What did you think would happen, after injuring yourself this badly?" Davorin, exasperated, raised his eyes to stare her down. Such wounds didn't appear painlessly. "What happened?"

Lada thought the answer quite obvious, but she knew what Dragon Supreme meant by his question. Embarrassed, Lada wrung her fingers in the part of her dress still intact. "I wanted to locate the source of the palace vines. If I find their root, it might be possible to save them."

Dragon Supreme listened, but heard no explanation in what she said. Therefore, he remained silent, waiting, hoping to hear the end of the story.

Lada didn't disappoint. "You see, I have a problem. When I focus on one thing, I think only of what I'm focusing on. So, when I set my sights on helping your poor, sick vines, I forgot to pay attention to my surroundings."

"Do you mean," Davorin asked as softly as he had ever asked anything, "you did not realize your feet were torn and bleeding?"

Were that possible, surely Dragon Supreme would have heard of such things. He had seen the world. He had seen war, his first battle fought when he had only survived ten winters. Dragon Supreme knew of truths that others thought to be myths. Yet, he had never met a creature quite like Lada of Flora Master's Hall. For that reason, only, her excuse rang sincerely in Davorin's ears.

If he hadn't seen her in action, Davorin would never have believed it.

"Did you believe I did this on purpose?" Lada asked, no trace of malice or defensiveness in her voice.

In fact, her voice sang gently in a way that made Davorin Astrophel, Dragon Supreme, feel a twinge of guilt for doubting her in the first place. Could it be that she never meant to hurt him, as she had said?

Naive thoughts came from naive people. If Lada of Flora Master's Hall believed he had decided to be good to her for the sake of kindness itself, she was indeed naive. But, for that matter, he had already decided to use her naivete to his own advantage. If he kept her safe, warm, and healthy, Lada of Flora Master's Hall would surely grant him what he wanted in return.

Soon, Dragon Supreme mused, he would have the key to enter Amaryl Tribe's borders.

"I didn't do it on purpose."

Davorin, unable to find any comforting words that he felt able to say, gave his head a shake. "You shouldn't have ventured into Firesbreadth Hall."

"My Lord," Cadfael interrupted to extend a handful of medical supplies. A jar of salve. Cloths to cover the wounds.

Dragon Supreme knew how to manipulate a war, how to win a battle, but Cadfael had more experience with the fairer sex. It had been Cadfael, after all, who had graced Lada with dresses in the name of his master. The way to a woman's heart was fragile, but clear. Dragon Supreme had no light hand, but he had Cadfael to pave his way. If not for the foundation of kindness Cadfael had laid, Lada of Flora Master's Hall might hold more suspicion toward Davorin Astrophel.

Cadfael felt no shame in helping his lord and master achieve his ultimate goal.

Dragon Supreme, though he would never admit it, felt a twinge of something sharp and nagging near his heart.

Choosing to ignore the glimmer of a conscience he had left, Dragon Supreme took the supplies from Cadfael's hands.

Over the past months, Dragon Supreme had recognized the importance Lada placed on kindness. To allow Cadfael this golden opportunity would be a waste. In order for Lada of Flora Master's Hall to willingly give him what he wanted, Dragon Supreme needed to be in her good graces. Bandaging her feet—which must ache and sting—would be a marvelous inroad toward winning Lada's favor. Anyone in the entire nation of Qranbu, throughout every household of Dragon Tribe, would fall to their knees under the weight of the immense honor of Dragon Supreme stooping low enough to give them aid.

Lada, who didn't understand Dragon Tribe and had never succumbed to any expected reaction, stared at the top of Dragon Supreme's head as he wrapped her wounded feet. To Lada, the action appeared sincere, as if he felt sorry for the suffering she went through because of the vines.

"I really didn't mean to injure myself." Lada's explanation revealed nothing new to Davorin. "I'm sorry."

The apology came unbidden and fell like coals atop Davorin's head. Dragon Supreme heard apologies all the time. He lived for the moment when his prey begged before him. Lada of Flora Master's Hall, on the other hand, announced her apology with such sincerity that it rendered Dragon Supreme momentarily speechless.

"Please, don't be angry."

As quickly as the apology had stunned him, Lada's request revived his senses. Anger, Dragon Supreme knew well. It embraced him as closely as his mother had held him as a babe.

"Fool woman," Dragon Supreme hissed. "How can you not feel it when you're being torn asunder?"

Lada pouted, unaware of the purse of her lips or the tears in her eyes. "I told you. I tend to focus too intently. It's a problem of mine."

"Don't do it again."

"It's difficult for me to have a say in such matters."

Dragon Supreme raised his eyes to glare up at her. "It affects my ability to perform my duties."

"Oh." Lada folded her hands neatly in her lap, prepared to promise the world for the sake of niceness. "I will try my best to remember where I tread."

"Tread with shoes on."

"I don't like shoes." Lada slumped where she sat, all semblance of posture lost to the dejection of having to cover her bare feet.

"Your wounds are my wounds," Davorin reminded her, agitated she didn't understand the premise of his requirements. "You are too easily injured."

The muttered words, tagged on as the thought came to Dragon Supreme's mind, hadn't been meant for Lada to hear. Unfortunately, Lada's hearing far surpassed that of Dragon Tribe women. She understood each word he said. Or, at least, believed she understood them.

"I'll *try* to wear shoes," Lada huffed. "But I make no guarantees of my success."

It was the first promise Lada offered to Dragon Supreme. The first time she took the initiative to say or do anything with a definitive answer. Davorin took it as a success to hear her say she would attempt something she detested for his sake.

Dragon Supreme decided, rather than do something amiss, he

would not react at all. It was, after all, a sure way to keep the upper hand. He tied the final knot in the bandages around Lada's feet.

Lada studied the bandages on her feet, dismissed the torn skirt of her dress, and tapped a hand on Dragon Supreme's shoulder to get his attention. As he had pointed out earlier, her injuries were also his. He had been so kind as to wrap her wounds. Lada should return the favor.

Dragon Supreme looked up, his eyes catching a ray of sunlight from Lada's open window, and once more Lada swore she saw his pupils turn gold. As quickly as they changed, they returned to their usual black, and Lada moved on to her original purpose.

"Have a seat, Your Majesty. I'll bandage your wounds."

"It isn't necessary," Dragon Supreme protested as he stood. "I've been through many batt—"

Lada leaped to her feet, wincing at the pain in them but ignoring it for the greater purpose of planting her hands on her hips. Her most intimidating stance. "*Have* a *seat*, Your Majesty."

And though both knew Lada pushed every boundary Dragon Supreme had, neither were in the mood to address her rebellious attitude. For the first time, Lada got her way. For the first time, Dragon Supreme obeyed without question what the Little Florist demanded.

CHAPTER FORTY-SIX
Healing Zohana

The aftereffects of Border Fog were nothing to be trifled with. Thus, Valor of Champion's Post did not rush the healing process. This agitated the woman taking refuge in his home, but Valor knew better than to push her too far.

Her wounds had drastically improved after her lucid dreams slowed down. Peace in one's mind created space for peace in one's body. Valor's sole focus had been on calming the woman's mind so her body could heal itself. As it turned out, the process worked. The terrifying effects of border fog could be subdued with the proper medicines and a heaping dose of blind luck.

Destiny must be on the woman's side, for though she slept long and fought arduous dreams, eventually the hallucinations began to fade. The dreams began to subside. It had been days since Valor saw the evidence of night terrors.

Day by day, the woman's body had recovered. Valor hadn't given her a sedative in almost two weeks, and she had managed to sit up on her own during the day prior.

The slow, frustrating process had begun to culminate in her complete restoration. The Orafel woman had passed the first hurdle in her journey toward life.

Valor found himself both relieved and terrified. Because of his conflicting emotions, he lingered too long outside the door of his own residence.

Within, Princess Zohana lay beneath Valor's quilt, concentrating her focus on the desk across the room from her. Every fiber of her being desired to move. Princess Zohana had never rested for so many days in a row. Since young, she had been trained to survive as a wife of Dragon Tribe. Resting didn't rank high among her priorities.

Having lain abed for many more days than she had been awake to count, Zohana could stand it no longer. If her childhood had taught her nothing else, it had taught her to fight.

After her first experience with waking up, Zohana had found more control over her body each time she came to her senses. Yesterday, she had sat awake for hours, silently strengthening her core for the day when she might need to escape. Today, Zohana had other plans.

Limbs and heart shaking like a leaf, Zohana rose and slid her feet to the floor.

She had left innocents behind in order to save them, but Zohana doubted her only friend could survive in Dragon Tribe without a proper patron. Lord Kavindra may have lost his head. Her guards wouldn't be far behind him. If Zohana returned to her place only one day sooner, another life may be saved. Zohana would do anything end the killing.

It was time she learned what kind of dire straits she lay within.

353

Shifting her weight to her feet took enough effort. Forcing her legs to stand was excruciating. Muscles and tendons, dormant for too long, spasmed and complained. Zohana bore it all with the practiced grace of a girl who had fought to stay alive.

Sweat beaded upon her brow with each step—no, with each intent to make a step. Her lungs burned with the exertion of walking. Zohana kept her sole focus on the writing desk. If she reached the desk, she would be one step closer to the door. If she reached the desk, she could take a break.

Five steps. Eight. Zohana clenched her hands at her side, her nails biting into the palms of her hands. Eleven steps.

Crash.

Zohana went down with the force of every inch of her body giving up. Her arms caught the edge of the writing desk, sending scrolls and pens careening to the floor.

But she had made it.

Having heard the commotion, Valor flung open the door.

The sight that greeted him tugged against the strings of his heart, in the perfect rhythm for a mourning ballad.

Hair piled over Zohana's shoulder and pooled between her hands, which were the only things keeping her upright. Her legs shook so violently Valor heard the bones in her knees as they knocked together. Moisture dripped from her chin like tears, though her eyes remained dry. That, Valor expected. Even when she woke in a strange place, without the ability to move herself, this Orafel woman had never cried.

"You shouldn't rush things," Valor chided softly. On instinct, he reached out to help the woman up.

A feeble swing of her arm swatted at his hand. "Don't touch me."

"Ah, you've found your tongue back."

Valor ignored her harsh words in favor of scooping her from the chilly floor. The drafts would not assist her recovery. She had not the strength to fight him and win.

Zohana knew this too. For that reason only, she said no more and did not try to escape the man's grasp.

Valor settled her back on the bed and pulled the blanket over her legs. "Since you can speak now, it's time you and I had a decent conversation."

Zohana agreed wholeheartedly, but her wary personality refused to allow this man the upper hand. Therefore, she asked the first question.

"Where am I?"

Valor stifled his laugh. The Orafel woman would not take kindly to his amusement. In Valor's experience, women other than Lada of Flora Master's Hall had emotions which fluctuated easily.

"We should begin with introductions. My name is Valor. How may I address you?"

Princess Zohana hated losing the upper hand, but Valor phrased his words so nicely that she couldn't stubbornly refuse to speak. Nor could she mention her heritage.

"I am Zohana," she finally answered, omitting her title lest it cause more problems.

"Zohana," Valor repeated. "You are blessed, Zohana of Orafel, for you have regained your life after it was lost to you."

Zohana had never heard it put quite that way before. Regaining life after she had lost it? She didn't know about all that. Fighting had always given her an advantage. Running away had been the coward's way out, but at the time it had been her only choice.

Valor gave Zohana time to think. About what he had said to her. About what she wanted to say to him. Over the years Valor had found that, sometimes, allowing others to process their intentions led to deeper and more meaningful conversations. If he were to extract any truth from the Orafel woman, she would have to give it willingly.

Over the time he gave her, Valor rose to retrieve Zohana's morning medicine. If she did well over the coming days, he would change the prescription to something lighter, but for now Valor held caution toward a resurgence of her illness.

When he had returned to her bedside, Zohana's brow had smoothed out, her chin had lifted, and her shoulders had straightened. Time must have done its duty to her, allowing Zohana to feel comfortable enough to show her stubborn nature.

Valor chuckled to himself. Only those with stubborn natures survived the hallucinations associated with Border Fog. Valor had expected her to be a tenacious woman.

"Your questions can wait a moment longer." Valor settled himself on the bed's edge, holding out the bowl of medicine. "Drink this first."

Zohana bit her tongue to still the harsh words she wanted to spit. Here, she reminded herself, she bore not the authority to act like a spoiled child. If she were to survive, she must adapt, and tear down the guarded walls of her captor's suspicion as well.

As obediently as she could, Zohana retrieved the bowl from Valor's hands. His medicine had not harmed her in all her time there, and thus she trusted it would not harm her now.

Gulp by gulp, the medicine ran down Zohana's throat. Valor watched each swallow with a silent satisfaction. Even if she told him nothing of what had been done to her, she had trusted him enough to continue her medicinal regimen. If nothing else came from their conversation, Valor would still consider it a victory.

"Your wounds," Valor started cautiously, "were not only from the river's turbulence." He dared not to ask what happened unless he needed to be forthright.

Zohana paused, only a swallow of medicine left in the vestiges of her bowl. One last drink of nourishment that would send her on her way toward being whole.

With one swallow, she drank it up. "Thank you for tending them, regardless."

Zohana of Orafel didn't wish to tell him. Valor understood how speaking of trauma to a man she did not know could be a frightening position to a woman. Thankfully, Zohana had given him an olive branch to use to bridge the gap between them.

"When you arrived here, you sought Lada."

Zohana raised her gaze, staring at Valor with all the suspicion and confusion permeating her heart. He uttered the name casually, so familiarly that it appeared he had no doubt about Lada's identity. Few would speak of her with such confidence and, thus, Zohana found her mind spinning with the possibilities of Valor's identity.

Better to play a fool than to give up her only friend to one who might seek her harm.

"When I arrived here, I was as good as dead, you said so yourself." Zohana set the empty bowl aside, then folded her hands atop the blanket on her lap. "What makes you believe anything I said was truthful?"

Valor studied the woman, admiring the way her lies revolved around questions. How her avoidance allowed room for interpretation. She had not answered any of his questions, but she used questions of her own to circumvent his curiosity.

In such a situation, Valor found it necessary to offer a truce. After all, this Orafel woman could do little to harm him and even less to hurt the country to which he swore allegiance.

"I think it's time I show you something." Valor rose to his feet, intending to scoop Zohana up and take her with him.

Zohana held out a hand to stop him, her eyes as tremulous as her fingers. "What are you doing?"

Valor gently took hold of her wrist, lowering her hand back down into her lap. "If I wanted to harm you, I would have done so before now. I've treated you kindly. Won't you offer me the smallest amount of trust in return?"

Trust had failed Zohana in so many ways that she long ago lost count. Since childhood, she had learned the lesson. To trust meant death. To fight meant life. Yet, here and now, a man stood before her wearing the most earnest expression she had ever seen. His hands had treated her wounds and his song had lulled her to sleep. For a brief but infinitesimal moment, Zohana wanted to experience what trust felt like.

So, she gave in.

Valor took the opportunity while it lasted. Zohana couldn't walk on her own, she had not the strength. Thus, he lifted her into his arms and turned for the door, willing to be the legs for both Zohana and himself. When they reached the doors, Valor stopped to speak.

"Allow me to reintroduce myself." Valor kept his voice calm and low, as soothing as possible for the woman who woke in a strange place. "I am Valor of Champion's Post." A light kick sent the door swinging open. Valor stepped into the late morning sunlight. "Welcome to Amaryl."

For the first time, Zohana gazed upon the magnificent expanse beyond Valor's front door.

Trees greeted each other with the warmth and intimacy of a family. Creatures of various shapes and sizes roamed the branches or the moss and grass beneath the residence, unafraid of the open air. The forest sang with the harmony of a thousand living things and there, in the midst of it all, Zohana found herself not an outsider but a new member of nature's choir.

Valor could not take his eyes from the awe washing over Zohana's face. Her eyes glistened with tears in the light of the world around her. Suddenly, Valor looked out upon his homeland with the eyes of one who had never seen it before. Did Orafel not have the things Amaryl cherished? What if Zohana had never seen butterflies or hummingbirds or flowers in their natural habitat? Were those the things that inspired the wonder in her gaze?

A moment later, Zohana returned to her senses. "This is Amaryl?"

"I would not lie." Valor settled Zohana on a stool at his carefully crafted porch table. "You ask yourself why I know the name Lada, do you not?"

Zohana wished not to lie about it. Neither did she wish to admit it aloud. She nodded her head instead.

"Lada of Flora Master's Hall. She is sister, mother, and friend to all of us."

Once upon a time, she may have meant more to Valor than that, but Lada's destiny must stretch farther and wider than anyone knew.

If not for destiny, she would not have gone from her mother's residence. Every Amarylite knew destiny could not be battled against.

Valor's words made sense to Zohana. Even knowing Lada for such a short period of time, Zohana sensed the familial bond she drew from all who ventured near her. Her own people must feel it a thousand times stronger than foreigners.

"It is likely the Tribute Parade took her to Qranbu. It must be there that she remains."

"I know." Valor stoked the fire beneath a pot of Zohana's medicine, scheduled to finish brewing later in the day. "The Elders have sent someone to watch over her. He trailed her as far as the gates of Isonpool Palace."

"She arrived in my stead." Should Zohana allow it, the spiral of blame and guilt would tug her down with it. If she had not acquiesced to the threat made upon the caravan, Lada would have arrived safely back in Amaryl. "I should have done the duty I was prepared to fulfill."

Several puzzle pieces connected in Valor's mind. Zohana had been part of the Tribute and had failed to arrive in Qranbu where she allegedly belonged. If it was her duty to fulfill, then...

"You are the Tribute Bride."

Valor swallowed, recognizing the gravity of the situation. No wonder she had arrived broken and bruised. Someone sent as a bride to a place such as Dragon Tribe... every hallucination Zohana had survived now made sense. They had not been fears or terrors. They had been regrets, memories.

"I must return to my place so Lada can return to hers."

"You cannot leave Amaryl."

Valor and Zohana turned to each other, both startled by the revelation. Zohana, because she rarely met anyone willing to disobey her commands. Valor, because he had not meant to say it aloud.

Valor recovered first. "You have not yet overcome the effects of Border Fog. You cannot venture through it again, perhaps not ever."

"I cannot sit here and do nothing to help. Have you any idea what Dragon Tribe will do to someone like Lada?"

"Have you any idea what Lada will do to Dragon Tribe?" Valor's smile was more pain than mirth. He understood both sides of the situation, and no possibilities held much hope. Not without intervention. "Perhaps you may be of assistance, anyway."

Zohana sat straighter, focused harder. "In what way?"

"You must have trained to enter Dragon Tribe as the bride." Valor reached for a dagger and his current piece of whittling work. "Tell me about Isonpool Palace and those within. We will create a way to rescue Lada."

CHAPTER FORTY-SEVEN
Border News

Davorin Astrophel, Dragon Supreme, inspected the bandage caging his foot for the fortieth time in the last hour. Used to military doctors only, he had only once seen a bandage tied in so pristine a fashion. Dragon Supreme understod, of course, that Lada of Flora Master's Hall knew herbal medicine as well as she knew her own name. Nothing could have prepared him for the way she tied a bandage. Knot tied squarely, ends tucked neatly.

Just like his mother had tied bandages.

Like the only cloth Davorin had tied in such a way. Gently, neatly, firmly around his mother's neck.

Lada couldn't have known, but the coincidence hit Davorin too firmly to ignore it.

A knock on Davorin's study door interrupted his journey down the rabbit hole of self-loathing.

"Enter," Dragon Supreme barked.

Easier than most, Cadfael read Dragon Supreme's mood. Dragon Supreme often used harsh words. More often, he used his blade to speak. Yet, this brand of irritation only came from the scraping of Dragon Supreme's deepest festering wound. The one wound that had taught him never to trust and never to show weakness.

Knowing better than to touch the aching emotional scar, Cadfael stepped into the room prepared to speak of nothing but business.

"My Lord, Dragon Supreme." Cadfael rested his hands in the standard phoenix salute and gave a deep bow. "Another message from the border."

"From General Branko?"

"I'm told this missive arrived at the behest of General Dalibor." Cadfael held out the letter, neatly folded but crumpled from the days spent in a courier's pocket.

Dragon Supreme momentarily set aside his consternation over the clash of past and present. In the line of priorities, the safety of Qranbu's borders came first. Without a strong border, nations crumbled like paper in fire. If only Dragon Supreme's ministers paid attention to such matters instead of obsessing over trivial court politics.

If not for their firm foothold in Dragon Tribe's finest families, Dragon Supreme would get rid of all his ministers posthaste. Longstanding traditions were difficult to overturn, and thus his board of ministers remained.

"My Lord?" Cadfael gave the letter a slight shake to garner Dragon Supreme's attention.

Davorin sighed, a world-weary sound that echoed in the empty study. Without ceremony, he snatched the letter from Cadfael's hands and tore open the seal.

Beshotan again, judging by the words of General Dalibor. It seemed odd, to Dragon Supreme, that Beshotan would work their way along the border without defeating their weakening enemies along the way. Only a few weeks ago, they had won a battle against General Branko. Had they not stayed to finish him? Beshotan's movements did not make sense tactically. In that, Dragon Supreme found the greatest vexation.

"My generals have managed to keep them at bay for now," Dragon Supreme told Cadfael upon seeing the aide's concern. "But I have no patience for the way their military is playing this game."

There were only two reasons for such trickery. Neither boded well for the future. Either left Dragon Supreme with a singular choice.

"I will journey to the border myself."

Cadfael, though surprised at the announcement, dared not argue with Dragon Supreme. He had not said it as an order, but it had been his intent to inform, not to ask permission.

However, Cadfael could not sit back and do nothing. "Leaving Isonpool Fortress will cause quite a stir and allow open space for anyone to attempt to overthrow your throne."

"Which is why you and I will leave secretly."

"Secretly?"

It had been done only once before. Dragon Supreme and Cadfael had been younger and stupider at the time. To leave without informing the ministers or setting a regent in place would backfire on them if discovered.

Dragon Supreme snarled at the question. "If I am to accomplish anything at the border, we must undertake the journey in this way."

"They will notice your absence," Cadfael advised.

Dragon Supreme allowed a slow, lazy smile to snake its way onto his lips. "I have a plan."

A plan that would make Cadfael worry, but a plan that would kill a whole nest of problems with a single stone. Dragon Supreme never moved without a plan, much less so when it involved the safety of his nation. His people. Isonpool Palace had seen too much death. They need not see another war. Nor would Dragon Supreme allow them to lose any more cherished members of the royal family.

This time, Dragon Supreme knew what he must do, both at home and at his border. The journey would not last long, but in order to make his absence invisible, he would have to rely on someone for the first time since his childhood.

CHAPTER FORTY-EIGHT
A Favor to Ask

Ironpool Palace stirred differently after Lada's excursion to Firesbreadth Hall. Nobles visited less often. Servants spoke more frequently. The rumor of Dragon Supreme's involvement with Lada of Flora Master's Hall scattered to the tiniest mouse-hole and rose to the top of the highest vine. And yet, it had only been a day since Lada injured her feet in the corridor.

For one whole day, Lada neither saw nor heard from Davorin Astrophel, Dragon Supreme. Given their recent rapport with one another, Lada found his absence strange. Nary a day went by that Dragon Supreme didn't come searching for clumsy Lada.

Though she remained mostly abed as per the doctor's orders, Lada did manage to trip over a stool twice and her own feet almost a dozen times. The tripping had broken open a number of scabs on her feet. That Dragon Supreme did not come to investigate meant he either cared not, or bad tidings had befallen him.

Lada had begun to suspect the latter as the sun set. If left alone for much longer, she might have gone in search of him.

The Orafel maids recognized her anxiousness. Lada would do as Lada pleased, but none wanted another confrontation with Dragon Supreme. Lada's willfulness was permissible due to her bond with Dragon Supreme. The maids had no such bond. Their lives hung in the balance each time Lada ventured off alone. They prayed she would not do so again.

Their prayers were answered in the form of a knock on the chamber doors.

Lada perked up from her huddled position beneath layers of blankets.

The maids muttered their concerns to one another, choosing one by vote to answer the summons. Enni lost.

Timid, cautious Enni tugged the door open to see the visitor on the other side.

The other maids shuffled closer to hear the words being said.

"...allow us to bring it within."

All the Orafel maids knew the voice by now. The Palace Administrator had come on several occasions, to scold or to deliver messages. Never had he delivered more than words.

"Who is it?" Lada asked from her perch at the far end of the room.

Those who visited her were rare and far between. Add that to Enni's cautiousness, and Lada's curiosity reached the sky.

The Orafel maids, knowing they could not send the Palace Administrator away, sprang into action. Sina moved Enni out of the way while Mitsie took hold of the door and swung it wide.

"Please enter, sir."

The Palace Administrator rolled his eyes, but in an odd turn of events he did not pick an argument with the Orafel maids. A brush of his fly whisk sent Mitsie skittering aside, but his lips remained closed as he breezed into the room.

Behind him, a line of servant girls followed. Each carried a tray laden with the most exquisite dishes. None took time to note the Orafel maids in the corner.

Yet another surprise came behind the servant girls, as a quartet of strong young men hauled a table into the chambers. Not a rickety old one like the tea table in place, but a sturdy wooden dining table with exquisitely intricate carvings.

The hustle and bustle continued as the Dragon Tribe servants removed the tea table and put the dining table in its place. The dishes went atop. From somewhere, a pair of chairs arrived.

The Palace Administrator shooed everyone out. Only he stopped, taking up a position inside the door.

A clearing of his throat. A raising of his chin. And then the announcement, "His Majesty, Dragon Supreme, arrives."

Unused to the pomp and circumstance, Lada merely tipped her head like a bird surveying her surroundings. Dragon Supreme had never come to her in such a manner. Lada wondered if he expected her to react a certain way. If so, he would be disappointed. Lada didn't know how to react to this new state of things, except to enjoy the friendship he offered.

Dragon Supreme's boot landed silently against the floor on the inside of the chamber doors. His robes hardly made a sound, save the swish of silk as it brushed over the threshold.

Lada tore her eyes from the food before her to smile at the Dragon Tribe monarch. "Your Majesty! To what do I owe the honor?"

Davorin's gaze went past the food to land on the bundle of a girl behind the edge of a gauzy curtain. A thousand questions raced through his head. Only one graced his lips.

"Are you ill?"

Lada blinked, trying to decipher why he would ask such a thing of her. A glance down reminded her that no less than three quilts shrouded her from neck to toe.

"Oh. No, I'm not ill. Thank you for inquiring about my health, Your Majesty."

Dragon Supreme had made such progress in the past weeks, Lada mused. When Lada had arrived as the princess instead of herself, Dragon Supreme held no concern or curiosity about anyone other than himself. Now he even observed closely enough to inquire about her health.

Of course, none of those thoughts ever entered Dragon Supreme's mind. He wondered only why Lada of Flora Master's Hall spent so much of her time being obnoxious and unpredictable. After sending a feast of royal proportions, Davorin had expected her to be up and flitting around, full of joy and energy. Instead, he found her hiding beneath blankets so thick she might suffocate.

One way or another, he would have his answers.

"Leave us," Dragon Supreme threw the instruction in the Palace Administrator's general direction.

The Palace Administrator, as per usual, gave an exaggerated huff. He pointed his fly whisk at the Orafel maids. "You heard His Lordship. Off with you!"

"Not them." Dragon Supreme leveled a smoldering glare at his Palace Administrator. "You."

"Me?" The Palace Administrator gaped at his sovereign. "Me?!

Who will be here to look after you? Who will watch after your interests—"

"I am perfectly capable of taking care of myself."

"But for security and propriety—"

"I have Cadfael. The maids are still here. I assure you, I will have no need of your services." That was the final word, thus Dragon Supreme removed his attention from the Palace Administrator and placed it back on the Little Florist. "You refuse to eat?"

"Oh, no, not at all!" Lada fiddled with the blankets, meaning to remove them but only managing to entangle herself further.

"My Lord!" The Palace Administrator interrupted.

As a man who hated insurrection, Dragon Supreme had no tolerance for the rebellious servant behind him. With a growl, he spun, his feet eating up the distance between the table and the arrogant Palace Administrator.

"Did you not hear my commands?" Dragon Supreme bellowed.

Surprised by the treatment and more than a little afraid, the Palace Administrator scuttled back a handful of steps. "I-I did hear you, indeed, My Lord."

"Then why are you not obeying?" Dragon Supreme continued his advance, each step more menacing than the last. "As I have not slain anyone in the past weeks, you all believe I've gone soft? You think you can do as you please?"

"N-no, Your Majesty, Dragon Supreme. I wouldn't dare..." The Palace Administrator shuffled away again, only to be pursued.

Lada stopped trying to escape her blankets. She had never heard Dragon Supreme so furious, and it bore the question of what had enraged him. He had been behaving nicely only a few moments ago.

"Do you think yourself above me now?"

"How could I?"

"Then stop babbling and *get out*."

The Palace Administrator tripped over his own feet and the threshold, landing him square on his buttocks in the hall.

With a *crack* that spoke more finality than any words he could utter, Dragon Supreme slammed the chamber doors closed.

Lada stared at him, wondering if something had truly infuriated him lately. It had been a long while since she had seen Dragon Supreme so worked up, the last time being the day she had forced the Mirror Needle upon him.

"Are you alright, Your Majesty?" Lada asked.

Dragon Supreme closed his eyes, inhaling deeply to calm his fury. His people—especially his servants—rarely rebelled, and he liked it better that way. For the Palace Administrator to self-centeredly insert himself in Dragon Supreme's affairs meant that Davorin must have been lax in discipline. He would rectify the matter later. For now, important matters demanded his attention.

Upon opening his eyes, Dragon Supreme found the Little Florist still staring at him from beneath her mass of quilts.

"It is but a trifle," he sighed, determined to use his best manners for the sake of his better interests. "Won't you come out and dine with me?"

"I would love to, Your Majesty." Lada paused, taking stock of her current situation. "I am uncertain I have that capability at the moment."

"Explain."

Dragon Supreme folded his arms and waited. He had learned, quite quickly, that if given a broad topic to speak upon, Lada of Flora Master's Hall would offer all the information she knew. If asked to wager whether the woman knew this flaw of hers, Dragon Supreme would bet his entire treasury that she had never realized. Nor would she.

Proving her obliviousness, Lada gave a huff and began her rant. "The room is damp and frigid, and as I've told Your Majesty, I dislike the cold and wet. Mitsie offered to fetch blankets, which was kind of her, yet I couldn't bring myself to allow her to stoop so low as to swaddle me like an infant."

None of this had anything to do with the question, but Dragon Supreme had learned that Lada would eventually come around to the point of the matter. If only his patience lasted.

A determined peek of her tongue between her teeth interrupted Lada's story. Bit by bit, she wiggled one arm out of the pile of blankets. "Thus, I wrapped myself in the warm blankets to dispel the cold and dampness. However, *someone* came barging in with food and furniture and if you know about me, you know that my curiosity often gets the better of me. Curiosity propels me to move to see the things I'm pondering. I seem to have..." Another arm came wiggling out, "...entangled myself too thoroughly to escape the bindings."

Not for the first time, Dragon Supreme found himself questioning his own sanity. In time of need, why must his perfect plan depend on a girl such as this? The Little Florist couldn't extricate herself from a pair of blankets. How, then, would she handle the most important task Dragon Supreme had to offer her?

Lada, on the other hand, had no such worries. She had managed to free her upper body from the cocoon of her own making, but the blankets and her skirts were too tangled up together to do much about it.

"My apologies, Your Majesty." Lada offered a sheepish smile to appease him. "It might take a while longer."

Having stood for far too long awaiting a clumsy oaf from Amaryl, Dragon Supreme's patience left him. No longer would he wait for her to arise from her bed. If he did so, they would never manage to arrive at the true purpose of his visit.

Resigning himself to his fate, Davorin marched to Lada's bedside, scooped her up from the bed itself, and deposited her in a chair at the table.

Lada, surprised at suddenly being moved from one location to the other, stared up at Dragon Supreme in sheer confusion. "You could have helped me untangle the blankets instead."

"This ensures you won't go running about and injuring us again." Dragon Supreme settled on his side of the table, perusing the dishes he had specifically requested.

Every dish before them had one thing in common. Over the past month (or so), Dragon Supreme had taken careful note of Lada's preferred foods. Bit by bit, he had narrowed down her favorites. Now, before them, lay the dishes that Lada had loved the best during her stay in Isonpool Palace.

A bribe? Dragon Supreme wouldn't refute the accusation. Bribes, when used appropriately, were most useful.

"Running has been... tricky." Lada reached for a fluffy white bread roll. "It's a shame you don't have any Caramun. The wounds wouldn't ache if you did."

Dragon Supreme resisted the urge to roll his eyes. At these times, he was reminded of Lada's profession. Only physicians could make an offhanded comment into an insult. Nevertheless, Lada of Flora Master's Hall was less troublesome than several battlefield doctors Dragon Supreme had known. Less troublesome, by a hairsbreadth.

"Pardon my complaints." Lada tore the roll in half, giggling in glee when steam swirled up and around her face. "Your Majesty has deigned to dine in my quarters this evening. To what do I owe such honor?"

Lada, though dense, paid attention to abnormalities. Dragon Supreme, since the beginning of her time in Isonpool Palace, had never lowered himself to come to her. He had always summoned her to his territory. Lada found it peculiar he would choose to enter her chambers now, when he faithfully avoided them on other days. A gentleman didn't spend time alone in a lady's chambers.

Lada had come to discover that Dragon Supreme did indeed possess the qualities of a gentleman. If only he could tamp down his anger once in a while.

Dragon Supreme, for his part, could only stare at the woman he found so foolish. She never ceased to surprise him at the most inopportune moments. Perhaps, he thought to himself, trusting her with this one task would have a better end than he anticipated.

"You have seen through my façade," Dragon Supreme began tentatively.

Lada, her cheeks stuffed with bread, managed only to nod. Any attempt to speak would spew crumbs everywhere. She did not expressly mind looking unmannerly, but Dragon Supreme would blame her for her bad manners nonetheless.

Plucking a berry with one of his claw rings, Dragon Supreme leaned back in his chair to study the fruit. "I find myself requesting you do me a favor these few days."

Lada found it peculiar that Dragon Supreme would ask her for a favor, but he had done nothing to harm her recently, so she mulled over the question. By the time she had swallowed her bread, Lada had decided to ask only one thing in return.

"May I be released to go home afterward?"

The forest called to her. Soon, Mirror Needle's effects would begin to fade. Lada doubted she would have such a foothold in Isonpool Palace once her hold over Dragon Supreme went away. Dragon Tribe would capture or kill her on his behalf if they knew of her trickery. It was past time she make her escape, but Lada had stayed on to heal of various injuries and to repay the debt she owed Dragon Tribe's leader.

Dragon Supreme turned his gaze from the berry to the woman across from him. It had been weeks since she last mentioned her home. A small part of Davorin Astrophel didn't want to allow her out of his grasp. It had been so long, after all, since he acquired such an interesting plaything.

"You may return."

"Truly?" Lada leaned forward in her seat, searching Dragon Supreme's face for signs of deceit or ill intent.

"But you have to guide my men and I across Amaryl's border." Dragon Supreme popped the berry into his mouth and chewed, slowly, awaiting Lada's reaction.

Lada flopped back in her seat, her mind whirling with possibilities and answers to questions she had never asked.

How did he expect her to guide him into Amaryl? Lada could never do it. To take Dragon Tribe soldiers across the border meant to betray her country and her people. With loyalty so deep it was carved into her bones, Lada could scarcely imagine how such a feat would destroy her.

"If he's being kind to you, it means he wants something from you." Nerys's words echoed in the back of Lada's head.

To dispel them, Lada gave her head a shake. It did not quell the encroaching dread.

Perhaps Dragon Supreme had been making the comment flippantly or as a joke. Lada might be able to understand, then. But she could not repay him as he asked.

Dragon Supreme, seeing her distress, heaved a mighty sigh and reached for another berry. "But that is not the favor I seek to gain this evening."

Lada snapped her full attention to the king seated across from her. "It isn't?"

"No. Tonight, I ask only one simple task." Dragon Supreme popped the second berry into his mouth.

Lada swallowed, now concerned with the conversation's direction. "What is it?"

"These coming days, dine in my study."

The simple request caught Lada off guard, eliciting a stare much like a startled deer. "Is that a favor?"

Dragon Supreme chuckled. "I will not be there. It is your task to make others believe I have hermitted myself away to study."

"You want me to lie to everyone?" Lada grasped the situation, but she didn't like to lie. She had found that she did not lie well. Not ever.

"All you have to do," Dragon Supreme assured, "is to eat in my study. Ensure that it looks as though two of us have dined there."

"That will mean a lot of eating for me. I cannot throw away the food, they will discover it." Lada tried processing out loud, but it still didn't quite make sense. "Where will you be?"

"Out." Dragon Supreme leaned forward, over the table until his face was level with Lada's. "I scarcely believe eating two portions will be difficult for you. You forget, I've encountered your appetite."

"Is it very important that no one knows where you are?" Lada's voice lowered to a whisper she felt more appropriate for their close proximity.

"Oh, yes." Dragon Supreme reached out a finger, topped with his claw ring, and ever-so-lightly stroked it down the curve of Lada's cheek. "Will you not do this for me, after all you've done against me?"

Lada wet her lips, weighing her options and finding she didn't really have a choice. Dragon Supreme had a point. She owed him many debts. Debts she would pay in full before she made her escape. For if this interlude had taught her anything, it was that escape was imminent. She must flee before she no longer had the courage to walk away.

Therefore, she would do this favor and one other. Then, Lada would disappear from Dragon Tribe forever.

A smile flitting up onto her lips, Lada gave a single nod. "This favor, I will do. May your journey be expedient and may you return safely."

Dragon Supreme, with no idea about Lada's thoughts of escape, grinned back. He always got his way, somehow. This time it had been no different. But, most of all, it pleased him that the Little Florist supported him so wholeheartedly.

CHAPTER FORTY-NINE
Border Battle

Davorin Astrophel, Dragon Supreme, sneaked out of Isonpool Fortress an hour after assigning the Little Florist her task. As discussed with his trusted guard Cadfael, it made no sense to waste more time than they already had. The sooner they left, the sooner they would return, and so Dragon Supreme and Cadfael found themselves hastening along their way.

The journey to Qranbu's border would take normal travelers, using well-established roads, many days. Dragon Supreme and Cadfael, using shortcuts and paths that others did not know, raced for the border over the course of a mere forty-eight hours.

Their treacherous race was more necessary than they knew.

For at the border they sought, another battle had begun.

Dragon Supreme's border generals were known for their quick wit and accurate intuition. After all, they served Dragon Supreme more loyally than any of his ministers or relatives. If Dragon Supreme could not trust them with the care of the nation, itself, they would lose both career and life.

Letters had been sent, replies received. The border generals quickly recognized the pattern in Beshotan's attacks. Like Dragon Supreme, they came to a conclusion that boded badly for everyone. Also like their ruler, the border generals made haste to stop the next attack before it began.

Their efforts, though not in vain, were not fast enough.

Beshotan attacked only half an hour after the next border town locked its gates.

Dragon Tribe stood firm and strong, as they always had, but a nagging doubt loomed in the backs of the entire city's minds. They had not asked for reinforcements. Would the Beshotani battalion outside their walls overpower them by sheer force?

Three cities had already lost their fights. Dragon Tribe could not lose another border battle.

General Dalibor, standing tall and proud atop the city wall, knew this better than most. He had seen victory, and he had seen defeat. Of all the border generals, General Dalibor knew best how a battle should be fought. How opposing sides should be treated. What it took to win.

Below him, his horse prancing beneath him, an arrogant Beshotani shouted up to the sentries. "Surrender now and the women and children will be spared."

Surrender without a fight? All standing at the top of the city wall knew better. Their honor depended on it. Beshotan may or may not keep their word. Better to hold still until they could hold no longer.

General Dalibor didn't budge. He simply examined the smug creature outside the gates. "Identify yourself."

"Lieutenant in charge, Heskel," came the immediate, conceited reply.

General Dalibor had already deduced that the man didn't hold a rank high enough to merit invading a country. If Beshotan had any respect or fear for Dragon Tribe at all, they would not send a man ranked less than a general. Every bit of this reeked of disrespect and self-importance. Beshotan suddenly thought themselves better than Qranbu and all the people in its Dragon Tribe. And for what? Because Beshotan had managed to survive the war thirty years prior? Because Dragon Tribe had not crushed them back then?

"Make your choice!" Lieutenant Heskel shouted as though he had the power to smite them all. "Surrender or death."

A decision had to be made. The city could hold out for no more than a week without more supplies. They could wait for those who would not come, or they could fight.

Without reinforcements, the Beshotani battalion outnumbered Dragon Tribe's available soldiers. But they would never break Dragon Tribe's will.

Thus, General Dalibor gave the order. "Fight."

Hundreds of men who had stationed themselves against the exterior of the wall rushed forward. Past the pikes used to protect the city gates. Out into the open expanse between fortress and their certain doom. Not one hesitated. They fought not only for themselves but for their country and their loved ones.

The first Dragon Tribe soldier fell, cut down by Lieutenant Heskel's own sword.

The Beshotani battalion raced into the fray.

Swords clashed, their metallic ring echoed in the sound of war cries and death. Blood pooled on the battlefield and leapt upon every man's carefully crafted armor. Both sides suffered. Soldiers who fell could no longer be distinguished if not for the unique colors on their helmets and shoes.

For this reason, General Dalibor saw the approaching loss. Beshotan's battalion had come prepared to kill every Dragon Tribe soldier who opposed them. They would leave the city in confusion and fear. The tactic worked, always. And it humiliated the one who lost the battle yet had to live another day.

General Dalibor weighed the option of calling a retreat. He weighed the decision of fighting to his last breath. Neither appealed to him, and thus a moment of hesitation delayed his commands.

From the back of the battlefield, a pair of hoofbeats resounded against the hard-pressed dirt. Through the sea of blood and foot-soldiers, two enormous war steeds appeared.

The battlefield split like a sea before them, each soldier remiss to find himself crushed beneath the horses' powerful hooves.

Dragon Supreme, his sights set on the city gate and the Beshotani fool before it, drew his sword from its sheath. The blade sang through the air to cut down those who dared stand in his way.

Lieutenant Heskel turned his horse, his own sword drawn and prepared to fight. He did not anticipate what tragedy next befell him.

Cadfael aimed for the Beshotani Lieutenant's steed.

The beast cried out, first rearing and then falling, and trapping one of the lieutenant's legs beneath its side. The lieutenant struggled, crying out in agony and anger. His struggling only landed him on his back, one free leg kicking as if the horse could get up.

A flutter of midnight cape wrapped around Dragon Supreme as he dismounted his steed. With a single motion, disregarding the

Beshotani lieutenant's cries to kill the Dragon Tribe soldiers, Dragon Supreme plunged his sword into the man's chest.

The screaming stopped.

"Your leader has fallen, will you still choose to fight?" Dragon Supreme's voice rose loudly and resonated out across the battlefield.

Those closest to him stopped to stare at the scene before them.

Like a ripple in a tumultuous lake, victim and victor alike lowered their swords. War cries ceased as swiftly as they had begun.

Dragon Supreme retrieved his sword, wiping it on the sleeve of his battle armor. "Surrender."

Confused, the remaining Beshotani soldiers looked to their Dragon Tribe opponents. The soldiers, though confused by this man's arrival, knew better than to allow Beshotan time to think. Swift in action, the Dragon Tribe soldiers took hold of the flabbergasted Beshotani men before them.

General Dalibor, having recognized the demeanor of Dragon Supreme, had long since left his post at the top of the wall. The city gates flew open, allowing General Dalibor to rush out into the open.

He fell to his knees as he reached his sovereign. "My Lord, Dra—"

"Rise, General. I wish no one to know my identity."

General Dalibor scrambled to his feet, feigning an injury to explain why he had knelt. Had any soldiers seen his reverence to the man before them, they would suspect. General Dalibor knew better than others that Dragon Supreme had killed men for less than exposing his identity.

"We will speak within the city walls." Dragon Supreme sheathed his sword. "Tell the men to take the remaining Beshotani soldiers to the prison."

"Yes, My Lord." General Dalibor quickly stepped forward, sliding past Cadfael to address the Dragon Tribe victors. "Congratulations are due. My fellow compatriots, we have won! We have shown that Dragon Tribe is not to be trifled with!"

A shout of triumph went up around the field. The distraction had worked.

General Dalibor continued, "This calls for celebration! Imprison your captives and prepare your families to feast tonight. No expense shall be spared for those who defeated these fools."

The promise of time with their families and luxury they did not often receive would overpower any suspicion the men had about their savior. They would remember him as an anonymous soldier who ended the border battle, nothing more.

As for the men who had died in battle, their comrades in arms would bury them and see to their families on their behalf. A mixture of joy and sadness would flood the city now. None could explain how they coexisted, only that they did.

General Dalibor turned to Dragon Supreme and his bodyguard. "If you would follow me, My Lord."

A nod gave the permission needed. General Dalibor led the way back into the city.

Thankfully, but unfortunately, the citizens were too preoccupied with finding their fathers, sons, and brothers to worry about the stately pair leading their horses through the center of town.

Dragon Supreme understood their fears. He didn't want them to recognize him, anyway. If word spread back to Isonpool Palace that Dragon Supreme had left without notifying his ministers, there would be trouble not only for him but for those within the palace helping him.

"This is my residence. You will be safe here." General Dalibor motioned to the gates of a large but plain mansion. "Stable boy! Come take the horses for food and water."

A teenage boy came running to help.

Dragon Supreme and Cadfael handed over their horses in order to follow General Dalibor inside.

They had not made it five steps beyond the threshold before General Dalibor spoke again.

"My Lord, Dragon Supreme. I never imagined you would come."

"My borders are being toyed with. Should I stay at home and rest?" Dragon Supreme took in the frugality of General Dalibor's mansion. Fitting for a man of his status. "You discovered they have been teasing us, as well, did you not?"

"Forgive my incompetence, My Lord. I should have handled it before the necessity arose for you to journey this far."

"This kind of situation requires the hand of a nation's leader." Dragon Supreme bypassed General Dalibor and entered the main parlor. "I will now handle all affairs concerning Beshotan's impudence. Hear my first order."

General Dalibor knelt, awaiting Dragon Supreme's command.

"Send this dead commander and his steed to the Beshotani military encampment, along with my message." Dragon Supreme sank into a chair and reached for a glass and a pitcher of water. "'Should Beshotan attack, regardless of city or province, they will receive the same gift'."

"It will be done as you have ordered." General Dalibor rose from his knees, clearing his throat as he did. "Although, if I may say something frankly, Your Lordship?"

"Speak."

"I doubt this will do much to dissuade the Beshotani army. Indeed, I fear it will do nothing but incite their rage."

"As they have incited *my* rage." Dragon Supreme set aside the glass of water. "Nothing to worry about, this is but a first step. I plan to stop the invasions within a fortnight."

Davorin rarely felt the need to explain his plans, but for his border generals he would break his habits. They secured his country and protected those within its bounds. Dragon Supreme would not lay down their lives for his own selfishness. If he could not trust his border generals, they would not trust him in return.

"Your Lordship is magnanimous." General Dalibor dipped another bow. "I will see to it that all is done. Someone will bring food for Your Majesty, Dragon Supreme."

A wave of Dragon Supreme's hand dismissed the general.

Left alone, Cadfael asked the only question he had thought of during the conversation. "Can you stop the invasions that quickly?"

"I'll stop them in a week if I put my mind to it." Dragon Supreme leaned his head back, allowing himself to relax for the first time since he left his palace.

"Isn't it too little time?"

A laugh escaped Dragon Supreme's lips, both mirthful and sarcastic. "Do you think the Little Florist can hold out on her lies any longer?"

With a point well made, Dragon Supreme had ended the inquisition. They must not remain outside of Isonpool Palace for long, else the ministers would notice. No one wanted chaos. Lada of Flora Master's Hall would have to hold on as best as she was able, no matter their speed of return.

Cadfael—and especially Dragon Supreme—could only hope Lada managed to keep the ruse and stay away from the suspicious ministers. If not, the secret could turn into calamity.

CHAPTER FIFTY
The Root of All Wistning

"My Lady, it is near time for you to sup in the study." Sina tugged a shoe out of Lada's hand. "Will you truly force us to run amok in the farthest parts of the palace?"

"Of course not."

Sina sighed, relieved her mistress had finally seen sense.

Lada, smile intact, snatched the shoe back and reached to slide it onto her foot. "I'll go by myself."

Sina's sigh became a groan, loud enough to express her agitation to the lady she served. "Lady Lada, it is improper for you to run off by yourself. What if something should happen?"

"Nothing will happen to me." Lada wrestled the shoe onto her foot with much difficulty. If not for the necessity of safety, Lada wouldn't have bothered to put them on. "Everyone in the palace knows that I am a tribute piece. Even if they did not, I believe the anticipation of His Majesty's wrath would keep them from mistreating me. Everyone in the palace has been lovely thus far."

Sina could have cried at her lady's eternal optimism. After all the injustices and all the rumors spread about the outsiders, Lada described the Isonpool Palace servants as *lovely*. Had the victim of this strange and twisted fate been any other aside from Lada, they would have given up hope by now. But not Lada of Flora Master's Hall. She saw nothing but goodness in the hearts of even the cruelest person.

Lada, hearing only silence from the maid, took it as a sign to continue her mission. This much, she owed to Dragon Supreme. He had put up with her tricks and tactics with surprising grace. As an herbalist, she should do him at least this one favor.

Given the sheer number of dying vines within palace walls, Lada surmised that they held a meaning to Dragon Tribe. She had never seen this plant before, but Lada had read extensively. With her knowledge, the vines could survive. She must save them before she left.

Such a favor would surely cover her debt to Dragon Supreme.

"Prepare the meal as usual," Lada instructed the worrying maid. "I will return to the study on time. I promise you."

Had it been the other Orafel maids, an argument might have ensued. After all, leaving Lada to her own devices had never been a wise idea. Her feet hadn't fully healed from the last time she ran off alone.

Alas, the other two maids had gone to fetch supper and run errands, leaving Sina with Lady Lada. Sina, though diligent in her work, disliked wandering farther than she absolutely had to. Given the choice between scurrying after her energetic mistress or taking a break in the room, Sina would choose the latter.

"Are you quite sure you won't be late?" Sina double-checked, to make it appear as if she might choose to follow Lada.

Lada jumped to her feet, stumbling sideways to regain her footing. "I promise I will arrive promptly."

She should refuse to go along with Lada's plan. Sina's laziness got the better of her. She turned her back, knowing Lada would run off at the first opportunity.

"If that is how it must be..."

Fully living up to Sina's expectations of her, Lada crept toward the door while Sina busied herself with the folding of a haphazard blanket. It was easier to sneak out of the chambers when the maids allowed it.

Lada paused to glance between the two guards outside her door. They might be troublesome if they followed her.

As usual, the guards didn't glance her way. They never did, but they always knew to trail her. Lada couldn't fault them for doing their job, but they could be friendlier.

"Are you going to follow me again?" Lada ventured to ask the guard on her left.

"That is our duty," he replied.

To the other, Lada leaned in to whisper, "Are you certain you wish to accompany me around the palace?"

This one raised his hand to the hilt of his sword. "We have orders."

They used to sigh and ignore her, yet they had warmed up enough to answer her questions now. Lada clapped her hands gleefully. If the stoic Dragon Tribe guardsmen had decided to tolerate her, others must follow suit. Perhaps even Dragon Supreme, himself, would crack a smile one of these days.

Too late, Lada remembered she may not be around to celebrate such an occasion. If she did not leave promptly, she would outlive her usefulness in Isonpool Palace. Perhaps she would not see his smile, after all.

The thought sobered and saddened Lada. She had so wanted to see Dragon Supreme's happiness.

Lada quickly recovered to return to the matter at hand. Summoning all the fierceness within her, Lada stood to her full height and folded her arms across her chest. "Do you work for His Majesty or do you work for me?"

"His Majesty, Dragon Supreme," the guards answered in unison.

Lada's façade fell away as swiftly as her arms fell back down to her sides. "But aren't you here to protect me?"

"Our duty is to guard His Lordship's Tribute Treasure." Guard One answered.

Guard Two gave an affirmative nod. "If he had not assigned us to you, we would not protect you."

"That seems unfair." Lada pointed it out before she saw the usefulness of their words. Springing into action, Lada wrapped a hand around Guard One's arm, tugging him toward Guard Two so she could pull both close. "But as it is such, could you do me a tiny favor?"

Both guards stared at her as if she had lost her mind. Both thought she might have. Lada of Flora Master's Hall had no idea the troubles she might stir just by standing too closely beside Dragon Tribe guardsmen. Dragon Supreme took the care of his treasure very seriously, to the point any misunderstanding would see their heads roll.

As one, the two guards tried to pull away.

Lada wrapped her hold tighter around both of them. "If you let me go exploring by myself, I'll heal your chronic backache," she glanced to the second guard, "and prescribe something for your stomach problems."

It paid to watch the guards closely. Lada had seen their problems within a fortnight. Dragon Tribe physicians were skilled, but none had the know-how of an apprenticed herbalist. Especially not when that herbalist came from Amaryl.

The second guard hesitated. "But, His Lordship—"

"I have a meal with him every evening in his study. There is less than an hour until I must arrive there. If I fail to dine with him and he turns his anger toward you, I will single-handedly take all the blame for my mistakes." Lada grinned like a wildcat about to catch its prey. "Either way, I will heal your ailments."

None of the three misunderstood the quality of such a deal. The guards, especially, knew they were on the better end of the bargain. Such a curious and energetic creature as this Amaryl Mystic was difficult to keep an eye upon. If she failed to please Dragon Supreme and found herself under a death sentence, they would be transferred to an easier job. Whether she displeased Dragon Supreme or not, they would be treated for longstanding ills.

With their usual sigh, both guards tugged their arms out of Lada's hold.

Guard One motioned down the hall. "For one hour only, we are blind, dumb, and deaf."

"Thank you!" Lada gave each of them a pat on the shoulder, then raced off as fast as her shod feet would allow.

Neither guard would admit to a slight fondness for the eccentric Amaryl fairy, but both understood their growing attachment. Women, like exotic flowers, bloomed brightest in the strangest of places.

Entirely on her own for the first time in weeks, Lada wasted no time in reaching her destination. The vines had taught her where to go to locate the things she sought. Thus, Lada found herself once more at the threshold of Firesbreadth Hall.

Should something go wrong, Dragon Supreme would know in no time. Lada didn't mean to anger him again, she meant only to help, and thus she stopped to check the security of the shoes upon her feet.

Where the soles of her feet had torn immediately upon the shards and stones, the thick platform of the well-sewn shoes would take longer to tear asunder. It would be enough.

Assured of her own safety and determined to find the vines' source before dinner, Lada marched forward over the stunning but dangerous path. This part of the palace contained no servants, Lada had found. The lack of living persons roaming about the space lent an eerie silence to the hall. A silence broken only by Lada's breathing and the cautious trod of her feet.

A pair of double doors at the end of the hall caught Lada's attention. They were unlike anything else Lada had seen within Isonpool Palace. Made of iron, as all the doors within the palace were, these bore designs beyond imagination. From top to bottom, the epic illustration of triumphant battles flowed like a river. Decades— centuries—of the story of a dominating nation. They were beautiful and historical, drawing Lada in to their show of determination and might. She dared not touch them lest she soil their legacy, yet...

Lada squared her shoulders, rubbed her hands together to warm them, and gave the double doors the hardest shove she could manage.

Without a sound, not even a creak of its hinges, the doors swung inward for Lada to squeeze through the opening. They slammed behind her with a metallic thud.

Lada startled at the sound, but her fear quickly gave way to curiosity and trepidation. Trespassing through the doors had brought her outside, and before her lay a set of open-air stairs lined with columns. The vines she had been chasing throughout the palace wrapped up and around each column, toward the top of the mysterious steps.

Despite the cold wind surging around her and the foreboding path before her, Lada had not come this far only to give up. Lifting her skirts in her hands lest she trip over them on her ascent, Lada cautiously moved forward. Each step took her higher, caused the wind to blow more brutally over the staircase.

Lada ignored all the inconveniences, her sole fixation on the shriveling vines. Up, up, up she ventured, until she found herself facing yet another set of doors. The tales on these were scarcer, more focused on love and loss than they were on war and vengeance.

And though a small voice within her whispered *"Do not enter here,"* Lada whisked it away like a pesky fly.

These doors, too, granted her entry without a complaint.

Lada stumbled into a room as black as night. The doors that closed behind her had plunged everything into darkness, save a shaft of late afternoon glow spearing from a far wall. Lada stepped into line with that light, allowing it to lead her to the crack it originated from.

On closer inspection, Lada found it was not a wall at all, but a pair of wooden shutters beginning at the floor and extending to the ceiling. With some finagling, Lada managed to open the latch and swing the shutters inward.

Suddenly, what had been steeped in darkness came into the sun. The evening sky, blazoned with hues of purple and pink, greeted Lada amidst a gush of cold wind. Below stretched stories and stories of open air, which ended at a river running directly below the tower.

Pleased at the presence of the light she sought, Lada turned to inspect what she had found. Never would she have predicted the extravagance hidden in the blackness.

Directly opposite her stood a canopied bed, furs and silks scattered over it in a haphazard fashion. A table made of dark wood and inlaid with gold and jewels sat regally in the center of the room. It matched the desk near the wall to her left, and complimented the lavish, throne-like chair in the corner. Fur rugs covered the floor beneath every piece of furniture.

And, climbing each wall and encompassing the bedframe and mirror, hung endless withering vines.

With nowhere left to go, the vines had to take root somewhere in this room. Lada planted her hands on her hips, as that gave her an advantage when thinking. The action didn't fail her this time, either.

Upon closer inspection, Lada noticed the Planting Boxes built into each wall, in regular intervals. Rising from each to cling to the walls and spread forth were the roots of the vines.

Lada grinned. She had found it. The source of all the palace's vines. It never occurred to her to ask who owned the room or why the vines started there. It didn't matter. With the root located, Lada could make a diagnosis about the vines and, with a turn of good fortune, could heal them on behalf of His Majesty, Dragon Supreme.

With the sun rapidly setting and her time running out, Lada set to work to investigate the cause of the dying vines. Only when she reached a conclusion did she leave, though she would be late to the study even if she ran.

Perhaps, for that reason alone, Lada did not pay enough attention upon exiting the battle-tale doors. Or, perhaps, the pair of beady dark eyes watching her from the darkness at the end of the hall could not have been seen by anyone.

CHAPTER FIFTY-ONE
A Heaping of Doubt

ada found herself busier than she had been in months, all over a promise and a favor.

In the evenings she consumed the portions of two grown adults to cover for the absent Dragon Supreme. During the afternoon, she left the assigned guards behind to tend to the undernourished vines. They had not responded to her gentle touch yet, but Lada spoke kindly to them and trusted they would receive her care sooner rather than later.

The mornings, she had left mostly for her own enjoyment, rare as it may be. The guards stationed outside her door visited each morning, as well, to receive treatment for their chronic ailments. Lada took pleasure in the company of her new friends.

Over the course of several mornings, the two guards had become more open toward her. Now, they would carry a pleasant conversation with the Amaryl Tribute Piece. Lada relished the company.

Yet she found, deep down, she missed keeping company with His Majesty.

If she allowed herself, Lada could imagine a future here. She would never allow such a thought. Even if she did not return to Amaryl, Lada had never meant to stay in Isonpool Palace forever.

Anticipation and sorrow warring within her, Lada did not pay attention to the time or circumstance surrounding her. The maids recognized Lada's melancholy mood. Blankets were brought to keep her warm, braziers lit to dispel the dampness. Lada whiled away her time tending to a potted plant she had found in the garden.

When one day she did not arise to set out on her usual afternoon adventure, everyone realized the gravity of Lada's thoughts. The guards could do nothing but watch over her door. The maids could only wish that their mistress would share her burden.

Alas, though all wished to help, none found the courage to speak out before the unexpected intrusion.

It had been over a week since anyone had seen Nerys Galashiel enter Isonpool Palace halls. Thus, her appearance at the door of Lada's chambers came as a shock even to the stationed guards.

"Announce my arrival," Nerys commanded.

Knowing their station, the guards could not refuse the order. Thus, with a trepidatious clearing of his throat, one obeyed.

"Minister Galashiel has arrived."

Without waiting for a "please enter" or a "by your leave", Nerys shoved open the iron doors and sailed into Lada's drafty chambers.

Nerys had come expecting the idiot Amaryl girl to have figured out her tricks. She never could have predicted the despondent atmosphere she found before her now. The Amaryl girl smiled at everything and trusted all that others said. Nerys could hardly fathom what made the imp pluck so dejectedly at the weed before her.

Never mind what had happened, Nerys found it worked to her advantage with the information she had gathered.

"He still has you locked up in this place, I see."

Nerys didn't bother to hide the derogatory tone with which she said it. This Tribute Piece had never heard Nerys's sarcasm, even when it had been dripping from her lips.

Lada looked up at the sound of a familiar voice. Growing up, Lada had seen different people every day, it seemed. Here in Isonpool Palace, she had a limited group of friends. No one dared get close to her on account of Dragon Supreme's wrath. Lada missed helping others instead of helping herself.

Thus, when Nerys arrived at Lada's lowest moment of longing, Lada opened her mind and heart to a woman she saw as a friend. After all, Nerys had apologized. Lada's mother had said that an apology meant the person had made a change of heart. Those who had been a threat would no longer be such if they changed their heart.

Lada believed firmly in the power of change.

"Nerys." Lada rose to her feet and dipped a short curtsy. "It has been long since you visited."

"I found myself worrying over what trouble you might cause." Nerys flicked an invisible piece of dust from her sleeve. The insolent girl didn't have manners befitting a mouse within the walls. "Do you force all your guests to stand at attention when they arrive?"

"Oh, of course not! Have a seat." Lada motioned Nerys to a chair across the table. "Mitsie, would you fetch some tea? I'm sure that Nerys could use refreshment."

Mitsie, didn't trust the female minister any farther than she could throw her, but had no choice other than to obey her mistress. With a glare at Nerys Galashiel's back, Mitsie left Lada in the care of Sina and Enni.

Nerys settled into the chair, but it did little to still her agitation. Last time she had been there, Lada's chambers held a dilapidated old tea table and a few stools. Nerys knew full well where the fine table and cushioned chairs had come from.

Would His Majesty, Dragon Supreme, never cease to bestow the lying wench with favors? If he had granted so many of his own treasures to her, what might come next? Nerys wanted no chance to remain for Dragon Supreme to grant this imbecile something as important as his heart.

Lord Velimir had been right. She must ensure Lada of Amaryl never loved Davorin Astrophel.

"I hear you have not heeded my warning about His Majesty, Dragon Supreme," Nerys commented casually.

Lada stopped to ponder. Their conversation had been brief before, but she remembered Nerys's warning to the last syllable. *"Be wary of him, please. His kindness means your demise."*

"It isn't that I haven't heeded your words," Lada explained. "I simply think you may be wrong. His Majesty hasn't done me any harm."

"Oh, hasn't he?" Nerys rolled her eyes heavenward, praying to whoever would listen that this moron's brain worked well enough for her to hear reason. "He has said nothing about Amaryl?"

"No, he has—" Lada stopped, her eyes falling to the table before her.

"...you have to guide my men and I across Amaryl's border." His Majesty had sat in the chair that Nerys now occupied when he said it. One of the last things he had said before he left.

"He was only joking," Lada tried to convince both herself and Nerys.

In the moment that he said it, Lada had known. Deep down, she had understood he meant it when he said he wanted that favor from her. That's' why she had to flee. It was why she must extract herself from Isonpool Palace as quickly as she dared. Because if she did not, Lada might grow to consider such an absurd request. She would never betray her people. They were her only family.

"His Majesty, Dragon Supreme, does not *joke*," Nerys spat back. "Think you not that he will ask something terrible of you? He cares nothing for familial ties, much less does he cherish a useless woman such as you."

"I don't expect him to *cherish* me..." Lada found herself pouting, trying to put her thoughts together. "Neither do I have familial ties to him. We are friends—"

"You are not friends." Nerys slapped a hand against the table to gain Lada's full attention. "He's using you for Amaryl. Consider him your friend, and he will annihilate your entire nation."

"You've misunderstood him," Lada tried again. "His Majesty cares deeply for others—"

Nerys's barked laugh cut off Lada's attempt at reason. "His Majesty, Dragon Supreme, did not care for his own parents. He sought only a title, don't you know?"

Lada sighed, remiss to believe bad of anyone, especially a man who had taken her in and kept her alive. "I doubt it was all that bad. The title belongs to him since birth, anyway."

"You think he would hold the title Dragon Supreme at this age, only by doing as he was told?" Nerys laughed again. If the Amaryl twerp couldn't discern light from dark, how had she managed to survive within Isonpool Palace?

"I'm sure a tragedy befell those he held dearest—"

"He slew his father." Nerys lifted her eyes, purely to see Lada's reaction to the news. "He became Dragon Supreme the same day. No matter the lies you tell yourself, he will slaughter your people without hesitance or remorse."

Lada never wanted to believe anyone would lie to her, least of all a friend. Nerys had bluntly put forth facts before Lada, but she still wished to deny their truth.

The man Lada had begun to know, behind the pomp and circumstances and all the ruthlessness, would not do what Nerys said. His words and actions could be harsh and harmful, but he acted with objectivity and practiced neutrality. Such a man could not have slain his parents, in Lada's opinion. Nor would he kill her people. If he did, it would make him a man the likes of which Lada could never tolerate.

Yet, Nerys had no reason to lie to Lada about such things.

Nerys, calmly watching Lada's panic, chose not to expound further on the facts brought to light. A woman's imagination could be her undoing, if left to wander. Nerys had merely set it on a path. What conclusion came of it, came directly from Lada's own thoughts. Nerys's mission had come to a close.

Nerys rose from her chair. "It seems I have overstayed my welcome."

"Oh, no! Not at all." Lada rose, as well, but those beady eyes of hers didn't focus on anything.

Nerys watched the imp struggle to collect her thoughts, fight to believe what she wanted. It would never work if the girl listened to any inkling of the doubt eating her away like sulfuric acid.

Just in case the suspicion turned on her, Nerys found the necessity to act like a concerned third party. "I should not have overstepped my bounds. I'm only concerned for your well-being."

The lies rolling from Nerys's lips wrapped around Lada like a comforting blanket. For all her intelligence and all her knowledge, Lada could not change the part of her that demanded she believe others would tell her only truth.

Thus, a smile returned to Lada's face, wiping away her confusion but for a moment. "Thank you, Lady Nerys, for selflessly looking out for my better interests."

Part of Nerys wanted to gag at the stupidity portrayed before her. The other part basked in the knowledge that she had won. This Amaryl oaf believed every word that flew from Nerys's mouth. Lie or truth, it no longer mattered. Lada of Flora Master's Hall would destroy everything with her own hands. Nerys would see to that.

A smug sneer wormed its way to Nerys's lips. "It's my pleasure to be of help."

And, like the fool she was, Lada believed it.

CHAPTER FIFTY-TWO

Davorin's Return

easting in the town streets had broken out hours ago, due to the news that the signed armistice with the Beshotan forces had arrived. Men and women danced. Children sang. Fires were lit and animals slaughtered to be roasted. Davorin Astrophel, Dragon Supreme, observed the festivities from a distance, his own heart wary and suspicious.

The Beshotani army had signed the armistice too readily. Even with the tricks he had played, there should have been resistance. Beshotan had sought to toy with Qranbu, which meant their confidence for winning should be astronomical. Yet, they had willingly signed the armistice offered them after only one act of wrath on Dragon Supreme's part. Had they been afraid of him, they should not have had the courage to attack in the first place.

Thus, the quick end to Dragon Tribe's border problem worried Dragon Supreme more than the problem itself. Without the ability to read minds, he could not speak up about his misgivings. Others might accuse him of paranoia or a too-suspicious nature.

With a tentative armistice in place and with the border cities settled and safe, Davorin had no further excuses to remain. Nor did he have time to stay outside of Isonpool Palace's walls. It had been too long, already. So long that Davorin doubted if the Little Florist had been able to keep the ruse in place. The sooner he returned to his throne, the better for everyone.

"My Lord, Dragon Supreme." Cadfael arrived stealthily, but his ability to materialize had ceased to startle Davorin.

"Everything is in place?"

"The horses are being led around."

Davorin nodded, surveying his people for the last time before he returned home.

They would never know Dragon Supreme had graced them with his presence. They didn't have to know. Davorin would rather keep them safe than make a spectacle. After all, the weight of nations wore down on his shoulders. It was Davorin's duty to see to their safety. He would rather leave with a vision of their celebration than the weight of their mourning.

The imprint of the feast still forefront in his eyes, Davorin turned to Cadfael. "Let's go."

Together, both pondering their own version of the same problem, Dragon Supreme and Cadfael made their way to the back gate of General Dalibor's mansion.

The horses had been fed, watered, and rested over the past days. They would need the stamina given them by this process. Dragon Supreme had every intention of riding them as quickly to return as he had to arrive.

"Your Majesty, Dragon Supreme!" General Dalibor came tottering out from within the mansion. "Wait a moment."

Considering the camaraderie that had been established on the short-lived battlefield, Dragon Supreme overlooked the improper way General Dalibor made his request. He would not defame his border general in the eyes of the servants scuttling out behind him.

Cadfael kept a loose but wary stance, ready to step in, in the case of emergency. As always.

"My apologies, My Lord." General Dalibor bent a series of bows meant as apologies. "I could not in good conscience send you off without decent rations." General Dalibor beckoned the servants forward.

Dragon Supreme saw, now, what they carried in their hands and on trays. Bags of food, skins of water. A pack containing a change of clothes. All things anyone should carry on their journey, but Dragon Supreme had not ventured to bring along.

General Dalibor lifted a bag of food. "My wife and daughter made these themselves. No need for you to fret over treason or poison."

Dragon Supreme took the offering silently, biting back the things he wanted to say.

On the battlefield, he ate the same food as his men. At General Dalibor's mansion, he had never worried about poison or sickness. That was the bond of war. Before the eyes of death and the grave, every man stood equal.

"May your journey fly and may you arrive before anyone knows you've gone." General Dalibor bent a low, ninety-degree bow, showing respect and allegiance to his sovereign.

The servants behind him followed suit.

Through a filter of unease, Dragon Supreme took note of his loyal subjects. The ones who fed and clothed him, whose lives were dedicated to his service. In that moment, faced with incumbent danger and barely teetering on the precipice of peace, they still sought his well-being. The least Dragon Supreme could do was keep them safe from those who sought their demise. In that moment, Dragon Supreme made a conscious decision to see to it that the border attacks ceased. For good.

"Thank you for your hospitality."

The words rang sincerely from Dragon Supreme's mouth, spoken before he could think to deny them. Dragon Supreme rarely thanked anyone. He never felt the need to be grateful. But to his border general, who risked his life to keep their nation safe, Dragon Supreme would not offer a cold heart.

General Dalibor did not raise his head. He merely offered a few brief words. "It is what I should do."

For that reason alone, Dragon Supreme should have thanked him again. Instead, he turned away and mounted his horse.

"Cadfael."

Cadfael had already moved, sliding into his saddle seconds after Dragon Supreme. Together, the duo pointed their mounts toward Isonpool Fortress. Neither need say a word about their departure. General Dalibor would not rise until they had exited the gates. In this way, he would fulfill tradition that required Dragon Supreme to be sent off with reverence.

The mighty steeds' hooves thudded against the ground in a rumble of thunder that went unnoticed by those feasting in the street.

It didn't matter if they heard. It didn't matter if they saw. The townspeople had been fortunate enough to entertain their monarch. As quietly as he had come, he would go.

Then, from his throne within Isonpool Fortress, Dragon Supreme would see to it that Beshotan knew their place and remained there.

CHAPTER FIFTY-THREE
River Dive

The vines had yet to recover. Because of this, Lada had yet to make a plan of escape. How could she leave without accomplishing the last mission she had given to herself? When she had healed the vines, Lada would plot her exit. Not a moment sooner, she told herself.

For this reason, Lada donned the shoes she hated and made her way toward Firesbreadth Hall.

Every afternoon since she had found the vines' roots, Lada had made a habit of returning. Without knowing the owner of the room she frequented, Lada could not leave it in a state that would benefit the vines. When she left, she returned everything to how it had been when she found it.

Having never crossed paths with the room's owner struck Lada as odd. Lada had expected to be found. The chances were in favor of someone returning to the room while she visited. Yet, every evening for weeks, no one appeared.

Lada should have known no coincidence ever lasted.

Across the hazardous Firesbreadth Hall, Lada searched for any spying eyes. She checked a second time before swinging open the iron doors and scuttling within.

The second part of her journey didn't require caution. With a giggle of anticipation, Lada kicked off the offending shoes, gathered her skirts up in both hands, and raced her way up the open-air staircase.

As they had all the evenings prior, this second set of doors brushed open with barely a hiss. Lada swept inside, allowing the doors to close behind her.

The click of the latch closing sounded through the room like a firecracker. Lada, as per usual, ignored it in favor of feeling her way toward the floor-to-ceiling window. Lada fumbled with the closure there only a brief moment before she managed to swing the giant shutters open.

"So this is how you play when the master is absent."

Lada shrieked, spinning to face the far side of the room, where the voice had come from.

The gilded chair no longer sat empty, but housed a tall, dark man too familiar to frighten her further.

Davorin Astrophel, Dragon Supreme, lounged with his legs spread wide and his black silk tunic open over his bare chest. Gone were his usual dramatic cape and metal claw rings, leaving only the man who lived beneath the pageantry.

She had not expected his presence, yet Lada did not fear the man before her. Quite the contrary.

"Your Majesty, you've returned. Why didn't you say so? I've been worried."

Knowing every word Lada uttered to be utterly sincere, Dragon Supreme overlooked her chattiness. "Must I tell you when I come and when I go? If such is the case, how would I have the privilege to see such a show in my own chambers?"

"This is your room?"

Lada raised her eyes, studying the room in a brand new light. Of course it belonged to His Majesty, Davorin Astrophel. The opulence should have told her as much. Yet, Lada did not observe such extravagance and see a proud and arrogant king. Lada examined his chambers and saw only darkness and loneliness.

Dragon Supreme didn't give Lada time to remark about such things. "It is, and who allowed you to enter?"

"No one," Lada admitted sheepishly. "I followed the vines and—"

"Are you aware of the punishment for entering Dragon Supreme's private chambers of your own volition?" Dragon Supreme's eyes did not lift from his fingers. His tone did not waver.

That's how Lada knew. He was not in a mood to be trifled with.

"I didn't realize it was a forbidden area. I'm so sorry, Your Majesty. I'll leave, if that's what you want."

Lada shuffled two steps toward the door, only for her foot to land against something stiff and sturdy. Looking down, Lada saw a mass of black leather. Dragon Supreme's armor, cast aside in a dark corner where he would no longer be able to see it. It would have terrified any normal woman.

Lada, on the other hand, noticed only one thing. Patches of dark splotches littered the armor's plates.

"There's blood." Her gaze shot up, seeking Dragon Supreme before her feet began to move in the same direction. "Are you hurt?"

Dragon Supreme gave a derisive snort. "No, of course not."

"Then why were you bleeding?" Lada made it across the room and, given her propensity for overdoing things, took Dragon Supreme's arm in one hand to inspect it.

Dragon Supreme glanced up at her, surprised at her boldness, before he tore away from her hold. Did she not realize he was angry with her? Why would she ask? It should be obvious.

"It belongs to my enemies."

As much as Lada of Flora Master's Hall always had movement to her limbs, she now stopped. Frozen, as if her time had been suspended. Even Lada's voice came out slowly and quietly.

"You killed people?"

"I killed my own cousin," Davorin reminded her.

Neither Dragon Supreme nor Lada were under any misconceptions about that, or so Davorin believed. The tale of how he had slain his cousin ran rampant through the halls long after Lada had arrived. With maids such as hers, she would have heard the story.

Yet, to avoid that awful naive gaze of hers, Dragon Supreme returned his attention to the hem of his tunic. He had not expected Lada's disappointed gaze to have such an effect on him, made more dramatic by the time he had spent outside of her presence.

His blunt answer sparked only doubtful memories in Lada's mind. Words she had not wanted to believe. *"He slew his father. He became Dragon Supreme the same day."*

"Is it true then?" Lada asked, seeing clearly for the first time.

"Is what true?"

Lada swallowed, unsure why tears pressed up in her throat and eyes. Because she expected Dragon Supreme to be the man she wanted him to be? The one she saw beneath his hostility and violence. Or because she trusted easily and fully, though everyone had warned her not to make such a mistake?

"Is it true you slew your own father?"

"So you know."

Three words. Only three words, but they sliced Lada like a sharpened blade. She had expected an explanation Dragon Supreme would not give, even under penalty of death. Lada had expected his honesty and openness in return for her own sincerity. Both knew, now, that she would never receive such a precious gift.

"What about me?" Lada asked as quietly as she dared.

"What about you?" Dragon Supreme spat back.

"Are you truly using me to gain Amaryl?"

"What do you think?"

"Answer me plainly!" Lada demanded. "You wish me to guide you to Amaryl. Why? What will happen to my people?"

"I will make them my subjects by any means necessary."

"What does that mean? Will you... will you kill them all?"

"War is the same, always. One must eliminate the rebel factions in order to win."

Lada's optimism shattered around her like frozen petals falling from dead limbs. Her mother had told her that if she saw the good in people, they would reciprocate with generosity and kindness of their own. Now, Lada found Nerys's venomous accusations more plausible.

"Were you always using me?" Lada had a hunch the kind of answer she would get.

Dragon Supreme dared not to look at the woman before him, aware the agony he would see. Agony had never bothered him, not until Lada of Flora Master's Hall had tied her calamities to him. He would not turn soft now, not because of a mischievous forest imp.

"Or what else? Did you believe I liked you?"

His question slapped Lada across the face. This whole time she had been pouring out her heart and soul to someone she considered a friend and confidante. Yet, this whole time, he had only been lying to her. She had been wrong. He hadn't changed. He was still the cruel king who had starved her, poisoned her, and left her for dead.

"I thought we were friends."

"I never have friends."

"Why not?" Her last hopes laced into the question, Lada could do nothing but stare at the man who would not even look at her.

"I can't be bothered to care."

"Is that why you killed your family?" Lada wrung her hands together, unsure whether to comfort or accuse. Part of her still wanted to believe Dragon Supreme could change. "I thought you were less monstrous than the stories made you out to be."

So pure and innocent. So otherworldly. This ridiculous fondness for a woman holding him hostage could not be tolerated. His family? Dragon Supreme wouldn't stand for anyone speaking about the deaths of his family. Not in his kingdom, not in his palace. Especially not to his face, without knowing anything.

"Monstrous?" A chuckle spilled from Dragon Supreme's lips. His gaze lifted.

The sun outside the open window spilled into Dragon Supreme's eyes, and Lada realized she had never seen it wrongly. His eyes reflected back at her not black abysses, but golden fireballs. Those golden eyes landed on her face and didn't leave.

Like a beast rising from his slumber, Dragon Supreme rose from his chair, straightening to his most imposing height but never removing his gaze from her.

For the first time, Lada felt fear at the sight of him. She had seen the king, proud and regal. She had seen the man, lonely and reserved. But now, before her, Lada saw the monster. A cold and chilling devil with no mercy for his prey.

Lada took a step back.

Dragon Supreme took a step forward. "I am the strongest in Dragon Tribe. The most monstrous. That is my fate and my curse. *You* have landed in the center of my talons." He raised a hand, curling his fingers like the talons of which he spoke, then stretching them as if he could picture what laid within their grasp. "It would be the simplest thing in the world for me to—"

"Kill me?" Lada craned her neck, offering him the chance without hesitation. "You already killed me when you ordered me to betray my people."

If he had chosen to give in to the monster, she would no longer submit to his authority. She never belonged there, anyway. If he wanted her life, she would offer it, because she couldn't go back to her people no matter what she did. Lada would not put Amaryl at risk by returning through the border. Nor would she betray them by telling their secrets. No one could force her to do it.

Dragon Supreme's fingers landed around Lada's throat, but they did not hold as tightly as the first time he had done the same. If he injured her, he injured himself, and he knew it. *She* knew it. Clever and manipulative, this Amaryl florist. Dragon Supreme had long doubted her childlike mind. He should have known she had been faking it.

"I won't kill you, nor myself." Dragon Supreme released Lada's throat, but his fingers lingered as if they might do what he said he would not. "But you *will* lead me through Amaryl's border."

Lada had dealt with predators before, and only one option remained open for the weaker prey. Escape.

The tears welled again, borne of regret and sorrow and betrayal. She had grown attached to the fearsome leader threatening her and her people. He had broken her heart in two, yet Lada would miss him once in a while, after she had gone.

"I will not," Lada stated firmly, "allow you to hurt my people."

"You don't have a choice in the matter."

"The bond is weakening. Can't you tell?" Lada held up her hands, where various nicks and bruises had occurred over the past week. "The small wounds no longer appear on you. Soon, there will be no more Mirror Needle binding us together."

"A day to which I've long looked forward." Dragon Supreme heaved a breath, wishing he understood the change of subject.

Lada surveyed her own wounds, tears slipping down her cheeks as she assessed all the people she would leave without a word. "I am sorry I did this to you, but I am not sorry for wanting to survive."

Dragon Supreme waved a hand through the air, the moment of tension broken with her halfhearted apology. "I've heard all this before."

Dragon Supreme didn't bother to look at her. He traipsed his way back to the chair, prepared to take another rest. Arguing with the idiotic florist made his head ache.

"If I may say one—only one—terrible thing in my life, I want it to be this." Lada's voice quavered and shook, her fears and disappointments influencing her mental and physical state. "I hope this hurts you half as badly as you've hurt me."

"What does that—" Dragon Supreme spun to scold her, but stopped when he saw.

Lada had retreated to the open window, her bare feet resting only an inch from the sill's edge. The cold wind caught her hair, twisting it around her like a violent spring storm. Her hands shook and her legs trembled, but Lada did not waver. She merely gave a sad, sad smile and a teary intake of breath.

"Goodbye, Your Majesty."

Lada teetered, fell, and disappeared below the ledge before Dragon Supreme had time to reach out a hand to stop her.

For infinitesimal seconds, silence and open air were Dragon Supreme's only companions.

Then, impact. It hit Dragon Supreme's chest with the force of a battle axe finding its mark. Dragon Supreme went tumbling to the floor, the pain too great to stand any longer.

Davorin wanted to cough, to breathe, to move, but he could not. Oxygen froze in his lungs. His limbs begged for release, yet found none. Head pounding, Davorin gasped for air. The pain in his chest grew, expanding to his heart, worming its way into every fiber of his being. The world tilted, blurred, and finally went black.

Far, far below, a rushing river whisked Lada of Flora Master's Hall away from Isonpool Fortress.

CHAPTER FIFTY-FOUR
The Need For A Florist

Davorin woke to the sight of a starry, clear sky outside the window he never opened. He had never wanted to consider the beautiful things he would never be able to keep. Darkness was his friend, the black abyss his constant companion. He could not wish for more.

Yet, as she always had, Lada of Flora Master's Hall had shown him a different perspective. Davorin hadn't realized the night sky held colors and lights.

Perhaps it was her last gift to him, this realization that even darkness held beauty. Or, perhaps, he had known all along and had chosen to ignore it.

The Little Florist had gone, swept up in rapids too harrowing to survive. Yet, she had. Davorin knew it. Lada of Flora Master's Hall was not the type to die so easily. At the very least, were the Little Florist dead, Davorin should be laid up unconscious. Instead, he had awoken. If he believed in signs or fate, this would be the sign he chose to believe.

She had escaped Qranbu, Dragon Tribe, and the title of Tribute Piece. Fine. All for the better. After all she had done for him and all he had done to her, it might be better to end their bond.

Davorin Astrophel chose to let her go. May she live her life in peace.

Then, he rose to his feet, dusted off, and closed the shutters.

The breaking of a new day brought the Orafel maids scuttling through the halls in search of their mistress. In a moment of weakness, Dragon Supreme allowed them to keep their posts. In hindsight, it might have been said that he hoped for Lada's return. Dragon Supreme would never admit such a ridiculous fact.

That did not stop the palace from creating a rumor and spreading it like wildfire.

Dragon Supreme didn't dare to shut it down, as it agitated his ministers to hear of his saga of love. Another gift the florist had left him: the ruffling of every minister's feathers.

Days turned into weeks. Dragon Supreme shut the whimsical elf out of his memories. He ruled as he always had, with an iron fist. Executions were demanded. Wars were discussed. Yet, not a mention of Amaryl and his plans for them.

Not until the time came.

After the incident at the window, Dragon Supreme found himself habitually opening his shutters. As if the Little Florist had cast a spell demanding his cooperation, his change. If she had, it did not matter. No one knew what Dragon Supreme did during his private time.

That night, it rained. Dragon Supreme sighed at the humidity, turning away from the gloom of his mountaintop abode.

Had it not rained, he might not have turned aside. Had he not turned aside, he would not have seen it. As it was, Dragon Supreme thought he might be dreaming. However, upon closer inspection, he found his hallucination was very real indeed.

There, upon a vine, a Wistning flower strove to open its petals. The first flower that had grown on the Wistning Vine in nine years. The first sign of hope for the royal vines in over a decade.

Dragon Supreme rushed to check the other vines. All showed signs of renewed vitality, deep green life.

"Cadfael!"

Dragon Supreme went running, down the steps and into Firesbreadth hall in a whirlwind so fierce it slammed the iron doors.

"Cadfael!"

From the other end of the corridor, Cadfael came running, his sword out and ready for emergency. Only confusion sparked on Cadfael's face when he saw Dragon's Supreme's purposeful stride and determined gait.

"Yes, My Lord?"

"Call the ministers."

The request, so strange and so unlike Dragon Supreme's character, caught Cadfael off guard. "My Lord?"

Dragon Supreme did not slow his march. How could he when there were things to discuss and a plan to be made? "Do as ordered. I want them here in an hour."

"Yes, My Lord." Cadfael fell into step beside his master. "Is that all?"

"Summon the best carpenters, four at the least."

"Carpenters, My Lord?"

"To build a greenhouse."

Cadfael opened his mouth in an "O", as if he understood when in fact he did not. "To grow the Wistning Vine?"

Only then did Dragon Supreme pause, a breath entering his lungs as if it were the first he had drawn in nigh on a month. "To grow a florist."

Acknowledgments

As always, there are so many influences involved in the creation of this book. These are only some of the amazing people who helped to make this book possible.

My Lord and Savior Jesus the Christ – This book would not have been conceived, created, or published without the guiding of God's hands. Each step was led by the urging of the Holy Spirit and without Him my words would not sing like they do.

To my forever Alpha readers – Abbie and Isabel, you two made completing this book worth it. Thank you for always reminding me that the worth of my story is found in the story itself, and in the people who love it. Everyone who dislikes it is simply not my tribe. Both of you are amazing!

Various social media writers – You may not know this, but to everyone on social media that has befriended me and supported me through this journey, I will never forget your encouragement.

To my family – you are all special, specifically because you put up with me through editing month. I know my emotions run high during that phase, but you all handled it beautifully and I thank you for it.

My ARC readers, specifically Danielle and Amy – Thank you, thank you, THANK YOU for your emotional support. You guys are amazing human beings.

Finally, to my online following – I'm still amazed you're all with me. Thank you for supporting in any way you can. I hope you all love this book/series as much as I do.

A Note From the Author

This story started as something I was writing just for me. It began with the thought "go back to the beginning" and it has traveled so far from there.

For me, going back to the beginning meant remembering why I started writing and what I loved about it. I remembered being young and loving fairytales and princess stories, damsels in distress and epic sagas. Along the way, I threw in a sprinkle of my newer love for Asian costume dramas, a little bit of morally grey characters, and whole heaping of intrigue. What has come from that is this series, and I couldn't be more in love with it.

A Tale of Blood and Blossoms will not be *everyone's* favorite story. I know that. I acknowledge that. I did not write it for everyone. I wrote it for the girls like me. The soft girls. The ones who still love heroes and don't think the princess has to save herself. I wrote this for the old-fashioned girls, for the girls who forgive easily, love unconditionally, and who the world thinks are naive. You are all special, don't change just because other people want you to.

For all my hopeless romantics and the girls who want the man to save the princess, this series is for you. I hope this book finds all my people, and I hope you find something of yourself in these pages.

So much love and all my respect,
Megan